THE SORROW OF SHADOWS

MORGANA BLACK

BLACK DAHLIA PUBLISHING

Cover design and chapter headers by Selkkie Design
Hardcover artwork by Zoë J. Osik
Map artwork by Mytinybookshelfs
Portrait artwork by Tony Viento
Editing by Samantha Swart & Sarah Ward
Proofreading and formatting by M.A. Kilpatrick

Paperback 979-8-9911585-0-3
Hardcover 979-8-9911585-1-0

Black Dahlia Publishing

To those who were told you were too loud, too bossy, or too much—
this one is for you.

A NOTE FROM THE AUTHOR

Dear reader,

I believe in transparency and protecting your mental health. This is a dark fantasy romance and contains a lot of dark subject matter. I have done my best to compile any triggers, but I'm human, so I apologize in advance if any were missed. This book contains graphic sexual content, explicit language, death (both off and on page), physical and mental abuse by a parent, dubious consent, pseudo-family love interest (they are NOT actually related), poisoning, representations of grief, violence, attempted murder, drinking, misogyny, voyeurism, death of a small child, and bodily fluids.

If you have any questions, please do not hesitate to contact me at morgana@authormorganablack.com. PLEASE REMEMBER THEY ARE NOT RELATED.

THE SORROW OF SHADOWS PLAYLIST

Do you want an immersive reading experience? The Sorrow of Shadows playlist has songs curated specifically for each chapter, including the prologue.

https://open.spotify.com/playlist/4jXKAYbgOEAtXbpX u1hb08?si=09266ebc4a94448c

MAGIC SYSTEM

HEMONIA

Anything related to the physical body/energy

- Blood manipulation
- Life/death touch
- Energy siphoning
- Healers

KAMINARI

Anything related to the weather

- Lightning
- Storms
- Elementals (earth, fire, air, water, metals)

ANIMA

Anything related to the soul/mind

- Empaths
- Reading memories
- Sensing intentions/lie detection
- Coercion

VIZIE

Anything related to sight

- Visions
- Illusions
- Dream walking/manipulation
- Astral projection

MADILIM

- Light manipulation
- Shadow manipulation

PROLOGUE

Blood. There's blood everywhere. The tangy copper smell permeates the air as I let out an earth-shattering scream that I'm sure will wake the entire castle. My lungs struggle to take in oxygen, and my hands tremble as I stare at the sticky, warm, crimson life force coating my hands. I open my mouth to release the sob that is building in my chest.

I scream again, trying to wake myself from this nightmare. Except it isn't just a dream. It's a vision; a glimpse of what is to come. It's a warning I've been sent no less than a dozen times, both while sleeping and awake. This time is the most vivid of all. I stare down at my hands and rub them together as if to rid myself of the blood.

The vision is the same every time. It is fuzzy at first, but more and more pieces become visible with each occurrence. The people of Rimor gather in the streets of the capital city, Ciyoria. In the next breath, those same people scream as they lay dying in the streets. The bodies of males, females, and children are piled high because evil does not discriminate. The city and castle are burning, the fire climbing toward the sky. At the center of it all, I see King Raynor Rozaria. His eyes are cold, colder than I've ever seen *them. It's as if all humanity has escaped him as I watch a sinister, cruel smile creep onto his face. The vision jumps forward, and I'm covered in his blood. There's always so much blood. I fear it will never wash off. The message is clear. King Raynor will be the end of this kingdom unless I stop him.*

I shoot up in bed, my hands trembling as the realization hits me. Bile crawls up my throat, and I fight to keep my supper down. I swore an oath to the kingdom and its people. First and foremost, it is my responsibility to protect them, which I will do even if the cost is my soul. Because I'm about to commit regicide.

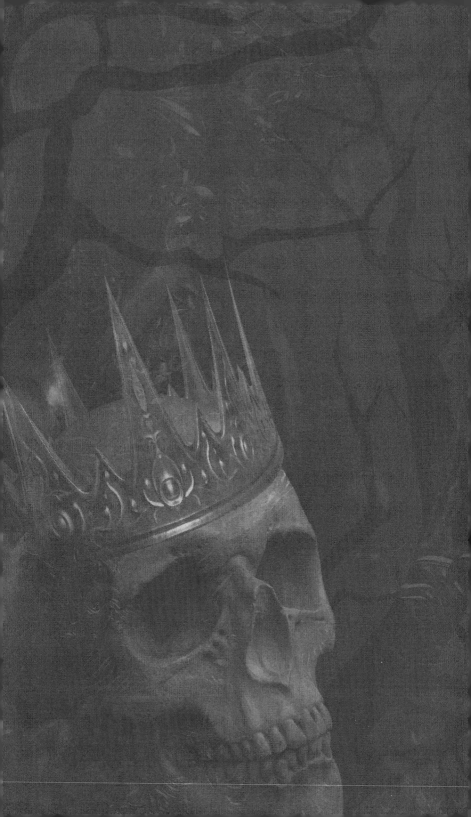

CHAPTER ONE

BREYLA

This blathering fool really should watch the way in which he addresses the grieving, widowed queen in his midst. The others may not notice, but I see the tremble of her lip and the ramrod-straight spine she keeps as she tries to hold herself together. "Queen Genevieve, are you listening to a word we are saying?" Lord Seamus all but demands. He may be one of the longest-standing council members, but his tone is one that would have seen me reprimanded as a child.

Elijah shoots him a glare that says as much. King Raynor was found dead not even a fortnight ago, and now his widow—my mother—sits with the King's council, having a conversation none of us want to have. Decisions must be made, but I wouldn't wish them on anyone. Especially not while you're supposed to be grieving.

I watch the council meeting unfold through the eyes of Elijah. Apart from him and the queen, no one knows I'm observing. Currently, I'm miles away from the capital city of Rimor leading the royal armies in battle against the neighboring kingdom of Prudia.

"Of course I'm listening," Queen Genevieve snaps. "I just don't see the point in this conversation. Quite frankly, Seamus, I'm not particularly fond of your tone. I suggest you fix it, unless you prefer I do it for you." The dark circles under her sky-blue eyes and messy golden hair give the appearance of a female broken, but my mother has never been weak. I can't help but notice she purposefully left out his full title, which I'm sure irks him but forces me to hide a smirk of satisfaction. *Pompous prick.*

"My apologies, My Queen. It's just that the law states that while a female may inherit the throne of Rimor, to main—"

"But to maintain it, she must be wed to a male of high noble ranking and power. Yes, I know the law quite well. Or did you forget that I am the one with royal blood flowing through my veins? That throne is rightfully mine. That law is archaic."

She's not wrong. Thousands of years ago we were a kingdom of just humans, then the Fae arrived and blessed us with The Gift. We received the ability to use magic, enhanced healing, and somewhat enhanced senses. The Fae worked and lived alongside us for a time, but they disappeared soon after arriving. They shared their culture and ideals with us, and as a result, ours had begun to evolve. Theirs was a matriarchal society that allowed females to not only rule but also lead armies and train alongside the males. What they left us with was their Gift and a society stuck somewhere between the old ideals of humans and the enlightened ideals of the Fae.

"Be that as it may, My Queen, the point still remains that you must remarry a male of high ranking and power to remain on the throne." Gods, this male is insensitive, but I have a feeling I know what he'll say next.

Before he can spew more useless knowledge of outdated laws, Elijah speaks gently, "My Queen, might I suggest you step down and let Princess Breyla rule? She is more than of age at twenty-seven, and she leads our armies just as well, if not better, than her male predecessors. She is equipped."

If I could reach through our connection and punch him for that suggestion, I would. His faith in me is touching, but I do not want the throne. I will have no choice one day, but that would not be today. I suspect the suggestion only came as a way to appease the snake sitting to the left of the queen.

The queen smiles softly at Elijah. "I know your faith in Breyla is high, but it's not her ability that keeps me from stepping down. Even if I passed the rule to her, the law still dictates that she would also have to marry. You know as well as I that nobody, not even her queen mother, tells her what to do. Though I found great love in my own arranged marriage, I would never force that upon her. I will let her find love in her own time." Her tone is gentler with him than the others. Perhaps it is that she feels something akin to motherly affection toward Eli. We grew up together and were the best of friends but prone to causing mischief. That's a fact that hasn't changed much over the years.

"You're right, My Queen," Elijah agrees. "No one tells Breyla what to do. It makes her a damn good general," then adds under his breath, "and a much larger pain in the ass."

"Besides..." the queen continues, "the point is moot as I have already planned for this. I sent a request to Lord Aurelius requesting his allegiance through marriage. I just received word this morning that he has accepted my proposal and is on his way here as we speak. This conversation, my lords and ladies, is over."

However, this doesn't satisfy Lord Seamus, and he rises quickly to speak. "Pardon me, My Queen, but did you say Lord *Aurelius*? As in the king's younger brother? Surely, there are better-suited matches available. I could—"

"You could do nothing, Lord Seamus. Lord Aurelius is only the king's adoptive brother. He is more powerful than most of you sitting at this table and twice as cunning. He is a brilliant strategist, which I am sure will be useful in the war with Prudia that's knocking on our door." Her exhaustion is apparent as she rubs tiny circles on her temples to assuage the brewing headache. How she's even having this conversation is beyond me. She sighs deeply and speaks with finality, "This meeting is over," before turning to leave the meeting room.

Finally. These council meetings are painful on the best of days, but today was worse. There are far more interesting things Elijah's Gifts are better suited for, but he keeps this position on the council to support the queen against the wolves in sheep's clothing. He is my eyes and ears when I'm away from court.

Elijah exits the meeting room, deep in thought, and makes his way toward his quarters in the east wing. When he's out of earshot from the rest of the council, he says, "I respect the queen and her decisions, but something seems off." He's voicing his thoughts to me, even if I can't respond to him through our connection. If I could speak to him right now, I would tell him I agree. He seems to read my next thought, though. "I understand why she would want to choose her suitor, but why Aurelius?"

Why Aurelius, indeed. While he was everything my mother described, he also had quite a reputation. We also had history—most of it not good. His ability to bend blood is what gave him his high rank in court, but he was rumored to have a secondary power that made him even more coveted by the lowborns and nobles alike. He was raised alongside the late king—my father—but bore no blood relation. It had been years since anyone had seen him at court, making me question both my mother's choice of suitor and why he would accept her proposal.

Elijah is nearly through the door when a royal guard stops him. "My Lord," his voice waivers, "there's something—more so someone we think you should see..." His voice trails off, and he looks shaken and pale.

Slightly confused by his statement, Elijah raises an eyebrow at him. "Who is it? And where are they?"

"Well, that's just it, My Lord. He's not always there, but several maids swear they've seen King Raynor's ghost around the princess's chambers. I would have thought it nonsense if I hadn't seen it myself. Then Alexander right here was telling me he—"

Elijah raises his hand, stopping the guard mid-sentence. My jaw drops alongside Elijah's, and he tries to form the words to tell the guard there's no need to convince him. Behind the two guards appears what looks to be the late king's ghost. Since he can't seem to form the words, Elijah just points behind them. The guards slowly turn to see what he's pointing at. While magic is commonplace, seeing ghosts is not. A strong sense of unease floods me as I stare at the apparition. The transparent form wavers, hovering just above the ground, staring straight at me. The first guard, Nathaniel, swallows hard and says quietly, "Yep, that's exactly what I was trying to tell you."

The ghost isn't trying to communicate, and it doesn't seem like he's there to harm anyone. He slowly starts to fade away, and I realize I can no longer avoid going home.

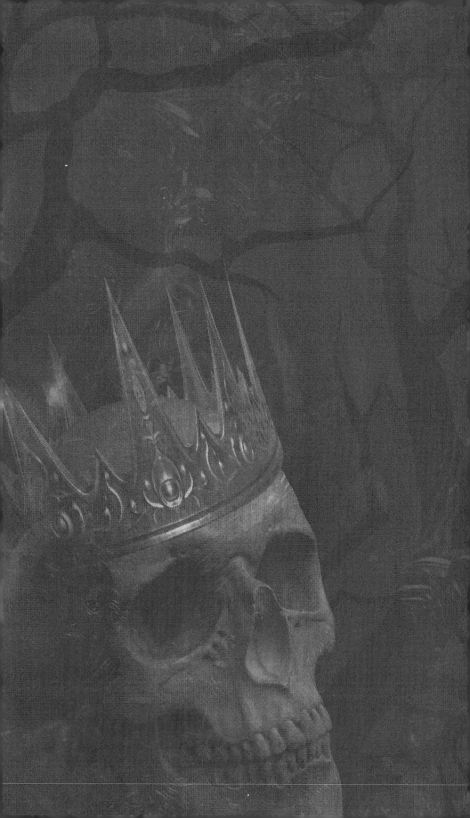

CHAPTER TWO

BREYLA

I didn't return home when my father died. I planned to, but I wasn't sure how to face that place with my father no longer roaming the halls. He had been found in the bed he shared with my mother a few weeks ago. Though it was uncommon to die as young as he had—barely into his fifth decade of life—we weren't immortal beings, and there had been no signs of foul play. It was simply a tragedy.

My quick thinking and strategic mind led me to be appointed as the royal army's general. I got that all from him. As a child, I had been teased endlessly because I favored swords and breeches over needlepoint and frilly dresses. I wanted to learn to fight battles, not flirt with noblemen. It was in those moments, in the training yard, that I formed my connection with him and earned the soldiers' respect.

Reflecting on the most recent council meeting, I find myself both surprised and slightly disgusted. My parents loved each other deeply, so how my mother could announce an engagement not even two weeks after my father was found dead is something

I can't even begin to understand. And of all people, why did it have to be *him?*

Aurelius.

My father's younger adopted brother. Emphasis on adopted, because there is no possible way I could be related to that male. Aurelius was found as an orphan when he was an infant. The only reason he ended up under my grandparents' care was because he showed immense power as he grew into adolescence. Our people value power over just about anything else.

All people had basic magic—the ability to create Faerie lights, levitate objects, lock doors, and create sound shields. Usually, the ability to use magic manifested sometime around puberty. Those blessed with additional Gifts typically developed them earlier, but not always. Some developed more than one power, but most kept additional Gifts secret. There were five main branches of magical Gifts: Hemonia, those relating to the physical body or energy; Kaminari, those relating to the weather or elements; Anima, those relating to the soul or mind; Vizie, relating to sight or vision; and Madilim, the ability to manipulate shadows or light.

Kaminari Gifts were the most prevalent, while Madilim and Hemonia Gifts were scarce. The rarer and more useful the Gift, the more sought after the wielder was. The Gift of the parents didn't determine what ability the child would receive, but two powerful parents tended to produce more powerful children. While I was known for my Madilim Gift—in my case, the ability to manipulate shadows—Aurelius was known for his Hemonia Gift. He was the only known blood wielder in our kingdom, but I didn't know the extent of his Gift.

My grandparents were the most powerful family in the town of Pelanor, so naturally, they had the most resources and agreed to take him in. He came to live with us at the palace after their parents determined he needed more training to learn how to control his powers. By that point, he was twenty and completely insufferable. To learn that my mother was now engaged to him, bile crept up my throat.

My second reason for being here was arguably more intriguing. A ghost appearing in the form of my father? That was something I had to see in person rather than through Elijah's eyes. I wasn't sure I believed in ghosts, but it sounded like the kind of fuckery I didn't want to miss out on. When he hadn't tried to communicate with anyone, I wondered if he was looking for someone who wasn't in the castle. The fact that he was usually found outside my chambers suggested that person may be me.

Which is why I'm standing outside the castle gates. Sure, I have questions for my mother, but I'm really here to see the ghost wandering the halls. It was a three-day ride from where I was posted in the village of Caedal, on the border of Rimor. I rode through the night, accompanied by only two of my most trusted guards, Ryder and Zion.

"State your business," a gruff voice says from behind the gate. I let out a soft chuckle and smile brightly at the older guard, who hasn't bothered to look up at us yet.

"I know you're getting up there in years, old male, but I didn't think you'd forget my face that quickly," I say to Nolan. That catches his attention, and his eyes snap to mine.

"Kid, is that you?" Nolan asks. "Well, I'll be damned. I wasn't expecting you for several more days. Come right on through."

Once we pass through the castle gate, I dismount my horse and turn toward Nolan. Before I have both feet fully on the ground, I feel Nolan's arms wrap around me, surrounding me in a warm, familiar hug. Nolan had been responsible for much of my training as a child and young female. I may have teased him about being an old male, but he could still easily best most of my soldiers without breaking a sweat. A few years ago, when he found out his wife River was expecting, he requested I remove him from active duty. I obliged with the condition he oversees the training of all new recruits, even if he wasn't the one directly training them. He was too much of an asset to let go completely.

"It's been too long, kid. I'm surprised I didn't see you back home sooner, all things considered..." Nolan's voice trails off like he's trying to be gentle with me.

I grimace. "I should have come home sooner. I just don't know how to be here without him. Then I received word from Elijah that there had been some developments I needed to see to believe."

"Ah, yes...that development arrived just yesterday." He clears his throat. He thinks I mean Aurelius, not the alleged ghost of my father. "Fair warning, I heard they've put him in the chambers next to yours."

I resist the urge to roll my eyes, but Nolan already knows how I feel about Aurelius. "How delightful," I say with as little sarcasm as I can muster.

Ryder and Zion stifle laughter behind me, and I narrow my eyes at them. "Well, you better get going. I'm sure you're tired after the journey. You'll need your rest to deal with the new *developments*." Nolan smirks at me.

This time, I roll my eyes at him, and he lets loose a deep belly laugh at my expense. I turn back to Luna and slide my left foot into the stirrup. Before I can lift myself onto her, I feel a firm but gentle hand on my bicep. Nolan has a serious look on his face when he says softly, "If you ever want to, er...talk...or you need anything at all, you know I'm here for you. River, too." He's about as good with emotions as I am. That is not good at all, but I know he means it. Tears try to well up in the corner of my eyes, but I refuse to let them fall. I blink them away, locking the feelings away for another day.

"Thank you," I whisper as I finish mounting Luna. Zion, Ryder, and I make our way to the stables and the chaos that no doubt awaits us.

Freshly showered, I step out of my bathing chambers and into my room. I let out a startled yelp when I see my best friend, Elijah, casually reclined in the center of my bed. "Gods dammit, Eli, give a girl some warning before you just show up in her bed," I say, exasperated.

"Now, why would I do that when I just love to hear you scream, Princess?" He grins widely at me.

I narrow my eyes at his innuendo, which makes his grin widen. "Anyway...Why are you in my room? Is there something so important it couldn't wait for me to be clothed?" I glance down at my body, as if noticing for the first time that I'm only covered by a towel that barely covers my ass.

"While we have important matters to discuss, I just wanted to see you. I didn't realize you'd be naked when I sent your maids away and snuck into your room. That's just a bonus." His eyes twinkle. There's nothing remotely romantic between us, but that's never stopped his shameless flirting. He's my oldest friend and closest confidant, so I tolerate the behavior with minimal opposition.

"I missed you too, Eli. Now turn around so I can dress myself."

He begrudgingly averts his gaze and allows me the privacy to dress. Despite being back at the castle, I still opt for my fighting leathers over a dress. They allow me to move freely and bring a sense of security that no dress could give. The material forms to the thick curves on my five-foot-seven frame, hugging right where they need to. I have never been petite, but my muscles are toned from years of training and battle, and these pants definitely show off that arduous work. I quickly try to tame my gold-streaked auburn waves into something resembling a braid.

I sneak over to my bed, where Elijah is still lying with his gaze averted. I jump onto the bed and wrap my arms around him, inhaling his spiced cocoa scent, which feels like home.

"Hey now, I never agreed to be the little spoon in this relationship," he says as he turns to look at me again. His chocolate-brown eyes roam over me, and I can tell he's trying to read my face for any signs of what I might be feeling. The mood suddenly shifts from playful to something more serious.

"I'm okay," I whisper, giving him a soft smile.

"No, you're not," he replies, calling my bluff. I'm not surprised by this; Elijah knows me better than anyone, probably even my mother. "But I wouldn't expect you to be. Whatever emotions you have are valid. Feel however it is you're meant to, let it out. I just hope you never feel alone because I am *always* by your side."

"Are you sure you're not an empath?" I joke, trying to lighten the mood.

Elijah snorts and gently grabs my chin with his thumb and forefinger. "Nope, I just know you like the back of my hand," he says confidently. "You'll refuse to talk about it or actually feel any emotions until it all builds up and boils over, and you melt down in epic proportions." He releases my chin to tap me on the nose.

Did this male just boop me like I'm a cute kitten?

I bring my hand to my chest in fake outrage before gasping. "That doesn't sound at all like me! You must be thinking of your other best friend."

He rolls his eyes this time but knows I'm done with this conversation for now. He clears his throat, working up to whatever he will say next. "Your mother's betrothal to Lord Aurelius."

My face falls because this is the last thing I want to discuss. "Do we have to talk about stepdaddy dearest?" I groan.

"I dare you to call him that to his face," Elijah chuckles. "But unfortunately, yes. We do need to talk about it."

"I just don't understand how she could so quickly turn around and announce a betrothal to *him*. Of all people, his own brother? I know my parents loved each other; that was obvious. Not even two weeks after my father dies, she's engaged? It seems disrespectful..." I trail off as my voice quivers. I'm clenching my hands so tightly I can feel my nails digging into the flesh of my palms.

A moment passes before Elijah speaks again. "Do you need friend Elijah right now, or do you need your advisor, Brey?"

I sigh, knowing as comforting as *friend* Elijah might be, protecting my feelings will get me nowhere. "Advisor Elijah, please," I mumble.

"Your mother loved your father; this doesn't change any of that. You know the law says she must remarry to stay on the throne. I think she only moved as fast as she did so she could maintain control over who she had to marry without the council shoving their noses into the matter. I can't begin to guess why she asked Lord Aurelius or what his motivations are—you'll have to ask them that. I don't think she intended to hurt you or diminish your father's memory. It was simply something that had to be done, and she took control of the situation. I figured you, of all people, General, would understand that."

I don't miss his use of my title to appeal to the part of me defined by logic. I sigh, defeated. "I see your point."

Elijah isn't done, though. "If I were you, I'd be more concerned with why Lord Seamus has such an interest in who your mother marries. That's what I can't seem to work out." His hands run through his long, golden locks. His hair typically remained tied up in a knot, but it was free and messy right now. I could tell he was frustrated at not having all the answers for me and was holding something back.

I lay a hand on his cheek and press my forehead to his. "You may be my eyes and ears, but I don't expect you to have all the answers. That bit about Lord Seamus is odd, but he's always been a nosey bastard. He often reaches too far, so we shall see how that plays out. What about this supposed ghost, though? I must admit I'm skeptical, so enlighten me. Seeing ghosts isn't normal—are we sure that's what it is?"

"You saw it that first time through my eyes, but he's appeared several more times since then. If I hadn't seen it for myself, I wouldn't believe me either. But I assure you, Brey, it is real. He still hasn't said anything. I don't believe he will take long to appear for you. He's almost always outside your chambers. I think he's been waiting for you." I can tell by his confident tone that he believes it. Whether or not it is the ghost of my father—or something more sinister—remains to be seen.

A few hours later, after Elijah and I had finished catching up and fallen asleep in the process, I step out of my chambers in search of food. It's well past supper, so I venture down to the kitchens to see what I can find. The room is pitch black when I enter, the staff having retired for the evening. I quickly cast several Faerie lights and send them to the corners of the dark space. I let out a soft gasp as I realize Lord Seamus's son, Lord Layne, leans against the counter, a bowl in his hand, with what looks to be a scoop of beef stew lifted halfway to his mouth.

"I'm sorry, I assumed I was alone in here, there being no lights on. Are you eating cold soup in the dark?"

Layne drops the spoon back into his bowl and looks at me

momentarily before answering. "I was in a meeting with my father that ran late, so I missed supper. I would have just waited if I weren't leaving in the morning, but I was starving. And it's not that cold, more like lukewarm."

"I suppose it all goes to the same place anyway, doesn't it?" I say as I reach past him to grab a clean bowl. My arm grazes his shoulder, and I feel him tense beside me. I look over to see his eyes wide and mouth open slightly. He doesn't say anything further, dropping his bowl to the counter and turning away from me before hurrying out of the kitchens, his bowl of soup forgotten.

That was strange. I fill my own bowl with room temperature beef stew and head back to my room.

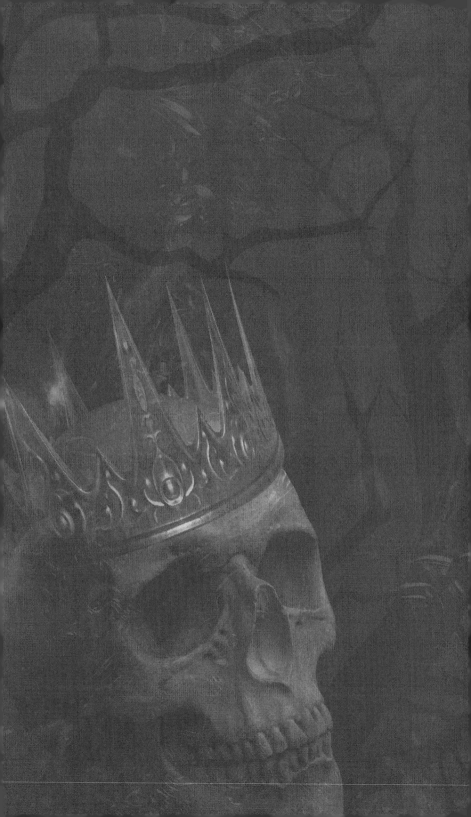

CHAPTER THREE

OPHELIA

I sit beside my window, my nose buried deep in a novel. I'm hiding. Father mentioned wanting to speak with me at breakfast, and I can't think of something I'd like to do less than have another one of his chats.

"My Lady, Lord Seamus sent us to fetch you," my maid says from the doorway. I sigh heavily and close my book. My disassociation shall have to wait.

"Yes, yes, I'm coming now. Best not to upset him further." I say the last part under my breath. There are very few people in this castle I can trust. Everyone fears Lord Seamus because of the lightning he wields. If only they knew how right they were to fear him.

I follow my maids, Ani and Maeve, out of my quarters and down the hall. I knock twice, then hear a gruff voice. "Enter." He's sitting in a wingback chair near the fireplace. It's the height of the summer season, and he insists on having a fire lit in the middle of the day. Add that to the list of things that make me question his sanity.

"Sit down, daughter," he says, gesturing to the chair opposite his. I cross the room and sit where he instructed. I can tell he is still deep in thought as his gray eyes—the same gray as mine—flicker back and forth across the flames dancing in the fireplace. I'm grateful our eyes are the only thing we share. Where his hair is brown and shaved closely to his head, mine is so black it almost looks blue and hangs straight past my waist. Where he is muscular, I am petite. Where he is powerful, I...am not. I possess the basic magic that all our people have, but as a highborn, I am expected to display additional Gifts. My father never misses a chance to remind me of my diminished value since I have shown no signs of other magical abilities. To him, I am little more than a burden to eventually be married off to whatever nobleman will take me.

"Have you developed any other magical Gifts?" I'm not surprised by this question, considering this should have happened years ago.

"Not since you asked me two days ago." I do my best to keep my voice and expression even. He's not fooled, though. Lord Seamus is never fooled.

"Pity." A one-word answer. Not usually a good sign. My body tenses as he shifts in his seat. "That's not why I called you here, though." A change of subject is my saving grace.

"What can I help you with?" I ask, wishing to be done with this conversation.

A grin starts to form on his face at the question. "Help me, indeed. I need you to get close to Princess Breyla. I have petitioned Queen Genevieve to make you one of her ladies-in-waiting. Maybe you'll be good at something for a change..." The last part comes out under his breath.

I ignore the remark as he continues, "I don't trust her intentions. She doesn't return home after the death of her father, yet rides through the night when her mother announces her engagement to Lord Aurelius. No, she's up to something. I need to know what, and you're the perfect person to find out."

"So, what exactly should I be looking for?" I'm not sure where he's going with this, but I know he's not giving me a choice in the matter.

"Any behavior out of the ordinary, conversations that seem unexpected, who she talks to, where she goes. Anything that might let you know her true intentions for being here." So, he doesn't really know what he was looking for. Got it. Super helpful.

"As you wish, Father," I say, hoping to end this conversation.

"You are dismissed."

Thank the gods.

I breathe a sigh of relief as I turn to leave. I'm nearly safe when I feel him catch my wrist and squeeze hard. I do my best not to react to the pain, but I know I will have bruises that will need tending tomorrow. "Do not disappoint me in this, Ophelia. I can think of much worse fates for someone as weak as you."

"Of course not. I will not disappoint you." That's all I manage before he releases me. I quickly make my way out of his chamber, rubbing my wrist as I go.

I'm nearly to my chambers when I notice the door ajar. I creep closer, keeping my feet light and listening to see if there is someone still in my chambers. That's when I hear, "I can practically taste your trepidation from here. It's just me, sister," come from the other side of my door.

I release the breath I was holding and enter to find my brother, Layne, leaning against the wall. His lean, six-foot-one frame towers over my five-foot-two self, but that doesn't stop me from wrapping my arms around his torso in a tight hug. "You're leaving again, aren't you?" I ask into his chest. He looks down at me, his chestnut curls hanging in his eyes. Luckily, he has our mother's eyes—a deep blue like the night sky just as the sun has set.

"Don't be sad, O. I'll be back before you know it."

I step back, frowning slightly. "Stop reading my emotions. You know I hate that," I protest. Layne is an empath. It comes in handy in court, which is why Father has him traveling so often. His power is known in the kingdom of Rimor but not outside these walls. That makes him even more valuable, and dangerous.

"Sorry, O. It's hard not to when you broadcast them so loudly."

"You're the only empath in court, so I don't see how it matters," I retort.

His expression turns serious. "I'm the only empath we *know* about in court. Another could easily be hiding. You need to learn to guard your thoughts and emotions."

I sigh loudly and ask, "Is this the only reason you came to see me? To lecture me on my mental shields?"

"Of course not. I wanted to say goodbye, but I also come bearing a warning."

I raise an eyebrow at him, waiting for him to continue.

"Stay away from Princess Breyla." *Crap.*

"Well, that might be difficult, seeing as Father just asked me to spy on her. He wants me to befriend her and report back to him on anything out of the ordinary. Where is this warning coming from?"

"I'm sorry, he what?!" Layne's eyes widen as he takes in this new information.

"He doesn't trust her. He thinks she's here with ulterior motives. He didn't say what he thought those motives might be but wants me to report on everything she does."

"I'm begging you, Ophelia. Stay away from Breyla. Knowing Father wants you to get closer to her makes me want you even farther away from her. I ran into her shortly after she arrived. I didn't mean to, but I read her emotions...except there was nothing there. I couldn't get any kind of emotion from her. That worries me more than anything. She's dangerous."

"She's the general of the royal armies. She's supposed to be dangerous. You know I can't ignore Father's orders. I can't disappoint him again. But I will be careful. Don't worry about me, brother." It's the only reassurance I can give him, and he knows it. My hands are tied when it comes to this.

Layne sighs deeply before responding. "Very well. I had to at least try. I'm leaving tomorrow, but I will return as soon as I can." He shuts the door to my chambers on his way out, leaving me alone to figure out how I'm going to get close to the princess. No pressure.

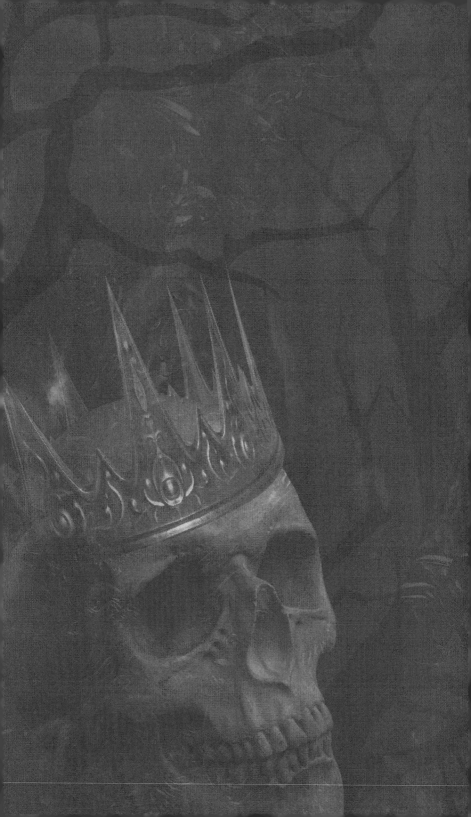

CHAPTER FOUR

BREYLA

"What about him?" I ask Elijah, pointing to the copper-haired male in the corner of the tavern. He's beautiful, really. Tall, bronzed skin, light brown eyes, and toned. My guess is he's not a soldier but perhaps a laborer by the defined curve of his muscles. Someone who could throw me around in the sheets, but not necessarily one whose name I'd remember.

We'd been drinking all day, having shirked all our courtly and general duties in favor of getting drunk and forgetting the current state of things. Now, we sat in Luella's tavern playing a game of truth or dare. In this version, though, if we fail the dare or don't answer the question, we must take a shot of rum. Considering we knew each other better than anyone else, it was mostly just a game of dares. Elijah and I had a way of escalating the challenges, letting our competitive natures get the better of us. Before this, we had both been tipsy. Now we were one shot away from making fools of ourselves. I couldn't find it in me to care, though.

"Him?" Elijah quirks a brow at me. He had dared me to kiss the male I thought would be the best to take to bed. With a caveat being he had to approve of the choice.

"Did I stutter?" I give him an incredulous look.

"Someone clearly has a type," he says, smirking.

"What is that supposed to mean?" I scoff. Elijah didn't know every male I had bedded, but he knew most of them. I did *not* have a type. Unless the type was dominating, muscled, and good at what they did.

"Please, B. I'm not blind. That male bears a distinct likeness to your long-time lover, Ci—"

"He's not my lover." I glare at him over my mug of ale, silently telling him to drop it.

"And I'm not your best friend." He rolls his eyes, calling me on my bluff.

"That can certainly be arranged," I threaten. We both know I'm lying.

"Nope, sorry. It can't. You're stuck with me until the end of our days. Probably the end of your days since you're more likely to do something reckless that will lead to your untimely death."

I stare at him, my mouth hanging open. "Your lack of faith in me is disturbing."

"I have full faith in you, B. Your taste in males, however..." He trails off, implying he disagrees with my choice.

"Fine," I huff. "You choose one then."

He grins at me triumphantly. "That one," he says, pointing to a dark-skinned male in the opposite corner. "He will do just fine."

"And you said I had a type," I say, rolling my eyes at him. Elijah didn't discriminate when it came to lovers, but this male definitely fit the look of one of his repeats.

He shrugs at me, clearly not denying it. "Go." He shoos me away from the table.

I down the last of my ale before approaching the male. He

has rich brown skin, smooth and stretched taut over his muscles. As I near him, I can see he has deep brown eyes—so dark they're almost black. They twinkle in the light of the tavern as I close the distance between us.

"Can I help you, Gen—"

"Shh. Not the general right now," I interrupt him, covering his lips with a finger to hush him. "And yes, you can."

"Just tell me what I can do for you," he offers. His voice is low and melodic. I could easily fall asleep to the sound of it.

"Are you taken by anyone?" I ask out of respect.

His eyes widen and he realizes what I mean. "Not current-ly," he replies with a wink. "But I could be tonight."

I chuckle lightly at his brazenness. Technically, I started it. But it takes a lot to openly flirt with the general and princess of this kingdom. Leaning in closer, I whisper, "Perfect. I need you to help me win a dare."

Before I can overthink it, my lips are on his. They're full and soft and exactly what I need right now. This started as Elijah's dare, but I didn't need much encouragement. A warm body sounded perfect to take my mind off things. He wastes no time kissing me back, his lips pushing and pulling with mine.

The male clearly knows what he wants as he deepens the kiss, his tongue licking along the seam of my lips, begging for entrance. I gladly oblige, opening my mouth and deepening the kiss further. His hand grasps my hip, pulling me down into his lap.

He tastes of whiskey, and I pull his bottom lip into my mouth. I suck and nip, drawing a soft grunt from him. Strong hands squeeze my hips, urging me to rock softly against his hard-ening length. Happy to oblige, I roll myself against him, a breathy moan leaving my lips.

Breaking free from our kiss, he trails his lips down my jaw, alternating kisses and soft bites until he reaches the base of my neck. I feel him move one of his hands up my side, grasping my breast and kneading softly. Teeth dig into the soft flesh of my throat, and I moan, throwing my head back.

Lost to my pleasure, I had forgotten entirely we sat in a crowded tavern. Elijah hadn't, though. "You win, B. Now get a room!" he shouts at me.

The male's other hand laces through the hair at the base of my neck as he tugs softly, eliciting a whimper from me. This was growing far too heated for public, but I couldn't stop myself. I just needed more, needed to feel good.

He breaks the kiss, trailing his lips across my neck to my ear. "Let me take you somewhere more private." The low timbre of his voice sends chills down my spine. I nod in agreement, and he stands from the bench.

Wrapping my legs around his waist, I let him carry me through the tavern to the exit. Somewhere in the background, I hear Elijah whistle as we pass, but I'm too engrossed in my partner to respond. I want what this male promises and can sense it will be good.

The second we exit the tavern and turn the corner, he has me pressed against the wall of the nearest building. I thought maybe we'd make it to his home first, but this will do. His lips are on mine again, more desperate than before.

I feel his hands grip my sides, fumbling for the hem of my shirt. He pulls it up, slipping a hand under it and up to my breast. I writhe against him, my hips seeking friction against his growing erection. A low moan escapes his lips into our kiss, and I do it again.

I'm so caught up in the feel of him on me that I don't hear the footsteps of an approaching figure.

I startle and pull away when I hear, "Well, this looks familiar, Princess." Aurelius is feet from us now, a look of disgust on his face.

"I didn't peg you for a watcher, Aurelius," I mock, trying to get a rise out of him. My lips search for the males again, trying to make the message clear that Aurelius wasn't welcome.

"What's his name?" he asks. Suddenly, I'm thrown back to the first time he asked me that question.

"What's his name, Breyla?" Aurelius asked. He gave me a disappointed look. What the hell did he have to be disappointed about? He didn't give a shit about me.

"What does it matter?" I asked, looking away from the boy I had just been kissing. I was without a shirt and very close to being without pants. Aurelius had discovered us in one of the lesser-used passages of the castle right as things were getting good. He could have just kept walking, but no—he had interrupted us like the prick he was.

"It matters," Aurelius gritted out.

I crossed my arms over my chest, suddenly feeling very exposed. "I don't know," I said quietly.

"So, you were going to fuck him, and you don't even know his name. What's your name, boy?" Aurelius asked. I didn't miss the demeaning way he called him boy.

"Simon," he mumbled.

"Simon, fuck off," Aurelius growled.

Simon looked at me, trying to decide what he wanted more— to get fucked or not to piss off Aurelius.

Ultimately, Aurelius must have been more frightening than me because Simon dropped me to the ground. "Sorry, Princess. It's not worth it," he said, backing away from me.

"Are you serious?" I demand, trying not to scream in frustration.

"Another time, maybe." He winked and disappeared down the hall.

Pulling my shirt on, I stormed over to Aurelius, shoving him in the chest. "You're the fucking worst," I seethed. Aurelius grabbed me by my wrists, holding them immobile in the air.

"Not by a long shot, Princess." He smirked with satisfaction.

"I'll get you back for that, you ass."

"Why do you even care?" I ask, my focus returning to the situation at hand.

"Who said I did?" Aurelius retorts.

My partner runs his hand up my shoulder and caresses my cheek, turning my gaze back to him. "Sure seems like you do," he says as his lips trail up my neck.

I tip my head back in surrender to the feel of his lips on my skin, but I can't shake the feeling of Aurelius's eyes on us.

"Fuck off, Aurelius." My words mirror the ones he first used to chase Simon away years ago. That male never returned to my bed, and it started an exchange of insults between Aurelius and me. We would go back and forth, finding new ways to inconvenience the other, and our efforts would escalate each time.

"I don't think I will," he says.

"Fine," I say, the word coming out as a breathy moan as my partner slides his fingers down the front of my pants at the same moment. "Stay and watch for all I care."

Feeling his fingers trail lower, I roll my hips into him, wanting him to get on with it. Just as he reaches the spot where I want him, he's yanked from me.

"Get lost," Aurelius growls at the male. His eyes seem to glow from anger. An anger I don't understand.

Much like Simon, the male decides this isn't worth the hassle —that I'm not worth it—and leaves me alone with Aurelius.

"What's your problem?" I spit the words at Aurelius.

"You, Princess." His tone is calm, but his body is anything but. He has me pressed back against the wall in the blink of an eye. His presence occupies the one left by the male, but the way Aurelius fills it is suffocating. He dominates and commands the space around him. My chest heaves, lungs working hard to pull in the oxygen Aurelius has sucked from the air around me. "It's always you," he says, eyes narrowing on me.

"Good to know I'm still your problem," I respond quietly, venom lacing my tone.

Aurelius sighs in frustration, then uses his thumb and finger to grasp my chin and turn it to meet his gaze. "You are much more than just my problem."

I don't follow his meaning, but my eyes search his for some explanation. His face is unreadable, and he refuses to break eye contact. The space between us is almost nonexistent, and my lips part slightly on instinct.

It feels like he's stealing the breath from my lungs as we both stand there in silence, locked into a battle of wills for who will look away first.

"Let me go, Aurelius." My words are soft but demanding. He ignores them entirely, instead pressing closer.

"Why? So you can track down some other poor male that will leave you wanting?"

I scoff, "He would not have left me wanting."

"Are you sure about that?" he challenges.

"Who I fuck is none of your concern," I retort.

"Perhaps not," he concedes. His lips hover less than an inch from mine, and I wonder how we got here. I also wonder how his lips would feel against mine. Would they be soft and full like the other male's? If he were anybody else, I would lean forward and take what I wanted from him—what he robbed me of when he dismissed the other male. "But I could think of much better options if you're looking for someone to warm your bed."

"Oh really?" I challenge. "Like who?"

Realizing his mistake too late, Aurelius says nothing. I wait a few heartbeats longer before pushing him off me and striding away from the wall. "That's what I thought," I snicker and return to Elijah and the tavern.

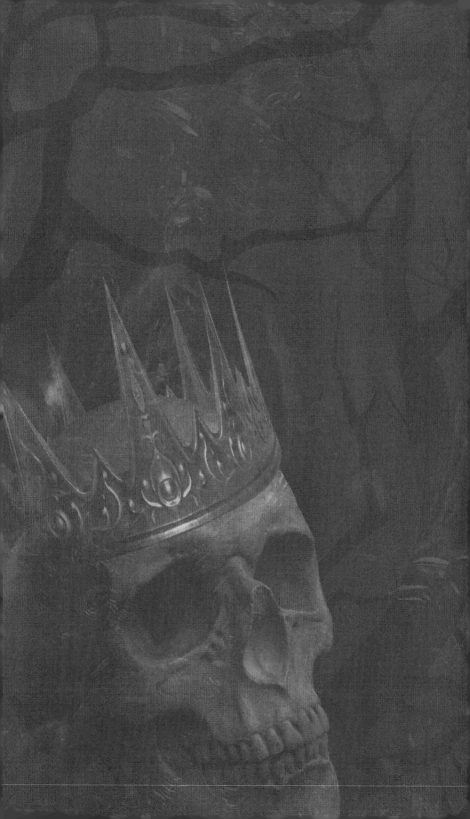

CHAPTER FIVE

BREYLA

I t has been nearly three weeks since I arrived at the castle, and I have seen no ghosts. Three weeks of watching my mother show affection for Aurelius, like my father meant nothing. Three weeks of avoiding everyone and drowning my grief in ale and wine.

"You win again," I say, exasperated. We've been playing various card games since lunch and are now well past dinner. Of the last eight hands, Elijah had won seven. "How did you win, again? It's statistically improbable!" I narrow my eyes at him.

He grins wide before answering, "Statistics don't take into account the six cups of wine you've had in the last two hours." He lets out a deep laugh at my expense.

My eyes narrow even further before I let out an unexpected hiccup, completely ruining the glare I was directing at my best friend. This only makes him laugh harder. Unable to contain myself any longer, I laugh with him, eventually so hard that I snort. My snort turns into me choking on my own saliva, then I'm coughing. I reach for my wine goblet, only to find it empty.

"On that note..." I stumble both with my words and with standing. Elijah gives me a questioning look as I trip over my feet on the way to my bedroom door.

"Are you sure you should be drinking more?" Elijah asks from his position, still on the floor.

My middle finger is the only response I give him as I exit my room in search of more wine. Trying not to trip again, I keep my eyes trained on the ground ahead of me. It would be easier if I created a few Faerie lights, but with all the wine in my system, it's taking all my focus to walk at the moment. I make it about ten feet before I trip over absolutely nothing. As I prepare for impact with the floor, I let out a rather embarrassing squeal.

Except I never hit the floor. I feel an arm wrap around my waist as I make contact with something hard. By the warmth under my fingers, I can tell it's not a wall or piece of furniture.

"I must say, I expected more grace from the general of the royal army. I'm not sure whether I should be disappointed or concerned for the safety of our kingdom." That voice—deep and melodic. It belongs to the asshole I've been avoiding for the past three weeks. This close to him, I can smell his spiced bergamot scent. It's intoxicating. My inebriated brain must be malfunctioning because I subtly breathe it in deeper as I push myself back upright, his hand still resting on my hip.

"Did you just sniff—"

Before he can finish that thought I cut him off with the best retort I can muster, "I expected the future King of Rimor to be...taller." *Real smooth, dumbass.* Aurelius stands several inches above six feet. He dwarfs me and most of the people in this castle.

Aurelius smirks at me. "Princess, clearly wine does not make you funny. Unless your goal was to make me laugh at you. In which case, mission accomplished."

"It may not make me funny, but it makes you easier to look

at. Has your face always looked that way?" I say. It's another lie, but anything said with enough confidence sounds like the truth.

"Your insult might have worked if you actually believed that was true, but we both know you're lying."

"Egotistical, much?"

"Only when I have reason to be."

We both knew he had reason to be. He had no shortage of options when it came to bed companions. Dark hair that curls slightly just above his shoulders. Tall and muscular. Not in the ridiculous way that Elijah is built, but toned and defined all over. I can't see his eyes in this lighting, but they're so dark brown they are almost black and laced with crimson flecks. If he were anyone else, I'd want to run my tongue all over him and claim him as mine.

Feeling his hand tighten on my side quickly disrupts my train of thought and brings me back to the situation at hand. "Well, as much fun as this chat has been, I really do need more wine. So, if you'll let me pass, I'll be on my way." With that he finally releases me and steps aside.

I make my way to the kitchen, feeling his eyes on me the entire time. By the time I return to my room, Elijah has passed out and is lightly snoring on my floor. I slip into my bathing chamber to change into my nightgown, then crawl into bed.

I'm not sure what time it is when I sense someone else in the room. I can hear Elijah still snoring from the floor, so whoever arrived is unwelcome. Very slowly, I reach for the dagger I keep under my pillow. I'm still slightly groggy from the wine and sleep, so I take control of the shadows in the room, willing them to sense out where the intruder is located. *That's odd.* My shadows find nothing.

Not wanting to waste any more time, I swiftly rip the covers back and jump to my feet in one fluid motion. Dagger in hand, I assume a defensive stance. Then my jaw drops because in front of me is my father's ghost.

He looks the same as the first time I saw him through Elijah, but clearer now. My breath catches as I take in his appearance. Every detail, every feature, even down to his clothing, is precisely as I remembered him. Red hair curls slightly around his ears, and hazel eyes stare back at me. His features are slightly muted by his mostly transparent form. I wonder if I could touch him or if my hand would pass right through.

He's staring at me like I'm crazy. Granted, I did pull a knife on a ghost, so maybe the look is justified. "It certainly took you long enough," I say, lowering my dagger and relaxing my stance.

"Time works differently when you're dead, my dear," he replies, and it feels like a punch to my gut. It feels odd to hear my father's ghost talk so casually about his death. My eyes burn as my throat constricts, and I choke back my tears.

"So you do talk."

"Perhaps I had nothing to say until now."

"I doubt that. More likely that you didn't have anyone worth speaking to until now," I say with a healthy skepticism.

"Clever girl. You're right," he says before pausing. "My death was not of natural causes." He has my full attention with that last statement. Something didn't sit right with me about his death, so hearing this fills me with an anger that burns like wildfire. What he says next has me shaken. "Aurelius is responsible for my death."

My eyes widen, and my pulse increases as I process his words. I stutter, "B-but why? He's your *brother*. Better question: how? As far as I'm aware, he wasn't even in the capital at the time of your death." The wheels in my head are working over-time as I try to wrap my mind around this new information.

"I don't know, my dear. I'm leaving that up to you to figure out. A word of warning, though: be cautious of who you trust. This castle is full of snakes." I didn't need his advice, but I would heed it nonetheless.

"I'm always careful, Father. But I don't understand. How do you know it was Aurelius?" Aurelius and I shared no trust, but this seemed out of character for him.

"I have limited time here, and it has run out."

Forget the questions; I wasn't ready to say goodbye to him yet. "Wait," I beg. "Don't leave yet."

His form wavers, starting to disappear. I take a few steps forward, arms reaching out like I could somehow keep him here. A soft smile forms on his face. "I'm already gone, Breyla. You can't keep me here. Time is up."

"I still have so many questions," I whisper, fighting the tears forming in the corner of my eyes.

"You'll find answers. I'm sure of that," he says as his form finally fades.

My king had given me a mission, and I would not disappoint him. There's a lot that doesn't make sense, but I will get to the bottom of it all. If he was murdered—regardless of who is respon-sible—I will avenge his death.

A knot forms in my stomach as I realize that I'll need to get close to Aurelius. I do not trust him in the least. But do I believe he was the one to murder my father? Of that, I'm not so sure. There are a lot of things that don't make sense with that situa-tion. It is, however, somewhere to start. If this is going to work, I can't let him—or anyone—know what I'm up to. As far as anyone is concerned, I am just a daughter mourning the untimely death of her father. My grief must be evident so my true actions are not.

I climb into bed, but I doubt I'll get any more sleep tonight. I must figure out how to get close to my mother's fiancé without arousing suspicion. I have other questions that need to be answered, but I will start with Aurelius.

CHAPTER SIX

AURELIUS

It's been over three weeks since my arrival in the capital, and the longer I'm here, the more questions I have. I swear Breyla's honeysuckle and citrus scent still clings to me from our encounter three nights ago. The servants whisper about a castle ghost resembling the late king, my brother, Raynor. Unable to sleep that night, I was wandering the castle hoping to find the ghost when Breyla ran into me. Though it was dark, I could clearly tell she was not the annoying pre-teen I remember from my time living in the castle. Gone was the lanky girl who didn't quite know what to do with her too-long limbs. In her place was the general with toned muscles, thick curves, and a mouth that just didn't know when to quit. She was confident in herself and her skills, and despite what I said about her balance that night, she was incredibly graceful when not piss drunk.

Breyla had been doing her best to avoid me since I arrived in Ciyoria. Not that I could blame her. I am betrothed to her mother, Queen Genevieve, but she doesn't have all the facts.

Closing my eyes, I replay the memory of my first encounter with the queen upon my arrival at the castle.

"Welcome to Ciyoria, Lord Aurelius." Queen Genevieve smiled, and though it didn't reach her eyes, I knew she was trying. Her husband had just died, and she was being forced into another marriage just to keep her throne.

"Please, Your Majesty, just Aurelius. We have known each other too long to be that formal with one another." At that, she smiled genuinely. I opened my arms, and she stepped into me, wrapping her arms around me tightly. I could feel the tension in her body start to melt away, even if just slightly.

"If that is the case, then I am just Gen to you. At least in private." She had always been Gen to me, but it had been years since I last saw her, so it was difficult to know where we stood.

Reluctantly, I pulled back from her and looked her in the eyes. "I'm not going to ask the bullshit questions everyone asks because they feel obligated. I know you're not okay."

She sighed. "Thank you, Aurelius."

"But I do have other questions."

"Of course. I would expect that."

There were so many I needed answers to, but the biggest one was, "Why me?"

"That's simple. You're the only one I trust."

I had agreed to the proposal for my own reasons; reasons Breyla—and everyone else—didn't need to know. Though Breyla had done her best to avoid me, I had been very closely monitoring her. She was drunk often, so it wasn't hard to keep an eye on her without catching her attention. I would have expected her to keep on her training, meet with her commanders about the looming threat of war from the kingdom of Prudia, or at least spend time with her grieving mother. She had done none of those things. She often slept late into the day, ignoring all responsibilities, and made a game out of trying to piss off as many of her mother's council members as possible.

My Hemonia Gift not only gave me the ability to manipulate blood, but also the ability to sense when something was residing in it, such as disease, infection, or alcohol. So, color me surprised when I noticed over the last three days, since our late-night run-in, that her blood had been entirely free of alcohol when she was seemingly inebriated.

To make things more interesting, my secondary Anima Gift —in my case, the ability to sense intention and truth—had caught brief glimpses of words and actions that didn't align. She had stronger mental shields than most, probably a result of her best friend, Elijah, also possessing an Anima Gift. For him, it was the ability to read memories. Very few knew I harbored this Gift, but it proved useful at court. The longer I spent in this castle, the more convoluted the situation became. This morning was a breaking point for me.

"Good morning, Princess," I said as Breyla plopped into the dining chair. Her emerald-green eyes shoot a glare my way. I don't think she liked it when I called her that, which made me want to do it even more. She looked broken and erratic. Her hair was braided in a crown, yet tendrils of her warm auburn and sun-kissed locks were sticking out and loose. It looked as if she slept on it. Her clothes were clean, but not pressed, and riddled with wrinkles. I'm not the only one that noticed.

"Darling, are you sleeping alright? You look troubled." The concern was evident in Gen's eyes. She was grieving her husband, yet still concerned with the wellbeing of others. I squeezed her hand lightly to reassure her. Breyla noticed, sneering at me. It was apparent she didn't approve of her mother's relationship with me, regardless of the nature of it. There was absolutely nothing romantic between her mother and me, but she didn't know that.

With a healthy amount of disdain, Breyla responded, "Sleeping just fine, Mother. It appears you've been sleeping well by the look of things." I didn't like what she was insinuating. I wasn't sure if it was what she said or the way she said it. What bothered me more was that she knew I occupied the chamber right next to her own, yet she still threw that insensitive jab at her mother.

Gen brushed it off and continued, "Do we need to assign you new maids? It looks like Lyla has lost her touch. I know her hands trouble her, but—"

"No need. I dismissed my ladies. I care for myself just fine when I'm away from the castle. I see no need for them here." Her words were abrupt. While they were true, it was also very unusual for royals or nobility to attend to themselves while in the castle.

"I see." Gen was upset. "Well, Lord Seamus has petitioned me to allow his daughter, Ophelia, to attend you."

"If Ophelia wishes to be my lady, she can speak with me herself."

Gen sighed deeply. "Very well. I believe Lord Aurelius has a matter he wishes to discuss with you."

She turned her gaze to me and, with a saccharine smile, asked, "Yes, stepdaddy dearest? How can I be of service to you?"

My nostrils flared at the tone in her voice and what it made me want to do to her. Such a brat. "I received word this morning that Prince Ayden II of Prudia attacked a village on the outskirts of Rimor. They say it was unprovoked, but your soldiers weren't far away and were able to end the skirmish with minimal casualties."

"I was aware of that, yes. My soldiers are well-trained. I am unconcerned. Prince Ayden is just throwing a fit because my father killed his in battle years ago."

Unconcerned? She was unconcerned. I could feel my temperature rising, but before I could say more, she stood and left the dining room.

I had been furious all day. How could she act so casually about the loss of lives? She is the general of our army, yet she can't be bothered to have a conversation about an open act of aggression against us. It's early evening when I find her lounging on a cushioned seat in the library.

I close the doors, locking them behind me, and lean against the frame. "Evening, Princess," I say, staring at the back of her head.

She sighs and slams her book shut. Turning to glare at me, she says, "Stop calling me Princess."

Knowing I'm about to start a war, I continue, "Sorry, no can do, Princess. I can't call you general, because from what I saw at breakfast the general isn't anywhere in this castle."

Stomping her way over to me, she demands, "What is your problem, Aurelius?"

She stands six inches from me, but I can still easily stare down at her. Something I know she probably hates. "My problem, *Breyla*..." I start slowly, "is you." She doesn't seem surprised, but I catch her jaw tick.

"What specifically is it about me that offends you so?" she grits out.

"It's your attitude that offends me so, Princess. You're a liar and quite possibly the most insensitive female I have ever met." I step into her space. Though she's tall for a female, I still dwarf her frame.

Anger flares in her eyes. "Oh, that's rich coming from you, asshole. You know nothing about me." She steps closer to me and shoves her finger into my chest to make her point. "Don't pretend otherwise."

This female.

In a move so quick she doesn't have time to react, I grab her wrist and flip her against the wall, pinning her hands above her head. I snarl as I lean close to her ear to whisper, "I know enough. You've been using your grief to justify your behavior since you've been at court. Although you pretend you don't care about anything, the truth is you care deeply." Her eyes burn into me, but I continue, "There are plenty of reasons for you to return to your soldiers and leave the capital. The report this morning wasn't the first we've received of this nature since you arrived. You should be out there with them, but there's something keeping you here. Despite your behavior, you are one of the best damn generals this kingdom has known, and you don't get that by not caring."

She scoffs in indignation, trying to jerk free of my grasp. I tighten my grip as I push closer, our noses almost touching. "I also know that the last three days, your blood has had no alcohol swimming through it, yet you let the entire castle believe other-wise. You're here for a reason—one you don't want people to know—so you're trying to disguise your actions." By the end, I'm almost yelling, pushed closer against her, and breathing heavily.

It's too late by the time I notice the shadows moving unnatu-rally around the edges of my vision. I feel something wrap around my ankles and knock me off my feet. I hit the library floor with a grunt as Breyla lands on top of me. She straddles me with a dagger pressed lightly against my neck. She may never admit it, but I struck a nerve with her. Her actions say every-thing her lips won't, so I take the opportunity to provoke her further.

"If you wanted me on my back, Princess, all you had to do was ask." I smirk at her.

Her shadows snuff out the lights in the room. I feel her lean in closer and press the blade harder into my throat. I swallow hard as she speaks softly in my ear, "You're still easier to look at in the dark."

I feel her nose run lightly down my jaw and my pulse jumps. But mine isn't the only one. A low growl escapes me as I buck my hips, throwing her off balance, and then roll her onto her back. I have my knee lodged between her legs and use my hips to pin her down. I lean down to speak low. "Liar." I can't help myself when I place a soft kiss on the spot between her neck and shoulder. She shivers under me, and I know she's affected. She can pretend she doesn't like looking at me, but my Gift effortlessly reveals her deception. "Now tell me what you're doing here," I demand.

"I have frequently caught myself wondering the same thing about you," she deflects. "I'll show you mine, if you show me yours." With that, she pulls her shadows back into herself, and light returns to the room.

There is a sharp knock at the door and a male's voice on the other side. "Breyla, are you still in there? Why is the door locked?" It's Elijah. I suddenly realize how the position we are in would look. I jump to my feet, straightening my tunic. This conversation is over, so I unlock the door with a twist of my wrist and fling the doors open.

"Lord Aurelius, I didn't realize you were in here," Elijah says with a suspicious look in his eye.

"The general and I were just discussing battle strategy," I grunt as I brush past him—noticing he smells subtly of lilac and honey—as I exit the library.

I shoot up straight in bed, my heart beating erratically and gasping for breath. Long auburn curls and the scent of honeysuckle are all that linger in my mind from the dream. The images are blurry, and I can't quite piece them together. *What had awoken me?* I look around the room, and that's when I notice it. Rather, I notice *him*. My brother, Raynor. He looks just like he had the time I'd seen him alive as he sent me to Prudia on official crown business—curls piled neatly atop his head with the sides shaved shorter, freckles spattering his face just like Breyla, the Rimorian crown resting on his brow. I'm doubtful that this is a ghost at all, having never seen one before, but I'm eager to hear what he has to say.

"It's about time you woke up," he says impatiently.

I stare at the ghost, dumbfounded. It's the middle of the night, and he's criticizing my timeliness in waking up? "Pardon me for sleeping. I'll do better next time. I've been here for weeks. It's not as if you didn't have ample opportunity to appear before now. Perhaps even at a time of day when I was already awake."

Raynor's ghost tsks at me. "Save your complaining for the living. I have something to say."

"I'm listening."

"I was murdered by someone in this castle," he says bluntly. I stare at him, and he continues, "You don't look surprised."

"I'm not surprised, brother. I noticed things were...not right the moment I arrived. From my first conversation with Gen—"

"Ah, yes. My wife, and now your fiancé. Tell me, how did that come about?" He seems genuinely invested in my answer here.

"She approached me about it. I only accepted her proposal to protect her. She apparently does not feel she can trust anyone on your council. Can you tell me why that is?"

"My queen's instincts are sharp. I cannot speak for everyone on the council, but I would start with Lord Seamus. I believe him to be connected to my murder." It's interesting what information this ghost has—and doesn't have.

"You believe? You don't know for sure who murdered you?"

"Unfortunately, I did not see my death coming. I can't say for sure, but I believe strongly that Lord Seamus had a hand in it. He stands to gain the most from removing my bloodline from power." His uncertainty about his murderer unsettled me, but his reasoning on Lord Seamus had merit.

"I'll look into it. Why come to me, though?" I figured he would go to Gen with this information.

"I do not wish to trouble my queen with this. It would only

upset her further. She needs to heal. Please do not mention this to her, I beg of you."

"You need not beg, brother. I will take care of Gen; she is always safe with me." I truly mean that. I love her, but not in the way he had. "There is something you should know about my engagement to Gen—"

"I do not wish to hear it. I love her, and I know you will protect her and Breyla. That is all I need to know."

I chuckle, thinking about the dagger the princess had to my throat just hours ago. "The princess has made it abundantly clear she can protect herself."

"That's my girl," the ghost says proudly. "Still, I expect my heir to be safe in your hands, Aurelius." He shoots a stern look at me.

"Of course, Raynor. I understand." With that, he was gone.

I lie back down, knowing dawn is still hours away, but I will get no more rest tonight. Lord Seamus might be suspicious, but he wasn't the only one. Breyla was here for a reason, and I was determined to figure it out. What mess had I walked into here? My duties as emissary were never this interesting.

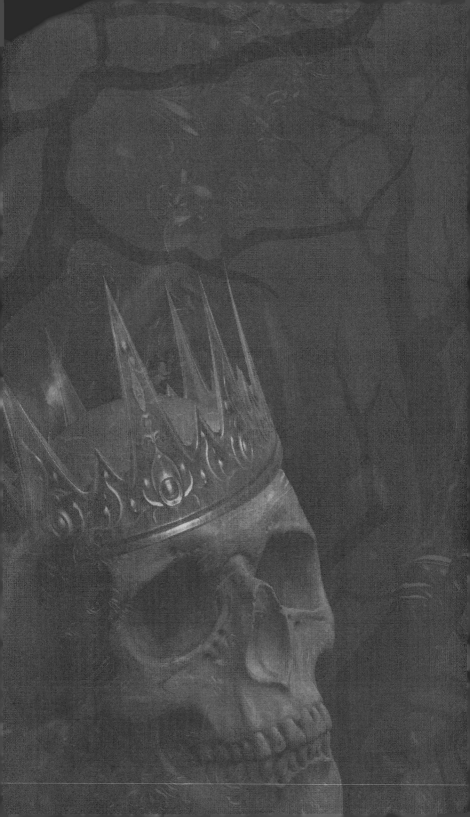

CHAPTER SEVEN

OPHELIA

Exhaustion fills every part of me. The white glow and tingling sensation fade from my hands as I remove them from Lyla. After Princess Breyla had dismissed her, she was reassigned to my father, Lord Seamus, as a maid. He had never been kind to his servants; this was the third time he had left her completely drained of energy this week. He was a leech, literally sucking the energy out of those he viewed as dispensable, but I feared if his Hemonia Gift were discovered we would be exiled from court. No law against such magic exists, but how he uses it would be looked down upon. It was why he let others believe he only carried the Kaminari Gift—in his case, the ability to wield lightning.

I am constantly cleaning up his messes. He would drain servants or other courtiers of their energy, unbeknownst to them, and I would find them near comatose, having to heal them with my own Hemonia Gift. When I was seventeen, I found a lady of pleasure laying naked on the floor of his room, near death from being drained while servicing my father. I barely had any grasp on my Gift at that time, but I was able to bring her back from the brink of death and send her to the court physicians for further help. A large sum was paid for her silence, but the madame refused to send more females to him after that.

I had been hiding this Gift from him for years, letting him think I was powerless so he couldn't wield me as a weapon. Healers were heavily sought after, but a healer I was not. I was something different, something more. There was no word I knew of for my Gift, so I settled on calling it the life touch. While healers' magic encouraged the body's natural healing at an accelerated rate, my Gift traded my life force for theirs. The energy it took me to restore others was immense. I imagine it would become easier the more I trained, but it was challenging to train with a power that you hide and required someone to be injured.

"Thank you, M'lady," Lyla says softly.

"Don't mention it," I say sternly but without intimidation. "Seriously, don't mention this to anyone."

"Of course. I won't say a word," she replies. "You best be getting to the princess. I saw her the day before last wandering the halls in just her underclothes with a half-empty bottle of ale. She was muttering about snakes, causing quite a commotion. She could use a friend, if you ask me."

I had not witnessed the event Lyla mentioned, but the imagery made me giggle. I try to hide it with a slight cough. "Ah, yes. I am headed to her now. I'll see if I can provide companionship to our distraught princess."

I'm not entirely sure what the princess needs, but I have to get close to her so as not to disappoint Father. I ponder how I should approach the princess as I make my way to her wing of the castle. I round the corner, deep in thought, and run directly into a massive form coming in the opposite direction.

"Umph," I grunt, looking into the warm brown eyes of Elijah. He reaches out to steady me. He usually wore gloves, but today they are absent. I can feel the warmth of his hands on my bare shoulders. It feels...nice.

"My apologies, Lady Ophelia. I did not see you coming." He smiles, his eyes sparkling in the mid-afternoon light.

"No apologies needed, Lord Elijah. I was not paying close enough attention. The fault is all mine," I say, diverting my attention downward.

He grabs my chin and lifts it gently. It is a bold move, but he is a notorious flirt. "Nonsense, the blame is mine, and that is the last I'll hear of it. Now, where were you headed? Perhaps I can escort you there?"

To spy on your best friend.

"Oh, that's not necessary. I'm just headed to visit the princess. I won't keep you from your duties," I stutter, trying to keep my voice even. I can't let on that I'm up to something more.

His smile falters slightly. Is he suspicious? Or is he disappointed I turned down his company? Surely, it must be the former. "Very well. Until next time, Lady Ophelia." He bows and turns to leave.

I finally reach Princess Breyla's chambers and raise my fist to knock. The door opens immediately to reveal a rather disheveled princess. A loose tunic hangs off her muscled shoulder, and stains that look suspiciously like wine cover the front. Her hair hangs loosely down her back in tangled curls. Deep green eyes sparkle in the light, emphasizing the gold streaks surrounding her pupils. I don't smell any alcohol on her, so I don't think she's drunk, but she is not the princess I was expecting.

"I knew you'd be back as soon as you realized you left these —" The princess stops mid-sentence, a pair of black leather gloves in her hands. "Sorry, I thought you were Elijah," she says before dropping her hand.

"I passed him on my way here, but he didn't mention where he was headed," I say, trying to be helpful.

"He'll be back later tonight; I'll just hold onto them for now."

She opens the door wider, gesturing to the open space. "Why don't you come in, Lady Ophelia." *He'll be back tonight?* Was Elijah sleeping with Breyla? Odd.

I step into her room and let the door shut behind me. "Thank you, Princess," I say politely.

"Please, call me anything other than *Princess*. Breyla works just fine. Now, how can I help you, Ophelia?" Her smile is kind. I feel like I could trust her, which makes the whole situation that much harder.

"I came to offer my service to you as a lady-in-waiting. Pardon my brazenness, but you seem like you could use a friend." I decide to be direct. Breyla seems like one who would appreciate that approach.

"I have a friend—Elijah. Why would I need another?" she quips.

"Is that what he is?" I ask bluntly.

"What else would he be?" The corner of her mouth quirks. Had I read that situation wrong?

"Perhaps more than a friend?" I suggest and raise a brow. She easily has half a foot on me and stares down at me with an intrigued look on her face. Until she bursts into laughter, her whole body shaking.

"Is that what you think? Eli and I?" She can barely get her words out.

I shrug my shoulders, readily accepting my embarrassment. "It's just how it looked. My apologies for misreading the situation."

"No need to apologize. That's comical. Almost as comical as you thinking I'd believe you are here on your own volition to 'be my friend'." She uses her fingers as air quotes for the last part. *Shit.*

"It is true! It was not my idea originally, but—"

"Please spare me your sugar-coated lies. You spoke plainly moments ago; let's not change that now. I know it was your father's idea." She is the bluntest royal I've ever met. I feel a growing spark of admiration for her.

"Very well. It was my father's wish for me to become one of your ladies. I won't pretend to understand his motivations, but I don't wish to disappoint him. He is...unpleasant to those who do not meet his standards," I say carefully.

"Now that I believe, but you aren't telling me everything. Allow me to be blunt. Ophelia, do you trust your father's intentions?"

"Not in the least," I reply without hesitation.

She accepts that answer, "And do you trust mine?"

"I want to. But to be frank, I don't know you well enough to answer that question." It was the truth. If she's surprised by my response, she doesn't show it.

"I like your intuition, Ophelia. You will need to trust it to survive," she continues. "Though I'm still not sure I trust you. So, you have two options. First, you can leave here and tell your father about this conversation. Or secondly you can tell him that you believe I intend to reach for the throne and remove my mother from power. Option two is a lie, but if you deliver that message, I will know you are loyal to me. I will have no one close to me that I cannot trust. I've already dismissed all my maids, and I will not hesitate to dismiss you as well. Choose your allegiances carefully, Ophelia."

She doesn't have to say anything further for me to know I've been dismissed. I have a difficult decision to make. I politely excuse myself as I contemplate what to do now. As I close her door, I glance left and see Lord Aurelius exiting the chambers directly next to Breyla's. I find it odd that he's not staying with Queen Genevieve, or at least next to her chambers instead. I acknowledge him with a slight nod and curtsey.

The walk across the castle is long as I contemplate the decision I must make. On the one hand, if I choose to deceive Father and he finds out, he will make my life miserable—and painful.

On the other hand, he's done nothing to earn my loyalty, and I think Breyla might protect me if I earn her trust.

"How did your meeting with the princess go?" is the first thing Father asks as soon as I have the door closed. He's in a mood; I can practically feel the electric current of his lightning filling the room.

"Very well, Father," I start, and he gives me a sinister smile. "There is something you need to know about the princess."

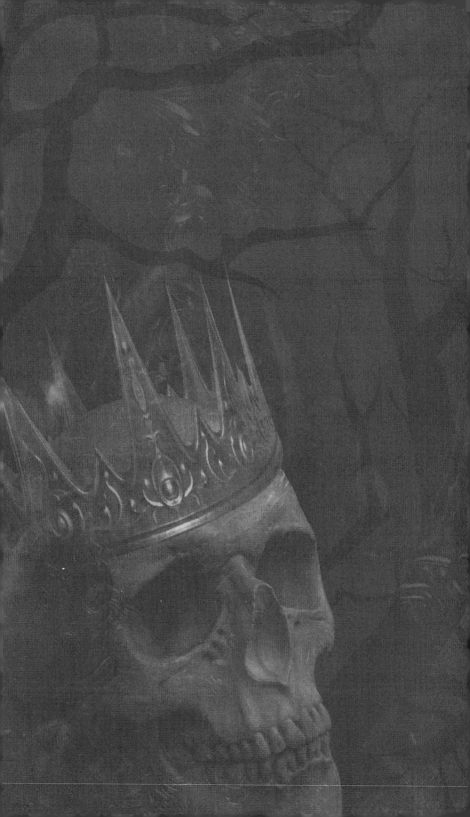

CHAPTER EIGHT

BREYLA

S weat pours down my back and forehead as I block another attack from Elijah's blunted sword.

"C'mon, General. I know you're better than that," Eli taunts and smirks at me. His golden locks are tied up in a knot on top of his head. I can see sweat forming on him, but not nearly as much as me since he's wearing substantially less clothing. I train in my leathers, but he only wears trousers and boots. His bare chest gleams in the sunlight, highlighting all the lines of the eight-pack lining his abdomen. Ryder and Zion stand outside the practice ring; both are also bare-chested and gleaming in the late summer sun. Eli catches me staring. "My eyes are up here, General."

"I'm just distracted. Did you get more abs since my last visit?" I ask, trying to flame his ego. I know how my friend works, and I just hope he doesn't realize what I'm up to.

"Why, I thought you'd never notice. Too bad I know what you're doing, and it won't work. No amount of flattery will distract me from kicking your ass," he says, winking at me.

Dammit. It was worth a shot. I take a deep breath before feinting right and going to his left instead. With a quick twirl, he blocks my sword and flips the blade from my hands. It sails several yards, landing out of my reach.

I suddenly feel eyes on me, and I don't have to look to know it's the future king watching from the shadows. He thinks himself inconspicuous, but I am acutely aware of every time he watches me. I turn my attention back to Elijah. I'm disarmed and running out of options. In a move that's as much for my comfort as it is a distraction to the males present, I remove the leather vest holding my tunic in place. I slip off the tunic as well, leaving me only in the wrap binding my breasts down. While the move is scandalous, I can't be bothered to care. I was the general of the royal army. It was something I did frequently amongst my soldiers, albeit not appropriate behavior for a *princess.* This was one of the many reasons why I hated that title and the expectations with which it came.

"Now that's not playing fair, B. If you wanted to get naked with me, you didn't need to get me into the training yard to do so," Elijah complains. How he manages to whine and flirt simultaneously is a skill only he seems to have.

"Stop flirting, and let's finish this," I quip back. He charges me, sword raised, but he doesn't see my next move coming. I rush at him, and at the last second, I drop down and slide under his outstretched sword arm. I spring to my feet and jump on his back, wrapping my forearm around his neck and squeezing just hard enough. He's forced to drop his sword to try and remove me from his back. *Perfect.*

"Yield," I demand.

"Never," he manages to get out. He immediately goes limp and falls backward onto the dirt. We both hit the ground hard, but I hit harder with his weight coming down on top of mine. I gasp for air, struggling to breathe deeply. I finally manage to get out one word.

"Ass."

Before I know what's happening, he's on top of me, restraining both of my hands with just one of his. "Do you yield?" he asks, a mischievous glint in his eyes.

"Never," I say, repeating his words back to him. It seems like that's what he wanted to hear, because he then uses his free hand to start tickling my bare sides.

Squirming beneath him, I make a sound that's somewhere between a laugh and a snort. "Not. Fair," I manage to get out. Elijah starts laughing at the embarrassing noises, and I take the opportunity to wrap my shadows around his torso and flip him onto his back next to me.

We laugh as we stare at the sky for several minutes until we're both out of breath. "You fight dirty. Those moves were downright unfair," I complain.

"Well, you know what they say about fair."

"And what's that?" I turn to my side and stare at him.

"Nothing in this world is fair, Breyla. It's impartial at best."

I let that answer roll around in my brain before asking, "What do you know of Lady Ophelia?"

"Not nearly as much as I'd like. Why do you ask?"

I quirk an eyebrow at his odd response but let it slide. "She came to me and asked to be one of my ladies. Said I seemed like I needed a friend."

He lets out a mock gasp. "Are you replacing me?!"

I elbow him in the side. "Of course not, you ass. I could never. You're like a bad smell that won't go away."

"Don't lie; you love my smell," he says with a grin before reaching over to pull me into a hug and shoving my head into his sweaty chest. Even with the sweat, I could still smell the cinnamon and chocolate scent that was uniquely Elijah.

"Okay, okay," I mumble into him, squirming to get free. "I love you, but you stink. What I meant was—do you think I can trust her?"

Elijah sighs. "I'm not sure. Lord Seamus, definitely not. She is his daughter, and if you had asked me this even two days ago, I would have said no."

"But?"

"But...I may have accidentally read her most recent memories when I bumped into her yesterday."

"Care to elaborate?"

"I didn't mean to, but I had left my gloves in your room, and when I saw her, I literally ran into her. I reached out to steady her, and because her arms were bare, I was able to see glimpses of her memory from right before she came to you. I saw her caring for Lyla. It wasn't clear what had happened to her, but it didn't seem like it was the first time. It was also a result of something Lord Seamus had done. I know we can't trust him, but someone who cares that much about the lowest of us has some good in them. I don't know her intentions, but I'd be more inclined to trust her."

I had known Eli long enough to know when he was hiding something from me. He wasn't telling me everything, but that's his prerogative. He would never keep something from me that could hurt me.

"You're probably right." I pause before asking my next question. "Does Lord Seamus seem overly interested in the line of succession and my mother's personal affairs?"

Elijah tears out some of the grass surrounding the training rings, which are really just dirt circles where the grass no longer grows. Technically, my mother could use her Kaminari Gift to make the grass cease its growth, but we had been training in these exact spots for so many years that there was no need. My father and Commander Nolan preferred the training rooms at the castle's bottom level, but I had always been partial to the open sky. Since my father's death, I have no desire to visit the spaces where his memory is the strongest for me.

"He's always been nosey, but yes, he does seem rather

invested in the matter. You saw him at the last council meeting, but that was just a glimpse of how he's been." Asking Elijah to be my eyes and ears at court rather than be by my side as I led the army was one of the hardest but most necessary things I had ever done. He's an exceptional warrior, and despite his flirtatious façade, he is brilliant.

"I can imagine. I plan to see what he's like at the next council meeting. I need to know what he's up to."

"I'll keep a closer eye on him for you in the meantime."

"What would I ever do without you?" I ask in the fakest swoony voice I can muster.

"Probably die of boredom," he responds like he's considered this answer.

"You think mighty highly of yourself." I smile at him.

"Someone has to."

"Half of the ladies at court seem to think so as well," I say, teasing him.

"Well, most of them probably have reason to." He grins like the cat that ate the canary.

"You're shameless." I slap him lightly on the chest, and he catches my wrist in his large hand.

"You know you'll always be my number one, B." Like I said, shameless.

"Funny enough...Ophelia was under the impression we were more than just friends."

He bursts into laughter. "I don't know what would have ever given her that impression."

"Probably your shameless flirting." I stare at him.

He continues laughing. "Probably, but I flirt with everyone. Her included." He was quiet for some time before he asked, "Did you know Aurelius summoned Julian and Jade to the capital?"

"He. Did. What?" I grit out. Julian and Jade, also known as the Twins of Death, were two of our childhood friends and now high-ranking captains in the royal army. Their skill in combat had earned them the nickname and their spot on my war council. I had entrusted my soldiers to them while I was away. Aurelius had pulled my number two and three away from where they were needed. Not only was it reckless, but it was also dangerous and stupid.

I use my shadows to search for the male I know is still watching me. Immediately, I pull the shadows away from where he's hiding and glare straight at him. I jump to my feet, Elijah behind me, Ryder and Zion not far behind him. I come to a stop just inches from him and shove him in the chest.

"How dare you!" I practically scream at him.

Aurelius smirks at me like he knows something I don't. "There she is." He trails a finger lightly down my jaw, tipping my chin up to look into his sparkling eyes.

"Excuse me?" I snatch his hand from my face, twisting it backwards in a hold that made most males whimper.

Not this male, though. No, his eyes widen in intrigue. "There's the general I've heard so much about," he says, grinning at me. It's at that moment I know I've lost this game. He sees straight through me.

Since the meeting with my father's ghost, I had carefully spent my time distracting the court so I could be free to roam the halls unbothered. I had already danced through the castle halls in my undergarments, given the children at the palace copious sweets before sending them to their parents, used the portraits of past monarchs as target practice, and set fire to the kitchens this week. The last one was a bit of an accident, but the kitchen staff had banned me from entering anyway. All that effort was wasted as Aurelius stared straight through me. He had purposely stroked my anger to elicit a reaction, and it had worked.

I release him with a snarl. He turns away from me and strides from the training yard. I'm breathing hard when Elijah says, "I could cut the tension between you with a knife."

Apparently, Aurelius isn't far enough away when he says this because we hear him yell, "That's not how she uses her knives!"

I feel an arm wrap around me from behind right as I try to take off after the insufferable male. "Whoa there, tiger. Let's not kill stepdaddy dearest today," Elijah chuckles in my ear.

"I wasn't going to kill him. I was just going to show him how creative I can be with my knives." This has all three males behind me laughing.

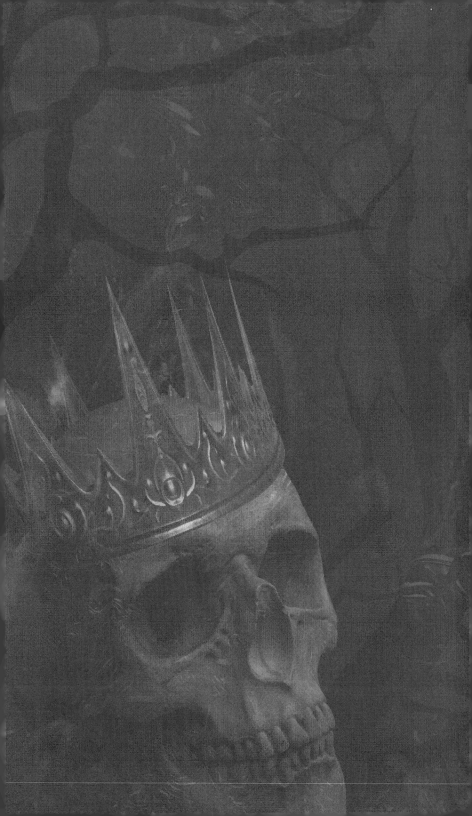

CHAPTER NINE

AURELIUS

I roll my head from side to side, trying to alleviate the stiffness that has crept into my neck. My investigation into Lord Seamus has gone nowhere. It's maddening how little I can find out about him. I had learned he wasn't kind to his servants and treated his daughter, Ophelia, almost as poorly. He appeared to despise all females, was exceptionally nosey, and a prick. I already knew most of this or at least suspected it. His son, Layne, was his glorified errand boy, often securing business contracts and acting on his behalf with merchants and contacts from other kingdoms. When I approached the spymaster, Lord Craylor, he had been tight-lipped. The most interesting thing I discovered was from my training yard encounter with Breyla yesterday. She had known I was there the whole time but still spoke freely.

It was worth noting that she and Elijah suspected something more was going on with Lord Seamus. They didn't speculate much on what he might be hiding, but they seemed to think they would learn more at the next council meeting. Which I will be attending in precisely two days. With any luck, the Twins of Death would arrive by then. It had been a bit of a calculated risk summoning them to court, especially with their general already here. I knew they were crucial in defending our people and borders, but I still don't trust Breyla's intentions. I thought bringing them here would stir up enough to make the princess show her cards.

A sudden knock at my door draws me out of my contemplation. "Well, speak of the devil," I say upon seeing Breyla outside my room.

"Yeah, I'm looking at him," she says shortly and pushes her way into my room. Before I can get a word in, she's yelling, "You had no right! They are my second and third in command. By bringing them here, you created a massive risk." I can feel her rage from here as I close the door.

"I have every right," I say calmly. My own rage flares inside of me, but she's hot-headed enough for the both of us, so I remain calm. "I am the future king, and as such, I will do what I deem necessary for the safety of our kingdom."

Breyla rears back and spits, her warm saliva landing directly on my cheek. "You are no king of mine." Her words are venomous as her eyes narrow.

My jaw ticks as she's nearing the end of my patience. I rub away the spit with the back of my hand and take a step closer to her. She's aware I've seen through her act. Still feeling the need to rub it in, I say, "There she is. I'm so glad we dropped the broken, mad, drunkard act. It was unbecoming. I much prefer the angry, possessed demoness in front of me."

Her nostrils flare, jaw clenching, and in a flash, she hits me square in the face. "I don't give a damn what you prefer," she seethes. *I was not expecting that.* "They are mine to command, not yours. How could you do something so reckless?!"

I rub my aching jaw, tasting blood on my tongue. "Be careful, little demon. I may not hit females, but I do bite. You are wearing my patience thin."

This time I see her fist, catching her hand in mine before it can make contact. I push her roughly into the wall, pinning her hands above her head. Fire dances in her emerald eyes. I stare intensely into them as I speak, "I took a calculated risk that was well within my rights as your future king. It was not one made lightly, and not one I would have made if I did not have full faith in the soldiers under your command."

I can still feel her heart overworking itself, the beats erratic, as anger courses her veins. She's wound tightly. A rational discussion with her like this isn't possible, and she isn't calming down on her own. She's been holding this in since yesterday, maybe longer. I let my Hemonia Gift seep out of me and into her. It immediately goes to work calming her racing heart to a normal level. A look of confusion crosses her face at the sudden de-escalation.

"Is that you? Did you just manipulate my anger?" she questions.

"Yes, that was me, but no, I didn't manipulate your feelings. I removed your body's physical reaction to the anger by calming your pulse. I can't make you feel anything; I just tempered your anger so we could converse like civilized adults."

I can tell I've piqued her interest when she responds, "I want to be angry right now, but I'm finding it impossible. That's incredibly invasive, but it's also...rather useful. What else can you do with that?"

An idea I shouldn't be entertaining forms, "Would you like me to tell you...or show you?" I quirk an eyebrow at her.

She bites her lip, trying to determine if my words have a hidden meaning. "Show me," she whispers. *Good girl.*

I slow her pulse considerably, to the point she's close to losing consciousness. "I can bring your heart to a near stop to make you sleep."

"Or kill me?" she asks with a yawn.

"That too." I bring her heart rate back to normal, then slowly increase it. "Or I can speed it up to make you more alert."

Her eyes dart back and forth rapidly as I once again return her back to normal. Next, I direct all the blood in her left side to flow away from her arm, rendering it numb and useless.

"Now that's strange!" she exclaims.

I return the blood flow to her arm and lean in closer. We're chest to chest, pressed against the wall, when I whisper, "I can make it flow to...other places, as well."

Her breath hitches, and she asks, "Like where?"

I work so slowly she's barely able to detect it. I wait until she realizes what I'm doing before I explain, "I can make more blood flow to your most sensitive parts. Increasing your pleasure and making it almost a need to be touched."

She's breathing rapidly as her arousal grows, and I smell it. I may have started this, but she's clearly into it. "If I release you, will you be a good little demon and not try to punch me again?"

All I get is a hesitant nod before I release her wrists but stay pressed tightly against her. As I lower my hands I run them gingerly down her sides, tracing every wonderful curve. My hands come to rest on her hips, and I squeeze tightly. "That's my good little demon."

Just like that, the wire snaps and her lips are on mine. A growl erupts from my throat when she pushes her tongue past my lips. She kisses like she fights—rough and dirty. It's all consuming, and I kiss her back harder, taking everything from her. I slip a hand into her auburn curls and tug hard, pulling her head back. She moans as I alternate kisses and soft bites down her neck, settling between her ample breasts.

I feel her wanting to fight against me, but also fighting how good this feels. I slip my knee between her thighs, forcing her legs to widen until I'm fit perfectly against her sex. It's clear her arousal is growing as she rolls her hips against me. My hand runs across the bare skin under her tunic, feeling my way up to her breasts, and I lightly flick her nipple with my thumb. She groans deeply and rocks her hips shamelessly against my thigh.

"That's it. Be a good girl and moan for me," I growl. I slip her breast out of the tunic and suck her nipple into my mouth. The noise she makes for me is decadent. Her nails dig into my side as she rides my leg closer to her finish. Her noises alone have me rock hard. I can feel my cock aching inside my trousers, begging to be set free. As if she can read my mind, she reaches down and grips me through my pants.

It's not enough for her, though. She slips her hand down the front of my pants and grabs my cock, pulling it out. She guides her hand up and down my shaft, her movements somewhat sporadic as she closes in on her own release. Completely lost in the feel of this female, I realize I am no longer using my Gift to heighten her pleasure. This arousal is all her own, and that thought has me releasing a feral growl. Her eyes began to close, and her hips move faster against my thigh.

"Fuck, Princess. Keep riding my thigh like you wish it was my cock."

This is both the best and most idiotic way I've ever used my Gift. It wasn't the first time I had used it in this fashion, but this female was the definition of off-limits to me. And I knew that this time would never be enough. I would want more of this beautiful creature in every way I shouldn't want her. She's the daughter of my late brother and my now fiancé, but none of that matters as I watch her writhe against me, chasing her release at my hands.

"Eyes on me, Princess. I want to see you when I make you come," I demand, and her eyes snap to mine. As if those dirty words are all she needs, I watch her tip over the edge. Her thighs squeeze my own, searching for something to fill her. I watch the aftershocks roll through her as I gently rub my thigh against her, ringing every last ounce of pleasure from her body. I grab her hand and shove it between where my thigh meets her apex and run it through the wet mess there. I bring her fingers up to my lips and suck them into my mouth. I groan at the taste. *"That's* what I can do with my power, Princess."

I release her, stepping back from the wall. My still-aching cock practically weeps as I shove it back into my pants and smirk at her. I commit the image of her flushed, disheveled, pouty lips hanging open in awe to memory. Something to relieve myself with later.

She finally opens her mouth to speak. "Can you please...stop it now?"

I give her a confused look before asking, "Are you still feeling aroused?"

She nods at me, and I grin widely. "I stopped using my Gift on you several minutes ago, Breyla. That arousal is all your own."

She has nothing left to say, her cheeks an even brighter shade of red. She turns to leave my room, but as she reaches the door she says quietly, "You will never be my king, and I will never kneel to you." For some reason, that remark stings more than I expect. The door slams behind her as she leaves.

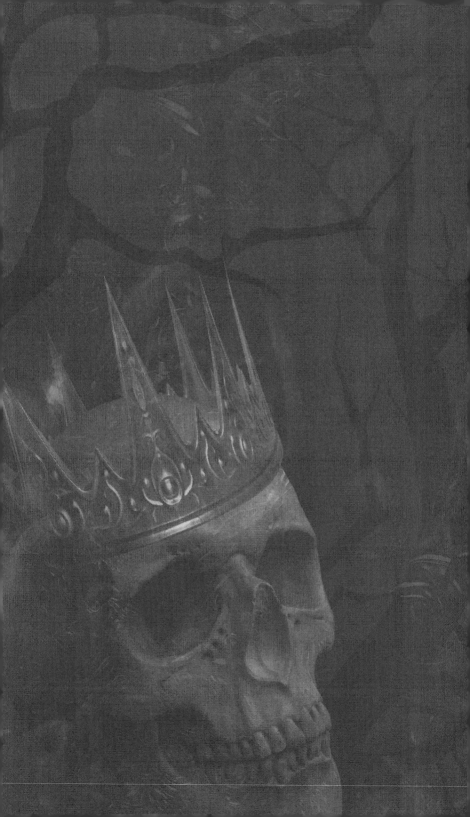

CHAPTER TEN

BREYLA

I wake the next morning feeling simultaneously rested and frustrated. Last night was the most sound I've slept in months. *Maybe I should have found someone to fuck before now.* I groan at the thought of having to face Aurelius at breakfast. I somehow know he will find a way to subtly remind me of what happened last night. Mortification rolls through me at not only what I allowed him to do to me with his Gift, but also how my body responded to his touch.

A shiver runs down my back as I recall his words from last night, *"Eyes on me, Princess. I want to see you when I make you come."* I should be disgusted, but all I feel is aroused. My mind wars with the Aurelius I know from the past and the one who brought me utter bliss last night.

"Why do you let her get under your skin, Aurelius?" my father asked. This was a conversation I wasn't meant to hear, but now I needed to know what they were discussing. I assumed this had something to do with our latest encounter.

I had no one to help me learn my newly manifested control—

or lack thereof—over shadows. I was the only one on record to have this Gift in several hundred years. As there was no one to compare with, it was difficult to know the extent of my power. I was rare and powerful in the eyes of society, but all I felt was alone. My parents were no help, since neither of their Gifts were anything close to mine, leaving me with only Cillian to teach me control.

His Gift wasn't one of shadows, but it was similar and equally rare, belonging to the Madilim power family. Together we learned to master our Gifts to the best of our abilities. This week he had shown me how to create a blindfold with my shadows and use it on others. Aurelius was my favorite—albeit unwilling—test subject. He had walked into a wall so hard he broke his nose on impact when I cast the shadow blindfold.

I thought it quite funny, but I was the only one. This conversation was bound to happen, but I doubted they expected me to be listening around the corner.

"I can't help it," Aurelius grunted. "She does it so perfectly I wonder when she has time for anything else."

"Yes, well." My father sighed before continuing. "She does rather excel at that." The way he said the last part almost sounded like pride, or perhaps amusement.

"And that does not concern you?" Aurelius asked, his voice rising in volume.

"Not particularly. I have always loved my daughter exactly as she is. She is half me, after all." My heart swelled at my father's words. He had never pushed me to be anything different than what I was. To better myself, yes, but he never tried to change what made me fundamentally me. He embraced my sharp edges and taught me to wield them as weapons.

"And I would not change her, brother. I simply wish to coexist with her peacefully; something she seems intent on never happening." I could understand Aurelius' desire, and a part of me longed for the same thing. But just as much as I got under his

78

skin, he got under mine. There was a push and pull between us that never relented. Anytime I was near him, I felt the overwhelming desire to be close to him, and I hated that. Aurelius gave as good as he got, though. Something many people seemed to overlook.

"What is the problem between you? Why isn't peace an option?" Father asked, attempting to understand the tension between us.

"She is the problem," Aurelius replied quietly. My chest tightened at his words. I shouldn't have cared what he thought of me. His words shouldn't have had any effect on me. But they did. I never wanted to be anyone's problem. The fact that he saw me as one hurt more than I wanted to admit. Not wanting to hear anymore, I turned and retreated down the hallway.

I shake myself from the memory and focus on the day ahead. I pull myself out of bed and into my bathing chamber. I quickly bathe and braid my hair in a crown around my head, the tail draping over my left shoulder. I have no plans to train today, so I forgo leathers and opt for lightweight trousers that hug my hips, but flow loosely down my legs. I pull on a deep forest-green tunic that brings out the gold and red hues of my hair. Tucking the tunic into my pants, I pull a strapless bodice around my torso and lace it up the front. Since I go nowhere unarmed, I grab a sheathed, slim dagger and slide it down the front of my bodice. It nestles snuggly between my breasts, undetectable.

When I reach the breakfast table my mother and Aurelius are already there. I sit beside my mother and across from Aurelius, careful to keep my gaze off the male. I reach for the teacup before me, letting the hot liquid warm my hands through the ceramic. Warm spices waft up from the brew; rich notes of cinnamon, turmeric, and ginger wash over my tongue as I take the first sip.

"Good morning, Breyla. You look rested. Did you sleep

well?" my mother asks as she takes a bite of the eggs in front of her.

"I did, thank you. How are you this morning?" I can make polite small talk. This is easy. A servant places a plate before Aurelius, causing him to wrinkle his nose in displeasure.

My mother takes notice of his expression. "Is something wrong with your breakfast?"

"Nothing is wrong, eggs just don't sit well with me." He smiles at her.

"We'll send it back and have them prepare something else." She smiles back, and I suppress an eye roll.

"Staff," Mother calls politely. "Please take Lord Aurelius's plate to the kitchen and prepare something else for him. Thank you."

Aurelius's plate is cleared away, and he folds his hands in front of him. I catch his eye momentarily and am surprised to see his face remains neutral. Based on our previous interactions, I would have expected Aurelius to be smug or find some way to taunt me for our clandestine meeting yesterday. Instead, I find only indifference.

"What was it you were asking, dear?" My mother's attention is back on me.

"Nothing important, Mother. Have you set a date for your wedding?" I'm trying to keep the attention off me, so I choose a topic I can fake interest in.

Aurelius coughs suddenly, choking on his tea. He clears his throat. "Not yet. We are in no rush." Did my question make him uncomfortable? Perhaps he isn't as indifferent as he pretends to be.

"I was only nineteen when I was engaged and married to your father. The wedding happened so quickly; I have no intention of rushing anything this time. The council seems content with my betrothal to Aurelius for now, as am I." Her answer surprises me a bit. With how quickly she announced her engagement to Aurelius, I figured they would also move for a quick wedding. "Speaking of, you know I would never force you into marriage, but you are twenty-seven, my dear. Are there any males that have caught your eye?"

This time it was my turn to choke on my drink. "I, uh—" I'm saved from having to answer by a shriek from the kitchens.

The screams continue as we all jump to our feet. Aurelius steps in front of my mother, his sword drawn. I draw the thin dagger from my bodice and make my way to the kitchens. When I arrive, the scene is horrific. The servant that cleared Aurelius's breakfast is laying on the floor, eyes wide. Foam coats her mouth and blood leaks out of her eyes, ears, and nose. It's clear the screaming came from the other servant on the floor next to her.

Wisps of blonde hair hang in a chaotic mess around her thin, heart-shaped face. Brown eyes fill with tears as she pulls in shallow, quick breaths. She's hysterical, crying and mumbling about the girl on the floor.

I crouch down to look her in the eyes and ask, "Can you tell me what happened? I'm sorry, I don't know your name."

"Melody. M-my name is Melody," she stammers. "I'm not sure exactly. One moment we're chatting, and the next Sera is on the floor, jerking uncontrollably, and b-bleeding. Oh gods...she's d-dead." She trembles violently.

I turn to Aurelius. "Can you help calm her down like you did me?" I may be questioned about that statement later, but I don't care right now. I need Melody to calm down enough to piece together what happened. He leans down and places a hand on Melody's shoulder.

"You're okay. I'm going to use my Gift to slow your heart rate to help calm you. Is that alright?" I can't help the respect I feel for how he explains himself first and asks for her permission. She nods slightly, and I can see the effects of his magic almost immediately. Her breathing slows, and the trembling stops.

She looks at us and whispers, "Thank you."

"Of course, Melody. Now can you tell me anything else about what happened? Did Sera eat or drink anything before this happened?" Aurelius asks, his tone soothing.

"She brought in your plate, Lord Aurelius, and ate the eggs. The chef usually lets us eat what's sent back, since it would just go to waste otherwise. I think that's it. I don't remember anything else." Tears are still running down her face.

"Okay, Melody. Thank you for your help. You are dismissed for the day. I'll make sure you're still compensated, but please go rest. You've been a great help." I smile at her, hoping she understands my sincerity.

"As you wish, My Lady. Thank you," she says quietly then pulls herself off the floor. She exits the kitchen, leaving me alone with a castle guard, Aurelius, and my mother.

"That poison was meant for you. Care to tell me what enemies you've made that wish you dead?" I deadpan.

"I'll let you know as soon as I figure that out," Aurelius says, his brow furrowing.

My instincts kick in, and I take charge of the situation, giving commands. "Alert Commander Nolan. No one enters or leaves the castle. I want all the kitchen staff questioned. Someone must have seen something. If the culprit is still in the castle, we will find them." The guard bows and leaves to follow my orders. I lean down and close Sera's eyes.

"At least she went quickly," I say to myself. "Which is a load of shit, because that fact won't make it hurt any less for her loved ones. It's just one of those things we're conditioned to think because no one is taught how to handle death."

Aurelius looks like he wants to say something but remains quiet. I still don't trust him, but I also don't think he'd go as far as poisoning himself. But it begs the question—*why* did someone want him dead? Sure, he made me want to strangle him any time he opened his mouth, but we have a special relationship. He was the royal emissary; his position was one intended to promote peace. An attack on him by a foreign kingdom would be considered an act of war. If it came from someone within our kingdom...it just didn't make sense.

Mother had remained silent through this entire ordeal. I look back to her to find her eyes wide and mouth hanging ajar. She looks shocked, which makes sense, but she was normally much better at not showing her true feelings. She was always stoic when it came to things like this. The ability to mask one's feelings was a skill that most royals were trained in, but one I failed at miserably. The situation must unsettle her.

"Are you okay, Mother?"

She snaps out of her daze and turns her eyes to me. "I-I'm okay. It's just a bit upsetting to have someone try to murder Aurelius so soon after Raynor's...death. I don't know what to think." I walk over and wrap my arms around her. She stands a couple inches above me, her warm vanilla scent cocooning me. I would be her support if she needed it.

"We'll figure this out. I promise," I reassure her, leaning back to look into her sky-blue eyes, now red and swollen. "I'm posting extra guards outside your and Aurelius's rooms." I hope that brings her comfort.

"I hardly think that's—" Aurelius begins.

"I'll decide what is necessary and what's not, Lord Aurelius," I snap at him. The look on his face suggests he doesn't appreciate my tone, but he isn't going to fight me on this.

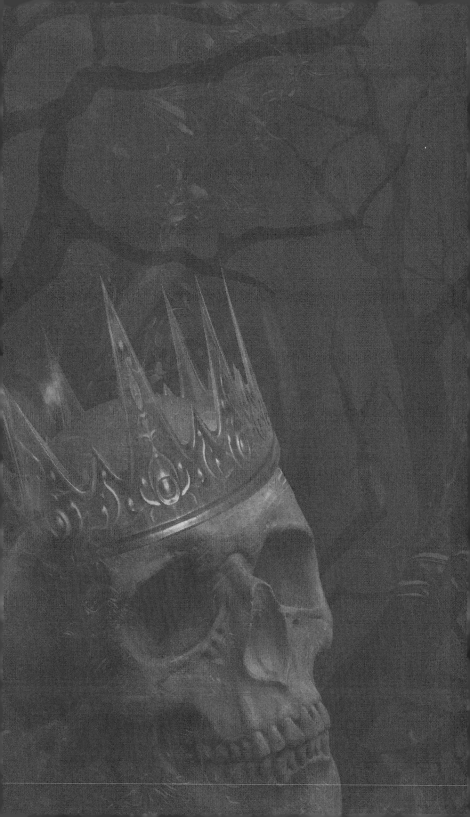

CHAPTER ELEVEN

AURELIUS

As the new day greets me, I'm filled with more questions than I know what to do with. I wasn't unaccustomed to death, but it usually wasn't coming for me. Who could be bold enough to attempt to poison the emissary and future King of Rimor? Perhaps it was the same person that took the life of the last king. That was a strong possibility.

Pulling the sheets back, I force myself out of bed. Today is the first council meeting since I arrived at court. I hope it will be more productive than all the investigating I've attempted so far. I slip on a pair of black leather trousers and a matching tunic. My hands run through my black waves, attempting to appear put together. Truthfully, I didn't sleep well last night, but I can't let that show.

I had summoned the twins, Julian and Jade, to court and they were set to arrive sometime today, hopefully in time for the council meeting. My hope is that they would be an asset here, even if I had originally only summoned them to provoke Breyla. They were powerful and had earned their positions as Breyla's second and third in command. Julian was not only skilled with any weapon handed to him, but his Gift allowed him to bend metal. Jade was equally gifted with a sword, but her Gift was far more valuable—the Anima Gift of coercion. With a simple touch she could bend others to her will. She could make you utter any truth, even cause you to turn your sword on your best friend. According to my sources, it was not a Gift she took lightly, reserving it for only the most necessary situations.

No matter how today goes, I expect I will at least be entertained. I exit my chambers, sparing a glance for the extra guards. I sigh, *damn infuriating female.* We both knew they were unnecessary, but she seemed to delight in exuding her power over me. When she was a teenager, we had come to blows more than once.

"Aurelius! You're needed in the king's chambers. Emergency council meeting or something!" Breyla shouted through my door as her fists pounded against it repeatedly.

I stared at the beautiful blonde with her head thrown back in lust currently riding me. Grabbing her hips, I rocked her back and forth, urging her closer to her release—and hopefully my own. For good measure, I used my Hemonia Gift to direct the blood flow to her clit and increase her pleasure. A moan left her lips that would leave no question as to what we were doing.

But Breyla already knew that. She had interrupted this very thing three times in the last several weeks. All in retaliation for when I interrupted her rendezvous with Simon a month ago. It was now a game to her; one I ruefully engaged in. We went back and forth, finding new and creative ways to inconvenience, interrupt, or insult the other.

Breyla hammered the door with her fist again and shouted, "Aurelius, you can fuck your whore later! You're needed now!"

"Fuck off, Breyla," I grunted, knowing damn well there was no emergency council meeting.

"Last chance before I break the door down and drag you out myself," Breyla threatened.

"Perhaps she's telling the truth," Elle said breathlessly above me.

"She's not, but she will break down that door," I said as I flipped our positions on the bed. "So, I'm going to need you to come for me." I growled and thrust into her. Leaving her no time to adjust, I quickened my pace and rubbed her clit in slow circles. Right as I felt her clamp down on my cock in orgasm, I heard the door slam open, splintering on impact with the wall.

"Woops," Breyla said with a shrug.

Elle's head is thrown back in pure ecstasy, but I'm still painfully hard inside her, no closer to my own release.

"For fuck's sake, Breyla." Throwing a blanket over Elle's naked body, I stood and stalked toward the infuriating princess standing in my room. "Was destroying my door necessary?"

"It was an accident. I don't know the strength of my own power." She batted her eyes in faux innocence.

"Fucking horse shit. I've seen you craft actual keys from shadows and open doors that way. You did that on purpose," I seethed.

She didn't reply but bit the inside of her cheek to keep from laughing. In an attempt to appear innocent, she cast her eyes down. Realizing her mistake too late, her eyes widened in surprise as she got an eyeful of my still fully erect cock.

"For the love of the gods, Aurelius, put some pants on," she said dramatically as she threw her head back to avoid looking at me any longer. I resisted the urge to wrap my hands around her delicate throat and squeeze the attitude out of her.

Sighing, I found the nearest pair of sleep pants on the floor and pulled them up my legs. Using every bit of my Hemonia Gift, I willed the blood away from my cock and let it soften, once again aching for the release she had denied me.

Bringing her eyes back to mine, she smirked. "They're waiting for you in the council room."

I pushed past her, off to a meeting I knew didn't exist, while I plotted how to repay her for this latest interruption.

She outranked me, but at that time she didn't overpower me, and I was prone to flaunting it in front of her, so making me submit was her way of getting back at me. Eventually, she would bow before me; I would get her on her knees one way or another.

As I make my way to breakfast, I pass a soldier that informs me that the twins have arrived but were already meeting with the general and would be unavailable until the council meeting this afternoon. I don't know if it's intentional, but Breyla has already worn my patience thin, and the day is still young.

My train of thought is interrupted by the soft voice of a servant. "Pardon me, Lord Aurelius. The queen has requested you join her for a private breakfast."

I wasn't expecting an invitation for a private breakfast with Gen, but it will help keep my thoughts away from how much I currently want to wrap my hands around the princess' throat. Giving a nod to the servant, I let them guide me to where the queen waits.

It's not typically used for eating, but a table has been set up near two stuffed armchairs. A fireplace occupies the center of one wall, surrounded by shelves housing various books and trinkets. Given the late summer season, the fireplace remains empty, but the windows have been opened to allow in the sunshine and a light breeze. There's an air of peace in the room, something that often accompanies Genevieve.

She's sitting in one of the armchairs, smiling warmly at me as I take my seat across from her. A spread of breakfast pastries, potatoes, sausage, and fruit has been set out for us on the table. I let out a sigh of relief at the absence of eggs. As the last of the servants leaves the room, Gen visibly relaxes and curls into the large chair, tucking her feet underneath her.

"Good morning," she greets.

I sit beside her and reach for a cup of steaming tea. "Good morning." I smile in return. Taking a long sip, I relish the warm herbal tea. "Lavender?" I ask, quirking a brow at Gen.

"I find it helps quell my nerves before having to endure council meetings." She finishes her cup, setting it down next to her, and reaches for one of the flakey chocolate-filled pastries she's fond of.

"The council makes you nervous? Since when?" Being born a royal, she's been dealing with council members since she was very young. Undoubtedly for longer than I have. I grab a dish full of raspberries, strawberries, and blackberries, then begin popping them in my mouth.

"Since I lost Raynor," she says solemnly. "Since I stopped knowing who to trust."

Her words cause something to click, and I set down my fruit. "You didn't just bring me here because I was the only one you could trust, did you?"

Her lips quirk in a half smile. "No, I didn't," she replies quietly, shifting uncomfortably.

I keep quiet, waiting for her to explain.

"With Raynor around, I always knew who I could trust. Now, I'm second guessing everything and everyone. You weren't here much before his death, but things had begun to change in recent months. Raynor confided in me less and in his council more. I can't logically explain it, Aurelius, but I feel something coming. Something big. I need your Gift to help guide me." Genevieve shoves the last chunk of pastry in her mouth as she finishes.

I'm saddened that she feels she couldn't share this with me before, but also concerned that she doesn't believe she can trust anyone. Given how she is feeling, it makes sense that she would ask for my help. My secondary Anima Gift allows me to discern the intentions of those around me and detect when others are being honest. Despite being known for my ability to control blood, my Anima Gift made me perfect for my position as royal emissary. Not even Breyla knew I harbored this Gift.

"I've already told you—I'm here for whatever you need from me. I must ask, though. Have you told Breyla any of this?"

"Which part?" Genevieve asks. She bites her thumb nail, a mannerism that betrays her nervousness. I haven't seen her do it since she discovered she was pregnant with Breyla. She had been so afraid of becoming a mother, but I knew she would make a great one. I was thirteen then and had little interest in babies, but my brother was delighted. It was the only thing he could talk about anytime he visited home. To see the nervous habit return after nearly three decades let me know how unsettled she must be feeling.

"Any of it," I clarify.

She sighs. "No. Breyla idolized Raynor. He was a good male, but he had faults. She never saw them, though. When she couldn't even come home for his funeral, how was I supposed to tell her any of that? I refuse to break my daughter's heart any further."

"And about the council? What have you told her about that?"

Her eyes drop to her lap, and a sad smile creeps across her face. "Nothing. I've tried to talk to her many times since she arrived, but she refuses to speak with me. The most I can get is indifference and barbed words. I don't know what to do, Aurelius."

Though I'm angry to learn that Breyla refuses to speak with her mother, I'm not surprised. Her recent actions align with that. "Trust me, I don't know what to do with that sharp tongue of hers either," I mutter.

That's not entirely true, though. There are a few things I could think to do with that tongue—but none of which I should be.

"Is she giving you trouble again?"

"When did she stop? That daughter of yours has been a menace since I arrived in the castle when I was *twenty*, Gen. How someone like you could produce a female so infuriating is beyond my understanding."

She chuckles, "If it weren't so true, I might be offended that you are speaking of my daughter this way. You forget she is equal parts me and Raynor. I'd say you two were like fire and ice, but that's not quite right. You're more like fire and fire, constantly locked in a battle of feeding each other's flames and hoping you don't get burned."

"That's accurate." Trying to shift the conversation away from the female I can't stop thinking about, I ask "What about Elijah? Breyla has always trusted him, and I've never felt any ill intentions from him."

"I trust Elijah completely. He might as well be my son. His parents—Olivera and Daniel—served on the council until they died unexpectedly when Elijah was four. Olivera was a dear friend of mine, so Elijah was already like family. It wasn't even a question to take him in. He and Breyla have been inseparable for most of their lives, and I know I can rely on him. He's smart but he's also young. I'm no fool, I know he only accepted the position on the council for Breyla's sake. He tells her everything, so it saves me from relaying information to her."

Some of this I knew, but some of it is new. Elijah's parent's death happened before my time at court, so I had no idea they had served before him—or that Gen was friends with his mother. It certainly explains why she is so fond of Elijah and why Breyla is so comfortable with him.

"Gen, I'm going to tell you something that's probably uncomfortable for you to hear, but it needs to be said." I was her friend first and everything else second. As her friend, it sometimes meant giving her the truth she didn't want to hear.

"Well, go on," she says.

"I know you mean well and want to protect your daughter, but you're not. You're only hurting her in the long run by keeping these things from her. I don't care if you say she won't talk to you—you're her mother and queen. You can make her sit and listen. She may be acting indifferent right now, but she needs you and you need her. I can only assume she doesn't understand the nature of our arrangement or relationship, as well. So, she probably feels betrayed that you would move on from Raynor so quickly. Keeping all these things from her is only hurting you both," I say as gently as possible while still getting my point across.

Gen's eyes welled up, and I almost regretted saying what I had said, but she needed to hear it.

"I can't, Aurelius. What if I tell her and I lose her, too?"

"So, you'd rather she remain indifferent and cold toward you?" I'm having trouble grasping how telling Breyla could be a bad thing.

"If it means she's safe, then yes. There are some things she's better off not knowing."

I slump in my chair and let out a deep sigh. While I may not understand her logic, this conversation is over because Genevieve rarely does anything without reason.

"Fine, Gen. If you want me to keep your secrets, I will. I don't understand your reasoning, but I trust you. However, I still think you should keep trying to talk to Breyla. You need each other." These aren't my secrets to share, but what are a few more to keep?

Nearly everyone is already present and seated when I arrive at the council room. I take the seat to the right of Genevieve, and across from Breyla. Standing behind Breyla is Jade and Julian. Though they share a similar bone structure, hazel eyes, and warm brown skin, it's easy to tell them apart. Julian keeps his raven hair trimmed short to his scalp, while Jade's silver-white hair hangs in braids that nearly reaches her waist. Julian stands almost as tall as I, while Jade is several inches taller than Breyla. They are an intimidating, yet breathtaking sight.

I look down at the table to find we are only waiting for Lord Seamus. I'm sure his late arrival is just a way to make himself feel more important than he really is. A few moments later he makes his appearance, a smug look on his face. *I wonder what that's about.*

"Well, now that Lord Seamus has graced us with his presence we can begin," the queen says, her voice full of irritation. "We have much to discuss."

Breyla speaks up first. "In case anyone hadn't heard, someone attempted to poison Lord Aurelius yesterday. Fortunately for him, he had sent back the tainted food, but it was rather unfortunate for the kitchen servant who ate it instead." Everyone has the decency to act surprised and horrified by this news, even Seamus.

"Were you able to discern who was behind it?" Lord Jaeson asks. He is powerful, but inexperienced in many ways. His Gift manifested unusually early at the age of eight. He's the youngest on the council—younger than even Elijah—at twenty-five years. So while he's had seventeen years to hone his power over fire, he's still learning the intricacies of court politics.

"Not yet. We plan to question the castle staff and guards today. Lord Aurelius will assist me, as well as Commander Jade." That catches their attention. They all knew what powers each of us possessed and what that would mean for those being questioned. "Rest assured, if those responsible are within these walls... we *will* find them," Breyla promises.

Lord Seamus clears his throat, "Do you suspect it to be someone within these walls?"

"I'm not ruling out any possibilities." Breyla glares at him.

"Lord Aurelius, surely you think this notion is absurd? As emissary, surely you have made no enemies in such a position." Seamus looks to me to side with him. I find it intriguing that he is adamant that it could not be someone within the castle. But I also find it offensive that he would try to rely on another male to convince the general she was wrong for thinking the way she did.

"Lord Seamus, I only find it absurd that you would try to rely on another male to undermine your princess and general. I agree with General Breyla's decision and line of thinking," I spit at him. "I do not believe my position as *emissary* has anything to do with why I'm being targeted." That earns me a heated look from Seamus and a slight smile from Breyla.

"Now onto the next order of business," Breyla starts. "The attacks from Prudia have grown in boldness and frequency. My commanders, Jade and Julian, have more information to report."

"My Lords and Ladies," Julian starts, "in the weeks before our arrival we suffered three separate attacks on border villages. We were able to fight them off, but not without heavy losses. They're not attacking females or children, but have no problem making widows and orphans. The odd thing seems to be the locations they're attacking. They aren't going for areas that would easily provide a foothold into Rimor. Their attacks are sporadic and spaced out...almost like they're trying to get our attention or provoke us."

The queen has been quiet, but finally says, "They sense weakness and want to test us. They're looking for something they think they're owed."

"That makes sense with the passing of King Raynor," Breyla muses. "But to what end? Even if they sense instability, they can't seriously think they can take on the full force of our armies.

They stand no chance of overtaking the capital, even if they make it into our lands."

"I wouldn't be so sure, General," Jade says. "I sent scouts out shortly before we were summoned to the capital. Their reports show significantly more troops than our last estimate. While our armies are better trained and far more powerful, they most likely outnumber us."

Breyla's jaw ticks before she asks, "By how many?"

"Three to one, if the scouts' reports are correct."

"Prince Ayden certainly has been busy."

"With much more than we realize," Genevieve adds. Breyla quirks an eyebrow at her but doesn't say anything.

"I'm concerned about the locations of these attacks," Breyla starts. "What if they aren't random?"

"What's their strategy?" I question.

"If they know they outnumber us, they could be thinning out our troops by drawing them to villages as far apart as possible. They take out as many of our people as possible, but the real goal is separating us so they can overpower us when they push forward." This explanation has everyone in the room quiet.

"For all of our sakes, General, I hope you are wrong," Lady Daphne says solemnly. She's an older female, soft spoken, but wise. She's seen a lot of fighting through her years, so I understand why she doesn't want to see war reach us.

"I hope so, too," Breyla replies. "Julian, has Prince Ayden requested any meetings with us?"

"Not so far, General."

"Perhaps a proactive approach would serve us better. We could invite Prince Ayden to Ciyoria to negotiate terms of peace." *Absolutely fucking not.* Breyla doesn't know what damage that could cause. The Prince of Prudia was finicky on the best of days. He was unpredictable and difficult from my experiences with him. Prior to Raynor's death, the king had me working toward a political alliance with Prudia that would bring peace for our two kingdoms. But that had died with the late king. Causing trouble was one of Prince Ayden's fortes, causing me to want him nowhere near this palace—or Breyla.

"A nice sentiment, but I would advise against that." I try to keep my voice even.

Her eyes dart to me. "Why is that, Lord Aurelius?"

"Forgive me, General, but you have not spent time there as I have. As emissary I have made numerous trips to Prudia. I feel I can speak to Prince Ayden's character at least a bit. For years he has been driven by one thing—vengeance for his Father's death. He does not care that King Raynor killed him in battle; he wants restitution. I fear if you invite him here it will be like letting the wolf into the chicken coop. It will cause far more damage than the alternative." I pray that's enough to convince her.

She mulls over my warning. "I will take your warning under advisement, My Lord," she finally says.

"Perhaps we should address why the kingdom of Prudia views us as unstable right now," Lord Rion suggests.

"Lord Rion is right," Lady Daphne agrees. "My Queen, you have announced your betrothal to your council, but you haven't made a public statement, set a date, or planned a betrothal celebration ball. You need to put our people's minds at ease and squash any sentiment of instability."

A few other council members agree. Lord Seamus has been uncharacteristically quiet. I glance at him and he's still wearing that smug look, like he knows something we don't.

"Lord Rion, you are approaching two centuries in life, correct?" Queen Genevieve asks. She looks exhausted. Dark circles are lining her eyes, and she seems thinner, her cheekbones more prominent than before.

"That is correct, Your Majesty," he responds, unsure where this is going.

"And you and your wife have been married since you were very young?"

"Since we were twenty-three," he confirms.

"So, you've spent nearly one hundred and seventy years together. How would you feel if you were to lose her, then find yourself being pressured into marrying another just a month after her passing?"

"I...I would call them crazy. There's no way I would marry so soon; it would be disrespectful to her memory."

"I was blessed with twenty-nine years with my soulmate. Twenty. Nine. Years. A mere fraction of what you have spent with your wife. I will take advice from you *only* when you have felt my pain. I am just out of the mourning period. It's been barely six weeks, and you want to rush me into marrying another? I will not disrespect his memory. I pray you never feel what I feel, but if you ever do, we can talk then. That is all I will say on the matter."

Just like that, the conversation is over. Council members shift uncomfortably, several rising to leave the meeting.

"I have something else I would like to bring to the table, Your Majesty," Lord Seamus says.

"Get on with it," Genevieve says impatiently.

He turns his attention to Breyla. "General, you didn't return home for your father's funeral—why is that?"

Breyla's face is completely unreadable as she responds, "I was unable to return home for his last rites, and the reasoning is my own. I owe you no explanation, Lord Seamus."

"Indeed, but I think you'll find I am not the only one wondering why you would bother returning now when you couldn't be bothered to see your father off into the afterlife." Lord Seamus' words are accusatory and laced with venom.

"Be that as it may, I answer to none of you. Remember your place, Seamus," Breyla growls.

Genevieve stands, resting her palms on the table as she stares down Lord Seamus. "What is your point, My Lord?"

"I have it on good authority that Breyla's true purpose in

being in the capital is to make a move for the throne herself. She plans to displace you as queen. It appears that she didn't care about the death of her Father, seeing as she couldn't be bothered to come home when he passed. She only bothered to return when she learned about your engagement to Lord Aurelius. How do we know she isn't the one behind his attempted murder? She wants the throne and needs the two of you out of the way."

I see a slight smile at the corner of Breyla's mouth before her, the queen, and Elijah are all laughing. The other council members look confused, but Seamus looks utterly irate.

Trying to catch her breath, Breyla gasps, "Who in the world told you that? I have no intention of reaching for *any* crown. I understand I will wear it one day, but I will do whatever I can to prolong that time." She winks at Lord Seamus. "Thanks for the laugh, though. I think we all really needed that."

Lord Seamus is fuming, his heart beating so rapidly I fear it might fail him. If only we could be so lucky. He opens his mouth to speak but is silenced by the whoosh of a slim dagger landing in the wood of the table barely an inch from his right hand.

Eyes wide, he looks up to Breyla, who is now wearing a sinister smile. "Oh, and Seamus?" she sing-songs.

"Yes," he grits out.

"If I were going to kill someone, I wouldn't use poison. I'd slit their fucking throat," Breyla says, turning on her heel to exit the room.

"Now, if you'll excuse us, we have servants to question and a murderer to find," I say, finally ending the meeting. I retrieve Breyla's dagger as everyone exits the meeting room. I'm a few paces behind Breyla, but quickly close the distance and grab her wrist, pulling her into an alcove in the hallway.

"Okay, Princess, start talking," I demand.

She smiles coyly at me. "Is that normally what people do when they're pulled into dark corners by dark sinful males?"

Darkness surrounds us as her shadows wrap around our bodies, helping blend us into the wall's stonework. Anyone passing by would see an empty alcove, and the secrecy of our conversation only contributes to the feeling that I shouldn't be this close to Breyla. Logically, I should be putting space between us, but my logic had a habit of fleeing when it came to her.

I lean in close, trapping her against the stone wall and whisper, "Oh, little demon, there are *many* other things I would prefer to do in this situation." I sense her heart beating faster and her eyes widening. "That's not the reason for this conversation. I need to know who wants me dead as much as you do—probably more. But what I really want to know is why you named me for questioning the servants? What value do I add in comparison to Jade?" It was a valid question; one that anyone would ask.

She grins widely at me. "Oh, Aurelius. I know your secret."

"Oh? Is that so? And what might that secret be?" I keep my tone neutral to not betray my panic. Thanks to Gen, I'm keeping more than one secret, so I'm eager to hear which one she knows.

"You may be known for what you can do with blood, but I know you have an Anima Gift. You keep it hidden well; I'll give you that. It was always impossible to lie to you, and I always wondered why, but one day it just clicked. It's not just me—you know when *anyone* lies." She smiles triumphantly.

A sigh of relief gets trapped in my throat. "That's not quite all of it, but it's the gist. I don't know how you figured it out, but please keep that to yourself."

"Of course, My Lord. It will be difficult to keep from Jade during the investigation, though."

I trail my hand up the wall next to her, letting my fingers nearly touch her, but resisting—just barely. When my hand reaches her neck, I wrap my fingers around her slender throat and squeeze. My grip is firm, but not painful, to accentuate my next point. "You can tell her if you must, but if I find out anyone else knows...you will regret it."

Her eyes flare wide as she asks, "Are you threatening me, Aurelius?"

"Never, Princess. Just stating a fact." I release my grip on her throat after a few moments, stepping back to put distance between us. Breyla's breathing heavy, her chest heaving and eyes roaming me in an assessing gaze.

"Oh, and Princess? You left this behind," I say as I flick her dagger back at her. Her shadows reach up and snag the blade out of the air before it can come close to her skin.

She narrows her eyes at me, and I give her a wink, turning from her and making my way toward the kitchens.

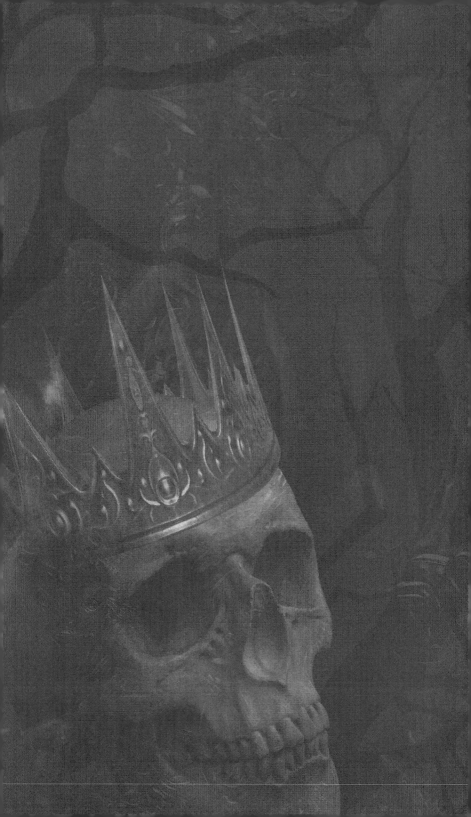

CHAPTER TWELVE

BREYLA

"You ready for this, General?" Jade asks.

Jade, Aurelius, and I had been interrogating the kitchen staff for hours. I would ask the questions, Aurelius would subtly alert me if he sensed a lie, then Jade would use her compulsion Gift to get the truth out of them. Or that's how it would have gone if we had talked to anyone who knew something about the attempted murder. We are no closer to an answer now than when we started.

"We only have a couple servants and the cook left, correct?" I ask with quiet desperation for this to be over.

"Correct. The cook is coming in now," Aurelius says as he lays a hand on my shoulder. It's meant to be supportive, but I can't help the reaction my body gives to the warmth where our skin meets. Arousal isn't what I should be feeling, but the goosebumps pebbling my skin suggest something is wrong with me. I know he feels it when his hand tightens slightly on my shoulder before it drops away entirely. I should be relieved, but disappointment is all I feel at the loss of his touch.

I roll my shoulders, trying to work out the knot forming between my shoulder blades. An older male enters the room, his apron covered in flour and other various ingredients for cooking. He sits in the empty chair before us, folding his hands in his lap. His hair is graying, and the wrinkles at the corner of his eyes show his age. I don't really know him, but he has cooked for the palace since my father was a child.

I smile softly at him. "Do you know why you're here, Mino?"

"I assume it had something to do with the poisoned eggs one of the kitchen girls ate?" he guesses.

"That would be correct. We have questioned most of the kitchen staff but have learned nothing of value. We're hoping you can help us determine the source of the poison meant for Lord Aurelius." The last part comes out almost like a plea.

"I'll do what I can. What would you like to know, Princess?"

"Start at the beginning of the day. Tell me everything you did, people you spoke with, anything unusual or out of place?"

"The day started the same as every other. I woke before dawn to prepare the bread and pastries for the day. The rest of the servants get there right at sunrise most days. They help with plating and delivering the food, some minor cooking if I trust them."

"Was there anyone new that day? Or just new in general?" I question.

"No one new in several months. All servants are vetted by Commander Nolan first and then assigned by Lord Elijah. We haven't seen a new face in the kitchen in quite some time." I had already guessed as much but wanted confirmation.

"And you didn't see anyone unfamiliar in the kitchens that morning? Someone who didn't belong?" Aurelius butts in.

"No, M'lord. No one except the kitchen staff and myself."

"Let's try something different. Mino, can you tell me where the food you use for the castle comes from?" I'm grasping at straws to get any kind of lead.

"Well, that's easy enough; most of our food comes from various farms and vendors in Ciyoria. Although..." he bites his lip as something occurs to him.

"Although, what?" I prod.

"Lately we've been getting more and more produce from one vendor than we have in the past. In fact, I don't recall them providing much until the last few months."

"What's odd about that?" I question.

"Nothing odd per se, but a few times I've caught them trying to sell us poisonous mushrooms that were mixed in with the rest. It's not so strange on its own—they look similar and grow close together. An honest mistake, but one that needs close watching. The most recent shipment we received from them was several days before the bad eggs, but I usually oversee and inspect the delivery to ensure no mistakes like that are made. I could not be there for the delivery that day, so I don't know who did the inspection."

That was finally something I could work with. I turn to Aurelius, and he gives me a slight nod. Everything Mino has said thus far has been the truth.

"Okay, Mino. Can you tell me exactly what was in that shipment?"

"Mostly produce. No livestock or eggs, I'm afraid."

"Specifically, what produce?" My tone is slightly elevated as I try to contain my enthusiasm for finally getting somewhere.

"Carrots, potatoes, celery, some parsnips I believe."

Alarm bells go off in my head. "Did you say parsnips?"

"I did, Princess. I use it in my stews."

"Please take me to where you store the produce. I need to see it *now*."

"Of course. Right this way." He looks slightly confused but leads us to the pantry. He gestures to a section of the wall. "This is all the produce, and right there," he points to the shelf third from bottom, "are the parsnips."

I lean down and pull out the box. It only takes me a moment to find what I suspected was there. "This whole box needs to be disposed of, Mino. These aren't parsnips—they're hemlock root."

Part of my training as a soldier was how to survive off the land. I was taught common poisonous plants and berries to ensure I didn't accidentally poison myself or others by eating the wrong thing. It's not a skill set needed at court, so I wouldn't expect most of the kitchen staff to recognize the difference between parsnip and water hemlock.

He stares at me wide eyed, "Of course, Princess. I—I had no idea. I n-never would have allowed for the delivery had I known." He's panicking, but I know it wasn't him. It might have been a slight oversight on his part, but it wasn't his fault it made its way into Aurelius's breakfast.

"I know, Mino. Thank you for helping us figure out what the poison was. Perhaps cut ties with this vendor." If I could figure out who the vendor was, I *might* be able to figure out who was behind this.

Once he is gone, I turn to Aurelius and Jade. "That's it for today. We've done enough for now."

"Perfect timing, because Julian will be here momentarily," Jade says matter-of-factly.

"How—"

"That twin thing still freaks me out," I say at the same time as Aurelius.

Jade just shrugs as Julian opens the door and strides in. "Made any progress?"

"As a matter of fact, we have," I tell him. "We still don't have a 'who', but we know what the poison was and potentially where it came from."

"Intriguing. Well, at least you have more information than you did yesterday." Julian rubs his chin, deep in thought. I take a moment to look him over. He, like his twin and myself, is dressed in fighting leathers. I typically only carry daggers when I'm at court—my shadows being the real weapon—but he wears weapons like noble ladies wear jewels. He has a dagger strapped to each muscular thigh and another smaller blade tucked into his right boot. Strapped to his back is his preferred long sword, Bella, her sapphire encrusted handle gleaming in the light. He named every blade, but I only remembered Bella because there were hundreds of them. I'm sure there were more that I couldn't see, knowing him.

I'm leaning against a kitchen counter, Aurelius to my left doing the same. "Now that we're all here, let's talk without the prying eyes of the council," I announce and clap my hands together. "Tell me everything you didn't say in front of Lord Smelly-us." I chuckle at my joke.

"That joke was exceptionally bad," Jade says.

"Did you really just call him 'Lord Smelly-ass'?" Aurelius looks at me incredulously.

"No, I called him Lord Smelly-us, but I think I like Smelly-ass better. It suits him."

"But why?" Aurelius side eyes me like I'm the crazy one.

"Because he's always got his nose in other people's business," Julian says as if that was obvious, which it is of course.

Aurelius rolls his eyes at the three of us and pushes himself off the counter. "Of course, why didn't I think of that? Now if you'll excuse me—"

"Not so fast, pretty boy." Jade puts a hand on his chest to stop him. He gives her a confused look, then looks over to me.

"You summoned them here to get an account of the current state of the armies. That's what they're here to discuss with me, so this is your meeting, too. Unless there was some other reason you pulled my second and third from the front lines," I challenge while picking invisible debris off my shirt. I glance up at him, waiting for an answer.

"Of course not, Princess." There's a glint in his eyes as if to say he's playing along for now. "That's *exactly* why I summoned them here." He dares to smirk at me, and I roll my eyes.

I catch the twins exchanging a look that tells me they are having one of those weird twin conversations that doesn't require words.

"Anyway," I say, dragging out the word. "Please continue, Julian."

"Prince Ayden is playing with you, B," he says bluntly. He's never had a filter and is always brutally honest. It's one of the things I admire most about him.

"He's always been fond of playing games," Aurelius says. Sometimes I forget how many people Aurelius must interact with as part of his position. He would have an insight into the disgruntled prince that most wouldn't.

"Elaborate," I say to both.

"The prince may be the one giving the orders, but we haven't had any reports of him present for any of the attacks. He's notorious for being alongside his soldiers, but he's nowhere to be found. It's extremely out of character for him," Julian explains.

"And it's not just that we're barely able to drive out his troops—they aren't even trying to advance. It's almost as if they've been ordered not to," Jade continues.

"Ayden will try anything to get your attention. That *is* very in character for him," Aurelius adds. "If it were anyone else, I would advise you to ignore his games, but I think that might cause him to increase his efforts."

"Then perhaps it's time we have a chat with him," I suggest. "Find out exactly what it is that he wants." I see Aurelius tense next to me.

"Maybe it's time to negotiate terms of peace," Jade adds. "Gods know I'm tired of camp food. I would love some peace."

"You'd be bored within a month if there wasn't a battle to fight or soldiers to train, Jade," Julian teases, but he's also not wrong. They were both busy bodies and couldn't stand sitting still. Case-in-point, Julian was currently using his power to bend the metal of one of his daggers into different shapes, while Jade paced back and forth.

"Alright, you two are too fidgety. Go find someone to train with and work off that energy."

"That's not exactly how I planned to work off the energy." Jade's tone is full of suggestion.

"Maybe you can find Elijah to 'train' with," Julian suggests using air quotes.

"Okay, that's enough of that conversation!" I am physically pushing them out the kitchen doors now. They both chuckle loudly before finally leaving to do whatever they needed.

"They are something else," Aurelius says once they're gone.

"Just remember, *you* are the one that brought them here. If the castle burns to the ground, you were warned." I fold my arms and stare him down.

"Princess—"

"Stop calling me that," I grit my teeth.

"Never."

I turn to leave, but he catches me around the waist and pulls me back against his chest. "What do you want, Aurelius?" I try to ignore how good it feels to be pressed against him, how well his body fits around mine, and how intoxicating his spiced bergamot scent is. "Let me go," I say, but there's no force behind the words.

"You don't actually mean that, Breyla." He presses his face into my hair and inhales deeply.

"No, I don't," I confirm quietly. "But I should."

"You can't bring Ayden here." He says it like a command, as if he has any say over my actions.

"Actually, My Lord, you'll find that I can." I pull away and turn to face him. "In case you've forgotten, not only am I general of the royal army, but I am *also* the godsdamned princess of this kingdom. It is well within my—"

I'm cut off mid sentence by his lips crashing onto mine. I push against him, trying to break away, but he just kisses me deeper. His hand weaves into my hair, which he uses to maneuver my head to the side and deepen the kiss. I stop fighting and surrender, parting my lips to allow him entrance. His tongue snakes out, tangling with my own as he backs me up against the counter. He tugs at my hair just enough to make me let out a soft moan, while using his other hand to trail up my side, caressing as he goes. He breaks the kiss suddenly, breathing deeply, and leans his forehead against mine.

"What I meant, Princess, was that it is a tremendously bad idea to bring him here," he says softly, no hint of a command present.

"Tell me why," I demand, trying to forget how right it feels to be with him like this. How this intimate position fills me with butterflies. I've slept with my share of males, but I've never experienced intimacy like this. It was all purely physical before, but I have to fight how right it feels just being in Aurelius' arms.

"You'll just have to trust me," is all he says.

"Sorry, handsome, but I don't have any reason to trust you so blindly," I say truthfully. I don't do secrets, and this male feels like he's holding more than one.

"You don't have any reason not to," he argues.

But I do. I still don't know his true reasons for accepting the marriage proposal from my mother. It doesn't make sense, especially with how he kisses *me.* Then there's the message I got from the ghost. I'm still not sure if he had anything to do with my father's death, but he is hiding something from me.

"Please," he says quietly.

"That almost sounds like begging. Typically, that's done on one's knees." I try to joke, pulling back just enough to look him in the eyes.

"If I'm getting on my knees for you, it will be for an entirely different reason, little demon." There is heat in his deep brown eyes. They are so dark they almost look black, and this close I can see flecks of crimson amongst the brown. *Such a beautiful and unusual color.*

"I will consider it," I say, trying to break the tension.

"Thank you."

It's not a promise I'm sure I can keep, and his insistence that I not bring Prince Ayden to court makes me want to do it even more.

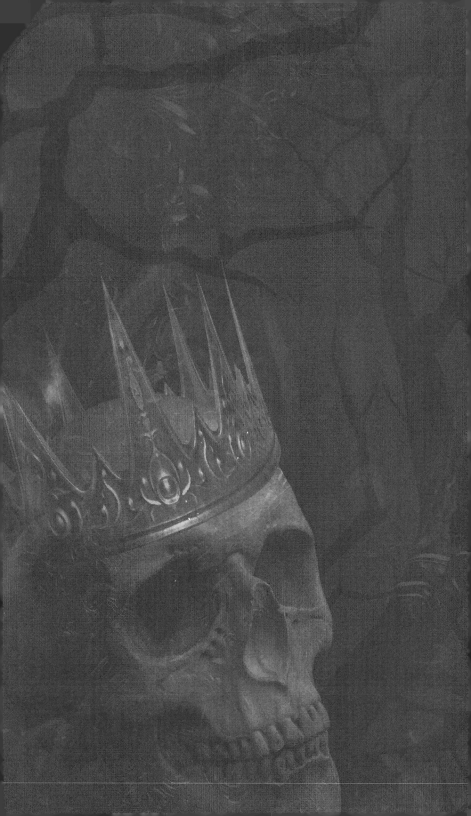

CHAPTER THIRTEEN

BREYLA

I find myself wandering the castle halls, lost in thought. The multitude of information I've learned over the last several days has left me more confused than before I arrived. Then, I just had a dead Father, a ghost, and distaste for my mother—or rather her decisions. Now, I have multiple bodies, at least one murderer on the loose, and an ache growing behind my eyes.

I sigh, rubbing my temples in an attempt to assuage the growing headache. Somehow I ended up in the long hall that houses the portraits of the royal family. Paintings of late royals stare at me, their eyes empty, yet somehow still assessing. It feels like the generations passed are staring at me, judging me for the state of my kingdom.

If they could see Rimor now, I'm sure they'd have things to say. "Yeah, I know, I'm disappointed in me, too." Thoughts of my father's ghost occupy my mind. He had seemed so sure Aurelius was behind his death, but I had yet to find anything that suggested such a thing. He was hiding things, but nothing fit together. I'm missing pieces of the puzzle. I sigh, moving down the wall to the next set of portraits.

This one is the most recent—a painting my mother had commissioned the day my father officially stepped down and handed the title of General to me. I smile softly at the memory of that day.

"Mother, please stop messing with my hair. Lyla has already perfected it," I grumbled, trying to push her hands away. She was just nit-picking, but I knew she meant well.

"I know, sweetheart. I'm just so proud of you, and I want this moment captured perfectly." She stopped messing with my curls, instead grabbing my gold and ruby diadem and placing it on my head.

"We already have family portraits. I don't understand why we need another," I mumbled.

She raised an incredulous eyebrow at me. "The last family portrait we have is from the day you turned seven, Breyla. I haven't been able to get you to sit for another in the eighteen years since then. You can indulge me on this."

"Listen to your mother, Breyla. She doesn't ask much of you." My father's deep timber was kind but left no room for argument.

"Fine," I conceded. If I gave her this, maybe she wouldn't bother me for another eighteen years. I could figure out how to sit for several boring hours in the same place.

My mother's soft hand gently stroked my cheek, and I let myself lean into her touch, savoring the feel of her peace.

"You know I only care so much because I love you, right? I couldn't have asked for a better daughter and heir. I'm so proud of you," she said, emotion choking her.

"We both are," my father agreed, wrapping his arm around my mother's shoulders and pulling her to his side. He softly kissed her forehead, and she relaxed in his embrace.

"I still remember this day vividly," my mother says, bringing me out of my memory. I don't know when she got here.

"I was just thinking about it," I say. This is my first time alone with her since I arrived home. The situation is one I've been avoiding for as long as I can.

"We were both so proud of you," she says.

"I'm aware." My tone is even as I say this, hoping it conveys the indifference I feel.

"Breyla, I think there's something—" she starts, but is interrupted by my blunt question.

"Was it hard pretending to love him, or was the hard part waiting two whole weeks to move onto his brother?"

I feel the sharp sting of her palm meeting my cheek before I ever see it coming. My mother never reprimanded me as a child —that was always my father's role. Guilt rolls through my gut, and my face throbs where her hand made contact. I touch it gingerly, honestly shocked that she hit me.

"How dare you," she seethes. Her eyes fill with tears as she stares down at me.

"I'm—" I start.

"No, you don't get to say anything. Right now, you get to listen," she spits at me, and I wisely keep my mouth shut. "I loved your father—still love your father—with my entire being. Not a day goes by that my soul does not ache for him. I never once had to fake my feelings for him. The *only* reason I'm currently engaged to Aurelius is to protect you. I am doing all of this to protect you, you stupid, selfish child."

"I don't need protection," I mumble, trying not to provoke her wrath further.

"Oh, how very wrong you are about that, daughter." She shakes her head at me, taking a step back. There's a pain in her eyes that I put there. Guilt grows in the pit of my stomach.

"Mother, I'm sorry," I say softly.

"No, you're not. You may feel guilty, but you don't feel remorse for what you said. You can find me again when that changes." She turns away from me and leaves the hall. I'm left standing alone, my face throbbing, and my gut churning.

Julian and Jade find me later that afternoon hanging from one of the trees that surround the training yard. At this time of day, the rings were empty, so I was enjoying the quiet and contemplating my words to my mother from this morning.

"Care to tell us why you're hanging upside down from a tree, B?" Julian asks, quirking a brow at me.

"I find it helps the blood flow better when I need to think," I answer flatly.

They look at each other, shrug, then look back at me. In true Julian and Jade fashion, they just accept the nonsense answer and climb up to hang with me. I sigh, then laugh at the three of us hanging upside down in a tree.

I'm reminded of the three of us in a similar position from years ago.

"What are you doing in the tree?" Jade asked from the ground. I had climbed the tree to escape the servants currently looking for me. My powers had manifested recently—just before my fourteenth birthday.

"I'm hiding," I whisper-shouted. "Now leave before someone sees you and comes to investigate."

The twins glanced at each other, sharing a look that was really an entire silent conversation, and climbed up the tree after me.

"What did you do this time?" Julian asked.

I sighed, swinging my legs back and forth. "I may have blinded Lord Aurelius with my shadows and made him walk into a wall."

"And it was on purpose?" Jade asked.

"Maybe," I replied.

They laughed simultaneously.

"Did he deserve it?" Julian questioned.

I rolled my eyes. "Doesn't he always?"

"Then I guess we're staying here until he forgets." Jade shrugged her shoulders.

"Then I hope you brought dinner because it will be a while."

"You know, I'm not sure this limb can take all three of our weights. We weigh more than we did at fourteen. If this limb breaks and we end up on the ground, I blame you two." That causes a new round of chuckles from the three of us.

"So, what's going on?" Jade asks after the laughing subsides.

I sigh, "I'm just contemplating my failures as daughter and general."

Julian rolls his eyes and says, "Pouting does not flatter you, B. Stop being so dramatic."

"Rude," I snort, giving him a slight shove with my elbow.

"Eh, he's right though. You're not one to seek pity, but right now you seem pitiful," Jade agrees from my other side.

"Wow, you two are really taking it easy on me today. Tell me how you really feel," I say sarcastically.

"We literally just did," Julian says flatly.

"To answer your earlier question—I said something to my mother today that was truly awful, but it was how I felt. Regardless, she probably didn't deserve it."

"What did you say?" Jade questions.

"I asked her if pretending to love my father was hard, or if the hard part was waiting two whole weeks to move on with his brother." I cringe as I repeat the words, realizing now how bad they truly were.

"Ouch," they say in unison.

"Yeah."

"Did you apologize?" Julian asks.

"I tried, but she didn't want to hear it. She said I may feel guilty, but I didn't feel remorse for what I said and that's what mattered. She doesn't want to talk to me now."

Jade hums, swinging her head back and forth slightly, and watches her silver braids wave in the air. "Frankly, I wouldn't want to talk to you either."

"Jade," Julian tsks.

"Julian," she says mockingly back at him. "What? I can't say I blame the queen for how she's feeling. That was exceptionally cruel."

"Perhaps, but I can't fault Breyla for how she felt either. She could have approached it differently, but they're valid feelings."

"Hm, that's fair," Jade concedes. "Do you feel remorseful now?"

"I regret hurting her," I start, "but I don't regret saying it."

Julian shifts his weight back and forth, swinging his torso until he's sitting upright on the branch. He drops to the ground below us and grasps my outstretched arms.

"What are you doing?" I ask.

"Come on, enough sulking. We're going swimming." He tugs me off the branch and into his arms before gently placing me on the ground.

In typical Jade fashion, she needs no help dismounting. She swings her body back and forth until she has enough momentum to flip herself off the branch, landing gracefully beside me.

"Show off," I tease.

She just shrugs and says, "Race you to the river. Loser buys drinks tonight at the tavern."

Jade and Julian both take off before I can respond, leaving me in their dust. I chase after them, my feet pounding the dirt and grass beneath me. Arms pumping, I push myself to catch up to them, but it's not easy when they're both so much taller than me.

I wind through the training yard and royal garden, savoring

the feeling of the earth beneath my bare feet. The late afternoon sun shines brightly, but the slight breeze makes it bearable. We reach the outer wall, the twins still several paces ahead of me. Once outside the gates, I push myself harder through the tall grass, desperately trying to close the distance between us.

As I near the riverbank, I realize it's a lost cause. Drinks are on me tonight. Jade and Julian are both there, already stripping out of their leathers before I even reach them.

"I'm feeling exceptionally thirsty tonight," Julian says, grinning at me.

I roll my eyes as I peel the sweaty layers of clothing off. Once we're all down to our undergarments, we take a running jump into the river. Calling it a river might be a bit of a stretch. It's closer to a stream, just barely enough to swim.

My feet dig into the soft mud at the bottom of the riverbed, and I let out a sigh of relief. The cool water provides the perfect reprieve from the hot sun and my troubled thoughts. I let myself float, the gentle current pushing me slowly down the river. The golden tones of my hair sparkle in the sunlight as it fans out in a halo around my head.

Jade and Julian are wrestling in the water a few feet from me, and Jade looks to be winning. She's currently on Julian's back, her arm wrapped around his neck in a stranglehold. Julian grunts as he attempts to pry his sister from his shoulders. After a few moments of struggling, he changes tactics and throws all his weight back, plunging them both under the surface of the water.

Waves ripple out from their impact, gently rocking me. When they don't reemerge, I get suspicious. I move into a standing position, my senses on high alert. It's not their safety I'm concerned about since we're all adept swimmers. No, I don't trust that they aren't up to something.

Something wraps around both ankles under the water, followed immediately by Julian popping up from the water right behind me. He wraps an arm around my torso at the same time that Jade yanks my feet out from under me. I'm immediately pulled under water, and the three of us hit the riverbed.

Fucking assholes, I think as I kick out to free myself from their grips. They let go easily, and I swim back up to the surface.

Wiping the water out of my eyes and brushing my hair back, I stand and face them. They're both grinning like idiots at my expense. I shoot them a half-hearted glare and flip them off, only making them laugh harder.

In our underwater struggle we have moved further down-river. My eye is drawn to the flower petals and leaves floating on the surface. I can identify most of them easily. Rue and daisies comprise most of the floating flowers, and I think the uniquely shaped purple petals belong to columbine. A flash of vibrant red catches my eye.

"Is that...Oleander?" I say out loud, mostly to myself.

"I didn't think oleander grew around here," Jades replies.

"It doesn't as far as I know, but that definitely looks like it." I take a few steps closer, following the trail of flowers downriver. Jade and Julian follow behind me, careful not to touch the dangerous red petals. They were typically only deadly if ingested, but they could still cause a rash from touch alone.

The further down the trail we follow, the more abundant the flowers become. A few yards down, we approach a large grouping of flowers along the bank, but as we get closer, I realize what else is among them. A startled gasp leaves my lips when I see a body nestled amidst the red, purple, and yellow petals.

The lifeless brown eyes of a castle servant stare up at the sky. She looks young, but it's hard to say for sure with her body bloated and face disfigured, suggesting she's been out here for several days. Most of her skin has also wrinkled from being submerged in the water, so it's hard to say her exact age.

The way the flowers have gathered around her head makes it look as if she's resting on a bed of wildflowers. The beauty of the petals serves as a tragic juxtaposition to her decomposing body.

"It looks like her throat was slit," Julian says solemnly.

Sure enough, there's a deep red line across her throat. What did this poor female do to deserve this?

"Have either of you heard of any servants gone missing?" I question.

"No," they respond in unison.

"But that's not saying much," Jade adds. "We haven't been here for long. I can ask around and see what I can find out."

"I wonder..." Julian starts, his voice trailing off.

"If this female is linked to the poisoning?" I finish his thought with a sigh. "I wonder the same. It seems like too much of a coincidence that she would turn up dead when we still haven't found the one responsible for adding the water hemlock to Lord Aurelius's eggs."

"And you don't believe in coincidences," Jade adds.

"No. I don't."

"Let's get her out of the water so we can figure out who she is and put her to rest," Julian says, taking a step forward.

I put a hand on his chest. "Stop. If you touch that you'll probably break out in a rash. I'll grab someone with a water Gift to move the flowers away from the body first."

Julian rolls his eyes and pushes forward anyway. "Really, Breyla? It's a bit of itching. It's a miracle the wildlife hasn't started eating the body already. Let's just get her out of the river."

He pushes past me, clearly disobeying my order, but I know it's pointless to argue. Since he's already in the thick of the flowers, I might as well let him finish. He scoops her body up and leaves the river. Avoiding the oleander, Jade and I exit a few feet up and follow Julian.

We're still sopping wet when we reach the spot where we left our clothing. I reach down, scooping up my and Julian's leathers.

The confused looks we receive from the castle guards as the

three of us reach the gates would be funny in any other situation. As it is, we have yet another dead body and more questions. My heart sinks at how much I feel I'm failing to protect my people.

Better is expected of me. My people should feel safe in their own kingdom, yet they aren't. I swore an oath to always put my subjects first, but I can't even keep them alive in my own damn castle.

Commander Nolan greets us on the other side of the castle walls. "General, I was alerted there was a body—" He stops in his tracks, seeing the bloated corpse of the servant in Julian's arms. "I see. How can I be of assistance?"

"Commander Julian will take the body to the physicians for further examination. I need you to find out who she is. Question the palace staff until you find out who was missing. By my estimations, she's been dead several days. An absence like that would have been noticed. Once you identify her, please let me know so I can alert her family."

"Very well, General." Nolan nods in understanding. "Do you have any idea what happened to the poor girl?"

I sigh, stepping closer to him. Voice low, I say, "She was murdered, throat slit. I think it could be connected to the attempt made on Lord Aurelius's life. I don't want to create hysteria, so please keep this quiet for now. If anyone asks, let them believe she drowned."

"Of course. You have my word."

I nod to Julian, silently indicating for him to take the body on to the physicians.

Nolan steps closer, resting a gentle hand on my shoulder. "You seem more troubled than I would have expected. You okay, kid?"

He's right, I am more troubled than I ought to be. I've seen more bodies than I could count; it came with waging war and leading an army. I should be used to seeing the dead—and in some ways I am—but it's still not easy. Each life lost inside the castle adds to my growing feeling of inadequacy.

"How am I supposed to keep my people safe from Prudia when I can't even keep them alive within their own home?" I ask softly. If anyone understands how I'm feeling, it's Nolan.

He pulls me into a firm hug and whispers, "This is not your fault. You've proven you're worthy of your position, so don't you for one second doubt the decision your father made. There's something else going on here, you just haven't figured out what yet. But you will."

Nolan's reassurance doesn't fully assuage my guilt, but it does lighten the load. In my father's absence, Nolan is a comforting presence. I spent almost as much time with him growing up as I did my parents. "You sure have a lot of faith in me."

He steps back and looks me in the eyes. "I better. I fucking trained you."

We both chuckle at that. "I should probably get some clothes on now that I'm almost dry," I say.

"Yeah, you're probably right. We can't have the guards getting distracted by their general waltzing around naked, can we?" he teases.

"I'm not *completely* naked. You try getting into leathers while soaking wet. It's physically not possible," I retort.

"Excuses, excuses," he admonishes. "Now get going, and I'll get to work figuring out who the servant was."

I bid him farewell and make my way inside. Once I'm back in the castle, I pull the shadows of the hallway around my body, essentially creating a robe made of darkness. The royal wing is on the opposite side of the castle from where I entered, so it takes me a while to return to my chambers.

Mentally, I'm exhausted and just want to hide in my room for the remainder of the evening. I owe Aurelius an update, though, considering I believe the most recent death to be connected to his attempted poisoning. I don't have the energy to track him down, so I pray he's in his room as I raise my fist to his door.

He opens on the third knock, an irritated look on his face. "Can I help you, Princess?" he huffs.

I cock a brow at him and fold my arms across my chest. The shadows move and twist around me like a living thing. His eyes narrow as he notices for the first time that I'm not exactly *decent.*

"I have something you need to know, but not here. Care to let me in?" I ask as sweetly as I can muster.

"Care to put some clothes on first?" he quips.

"Not particularly," I say, refusing to budge.

After a few moments, he groans and relents. "Fine."

I follow him in, letting the door click shut behind me. He walks to the desk in the corner of the room and pours a healthy measure of spiced rum into a glass. I inch toward him, trying to decipher why he seems so bothered right now.

I drop the leathers I'm carrying on the ground and stop directly in front of him. He narrows his eyes at the clothing on the floor, then turns the glare to me.

"Am I disturbing you, Lord Aurelius?" I challenge.

"That's one word for it," he says, taking a long drink of the amber liquid.

I snatch it from his hands and down the remainder of the rum. Setting the glass on the desk behind us, I cock my head to the side. "Now, here I am trying to share pertinent information about your would-be murderer and I'm somehow bothering *you.*"

His hand darts out, wrapping around my throat, but doesn't squeeze. I swallow hard as his other hand reaches out and moves right through my shadow robe. He caresses my waist softly, letting his hand finally rest on the small of my back. "How did you expect me to react when you showed up at my door, practically naked? My restraint when it comes to you is impressive, but I'm still male."

I can smell the spices of the rum on his breath, and it makes me want to reach out and taste it. I want to find out if the liquor tastes the same on his lips as it does from the bottle, to see if the rum is as intoxicating as his presence.

"It didn't seem like your restraint was all that impressive when you pinned me to the wall and made me come with your Gift." A warmth hums low in my belly at the memory of how hard I came to ruin at his will. I bite my lip, lost in thought at what he could do with more than just his hands.

"Oh, little demon. You're playing a dangerous game. If I had let my restraint snap that night, I would have had you bent over this desk, fucking you until you forgot you aren't supposed to want me." His words make the heat in my belly grow, my clit thrumming between my legs.

"I don't want you," I say, but my words fall flat.

His lips quirk in a half-smile. "I can smell how much that isn't true. Now quit lying and get to why you're here." He shoves me back, releasing my neck.

"We found another body," I start. "A palace servant."

"Any idea who it is or how it's connected to me?"

"We're working on identifying the body right now. Her throat was slit, and she had been left in the river behind the castle. By the looks of it, she'd been there several days."

He pours another measure of rum, bringing the cup to his lips in a long drink. "So, what makes you believe it's related to the eggs?" he questions, trying to connect the dots.

"I don't have any concrete evidence yet, but I don't believe in coincidence, and the timeline lines up too perfectly with the breakfast incident. I should be able to find out more once we can determine who she is and which part of the castle she worked in."

Aurelius nods in understanding. "Is that all of it?"

"For now."

"Then I suggest you leave before my restraint runs out. Regardless of whether it's right or wrong, the next time you show up to my door in this state, I will bend you over this desk." I can't tell if his words are a promise or a threat. He throws back the rest of his drink, obviously done with this conversation.

I smirk at the idea that crosses my mind next. Taking several steps back, I let the shadows fall from my body, leaving me standing in my undergarments. A maniacal laugh escapes me as I catch his nostrils flaring, and a growl erupts from him.

"Until next time, Aurelius," I whisper, leaving his room for my own. What an eventful day it's been.

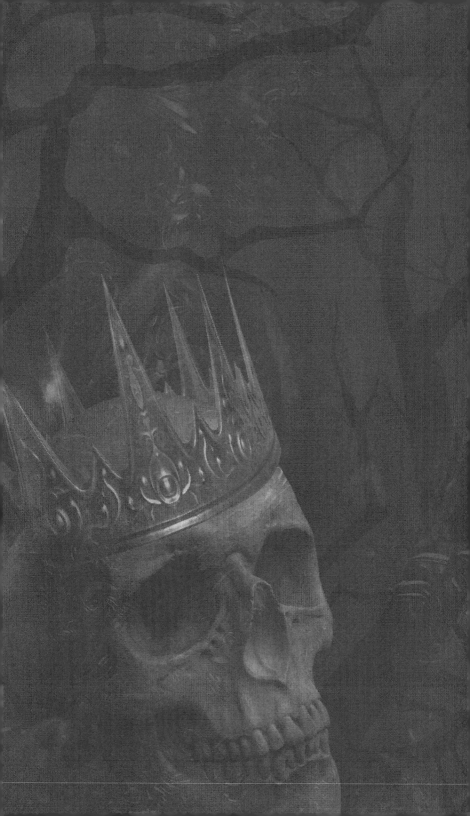

CHAPTER FOURTEEN

BREYLA

The setting sun casts red and gold tones throughout my room, bathing everything in a peaceful glow. I'm lounging in a wingback chair, my feet propped up on a cushioned stool as I read the first chapter in my newest book. It's a guilty pleasure I don't have the opportunity to indulge in when on the battlefield, and one that I desperately need after the last several days. The words paint a moving picture in my mind, allowing me to forget my current situation and breathe. Even if for only a moment, it allowed me to live in someone else's story, feel *their* emotions, and forget the world around me.

As the sun finally disappears and the light begins to fade, a knock sounds on my door. Standing swiftly, I close my book and cross my room, relishing the cool touch of smooth stone on my bare feet. I find Ophelia holding a pitcher of fresh wine on the other side of the door. She smiles at me softly, the last of the gloaming light catching her raven locks and highlighting the blue tones. Her gray eyes sparkle, and though she shares her deplorable father's eyes, hers were soft and welcoming, contrasting his cold and dead orbs. Where I'm toned curves and muscles, she's soft and feminine. Her beauty is truly magnificent. Power or not, it was a mystery why no one had pursued her yet.

"Someone left this outside your door," Ophelia says, lifting the wine jug to me in offering.

"Oh perfect, I've been waiting for that. Thank you." I take the jug from her outstretched arms. "Would you like to come in?"

"Thank you, My Lady." She enters and closes the door behind her.

"Just Breyla," I insist. I hadn't been a 'Lady' since I started training with my father's soldiers at fourteen. It felt strange being referred to in that manner. I pour myself a healthy cup of wine and reach for a second. "Would you care for a glass, Ophelia?"

"Oh, no thank you. Truthfully, I don't handle spirits well. It takes very little before the room spins and I make a fool of myself." She looks embarrassed.

"Are you trying to tell me you're a lightweight?" I chuckle.

"That's one word for it, I suppose."

"Oh, now that's something I must see at some point. You'll have to play drinking games with Eli and I sometime. If you drink with that one, it won't take long to build your tolerance." I see her eyes light at the mention of Eli. *Interesting.*

"Perhaps sometime." She's trying very hard not to show her excitement at the thought of Elijah.

I table that discussion and change subjects to what's been on my mind. "I must say, it was quite humorous to see your father accuse me of reaching for the crown at the last council meeting."

She smiles coyly, a gentle blush coloring her cheeks. "I heard it was quite the show. I wonder where he could have possibly come up with such a ridiculous story." If I wasn't sure about her before, I am now. I like Ophelia.

"Where, indeed." I sport a grin bordering on maniacal. "Sit, let's chat," I say, falling onto the bed and gesturing to the spot next to me. "You have earned my trust, so tell me more about yourself. I know you grew up in court, but I don't feel I really know you."

It's my fault, but I honestly didn't know many ladies. I had known early in life that I preferred swords and fists over needlepoint and gossip. My mother never pushed me to socialize with other girls my age, and my father encouraged my interest in training to take over control of the royal armies. I would have grown bored with the females at court very quickly. I lacked the ability to filter my thoughts around those that annoyed me, making it hard to relate to the women who spouted pretty words to hide their true opinions. Even if my mouth didn't say what I was thinking, my face certainly would. That was one reason I felt ill suited for the throne. Another being that I simply did not want to rule. For some reason I felt like Ophelia would get along with my brand of crude honesty just fine.

"That truly means a lot to me," she says, smiling shyly. "I'm not sure what you'd like to know. My mother died when I was young, and my father pays me little attention because I'm worthless to him without power. My brother, Layne, is really the only one I talk to. Father often has him away from court on business, so I don't get to see him much."

Most of this I already knew. "Your worth is not determined by your power. *You* determine your worth, Ophelia. Never forget that."

Unfortunately, most of our society would agree with her father. Our people value power over anything else. Those with stronger or rarer magical Gifts were more likely to be elevated in status—given titles, lands, better marriage prospects. It's bullshit and not something I heavily value with my soldiers. Sure, those with Gifts are valuable, but I care far more for those who have discipline and can follow orders.

"Thank you, Breyla. I wish more people thought like you."

"I do, too. Now tell me what you enjoy doing for fun, your hobbies, any males you fancy?" I wanted to know more about her. I had never really had female friends, so I was searching for common ground with her.

"I enjoy reading. I'll read practically anything I can get my hands on. Romance and adventure are my favorites." She was beaming now. This was something I could relate to easily. "As for males, there's been no talk of potential matches from my father. I think he believes he won't be able to marry me off to anyone of high enough standing, so he just doesn't try. There is someone at court, though, that I admire from afar. We haven't really spoken much, but he seems kind."

The last part had piqued my interest. "I love reading myself. I don't get to do it much since I'm on the battlefield. You shall have to give me some recommendations. Now tell me who this male is that you admire."

"Oh, no. I couldn't do that. It's not like it will go anywhere, so there's no point in telling anyone."

"Telling me won't hurt anything. I won't tell anyone, cross my heart."

"Fine," Ophelia groans, "but you can't tell him. Swear it."

"I swear; now spill," I demand.

"It's Lord Elijah," she mumbles.

I gasp loudly, clutching my chest. "You like Elijah?!" My words are teasing.

She grabs the pillow behind her and smacks me with it playfully. "This is why I didn't want to tell you. Now you're making fun of me," she pouts.

"Oh, come on now, I'm not making fun of you. If anything, I'm surprised Elijah has an admirer. He may be pretty, but he's a flirt and a complete ass." I try to reassure her. "You could do much better."

"I know he's a flirt, but he doesn't seem like an ass," she reasons.

"Oh, but he is. It's one of my favorite things about him." I grin over the rim of my glass as I take another sip. "Are you going to tell him?"

"Why would I do that?" She seems genuinely curious.

"Why wouldn't you tell him?"

"I have no power, so no one will want me. I'm just a burden at this point." Her insistence on coming back to this point was annoying. Mostly because that line of thinking irked me, even though it wasn't her fault. It was likely engrained in her seeing as that's how most people thought, so I couldn't fault her for it. I could try to break her of it, though.

I grab her hand and look her in her beautiful silver eyes. "Listen to me, Ophelia, you are not a burden." I enunciate every word to drive home my point. "I know that's what most people think, but they're wrong, and I would never have kept Elijah as my best friend for this long if that's how he thought. The choice to tell him is yours, but don't make it based on what you think he will believe. I promise you Elijah won't care whether you have power or not. That's not the kind of male he is."

I don't know if she believes me, but she seems to smile brighter. We spend the rest of the night talking about books and getting to know one another. I don't know if all females are this way, but I know that I want to keep this one around.

I'm unsure what time it is when I hear someone enter my room. Groggily, I reach for the dagger I keep under my pillow. Whoever it is isn't even trying to be stealthy. I hear their heavy footsteps cross the room to my bed. My eyes are open now, but unfocused as I try to leap from my bed to meet my attacker. Something is wrong, though. My limbs are slow to respond, and it feels like I'm moving through molasses. My normally graceful movements and agility are nowhere to be found.

The male in front of me grins and cocks his head at me, "Something wrong, Princess?" There's humor in his voice. I can't seem to focus on his face long enough to identify him. He's male, but that's all I can make out. My vision blurry, I swipe out in an arc attempting to cut him. My movements are slow, and he easily deflects, pushing my arm away from his face.

"Wha...do you want?" My words slur, but it's close enough for him to make out what I'm saying.

"From you? Nothing. Nothing, except your death, that is." He chuckles and lunges forward, burying his knife deep in my gut. It's not placed somewhere that will kill me immediately, but I will bleed out painfully. I grunt but take the opportunity to do my own damage by stabbing my dagger into his thigh. I don't have the strength to drive it deeply, but it'll still hurt.

"You bitch!" he exclaims while pushing me away.

The bed cushions me as I fall, the blade still lodged in my abdomen. The pain is excruciating, and I let loose a scream before my attacker can get to me to cover my mouth. There's a fire burning in my stomach where the knife remains lodged in place. My scream was loud enough for someone to hear. Extra guards were stationed right next to my quarters, outside Aurelius's room. How the attacker got past them is a mystery, and one I can't ponder right now. Instead, I pray someone heard me.

Black starts to creep into the edges of my vision, and I know I'm on the verge of passing out from blood loss. It's the scent of bergamot and rich spices that greets me and the words, "Stay with me, little demon," that I hear as I finally drift into the blackness.

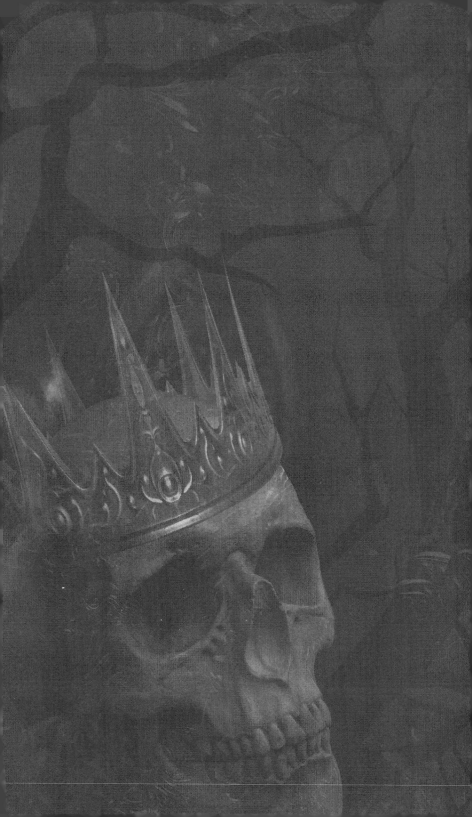

CHAPTER FIFTEEN

AURELIUS

I t was Breyla's piercing scream that woke me from sleep. What I find when I reach her room is so much worse than I imagined. She's laying on her bed, dagger protruding from her stomach and blood pooling around her. She's bleeding out and barely conscious, but I can see she's still breathing, at least for now. There are no guards stationed outside either of our quarters; that's something I'll have to look into later. Right now, I need to stop her bleeding. I'm kneeling beside her bed, applying pressure to the wounded area and cradling her neck.

"Stay with me, little demon," I plead, watching her eyes flutter shut. I feel her heart slowing, but her pulse is still there. I have never been so grateful for my Gift as I am now. I use my Hemonia Gift to slow the flow of blood to her wound, forcing it to clot temporarily so she doesn't lose any more of it.

"Guards! Servants! Anyone?!" I yell at the top of my lungs, hoping someone nearby will hear. I can't leave her now or she *will* bleed out. After what feels like hours—but is truthfully only seconds—a servant peers in through the open doorway.

Her long gray hair and withered hands tell me she's been serving the royal family for quite some time. I believe her name is Lyla, but I'm not as familiar with the staff as I should be. "Please, the princess has been attacked. She needs a healer, but fetch me the castle physician as quickly as you can," I plead. She nods her head and swiftly disappears.

Breyla's breaths are shallow and her freckled skin pale when Lyla returns. Following behind her is not the court physician, but a sleepy-eyed Ophelia in a nightgown. Ophelia seems to know what to do as my jaw drops in confusion. "I don't understand. Why is Lady Ophelia here? I told you to fetch the *physician*." The frustration is clear in my voice. "Breyla is dying, and you brought a female with no power instead?"

"I can explain later, but right now you need to trust me, Lord Aurelius. If you don't, the princess *will* die. I can save her, but only if you let me act now." Her face is serious and confident. I nod, putting my trust and Breyla's life in her hands.

She steps up next to me and covers my hand with her own. "Keep pressure here. Lyla, I need you to pull the knife from Breyla's stomach when I say. Be swift with it."

Lyla steps up behind us and wraps her hands around the knife's pommel.

"On my count," Ophelia starts. "Three, two, one...now!"

Lyla pulls the dagger straight out. I feel Ophelia's hand press harder into my own as the blood starts flowing more freely. It only lasts a second before a white glow comes from Ophelia's hand and rests on top of my own. It's only a few moments more before the blood flow slows and I can see Breyla's flesh knitting itself back together. I can hardly believe my eyes when after a few minutes it looks like there was never a wound there to begin with. It's common knowledge that Ophelia possesses no magical Gifts, but apparently that was incorrect. *How had she managed to keep her ability a secret?* More importantly—*why* would she keep this ability a secret? It would make her one of the most powerful females at court.

I look Ophelia in the eyes as Breyla's heart rate returns to normal. "Thank you," I whisper desperately.

"There's no need to thank me, Lord Aurelius. I care for her, too."

"Of course, I care about her wellbeing. She is the future of this kingdom," I stammer quickly in response.

"Of course." She smiles at me. "She will be out for several hours while she recuperates, but she should fully recover by then. She's very lucky to have you close by. She might not have made it if not for your quick action." Ophelia's shoulders sag, and she seems more exhausted than when she arrived. Her normally bright eyes are dull and glaze over as she looks at me.

"The crown is in your debt, Lady Ophelia. How can we ever repay you?" I question, not sure what she would want in payment.

"You don't need to. Just do me a favor and keep this between us. I don't need anyone else knowing about my Gift." Her tone is serious. She must have a good reason for wanting this kept secret.

"You have my word. But what am I supposed to tell the princess when she wakes? She's not stupid; she'll know this is the work of a healer."

"You can tell her I'm responsible, but if she wants the full story, she must come to me." She looks around the room, noticing the blood and disarray. "Lyla, will you help me clean the princess and change her sheets? Lord Aurelius, we can manage from here."

"No." The word is harsh, but not meant to be mean. "I don't know why none of my guards or hers were here to stop the threat tonight, but I will not be leaving her alone until we know why that is and who is behind the attack. You may clean her, but she will stay with me—in my chambers—where I can watch her. She is obviously not safe alone for the time being."

Once they have her clean, I carry her to my room. There are still no guards at our doors, something I will need to see Commander Nolan about later. For now, I just need to make sure Breyla is safe. I slide her into the unmade side of my bed, covering her with the silk sheets and comforter. The last thing I want is for her to feel threatened or startled when she awakes, so I lay on my side of the bed on top of the sheets, leaving ample room between us.

Lastly, I use my magic to lock the door and then levitate a heavy armoire in front of it, just to be safe. I watch her slow and steady breaths as the adrenaline from the night leaves my body at last. Exhausted, I fall into a deep slumber.

I'm greeted by Breyla's gold-flecked emerald eyes when I wake the next morning. Before I can even open my mouth, she beats me to the first word. "Aurelius, you better have a damn good reason as to why I'm in your bed without memory of how I got here." Her tone is serious, but she doesn't quite seem mad.

"How is 'you were stabbed last night and none of your guards could be found anywhere, so I saved your ass and then refused to let you out of my sight until we found the responsible party' for a reason?" I quirk an eyebrow at her. "Is that good enough for you, Princess?"

She gulps. "There's a lot to unpack there, but I suppose that will do."

"There's a lot we need to discuss, but first, how do you feel?"

"I feel fine. Great, actually." She stretches her arms out above her head.

"Good. What do you remember?" I push a stray auburn lock out of her face and behind her ear.

She leans just slightly into my hand. "Not much, honestly. I remember talking with Ophelia for hours, before eventually falling asleep. I vaguely recall someone entering my room, but from there it gets hazy...Wait, you said I was stabbed?!" There's alarm in her voice. She rips up her shirt to expose her stomach and runs her eyes over the unmarred flesh. She looks up to me, her eyes pleading for an answer.

"I found you with a dagger still embedded in your stomach. I was able to stop the flow at the wound, but I couldn't do anything about the blood loss you had already sustained."

"So who saved me? This goes beyond the court physician's ability, Aurelius. At the very least I shouldn't feel this good. Frankly, I should be dead."

"That is not my story to tell. For that you'll need to talk to Lady Ophelia. She is a very good friend to have." I leave it at that. "There is one blank I can't seem to fill, though. I have seen your reflexes, and I know you would never let anyone sneak up on you like that, even asleep. So how was your attacker able to get close enough to stab you?"

Her brow furrows as she ponders my words, "I think...I was drugged. I had requested more wine from the kitchen, and it was waiting outside my door when Ophelia arrived. Normally they hand the wine to me personally, but I didn't think anything of it. The only thing I can come up with is that someone switched the wine with the poisoned jug. It obviously wasn't intended to kill me, just knock me out enough to make me an easy target."

"We need to talk, Princess." My gaze pins her in place.

"About why I woke up in a male's bed fully clothed for the first time in my life? I think you may be confused about the proper intricacies of the bedroom. Typically, you get the lady naked first, then throw her in your bed to fuc—"

I cut her off by gripping her chin between my thumb and

141

forefinger. She's trying to deflect, but it won't work. I lean in close to her ear. "That filthy mouth of yours is going to get you into trouble," I whisper, and a line of goosebumps trail their way down her neck. "Now, stop trying to deflect, and have a big girl conversation with me."

That last command has her angry, her eyes glaring daggers at me. To add insult to injury, I add, "Good girl," when she doesn't speak any further. I catch the flare of her nostril and the sharp intake of breath.

"Someone wants both of us dead, but they've failed twice. I wouldn't think much of it, except poison was used in both instances. The question is who wants us dead and why?"

"I should think the why would be obvious." Breyla lifts an auburn brow at me. "We're both in line for the throne, Aurelius. Whether by marriage or birth, we are both set to one day rule Rimor. So, the real question is who benefits by disrupting the line of succession?"

"I have my thoughts on that, but nothing I can prove."

"As do I, but at least we know one thing."

"And that would be?"

"We are certainly not the ones behind it, otherwise you would have just left me for dead last night."

"That makes us allies, Princess. It means you have to start trusting me." I grin at her. "It means we have to work together until we get to the bottom of this." The thought excites me more than I want to admit.

She rolls her eyes at me. "Okay, partner. Where do we start?"

I slide my fingers into the hair at the back of her skull and tug gently until I have her full attention. "We start by laying ground rules, and rule number one is that you never roll your eyes at me. I can tolerate that mouth of yours, but the next time you roll your eyes you will discover what the end of my patience looks like."

She gulps, but her gaze doesn't waver. She's not scared of me. On the contrary, she's intrigued. It's then that her scent hits me. She's aroused. "Oh darling, I can smell how much that excites you." Her eyes widen in surprise.

"You can smell that?" She looks at me confused.

"I can smell a great many things, but your arousal is by far my favorite scent." I lean closer to her neck to prove my point and take a deep breath. The scent is intoxicating and has me instantly hard. I lift my torso so I'm leaning over her, my hand still entwined in her hair. She lets out a soft gasp as I tug harder, pulling her head back slightly to expose her neck. My mouth trails light kisses down her throat, peppering her with the occasional bite. With my free hand, I pull her against me, then hitch her left leg up over mine. Her nightgown has shifted up, exposing her ass and bare thighs. I run my hand up the back of them, squeezing and massaging as I go.

This female will be the death of me. Her curves are like something from a dream. She's toned from years of training, but in no way does it take away from her femininity. She's thick in all the right ways.

She's trying to hide how much I'm affecting her, but finally relents when I bite that spot where her neck meets her shoulder as I trail my fingers down her backside to find her entrance. She lets loose a moan as I trail my fingers around her opening, finding her drenched for me already. My fingers tease her, slowly inserting one finger at an agonizing pace. By this point, I'm sucking the skin of her neck, and I know it will leave a mark. She begins rocking her hips, begging for more from me.

I release her skin from my mouth. "Use your words, little demon. Tell me what you want," I say as I still my finger inside her.

"More." Her voice is raspy and full of desperation.

"Ah ah ah, darling," I tsk. "I need specifics."

"Please...make me come." I love hearing her so needy and desperate.

"That's good enough for now, I suppose," I concede. Before she can respond, I have her flat on her back with my hand at her entrance. I insert two fingers, making slow movements. My fingers curl, hitting that delicious spot deep inside her. She moans louder each time I hit it, and I know she's close. I grind my palm into her clit as I increase the pace of my ministrations inside her. My lips are on hers, my tongue demanding entrance. She opens her mouth to let out a moan when I apply pressure to her clit, slowly rubbing in small circles.

Breyla's hands fly up and grab onto my sides, her fingers gripping me tightly. She squeezes hard, her nails raking down my sides. The edge of pain has me moaning this time. Breaking the kiss, I lean down to her ear and demand, "Come for me, little demon."

The command does her in, and I feel her inner walls flutter, then clench around my fingers. As she hits her climax her moans grow louder. I slowly continue my movements, drawing out her release for as long as possible. Finally, I feel her go limp, her breathing deep. I remove my fingers from her and bring them to my mouth. She tastes divine. I suck my fingers in deeper, groaning at the taste.

As she comes down from her high, I see something flip in her eyes. Her mood has shifted from lust to regret faster than I can blink. She's no longer looking at me, so I do the only thing I can think of. I cradle her face in my hand and turn her head until her eyes are back on me. "I'm not done with you, Princess."

Her voice is cold when she quickly replies, "Yes. You are." It should leave no room for argument, but that's never been my style.

"And why is that?"

"Because this," she gestures to the both of us, "us being

together like this isn't right. You're engaged to my mother." The end of that statement feels like a dagger being thrust in my chest.

"Princess, there's something I've tried telling you before, and you need to hear it now—"

"No, there's nothing you can say that makes what we're doing right," she says, cutting me off.

"If you would just—" This time, a knock on the door interrupts me. *Damn it all.*

Reluctantly, I push myself off the bed and cross my room to the idiot interrupting an important discussion. I levitate the armoire away from the door and back into its rightful place on the wall. No one needs to see that Breyla is in my chambers, so I open the door just enough to see who is on the other side. My eyes glare daggers at Elijah and I spit, "What are you doing here?" It's then that I notice his face is lacking his normal jovial disposition. He looks...sad.

"There's been another murder," his voice cracks. "Have you seen Breyla? She's not in her chambers."

"Who—" I start to ask, but Breyla is already shoving me out of the way.

Elijah gives her a questioning look, but she ignores it. "Who is it, E?"

"Breyla..." Elijah's voice is barely more than a whisper. "It's Nolan."

Breyla goes still beside me. "How?" she demands. Nolan had trained Breyla, me, and most of the soldiers in the royal army. It wouldn't have been easy to take him by surprise.

"They found him outside the guards' quarters with his throat slit," Elijah explains.

Breyla nods in understanding. I see her knees shake, but before she can fall, I reach my arm around her back to support her. Elijah is just as quick, though, because he has her fully supported against his chest as she stumbles into him. Her wail pierces the air as she mourns the male who played the role of a second father to her. I know what Nolan meant to her, what he meant to this kingdom. He was simply someone who could not be replaced.

She throws her arms around Elijah's neck and sags against his body. A tingle of jealousy creeps through me at seeing how comfortable she is in another male's arms. Her whole body trembles and shakes with her sobs. Elijah's hand threads through her sun-kissed auburn waves as he gently strokes her hair and tries to soothe her.

As if a switch had flipped, her sobs stop. Her eyes are red and puffy. She stands on her own and pushes through Elijah to her chambers. It's my turn to look confused as my eyes meet Elijah's. He looks concerned, but not surprised at her sudden change. We follow to find her already half dressed in leathers, nightgown discarded on the floor. Her room is spotless, no sign of her blood from last night's attack. Ophelia and Lyla had worked pure magic.

Cautiously, I ask, "Breyla, do you think this could be related to last night's incident or why we could not find any guards stationed outside either of our chambers?" I was careful not to mention too much detail, so as not to expose Ophelia in the process.

"Wait, what?!" Elijah exclaims.

"Someone drugged and attempted to kill me last night. Obviously, they failed. That's why you found me in Aurelius' room this morning. Apparently, the broody, overprotective male thought I was incapable of sleeping alone," she says with cold indifference.

"Excuse me, Princess, if I find it hard to leave a drugged and unconscious female alone and exposed. Especially when they've already been attacked once and there are no guards to be found. Not to mention, she's both the general of the royal army, and the heir to this godsdamned kingdom." My blood is boiling as I finish.

This damn female.

"You *are* excused, Lord Aurelius." The use of my full title is a slap in the face. "I am perfectly capable of taking care of myself. I never asked for your help, nor will I listen to you simply because you are fucking my mother. I told you once already—you will never be my king." She's picking fights to avoid dealing with the emotions Nolan's death has caused. Fighting is all she knows, so she's sticking to that. Logically, I know all this, though my body and tongue have missed the memo.

Quicker than either of us can register, I have her pinned to the wall, my hand wrapped firmly around her throat. She goes still, not responding. "We are allies, little demon, so I'll forgive that last outburst, but the next time you decide to spew lies, I'll show you a much better use for that filthy mouth."

It's then that I notice the dagger she has pressed against my stomach. She's not applying any pressure, and that's how I know she's not serious. The irony of the dagger's placement isn't lost on me. It's the same place she was stabbed last night, and I can't help but smirk. "If you were trying to turn me off, I'm sorry to say you'll have to try harder."

Defeatedly, she drops her arm holding the dagger, and I release my hand from her throat, sensing her blood pressure has returned to a normal level. "Now get your shit together and start acting like the general and not the spoiled brat," I say loud enough for Elijah to hear.

I hear Elijah let a chuckle out at that last command. Breyla shoots daggers at him with her eyes. "Way to just stand there and watch."

"Oh no, I'm not getting sucked into this argument," Elijah insists. "Besides, I really wanted to see that play out."

"Dick," she grumbles at him, trying to hide a smile.

"But I'm your favorite dick."

"Careful, or I'll replace you," she threatens playfully.

"No, you won't," he says confidently as a genuine smile stretches across her face. How he can swing her mood so quickly is an enviable skill, one I find myself hoping to someday attain.

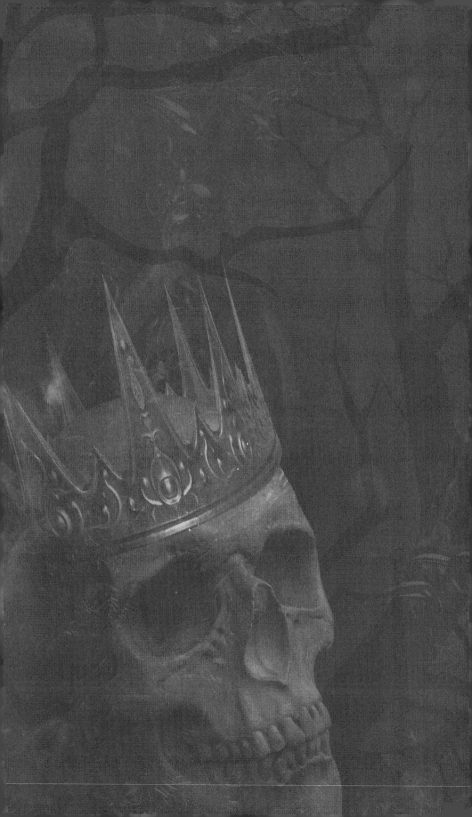

CHAPTER SIXTEEN

BREYLA

It's too damn bright for what we must do today. The sun is beating mercilessly on all gathered around the funeral pyre. I missed my own father's funeral. At the time, I hadn't been able to face my feelings and found every reason to avoid coming home for it. Nolan was like a second father to me, and I don't know if I could handle the remorse of missing another funeral. It had been three days since Nolan's murder, and we knew no more now than we did the first day. Nolan's body had been found outside the guard's quarters, throat slit, completely drained of blood. There was no sign of struggle, and he was found around the time of the guard rotation. No one had seen or heard anything. We had no leads, no witnesses, nothing. None of it made any sense. Now I had to stare his wife and young children in the eyes and tell them I still had no idea who had murdered their father or why.

I stand front and center, dressed in a black tunic, leathers, and full armor, sword strapped to my left hip. My hair is braided into a crown on top of my head. Elijah stands to my right, my mother on my left, and Aurelius on the other side of her. The guards and soldiers in attendance are also dressed in black with full armor. The rest of the attendees are in black formal wear. I know my mother would prefer to see me in the traditional black mourning gown, but outside of the fact that I hated dresses, I was the general. All the soldiers are looking at me and the example I set. The full armor signifies respect for the fallen, and Nolan deserved the utmost respect.

On the other side of Elijah stands Nolan's wife, River, and their two children. Briar is a girl of six, and Phillip a boy of four. These babies would never truly know their father. Not like I knew him. That thought makes it hard to breathe. As if he could sense my chest tightening, Elijah laces his fingers with mine, squeezing gently. It's a subtle reassurance to let me know I am not alone. Elijah would always be there for me. If soulmates existed, he was mine.

I glance down to see Briar, her eyes red and puffy. She's just old enough to understand what was happening but not old enough to know how to process her emotions about it. Phillip is more confused than anything. He doesn't quite know what is happening, so he keeps tugging at his mother's skirts and asking why his papa is sleeping on top of the sticks. Seeing them shatters my heart all over again, but I bite my cheek and hold it together. I have a job to do today. I can cry later. Maybe never.

I clear my throat, waiting for the last few voices to die down before I begin my eulogy. "Thank you all for joining us today to send Commander Nolan on to the next life," I start, feeling awkward. Elijah squeezes my hand reassuringly and I squeeze back. "Nolan was more than just a commander, though. He was an essential part of the lives of everyone in this kingdom. He trained me and just about every other soldier and guard here. He loved his two babies more than anything, but he was also a father well before they were even born." I glance at his wife and see a small smile on her lips as she nods in agreement.

"He was a teacher, a protector, a confidant, a friend, and so much more. Words truly cannot convey what he meant to me and many others here. This kingdom owes him many debts. If I can one day be half the warrior, teacher, and friend he was, I will consider that a success." I pause to take a breath. By this point there are not many dry eyes left. "This world will not be the same without you." My throat tightens as my eyes fill with tears. I raise my voice and speak with a confidence I do not feel. "From your first breath until your very last, may the gods grant you peace." Everyone around me chants back the traditional Rimorian tiding.

I take a step back and nod to my mother. She calls forth her element of fire, and a bold flame dances in her palm. Six of my guards step forward, holding unlit torches. One by one she sends her flame to each. Once all six are lit, the guards step to the pyre and touch them to the wood holding Nolan's body. It takes only moments for the fire to climb and envelop Nolan's body. Then, I hear River let out a wail that turns into an ancient Rimorian death hymn. The language is long forgotten, except for the translation of this one song.

May the mother keep you close
And the father protect you now
The tears that once were shed
Make the flowers grow
When the night is darkest
And the sun has ceased its shining
May you remember
My love for you is eternal
From your first breath
Until your very last
May the gods grant you peace

River finishes the first round, and as she begins again more voices join. By the end of the third round, every voice can be heard. The medley of voices sends goosebumps down my spine until everything eventually quiets.

As the crowd dissipates, leaving only Nolan's family, my own, and Elijah, I make my way to River. Finding words now is harder than giving the eulogy. "River, I just want you to know that I've arranged for Nolan's salary to continue going to your account indefinitely. When I said this kingdom owes him a debt, I truly meant it. I can never repay him, but I can make sure you and your kids want for nothing. I've also arranged for an inheritance to be set up for each child to do with as they please once they come of age. If there is ever anything you need, do not hesitate to come straight to me."

"Thank you," is all the teary-eyed widow can manage. I turn to leave when I feel a soft hand grasp my wrist. "Nolan was an excellent father to Briar and Phillip, but you should know that he always considered you a daughter. In many ways, you were his child first. He loved you and was so incredibly proud of you. His bloodline may live on through our children, but his legacy lives on through you."

The tears well up in my eyes as she turns to go, her somber children in hand. I lose the fight and feel the tears dance down my cheek. A warm, muscled arm wraps around my midsection and pulls me back. I'm greeted by the firm chest and rich spiced cocoa scent that is uniquely Elijah. I turn in his arms, burying my face in his neck. His dark, long golden waves are down today, so my tears are easily hidden. My arms wrap around to his back, my fingers clutching at his tunic. His grip tightens, giving me the security I crave to feel weak for a moment. Elijah weaves his fingers into my hair, softly playing with it in the way he knows soothes me. He grounds me. Like an anchor keeping a ship at bay, he keeps me from drifting off into the sorrow that threatens to drown me.

I don't know how long we stand there before I feel eyes on

us. I pull back, and Elijah kisses me softly on the forehead before releasing me. It doesn't take long for me to find that the eyes I felt belong to Aurelius. He looks concerned, but also...something else. *Is that jealousy?* I shake that thought off because he has no room to feel that way. The crimson in his irises seem more prominent as they burn into me. He doesn't move, so I break eye contact and move toward my mother.

Most of the crowd has thinned by the time I reach her side. "You spoke eloquently, my dear. I know your father would be proud." I know it's meant as praise, but it feels like a punch in the gut.

"There's something I wish to discuss with you, mother," I say, changing the subject to save myself.

"Drink up, assholes!" I shout as the coin I just bounced off the table lands in the goblet in the center of the table. I have many talents, and drinking games—specifically Remis and Goblets—are near the top of that list. We're several hours into the celebration soldiers have to honor the dead. Where the formal funeral rites are a somber event, the soldiers always honor the fallen in a way that celebrates life. Mostly we drink and revel and get up to all manner of trouble. Several guards bet me I couldn't make the coin in the cup ten times in a row. Honestly, it's insulting. I excel at drinking games—it's like they don't know me at all.

I hear a few grumbles, but mostly laughs as they all drink when I make the tenth cup. I stopped counting my drinks somewhere in the third bottle of wine. That was about two hours ago, but I honestly couldn't care. I would feel the hangover tomorrow, but tonight I would drown everything out. If I were lucky, maybe I could find someone to drown in. It wouldn't be anyone here; sleeping with the guards or my soldiers was not an option.

"Tell us another story about Commander Nolan, General," Jade prods. She's probably heard them all, but telling stories is how we keep the memory of the deceased alive. Ryder and Zion sit on the other side of her, Ryder's hand trailing up and down Jade's curves as she leans back into him. The bonfire burns bright, reaching at least ten feet into the air. I sit down on a bench across from Jade and adjacent to the flames. Elijah is already sitting when I lean back into him to start my story.

"Have I told you about when he caught me with one of my father's men?" I grin at her.

Elijah chuckles behind me, and Jade quirks an eyebrow at me. The other males and a few females gather around me to hear the story.

"I was sixteen, and at sixteen I was a...typical sixteen-year-old, let's say."

"She means horny," Elijah interrupts with a mischievous grin on his face. I elbow him in the side to shut him up, but he continues, "Honestly, I think she was hornier than I was. Unbearable at times."

I glare at him, "Are you telling this story, or am I?" He's still wearing that shit-eating grin but doesn't say anything else.

"Anyway, I was sixteen, horny all the time, but also training with my father's men daily. Not a good combination if you ask me." More people are gathering as I continue, "I hadn't hit my full height and certainly not my full strength by this point, so my father and Nolan had me training with the newest recruits. They were boys, a lot of them orphans. They were all gangly, awkward, and had no clue what they were doing on the battle-field let alone the bedroom. But I managed to find one with pretty eyes that showed promise with a sword. At sixteen, what more could a girl ask for?" This elicits a laugh from them all.

Julian takes a seat quietly on the other side of Elijah and

begins tracing swirls up and down Elijah's bicep. I can feel the shivers that pebble Elijah's skin at Julian's touch. The firelight catches his hazel eyes, and I see desire swimming in them. Too bad Elijah is currently my cushion, and he will have to be patient.

I continue my story, "I had been forced to train with the recruits, and it was a particularly humid day, so all of them were shirtless before lunch. A girl can only take so much before she breaks, so naturally instead of sneaking him to my rooms, I cornered him in a storage closet after training and took him there. Nolan walked in on us with the poor kid mid thrust, and the look he gave him had him soft in seconds. It would have been funny if it weren't quite so sad. Nolan looked at me and asked if it was worth it. I begrudgingly told him no. To which he responded, 'Just because the kid can hold a weapon, doesn't mean he knows how to handle *his* sword. That takes years of practice. Next time find someone who knows what they're doing. And for gods' sake, take him to your room.'" This has everyone full belly laughing.

"I was mortified to say the least. What he said the next day, though, was something I learned from. He pulled me aside and told me to be careful who I take to my bed. Not because he cared that I fucked someone, or even who they were. But if I wanted to someday lead the armies of Rimor, I would need to ensure the soldiers could trust my judgment. If I showed them that I would let just anyone with a cock into my pants, then they would think I was easily influenced. He said if I wanted to command their respect, I should show them that anyone I let close had to earn their position there. I wanted their respect, so I never took another of my men to bed."

"So that's why you always shot me down; I'm too pretty to say no to," Zion quips.

"No, I never took you because you take anything with a

heartbeat to bed. You shut that door all on your own, cupcake."
This has everyone laughing even harder.

"Aye! That's the damn truth," Julian chimes in. I shoot a
wink to Zion as I hear him grumble something about at least
knowing how to use *his* sword well enough.

I hear a breathy sound come from behind me and turn my
head to see Elijah's head thrown back. Julian's hand is fisted
through Elijah's hair and his lips are trailing down his stubbled
jaw. I feel Elijah's hand clench at my side, and something firm
presses into my back.

*Is that...*Nope. "No, thank you!" I say as I jump to my feet.
"Hard pass on feeling my best friend's erection."

They both smirk at me as I hear Elijah say, "Literally," at the
same time Julian tells me I can find somewhere else to be if I'm
uncomfortable. I glance over to Jade and Ryder to see they are
also...preoccupied. Zion has undoubtedly disappeared to find
someone to bury his sorrows in.

The flames from the bonfire lick at my cheeks as I feel eyes
on me again. Without turning I blurt, "How long have you been
there?"

"Long enough to hear that charming story of yours," Aurelius teases. "We need to talk, Princess."

I'm not in the mood for his shit tonight. I know why he's
here, but I'm going to make him work for it. "Ask nicely," I say
with a sickly-sweet tone. By the tick in his jaw, I'd say he doesn't
appreciate my sass.

"All that wine has really gone to your head," he says, making
his way closer to me.

I turn away from him and start to walk away, throwing a flip-
pant, "That wasn't asking nicely," over my shoulder as I go. I
make it to the tree line behind the castle before he catches up,
and my back is suddenly being pressed into the bark of an old
oak tree. *Damn wine, slowing my reflexes.*

A grunt escapes my lips as I stare into Aurelius' dark eyes.

The fire behind us really makes the crimson flecks of his eyes glow, almost unnaturally. He has both my wrists in one hand pinned above me on the tree while his other rests on the curve of my left hip. In any other situation this position would be hot, but the flames in his eyes tell me he is livid.

Even so, he leans in close and whispers, "Please," so softly I barely hear it. I can tell it takes everything in him to utter that word. He's pissed, so naturally I have to push him further.

"I like it when you beg," I chuckle in his ear. He growls in response and abruptly pushes away from me. Instantly, I'm stone-cold sober and I know his Hemonia Gift is to thank for that.

"Hey! I worked hard for that buzz," I pout.

"Too bad. You'll thank me in the morning when you don't wake up with a hangover." This male is insufferable.

"Fine. Talk," I spit out at him.

"You're throwing a ball to celebrate your mother's engagement."

"I am, but that's not what has you so worked up."

"It's a stupid idea, but you're right. What has me fuming, Princess, is that you seem intent on inviting snakes into our home," he seethes. I open my mouth to respond, but he isn't done. "I specifically warned you against inviting Prince Ayden anywhere near here."

"Near the palace or near *me?*" I challenge. His insistence on keeping Prince Ayden away from the palace makes little sense. No one else has pushed back against the idea as much as Aurelius.

"Both." His answer doesn't clear anything up for me.

"Why?" It comes across as the demand it is, not a question.

"You know why."

"You're avoiding the question, Aurelius. Tell. Me. Why." Now I'm just pissed. We're supposed to be allies, but he's keeping secrets.

"It's not safe for you!" he bursts out.

"That's bullshit! I'm the general of the fucking army, my shadows are the strongest in hundreds of years. I can protect myself, and you damn well know it!"

"Shadows that you currently have no control over," he grinds out. I look down and see that his wrists are bound by my shadows, holding him taut, and even more are seeping out of my fingers. I didn't even know I had called them. My jaw drops, then he says softly, "You can't protect yourself from him, Princess. You're just going to have to trust me on this."

I hesitate at his sudden change in tone and the pleading look in his eyes. But his non-answer still has me pissed. "I only trust those who don't keep secrets from me, Aurelius." With that I release him from my shadows and walk away. The night ruined, I make my way back to my rooms in the castle. My bed is calling my name.

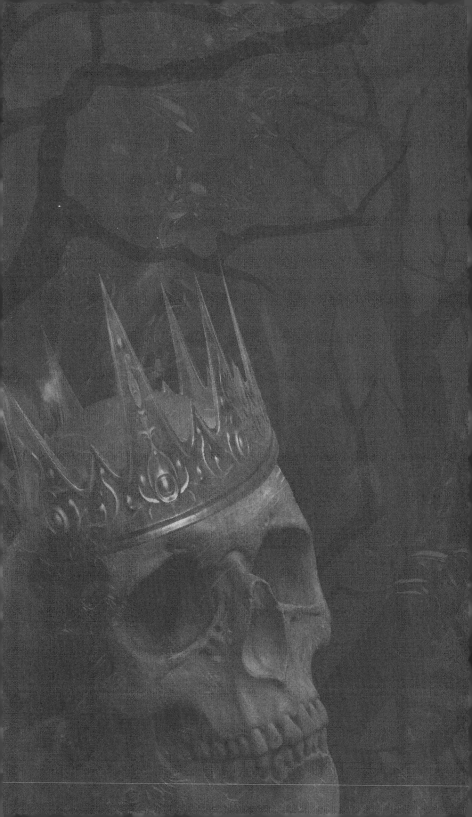

CHAPTER SEVENTEEN

OPHELIA

Pain courses through my entire body, and I bite my tongue to keep from screaming. A metallic tangy taste spills through my mouth when I bite too deeply. I would have hit the ground if I hadn't already been sitting. I still feel my father's electric currents traveling through my limbs as I gasp and struggle to pull oxygen into my lungs. This is significantly worse than previous punishments. Father is livid, and it's my fault.

"How dare you make me look like a fool in front of the council," he seethes. Truthfully, it had been long enough since the council meeting that I believed he had forgotten. I was wrong.

Still gasping for air, I can't respond so he continues, "The information *you* gave me was wrong. I made an idiot of myself accusing the princess of plotting against the queen." If I could speak, I might tell him that he didn't need my help to look like an idiot, so it's probably better that I can't form words.

The pain begins receding, eclipsed by a tingling sensation that travels down my fingers. "My apologies, Father. I didn't know it was false information." The lies roll off my tongue so easily. "Perhaps the princess does not trust me as much as we believed."

"Little good that observation does me now, stupid girl," he spits. "What else can you tell me? And don't even think about lying."

"She's hosting a ball to celebrate the engagement between Lord Aurelius and Queen Genevieve," I start. The information isn't exactly a secret, but word hasn't yet made its way around court. The look in his eyes tells me he's intrigued.

"Why? Does she have some ulterior motive?"

"I believe she wishes to meet with Prince Ayden II of Prudia. I'm not sure why, but perhaps it's a cover to conspire with him in some way." The last part is a lie, but close enough to the truth that it's believable. I see excitement dance in his eyes.

"Now that I can work with." A sinister smile spreads across his face. "See if you can find out anything more."

"What are you going to do with this?" I try to keep my tone even.

"That is none of your concern, girl," he replies, harsh and patronizing. His insistence on still calling me 'girl' grates against me.

I don't register the sound of crackling before it's too late. A fresh wave of lightning hits me, stronger than the last. His last words are muffled as blackness takes over my vision and I lose the battle to stay conscious.

When I awaken several hours later, the sun has begun its descent in the west. Every bone in my body aches, and my skin is sensitive to the touch. My nerves feel like they're on fire, and the effort it takes me to sit up causes bile to creep up my throat. After a few long minutes, I can finally push myself off the floor and onto my feet. I gently roll my shoulders, trying to stretch out the stiff muscles.

I examine my reflection in the mirror and find my eyes are streaked with red and the braided crown I had this morning is nearly undone. I look like I fought a dragon. Hell, I *feel* like I fought a dragon. And the dragon definitely won this round. I pull my remaining hair free from its braid and comb through the long ebony locks with my fingers. I splash cool water on my face from a bowl on the vanity, then smooth out my dress as best I can.

The walk to Breyla's chambers is short but allows me time to stretch my aching body. My knuckles wrap softly on her door, and it only takes a moment to fly open. A panicked-looking Elijah greets me.

"What's wrong?" I blurt, immediately on edge.

He groans, "Oh, thank the gods you're here, beautiful. Your princess needs you." His answer doesn't soothe my nerves.

"Would you quit being so dramatic?" I hear Breyla protest behind him. I peak around the mountain that is Elijah and find a half-dressed princess clutching a corset to her chest. I cock an eyebrow at them both. It's not Breyla being half-dressed that surprises me, but that she's wearing a dress at all. A dress she looks rather uncomfortable in.

"Mother insisted I wear a gown for dinner tonight. I don't actually know the last time I had to wear one of these horrible contraptions, and I couldn't find you so I asked Elijah to help me dress."

"I got my finger stuck in the laces and it started turning purple. I really don't understand these things." Elijah shudders.

"You probably can't even count how many corsets you've taken off, but suddenly you can't help me put on just one?" Breyla stares at him incredulously.

"Exactly, B. I *take them off.* Never do I have to help them go back on," he states matter-of-factly. This doesn't surprise me, but it does make a strange sensation settle in my chest.

"Well, if you're not going to be any help, get lost," Breyla huffs.

"You don't have to tell me twice, doll. I'll see you at dinner." Elijah makes his way to the door. He pauses next to me and leans in close. "Thanks for the rescue. Just let me know if you need help unlacing any corsets later." The last part is said low enough that only I hear it. Before I can process his words fully, I feel his lips on my cheek. The kiss is brief, but the feeling on my skin lingers as butterflies erupt low in my belly.

"What did he say to you?" Breyla asks, sounding intrigued.

"Um..." My cheeks warm as I stutter my response. "To let him know if I need any help unlacing corsets later."

Breyla throws her head back as a full-body laugh erupts from her. "He would say something like that. That male..." She shakes her head. "Now can you please help me lace this thing?" she practically begs.

I chuckle. "Yes, of course. You look absolutely pitiful trying to do it on your own." I get to work untangling all the knots Elijah left for me.

"How in the world did he manage this?" I question as I get the last of the knots cleared.

"I truly don't know," Breyla says, shaking her head.

I begin lacing it back up, starting loose and then tightening as I go. I weave the lace back and forth, over and under, until it reaches the top. By the end of it, my already aching fingers are trembling. "There you are, right as rain." I tie her laces off and tuck them in the back.

She turns to me, giving me a full view of the dress. It's a sleek, long-sleeved black gown, the neckline cut low and showing off the tops of her breasts. Light freckles dot from her face down her neck and collarbone. The rest of the gown is simple for someone of her standing. No embellishments or slits to expose her leg. I reach for the diadem sitting on her armoire and place it on her head with trembling hands.

I gently try to rub the pain out of my fingers and give her a soft smile. "Beautiful," I whisper.

As I drop my hands, I feel Breyla's lightly grasp my wrists. I fight a flinch and force my face to stay neutral. She doesn't miss it, though. She lifts my hands to inspect them, taking care to remain gentle and not cause any more pain.

"What. Happened." Each word is sharp and demanding, though I know her ire is not directed at me. She can't physically see anything on my skin, but the trembling in my hands and the flinch from the lightest of touches is something I can't hide.

"The information I provided Father was less than satisfactory," I admit.

A look of shock crosses her face. "This is because of me?"

"No. I made the decision, and I stand by it and the consequences." I give her hand a gentle squeeze of reassurance. "I have very little control over my life; I will not let anyone else take credit for *my* decisions. They are mine, and mine alone."

Breyla ponders this a moment then decides to let me keep what little autonomy I have. "I wish to discuss something with you that I should have brought up sooner."

Internally, I bristle, unsure where this is going. "Okay," I start softly and evenly. "About what?"

"I'm no fool, Ophelia. I know I should be dead right now. The night I was attacked, you healed me. Aurelius said I should speak to you."

I release my breath, unsure why I was nervous in the first place. It might be the number of times my father has started a conversation the same way and ended it with unrelenting pain courtesy of his lightning.

"I did," I confirm.

"And yet, the whole castle believes you to not have powers. Why is that?"

I smile sadly. "My powers manifested later than most. I was twenty-three, and by then my father already believed I was powerless. He has always treated me poorly, but when my powers didn't come in during my adolescence, his treatment of me grew worse. He made it clear through his actions that he wasn't above using anyone—especially his own daughter—for personal gain. I don't know the details of his business dealings, but I know my father is unequivocally not a good male. I refuse to be used by him. If he knew my true abilities, I have no doubt he would find some way to use me—probably to hurt others."

Breyla contemplates my words for a moment. "What an ass," she huffs.

A half-hearted chuckle escapes me. "That's an understatement."

"So, help me understand something. Can you not heal yourself?" She looks confused.

I sigh, "Unfortunately, it doesn't quite work that way. When I heal someone, it's more like I'm trading my energy for their healing. So, I might be able to manage small things, like cuts or bruises, but when he gets like this..." Hesitation fills my voice. "Let's just say I don't have the energy to stand, let alone try to heal myself."

"So, you're trading your life force for another when you heal them." I can see her making the connection in her mind. "Meaning when it's your own body that needs healing, there's nothing to trade."

"Essentially."

"I guess we have so few true healers that we don't know much about how their power works," she muses. "I see why you would want to keep the knowledge of your power to yourself. That information in the wrong hands..."

"Could be deadly."

Among other things, I think to myself.

"I can't in good conscience keep asking you to feed information to him." Anguish flashes in her eyes.

"Don't," I say, my voice stern, and she looks taken aback. "Don't you dare take that decision from me. I decide what risks to take and what my actions are. You will not take that from me," My guess is she didn't expect to hear this boldness from me. The truth is, she is one of the only people I feel safe enough with to expose this vulnerability.

She nods her head in understanding. "Alright, I can respect that. But if I ever catch him hurting you, I will make him live to regret ever laying a finger on you." I can feel the fire in her words as shadows dance in the corner of her eyes.

"Why would you protect someone you barely know?"

"I know your soul, Ophelia. I may not have known you for very long, but actions will always speak louder than words. I also know you volunteer your time with the castle physician, something no one would expect or ask of you. Your actions sing of a pure and genuine soul. You endured torture for me when you could have sold me out. I do know you, Ophelia. I will always protect those that have earned my loyalty." Tears burn the back of my eyes as her words fill something in me I didn't know was empty. Breyla pulls me firmly into her chest as her arms wrap around me. I squeeze her back, my head pressed firmly into her bosom. I listen to her heartbeat for a minute before I finally wheeze out, "Your breasts are smothering me."

Her breathy laugh escapes as she releases me and steps back. "I forget how much these dresses shove them out there. My leathers have bindings built in, but it's easier to dress myself and definitely doesn't accentuate my chest like these awful dresses."

"In all fairness, most of the people you're accustomed to hugging are taller than me," I say with a shrug.

"Most of them would also probably not complain if I smothered them," she chuckles.

"By most of them, you're talking about Elijah, aren't you?" It isn't even really a question, and we both know it.

"Touche." We're both laughing hysterically now.

"Now that our princess is properly dressed, let's get to dinner. I'm starving. Being electrocuted really works up an appetite," I joke. She cocks her head at me wide eyed, a disbelieving look on her face. I just shrug and usher her out the door.

As we make our way down the hall, she litters me with questions on what I believe Father is up to. "Given the situation, it's hard to say if he is being truthful. I did make him believe you had ulterior motives with throwing the engagement ball. I think he believed that."

"But I do have ulterior motives," she says, quirking an auburn brow at me.

"I know, but I let him believe you're scheming *with* Prince Ayden, not against him."

"Clever girl," she grins.

We continue in silence for several minutes. I notice eventually that every couple steps a bare toe pops out from beneath her skirts. It's not at all surprising that the general of the royal army would rather walk barefoot than be forced into ladies' slippers.

Breyla is a walking paradox to everything a princess should be. She speaks her mind, is foul mouthed, acts first and thinks second, roams the halls barefoot, and seems to detest everything that comes with being a princess. It makes me admire her even more. I've spent so long trying to do what is expected of me that I feel like I don't quite know who I am at my core. Being in her presence feels like permission to break those chains and discover myself.

"Join me for wine after dinner," she offers.

"As much as I would love that, I am actually looking forward to some peace and quiet. Father left the capital on business earlier today. I plan on reading and drinking all his most expensive wines, then replacing them with the bitter stuff the kitchen serves to the guests they don't like."

"He left on business?" She completely ignores my wine scheming.

I hum in confirmation and catch the look in her eyes. The wheels are turning, but I'm not sure what she's thinking. The gold flecks of her emerald irises sparkle in the soft fairy lights of the castle hallway. Just the corner of her mouth quirks briefly before her expression turns unreadable.

We finally reach the royal family's private dining room to find we are the last to arrive. Queen Genevieve is seated at the head of the long mahogany table, Aurelius on her right, followed by the twins Jade and Julian. Further down the table are a few cousins and distant relatives.

"Nice of you two to finally join us," Elijah teases.

Breyla just flips him her middle finger, and I shrug. "If you hadn't made such a mess of Breyla's corset laces it wouldn't have taken me so long to get her dressed." I don't miss the flare of Lord Aurelius's nostrils and the way his eyes dart to Elijah. Breyla takes her place between the queen and Elijah, sitting across from Lord Aurelius.

Elijah pulls out the chair next to him for me to sit. As I settle, he leans in to whisper, "I already told you—I'm much better at removing them."

Blood rushes to my cheeks as Elijah lets out a grunt. A look around Elijah shows me that Breyla has shoved her elbow into his ribs. "I heard that. Everyone heard that. Stop flirting at the dinner table."

Elijah runs a hand through his dirty-blond curls, hanging loosely down past his shoulders, and leans back in his chair. "Or what, Princess? You might hold your own in leathers, but what exactly do you plan on doing in that dress?"

It's the queen that surprises us all with, "Elijah, you very well know that my daughter can put you on your back regardless of what she wears. A dress doesn't make your opponent any less lethal; it makes them more dangerous. Most are just too ignorant to see that." This silences Elijah.

I wish my father were here to hear what was just said. It's not just me he undervalues and underestimates—it's all females. He's remarked more than once on how Breyla is unfit to command the royal army and how Queen Genevieve is inept and frail. My mother died when Layne and I were young and he never remarried. He claims it's because no one could ever replace her, but in truth I believe it's because females can't stand him. His hatred of them is disgusting.

Servants begin to fill the table with food—roast lamb, herbed potatoes, warm vegetable broth, freshly baked rolls, and port wine soon fill the dishes in front of me. The aroma permeates the room and my stomach rumbles. I finally realize how hungry I truly am. How long has it been since I last ate? Since before my encounter with Father this morning at least...so dinner last night? I wait patiently for the queen to take the first bite before digging into the mouth-watering foods in front of me.

As the sounds of silverware hitting plates ring out, I bite into a piece of roast lamb. The juices dribble down my chin, and I let out a small moan of food-induced pleasure. I am so much hungrier than I realized. I feel the heat of Elijah's gaze on me, and I turn to meet him. His eyes are trained on me in an intense stare, watching the juices on my lips run down my chin. Embarrassed, I reach for my napkin and clean my face. Luckily, most people are too involved in their meals to notice what is happening between us.

"Have you made any progress with figuring out who is behind Commander Nolan's death?" Lord Aurelius asks Breyla.

"Not much," Breyla grits. Her tone is clipped and guarded. "I'm following up on a potential lead tomorrow."

Aurelius's eyes scan Breyla, analyzing her. He lifts an eyebrow at her. "Who might this lead be?"

"That's classified, Lord Aurelius." Even I can sense the bull-shit in her words. She just doesn't want to tell him, but I have no idea why. It's difficult to read the situation with Breyla and Aurelius. He seems to care about her, but she fights him tooth and nail at every turn. At the same time, he knows exactly what to say to get under her skin.

His eyes narrow to slits, and I swear the fork in his hand bends. His next words are low and bitter. "Lying does not become you, Princess."

"And being a nosey insufferable prick doesn't become you, Lord Aurelius," Breyla snaps back.

"Enough," Queen Genevieve barks as the temperature in the room drops to a teeth-chattering level. I can see my own breath and hear the hiss coming from Breyla. The queen has frozen both Breyla and Aurelius's hands in place. She has teeth, a fact commonly overlooked until someone pushes her too far. Outwardly she was everything expected of a queen—patient, kind, gentle, and compassionate. She was also decisive, stern when necessary, and fiercely protective. She seemed willing to do what was necessary for the good of her people.

Breyla's face softens. "Yes, Mother."

Aurelius's expression doesn't shift, but he nods to the queen, implying his compliance.

The queen seems satisfied enough with their reaction that she releases the ice binding them, and the room returns to a normal level. Both Aurelius and Breyla rub the stiffness out of their hands, the color slowly returning from blue to their natural tones. Jade and Julian share a look and snicker, while Elijah's back silently shakes with restrained laughter. I get the feeling I'm either missing something, or perhaps this isn't the first time the queen has had to deploy this tactic with Breyla.

"Now, General, please share with us what details you can. These developments are intriguing." Breyla's whole demeanor shifts when her mother addresses her this way. There seems to be an added tension between them.

"There is a member of the court with...questionable actions as of late. I can't confirm or deny any connection to Nolan's death, but it is enough for me to look into. I also have my suspicions that the servant we found in the river could be related to it all." A pit forms in my stomach as I realize exactly who she's referring to. I can't exactly blame her for her suspicions, but I fear what this will mean for Layne and me if she is correct. History has shown us that people are anything but kind to families of traitors, no matter how innocent they may be.

I could recall an instance nearly eight hundred years ago. A heartbroken male named Myer had attempted to assassinate the entire ruling family. It was shortly after the Fae had disappeared from our lands, taking the male's mate, a Fae female named Elythia, with them. While we could, and often did, form mate bonds, it was rumored that the bonds with the Fae were far stronger and granted special connections or powers. To lose a mate was thought to be impossible to survive.

Myer and Elythia had two small children, and she was carrying their third when she disappeared. Myer blamed the royal family for the Fae leaving and the loss of his mate. Myer wouldn't live long enough to find out what it was like to live without his other half, and we have no idea whether he could have survived without her. He was successful in murdering King Grayson and Queen Amantia before the guards were able to subdue him. The three royal heirs survived, leaving Prince Ronan to ascend the throne at the age of fourteen.

Myer was executed the following morning, along with all members of his family—both parents, his siblings, and their families, and both his young children. Olivia and Finn were only two years old. In an instant, Myer's entire line was wiped from existence. None of them knew what he planned, but it didn't matter.

The crown didn't tolerate traitors or their families. It was a dark time in our history that most preferred to ignore.

Surely Breyla knew by now that I was loyal to her, but unease still rolled through me. I couldn't bear the thought of Layne and I becoming the next history lesson.

"I am dispatching one of my most trusted soldiers to follow them, track who they are speaking with, and see if their actions prove traitorous or warrant an arrest. For now, we are just observing. I hope to have more clear information soon." Breyla's voice brought me out of my own head. I had almost forgotten we were in the middle of conversation.

Queen Genevieve looks as unsettled as I feel. "Very well, I pray to the gods you are wrong, and we are not fighting an enemy from within our own court. I trust your judgment, though. You will alert me as soon as you have any more information." The queen pauses, before asking, "Why send your own and not the spymaster?"

Breyla wrinkles her nose and says softly, "I have my reasons, Mother. Most of them being Lord Craylor is vile and I do not trust him."

"Your father trusted him."

"Yes. And now Father is dead, so I doubt he has much to complain about now, anyway." It is stated matter-of-factly, as if this is of little importance to her.

The queen's face hardens, her eyes brimming with tears she refuses to let fall. "Indeed," is all she manages, and the conversation ends.

The rest of the meal is uneventful and passes in silence. I find that as ravenous as I was to start, my stomach has gone sour.

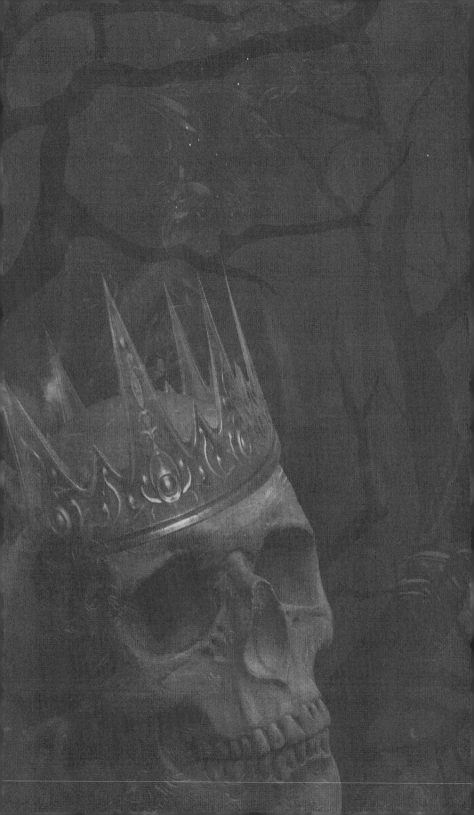

CHAPTER EIGHTEEN

BREYLA

"Ride swiftly, my friend," I say, grasping Julian's forearm and pulling him in for a quick embrace before his departure.

"Of course, General. I'm your fastest rider; that's why you're sending me." He squeezes me tightly. He's cocky, but he's right. He is the fastest rider, but he's also my stealthiest soldier. Part of what makes him invaluable as my second in command. I inhale his leather and fresh rain scent and hold him for just a minute more before releasing him. His amber eyes sparkle in the late morning sun, the green especially bright today.

"Keep your distance. I don't want anyone knowing what we're up to." We can't afford for anyone to learn who we were trailing or why. He was more than capable, but I couldn't help how my stomach twisted into knots. So much was riding on figuring out who was responsible for Nolan's murder. I have a feeling they will also lead me to what really happened with my father.

He rolls his eyes. "This isn't my first mission, B. No one will know I'm there." He leans in to hug his twin next, then Elijah. Gracefully, Julian hoists himself onto the back of his midnight black mustang horse, Nox, and swings his right leg over in one fluid motion.

I pat Nox's hindquarter, and Julian spurs him onto a trot, leaving us staring after him. When he reaches the castle gates, he briefly looks back and nods at us before disappearing through the castle's outer walls. I remind myself he knows what he's doing and what his mission is. Lord Seamus only left yesterday and isn't a fast rider. Julian will ride hard today to make up ground on him but will stay out of major towns or places where he could be easily recognized. He is simply there to observe and report back on with whom Lord Seamus is meeting.

Jade, Elijah, and I turn back to the castle and make our way inside. My mother is standing in an open window several floors up, watching Julian leave. Her face is unreadable. My gaze catches her sky blue eyes, and I notice they're rimmed in red, but she's not currently crying. The red tinge causes the blue of her irises to pop and shine brighter. She holds my gaze for a moment, her expression unchanging, then turns from the window and disappears into the castle.

"You're wound tight; let's go spar." Jade's voice breaks me out of my daze.

"Yeah, that sounds perfect," I agree, and we make our way to the training rooms.

Sweat pours down my back as I breathe deeply, concentrating on allowing the breath to expand through my core muscles and keep my heart rate steady. The sun is setting as we approach the gloaming hour, and everything dances with vibrant pinks, oranges, and deep blues. My hands shake as I put all my energy into forming my shadows into the shape of a small dagger. I'm alone so there's no one to see my humiliation when I finally shoot the shadow dagger at the training dummy, and it dissolves before impact.

I grunt in frustration—this should be something so simple I can do it subconsciously. I've used my shadows in this manner hundreds of times before, but lately I can't seem to maintain any control over this essential part of me. Before I can raise my hands to try again, I feel a strong forearm wrap tightly around my abdomen, and a hand covers my mouth.

For a moment panic sets in and I believe I'm being attacked again. I start to struggle but settle when the scent hits me—bergamot and warm spices.

Aurelius.

"Shhhh, Princess. You know exactly who has you," he chuckles. I hate the way my tense muscles easily relax and melt into him when I realize he's right.

I inhale sharply through my nose as his grip on my stomach loosens and his hand slowly trails down to rest at the top of my leathers, just below my belly button. I had moved outside earlier after everyone else had called it quits for the day, and anyone could easily find us. That thought should terrify me, but I find my core warming at the thought instead.

"Can you be quiet, little demon?" Aurelius whispers in my ear. I nod my head in affirmation.

"Good girl," he praises. His hand drops from my mouth as goosebumps erupt across my flesh. He notices and begins trailing featherlight kisses down my neck as his free hand rests on the curve of my left hip, right below my rib cage.

"What are you doing?" I ask softly. When I feel the sharp sting of his teeth on my neck, I let out a sound that's somewhere between a surprised yelp and a moan.

"I said be quiet," he growls, but answers my question

anyway. "I can sense how tense you are from a hundred yards away. I watched you train earlier, and it's obvious that the stress you're shouldering is hindering you. I can feel how hard your heart is pushing the blood through your body right now. I'm going to help you...unwind."

"Why? Why help me *unwind*?" I make air quotes with my fingers at his choice of words.

"Because, Princess. Though you seem to forget, we are allies. It's my responsibility to look after your wellbeing if only to keep you alive."

"Do you treat all your allies like this?"

"Oh, green looks good on you, my dear." The smirk in his voice is maddening.

"I'm not jealous, just not sure you understand the definition of ally."

"I'm perfectly aware of its definition, I just don't keep many of them. My position would suggest I am everyone's ally to an extent, but personally I don't let people that close."

"Seems like a lonely way to live."

"Indeed. But I'm not here to discuss semantics with you. I bear news that might upset you."

"Go on. I'm sure I'll love this."

"Prince Ayden is nearly at the capital. All reports suggest he will arrive tomorrow."

My skyrocketing heart rate suggests Aurelius knows my body's reactions better than I do.

"Tomorrow?" I stammer. "That would mean he was..."

"Either close by or expecting the invitation. Either option is not something I want to ponder."

Annoyed with this entire conversation, I roll my eyes and start to pull away from him. Before I get too far, I feel his hand tighten on my side as he pulls me firmly back into his chest. His right hand slides back down and slips in the front of my leathers. I nearly sigh in relief as his fingers slide between my thighs and circle my clit. He moves his left hand up, threading his fingers into my hair, and pulls. My head is forced to the side to meet his lips as they crash into mine.

His kiss is unrelenting. There is no question or request; he demands entrance into my mouth. His tongue dances with mine, and he swallows my moans as his tempo on my clit increases.

I grind my hips back into his hard length, the friction not nearly enough for me as his fingers move to my entrance. My teeth dig into his bottom lip when he slides a finger inside me. The pain only serves to increase his desire and he adds a second finger, pumping in and out of me in long, fluid movements.

He groans deeply and grinds his hard cock into my ass, meeting my thrusts while increasing the pace of his fingers. My body sings for him in a way I've never experienced before. It's like he knows me better than I do myself, and he plays it beautifully.

My inner walls clench, desperate for something more than just his fingers. I reach for my shadows, deciding I've had enough foreplay. The tendrils of darkness wrap around the hand he has tangled in my hair and pulls it back. Had he not been knuckle deep in me, I doubt I would have been able to catch him off guard for that to work.

I twist in his hold, so we're face to face. "Enough teasing, Aurelius. I want more."

My shadows wrap around us as I tear at the buttons securing his pants. His face is one of shock and curiosity as I drop to my knees and drag his pants down with me. His hard cock springs free and my mouth waters. I had felt him during our first encounter, but I didn't get the chance to fully appreciate him. I had accidentally seen him once nearly ten years prior, but under much different circumstances, and my memory had not done him justice.

Precum glistens on his tip and I hungrily lick it, savoring the salty flavor. He's not just impressive in length, but he's thick as well. I wrap my lips around his head and slide my left hand down his shaft, gripping him firmly at the base. I swirl my tongue around his tip, teasing him slowly.

A growl reverberates through his chest as his fingers wind through the hair at the back of my head once more. I pull him deep into my throat, as far as I can take him, and pump my hand up and down to meet where my mouth can't reach.

His hand works my head up and down his length, pushing me further than I think I can take him. Tears form at the corners of my eyes, and I hollow my cheeks, sucking him in even harder. Even though he's not even touching me, my pussy is throbbing for him, my need only growing in intensity.

I relish the stinging sensation in my knees from the twigs and hard earth beneath them as Aurelius's thrusts into my mouth grow more punishing. I glance up to find him staring down at me, the look in his eyes burning into me like wildfire. The red flecks in his irises seemed to glow as he grits out, "That sinful mouth of yours will be the death of me, little demon. This is not how this was supposed to go."

I let his cock pop out of my mouth and grin up at him. "Well, it's a good thing you aren't in charge here."

That was either the worst or best thing to say at that moment. Suddenly I'm being tugged off my knees, and my back hits the trunk of the nearest tree. I let out a slight gasp of surprise as he drops to his knees in front of me. With a strength I didn't know he possessed he rips my leathers down my legs. He hasn't just pulled them off; he's shredded them.

The part of me that wants to protest his brutish behavior is quickly silenced when he licks up the slit of my pussy and circles his tongue around my clit. The moan that leaves my mouth is surely heard by the rooms closest to the training yard. The sun has finally descended, so there's no chance for anyone to see us, but there's no question what's happening to anyone in the area. I'm too far gone to care.

I lace my fingers into his inky black locks, tugging him closer. A tongue like this should be outlawed. I'm nervous to voice the thoughts running rampant in my mind—*Aurelius, my future stepfather and king, is ruining me.*

His tongue flicks quickly across my clit, and he slides three thick fingers into my soaking center, fucking me with his hand. In no time at all he has built me up to that edge of bliss, and I feel the tingling start in my core. I go silent and my inner muscles begin to clamp down on Aurelius's fingers as he whispers the words that damn me, "That's right, my filthy little demon, come on my face as I fuck you with my tongue."

An orgasm explodes through me, and stars dance in my vision as I lose all control of my body. My legs tremble, my muscles unable to hold me upright as the violent tremors rack my body. Aurelius rises to catch me and sets me gently on the ground.

As I finally come back to reality, I see that he is standing in front of me and is still painfully hard. His dick is practically weeping as he strokes it from base to tip, twisting along the shaft. I know exactly where this is going and grin as his rhythm increases, and he throws his head back. I reach for him, and he swats my wrist away.

"Open," he demands.

I oblige and stick my tongue out as his hot length slides into my mouth moments before his hot cum shoots down my throat. I gladly drink down every drop he gives me, licking my lips at the end.

He tucks himself back into his pants and straightens his tunic. I finally find the strength to stand from the forest ground, using his offered hands to help. I glance down at my ruined pants in the dirt.

"Now what am I supposed to do?" I quirk an eyebrow at him.

A devious grin spreads across his face as he begins walking

toward the castle. "You're a clever female, General. I have no doubt you'll figure it out."

"Are you serious?" I raise my voice at his retreating form.

"Quite."

"Asshole! You didn't have to shred my pants, and you certainly don't have to leave me stranded here now."

"If you're not quiet, Princess, someone will surely hear you." His voice grows distant as he approaches the castle.

"I'm sure they've already heard plenty, you prick. How do you expect me to make it back to my rooms?"

"I expect you to walk, Princess. You are the one in control, after all." With that he was gone, leaving me alone and half naked in the dark of the training yard.

"So, tell me again how my best friend ended up half naked, tossing rocks at my window?" Elijah's grin spreads wide. I'm sitting on his bed in a pair of his silk sleep pants, avoiding returning to my chambers. I'm unsure what I would do if I ran into Aurelius right now. I was fortunate that Elijah's rooms over-looked the training yards and that he happened to be in them, but he was finding way too much enjoyment in this.

"I've told you half a dozen times already. I found someone to help scratch an itch, but we were in too much of a frenzy when removing our clothes. It was dark when we finished, and I couldn't find my pants. He's an asshole and left me alone, naked in the dark." It wasn't technically a lie, more a half-truth.

"Uh huh, maybe if you say it again, I'll believe it this time."

"I don't care if you believe it, that's what happened," I insist.

"Sure, and who was this body you used to *scratch your itch?*"

"Nobody you know." The reply is too quick, and we both

know I'm hiding something. "What's with all the questions?" I ask, trying to steer the conversation away from the *who*.

"I have the right to ask questions when my friend shows up naked at my window, requesting my help." He's laughing at me now. His point is valid, but that doesn't mean I'll answer his questions. "So, was this nobody at least a good fuck?" I see the questions aren't going to cease.

"We didn't get to that part," I mumble.

"I'm sorry, what?" he stammers.

"We didn't fuck. We did just about everything else, but his dick was not inside me. That mouth, though..." I trail off as the memory of his tongue on my clit sends shivers up my spine.

"So, you're telling me you got handsy with a stranger in the woods, lost your pants, and you didn't even actually have sex with him?"

"Something like that."

"No wonder he left you naked and alone in the woods," Elijah snickers at me.

"You ass, now you're being just as much a prick as him." I throw one of his pillows at him, but he ducks and catches it midair.

"Something makes me think you probably deserved it. At least a little bit."

"Nonsense, I'm an angel."

Elijah snorts at that. "No, you're a brat, and we both know it."

"That doesn't sound like me."

"The first time I beat you in cards you burned all my under-wear and told every female at court I had a rare pox that only affected my dick."

"Allegedly, none of that was ever proven. Besides, you cheated."

"I did not!" His jaw drops open.

I smile sweetly at him and shrug my shoulders. I'm just

happy to be talking about something other than why I had been naked outside.

"Did he at least have a decent dick?" Elijah has a one-track mind.

I groan. "The best. Like puts-all-the-rest-to-shame kind of dick."

He crosses the room and drops into the bed next to me. "Sounds like someone will be returning for seconds," he chuckles.

"It probably shouldn't have even happened at all. Besides, he's an asshole," I grumble.

"I think the lady doth protest too much," Elijah tsks.

"What's that supposed to mean?"

"It means I don't believe you. I think you don't want to like him, but the fact that he's an asshole turns you on even more. You just don't want to admit it, so it's easier to complain about it."

I stare at him, my mouth open wide.

"Truth sucks, doesn't it?"

"No, you suck. That's not it at all," I protest, and shove him with my shoulder.

Elijah chuckles and pulls me into his side, wrapping his arm around my shoulders. "So, what will it take for you to tell me who this mystery male is?"

"Why do you want to know so badly?" I challenge while snuggling into his side.

"Well, if his dick is as glorious as you claim, then maybe I need to see it for myself."

"Trust me, you are not his type."

"Why? Because *you* are his type?"

"Because you have a dick, amongst other things. Plus, aren't you interested in a different dark-haired beauty? I've seen the way you interact with her. You haven't slept with her, but I know you want to." I try to divert his attention away from my mystery male again.

"So, he's also a dark-haired beauty? Interesting."

Shit. I didn't mean to let that out.

"And yes. Ophelia very much intrigues me. She's delicate and beautiful, but so fierce beneath it all. She's the opposite of me in so many ways."

"Just do me a favor and don't break one of my only female friend's hearts. I'd hate to have to kick your ass for her sake."

"Like you could. You haven't beaten me hand-to-hand in years, B."

"That sounds like a challenge."

"It's only a challenge if the other person has a chance at winning." Gods, he was cocky tonight.

I push myself up and away from his hold, staring him in the eyes, "You. Me. Right here, right now."

"You're being serious?" He looks amused.

"You know I am."

"Fine, but no shadows. That's playing dirty. When I win, you won't just tell me who he is—you'll give me the memory."

"Agreed. If I win, you stop asking about mystery male and you have to take Ophelia to dinner in the city."

"You're punishing me with a date? Do you know how bets work?"

"I get to dress you for it." I grin widely. "The thought of you in a corset is rather satisfying."

"Fine, you sadistic—" He lets out a grunt as I tackle him off the bed and onto the ground. Taking him by surprise would be my only chance at an upper hand. I straddle his hips and make a grab for his hands, but I'm too slow.

He bucks his hips and flips me off of him before I can pin him. My hands are pinned to my sides against the floor with all his weight on top of me.

"Like I said, a brat." He rolls his eyes, thinking he's already won.

I know what I do next would never work in a real-life situation, but I'll use whatever I can to win. We already established that I don't fight fair. I pinch the back of Elijah's thighs that are currently pinning my hands and hips to the floor. If it weren't for the fact that he's in light linen sleep pants he wouldn't have even felt it. But he is, and I pinch hard.

It catches him just enough by surprise that he arches his back slightly and lifts enough for me to twist my hips and throw him off me. As he finds his footing I roll from my back and spring to the balls of my feet. He's ready for me when I start throwing punches at him. I don't go for his face because I may be a brat, but I'm not that cruel.

He's quick though, blocking every punch I serve him and not even trying to throw one back. I finally land one to his stomach, and I'm not even sure he feels it through the layers of muscle.

Realizing my approach is not working, I take a step back to reevaluate.

"Tired already? We can just call it now if you'd prefer."

"Never." I smile as a thought occurs to me.

Elijah's focus shifts to several feet away just long enough for me to land a hit directly to his solar plexus. The breath leaves his lungs in a rush, and he gasps for air. I swipe my leg behind his, taking him down to the floor.

This time I don't straddle him; I use my knees to pin his arms to the floor next to his body and smile triumphantly down at him.

He's finally caught his breath again but has no control over his arms.

"Yield," I demand.

"Never."

I realize my mistake just moments too late when one of his

free legs swings up and wraps around my torso. The room flips on me as he switches our positions. He has me face down on the floor, sitting on my back, with my hands pinned above my head. *Fuck.*

"Are we done here?" He sounds bored.

"I yield." I sigh in defeat.

He rolls off my back, and I feel like I can finally breathe deeply. He holds out his hand to help me up and shakes his head. "I can't believe you fought dirty and *still* lost. What shame, General."

"Yeah, yeah. I'm not usually fighting males your size or as well trained. I also usually have swords available."

"Excuses, excuses," he tsks at me. We settle back in his bed, pulling the covers up over our legs. "Now pay up."

Fuck. I'm not ready for this. "Okay, but first you have to promise to tell no one. I'm serious, E. This can't get out."

"My lips are sealed," he promises.

I sigh and drag his hand to my temple. His power works through physical touch. He can control when he reads memories pretty well, but occasionally he slips. When his power first developed, nobody was safe. He didn't mean to invade people's privacy, but it took time to learn control. As a result, I learned to build mental shields against all Anima Gifts.

I drop my shields and let his warm essence fill my mind. Most people probably wouldn't even recognize what it felt like to have him in their mind, but I had felt it enough times that I would always recognize him. Though the concept as a whole was invasive, his essence would always be a comfort to me.

I study his face as he watches the memory play out for both of us. I expected disgust, surprise, horror maybe, but what I see instead is pure humor and relief in his eyes. As the entire encounter comes to an end, he lets out a deep laugh, and I instantly regret showing him.

I start to turn my head away to hide the blush creeping up my cheeks when he pulls me closer into him and squeezes me gently. "I can't believe you thought that would be a surprise to me. You two have been at each other's throats since you arrived. The tension you two have could be cut with a butter knife. I'm just glad you finally stopped fighting it. That was painful to watch."

I'm speechless because I had no idea it was that obvious. "Wait, you knew this entire time?"

"I didn't have confirmation until just now, but I had a strong feeling there was something more going on between you. Nobody has chemistry that strong without doing something about it."

"Except we shouldn't be acting on it. He's with my mother." I groan and throw my head back. This situation makes my head throb.

"But is he?" Elijah challenges.

"He's literally engaged to her, E."

"Would you just stop and think about the bigger picture for one minute, Breyla?" Elijah's tone turns to frustration. "For one of the most strategic and accomplished generals in our history, you are awfully dense when it comes to what's right in front of you."

I open my mouth to defend myself, but don't get far.

"What do our laws say will happen if the queen doesn't remarry?"

"The rule would pass to me, and I would be forced to marry," I start. "But Mother would never force me into that position."

"Right. Do you really think she, of all people, wants to marry right now?"

I know what he's really saying. If I had lost my true love, the last thing I would want is to be forced into marrying another.

The whole kingdom was grieving, but she was having to plan a wedding. The thought has my chest tightening.

"No, I suppose she probably doesn't." It comes out barely above a whisper.

"I don't suppose you've thought about what happens if both you and your mother refuse to marry and leave the throne empty?"

No, I hadn't. My silence says as much.

"The rule would pass the next strongest family of noble standing. Any guesses who that might be?"

This one I do know the answer to. "Lord Seamus."

"Exactly. Now let's forget trying to keep you happy, and keep a power-hungry, sadistic male away from the throne. Let's look at Lord Aurelius. Have you even once seen him being affectionate toward your mother?"

"Yes, plenty of time—"

"In a way that wasn't exactly like us?" he clarifies, waving a hand between us.

"What's your point?" I grit out. I don't like where this is heading.

"My point, Princess, is that everyone around you is protecting you in some way, but you haven't once stopped to consider why." The frustration is palpable in his tone.

"I don't need protection," I grit out, my back molars grinding.

"You're wrong about that."

The way Elijah says that catches me off guard. "What aren't you telling me? Who do you think I need protection from?"

He sighs, "There's a lot going on that I'm not sure about right now, but most of all you need protection from yourself, B."

His words sober me, leaving me unable to form a response. I'm not sure I completely understand his meaning, but it leaves my stomach in knots either way.

Elijah pulls me into him and lays us down, wrapping me tightly to his chest. The lights extinguish themselves, and the room goes dark. I listen to the soft inhales and exhales of my best friend behind me as I ponder his words. His breathing is deep and even, letting me know he's found sleep as I continue to mentally replay our conversation early into the morning hours. When sleep finally comes for me, it's not restful.

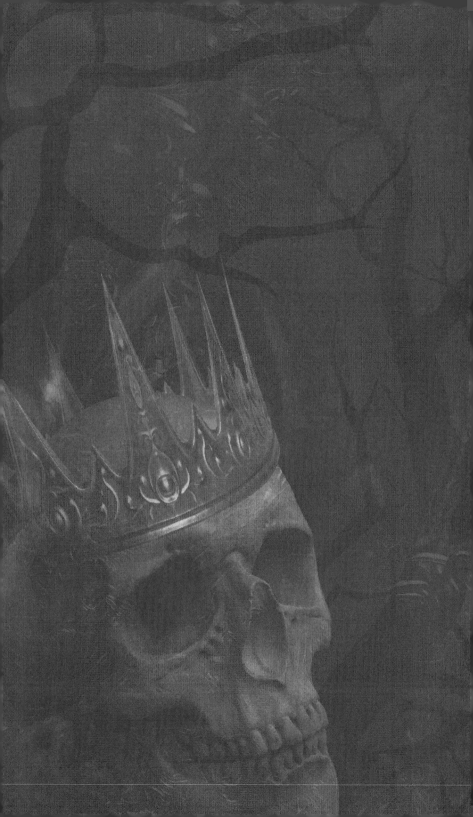

CHAPTER NINETEEN

BREYLA

I awake the next morning with a pounding behind my eyes and a stiffness in my limbs. Normally I sleep peacefully with Elijah, but I spent the entire night in a semi-conscious state, tossing and turning constantly. Elijah is already up and in the bathing chamber getting ready for the day.

According to Aurelius's sources, Prince Ayden is set to arrive today. The thought has my stomach knotting even further. There is so much I don't know, and the lack of control has me spiraling.

I slip from Elijah's bed and out of his chambers. It's early enough that I won't be seen by many. It doesn't take me long to reach the royal wing and my chambers. As I unlock my door, Aurelius's swings open.

Before I can voice my displeasure with him, I find myself pinned to my door, an angry-looking Aurelius staring at me. He leans into me and runs his nose along my neck, and I realize he's smelling me.

His deep voice betrays nothing as he asks, "What are you wearing?"

Then it dawns on me; I'm still wearing Elijah's clothes. I resist the urge to grin as I realize what's happening.

"Something of Elijah's," I answer boldly, and because I can't help myself, I taunt him further. "It's where I just came from, actually."

A growl escapes him as I feel the pad of his tongue lick up my neck. The feeling has shivers racing up my back, and I fight the arousal I'm feeling from his reaction. It's completely feral and should be a red flag, but I always did love the color red.

"Go bathe, Princess," he demands and nips my earlobe. "You smell like shit."

He opens my door behind me and shoves me in, slamming the door behind him.

I can't help the full laugh that escapes me as I realize I smell like Elijah. It doesn't matter that Elijah is more of a brother to me; it would appear Aurelius doesn't like the scent of any male on my skin.

As tempted as I am to taunt him further by keeping Elijah's scent on me, a bath sounds amazing. I still have remnants of our activities in the woods yesterday all over me. Small twigs and leaves are wound in my hair, and there's a slight ache to my muscles.

I quickly undress, dropping Elijah's clothing to the ground to be laundered and returned later. There's a fire burning, and I know I have Lyla to thank for still tending to me even when I had dismissed all my servants. I enter the bathing chamber to find the bath already drawn.

I sink into the warm water and let it relax me, washing away all of the events of the last twenty-four hours.

I take my time in the bath and emerge later, ready to face the day. Today won't be easy, but I'm more prepared to handle it now that I feel alive again.

With my hair wrapped in a towel and a thin black robe wrapped around me, I pad across my chamber in search of clothing. When I pass the fireplace, I notice something odd burning in it. I bend down to inspect it and grab the black metal poker from next to the hearth. I use it to move the mystery item until I can see it clearly.

"Is that...clothing?" I ask aloud.

I drop the poker and look behind me where I had dropped Elijah's borrowed clothing to find it missing.

That motherfucker. The jealous male had snuck back in my room to burn the other male's clothing because he didn't like his scent on me.

I sigh and move to my wardrobe. It's obvious that this day is going to try me in more ways than I originally anticipated. I select a fitted black tunic and red waist cincher to give me a feeling of security, without being completely confined by a bodice. I need support, but I also need to be able to move freely. I could also easily dress myself in this outfit, so there was no need to call for Ophelia. I slip into my normal black leather pants, savoring how they hugged my hips but allowed me to move fluidly.

Sitting on the edge of my bed, I pull on my boots and lace them up my calves. Lastly, I tuck my knives into their right places on my body—one hidden in my boot, one openly strapped to my thigh, and a smaller dagger tucked into the front of my waist cincher. Their proximity brings me a sense of peace, and I breathe deeply.

I wrestle my waves into a braid down the center of my back, securing the end with a strip of leather. As much as I despise wearing a tiara, I know it's proper etiquette when welcoming visiting royalty. I choose a modest gold piece with a blood-red ruby in the center. Placing the tiara on my head, I admire how the red and gold play beautifully off the golden strands that twist through my braided hair.

By the time I reach the throne room it's late morning, and the castle is bustling with activity. My mother is sitting on her throne, my father's seat next to her lying empty. On her right stands Aurelius, glaring daggers at Elijah as he gives his report. "Prince Ayden and his party were seen entering the city roughly a half hour ago. He should be arriving any moment."

The Queen's eyes remain distant, her mind seemingly a thousand miles away. She nods in understanding but doesn't speak. She's just as nervous as the rest of us, maybe more so. Her fingers lightly drum on the throne's armrest. As she glances at Aurelius, a look of understanding passes between them. I'm unsure what their eyes communicate, but I'll find out soon enough.

With that look, I'm reminded that I'm irritated with Aurelius and decide to play with fire. I stop next to Elijah and smile sweetly. "I'm sorry I'll have to replace the tunic you lent me. Something unfortunate happened to it."

Elijah must notice the glint in my eye, or perhaps it's the way Aurelius is looking at us both, but he seems to know what I'm doing. He grabs me by my hip and pulls me to his side before kissing my cheek softly. "No worries, B. It's just a tunic. You know I'm always there for whatever you might need." I know what he means, but the way he says it has Aurelius's jaw clenching.

I move to stand beside my mother on the opposite side as Aurelius. The throne room doors open as the herald enters to announce our guests.

"Now announcing Prince Ayden Mordet II of the Kingdom of Prudia, and his companions."

Prince Ayden enters the room, and I'm hit with a sense of déjà vu. I've never met this male, but something about him seems familiar. He stands tall, even with Aurelius, who stands eight inches above me. Deep brown hair frames his face, shaved closer to the side with longer curls adorning the top of his head. Amber eyes scan the room, and a grin tugs at the corner of his lips. Lips that draw my eyes to the strong jawline covered in a short but tasteful beard. *Holy hell, he's handsome.*

He strides into the room and crosses it with the arrogance every royal male seems to master. He comes to a stop in front of the dais, his guards and companions a few feet behind him. My mother rises to greet him. "Welcome to the kingdom of Rimor, Prince Ayden. We were not expecting you for several more days, but we are happy to have you. I hope you find your stay comfortable."

"Thank you, Your Majesty. I have very much looked forward to visiting your beautiful kingdom for quite some time. How lovely it is that we get to celebrate your engagement to Lord Aurelius. My condolences on the loss of King Raynor. I know how difficult death can be." He seems genuine, but I sense the bitterness of his words. His father's death came at the hands of my own. It was in battle, but he still holds that bitterness against our family.

Clearing her throat, my mother changes topics. "Prince Ayden, may I introduce my daughter, and general of our army, Princess Breyla." She gestures to me, and I step forward on the dais to greet him.

The white of his teeth shines as he smiles widely. "Well of course this beautiful female is your daughter. She is simply dazzling. Queen Genevieve, I could never mistake her for anything but your blood."

He takes my hand and lays a warm, lingering kiss on it.

When his eyes lift to mine, I smirk. "Do lines like that normally work for you, Prince?"

"Breyla!" my mother exclaims, but Ayden is unphased.

He quirks an eyebrow at me and asks, "I don't know, Princess, does it?"

I chuckle at his boldness. "It might if I were a softer female. You'll find nothing but rough edges here."

"Oh, I see plenty of soft edges on you, Breyla. At least, where it matters, that is."

I fight the amused grin threatening to take over my face and hear a snicker behind me. No doubt Elijah finds this as entertaining as I do. We're the only ones, though, as I hear my mother clear her throat uncomfortably. I glance over to see Aurelius's dark eyes pinning me, the red specks in his irises burning brightly. His hands are clenched, and I can tell he's exercising all his restraint at the moment.

"You must have had a rather long journey, Prince. Why don't I show you to your room?" I suggest, trying to ease the tension in the room. "You can rest and bathe before dinner."

"That would be lovely, Princess." Ayden offers me his hand as I step down from the dais.

Slipping my arm through his, I lead him out of the throne room and toward the royal wing.

We make our way down the stone corridors, the afternoon sun shining brightly through the open windows. It's nearly the fall season, and the days are a comfortable temperature. I savor the warmth and take a deep inhale. I'm close enough to Prince Ayden now that I catch a whiff of his scent—a woodsy citrus smell that's oddly warm.

"I must say, you are not what I was expecting, Breyla," Ayden confesses.

"So I've been told," I shrug. "I think most males are intimidated by a female in leathers."

He eyes me up and down. "I think I'd be far more intimidated with you *out* of leathers."

"You flirt shamelessly, Prince Ayden."

"So I've been told," he replies, parroting my words back to me.

I roll my eyes before teasing, "What? No pretty maidens back home to hold your interest?"

"None so pretty as you, darling."

"Wow," I say in awe.

"That's exactly what I thought when I first—"

"You're honestly worse than Elijah. I thought he was the biggest flirt in this court. I'm really going to have to keep my eye on you." I turn down the corridor that leads to my—and now Ayden's—chambers. *Having both Aurelius and Ayden in such close proximity was going to get interesting.*

"Oh, please do, Princess. Which one is Elijah?" he asks curiously.

"The one with the long blond hair and more muscles than should be possible." *Kind of like you.*

"Ah, yes. He is your mother's advisor?"

"One of them, yes. And my best friend," I explain.

"Hmmm," he muses.

"Here we are," I state as we arrive at his chambers. "This is where you'll be staying. My room is just across the hall." I motion to my door. "And Lord Aurelius is just next to me."

"Lord Aurelius does not stay closer to the Queen's chambers?" he questions, somewhat confused.

"Obviously."

"Why?"

"I suspect he enjoys making my life hell," I joke.

"So, she has a sense of humor," he says with a chuckle.

"She does. But in all actuality, I don't know. You'd have to ask one of them that question."

"I don't actually care that much," he drawls.

"Hence the reason I don't know the answer."

Prince Ayden steps into his room and looks around. "I think we'll get along just fine, Breyla."

"We'll see," is all I say before shutting the door and leaving him to prepare for dinner.

Dinner that night is nothing less than I expected: an utter shit show.

Due to Prince Ayden's early arrival and the large party of people accompanying him, we are forced to have dinner in the formal dining room rather than the private room reserved for the royal family. It easily sits thirty rather comfortably, and nearly every seat is filled when I enter. The queen sits at the head of the table, Aurelius to her right while the spot to her left is left open for me.

I cross the stone floor, the slight heel of my shoe clicking as I walk. I had changed out of my previous outfit and into a floor length blood-red dress. It's made of silk and hugs every curve down to my hips, then flares out into a flowy skirt. The neckline is a sweetheart cut with lace details that accentuate my breasts. Full-length sleeves made of the same lace end in a design that loops around my middle fingers.

I left my hair as it was, my gold and ruby diadem still sitting in place atop my braid. As I reach my seat, I notice that instead of Elijah to my left, Prince Ayden occupies that spot. To his left sits Ophelia, then Elijah with his arm slung across the back of her chair, his fingers tracing the curve of her shoulder. Across from Prince Ayden, a beautiful golden-haired female sits next to Aurelius.

She smiles sweetly then casts her gaze on Aurelius. "Hello, Aurelius," she practically sings. Her voice is sweet and smooth like honey. It rings with a tone of familiarity that catches my attention. *Who is this female?*

"Princess Breyla, I don't think you've been properly intro-duced to my cousin, Lady Charlotte," Prince Ayden announces.

"Of course, you're already well acquainted with Lord Aurelius, Charlie. No need to introduce you."

Both Aurelius's and Lady Charlotte's eyes narrow at Prince Ayden. Prince Ayden just smirks as he takes a sip of his wine.

A blush creeps up Charlotte's cheeks, and she clears her throat. "It's a pleasure to meet you, Princess."

"Please, just Breyla. Or General if you prefer. And likewise," I force out as evenly as I can. The heat I feel coursing through my veins would suggest it is *not* a pleasure to meet her.

Her blonde hair shines in a way that I know it would be silky to the touch. Her eyes are a shade of blue that reminds me of the baby's breath that grows outside the palace walls. Alabaster skin, so smooth and flawless, serves as a reminder that mine is scarred and calloused by years of battle and training. She's lean with a petite frame, not an ounce of fat—or muscle—on her. While I'm above the average height of women in our kingdom, she stands several inches taller than me and has the legs any male would want to part. *Ones that, apparently, Aurelius has already parted.*

Charlotte is everything I'm not. Her resemblance to my mother doesn't escape me, and it has my gut churning. Where Aurelius is dark like my shadows, they are both bright. They contrast him in a way that's beautiful and just seems so natural. They're both graceful, soft spoken, and carry themselves in a gentle manner. I'm loud, mouthy, and sometimes brash. I've never been insecure about my looks, and honestly, I shouldn't even care when it comes to him, but I can't help but wonder why he pursues me. He clearly has a type—a mold I don't fit.

"Though she doesn't look like it, Charlie has quite the mind for strategy. She serves as one of my advisors. From what I hear about you, General, you might find you have more in common than you think." I don't miss the insinuation in his statement. I immediately tense, because there is no way he should know that we have *that* in common.

I glance around to see if anyone else understands what he is suggesting. I see Elijah giving him a curious look, but he doesn't say anything.

"Ah, so we have her to thank as well for the attacks on our border villages?" I challenge. Everyone stiffens, as if they didn't expect me to call him out over our evening meal.

Prince Ayden lets out a loud laugh as he turns to me, draping an arm around the back of my chair. "I'm quite sure I don't know what you're talking about, General." His amber eyes stare directly into mine, almost urging me to continue my accusations.

Before I can let my mouth run wild, I'm interrupted by the servants entering with the first course. I turn my attention to my wine, drowning my unease in the crimson liquid as a warm, hearty vegetable soup is placed before me. The smell has my mouth watering as I patiently wait for everyone to be served.

As the warm broth fills my belly, I hear my mother speak for the first time this evening. "So, Prince Ayden, when might we expect to hear of a coronation ball for yourself?" Her tone is polite and inquisitive, but I know she's probing for information.

The spymaster, Lord Craylor, sits several seats down from Charlotte, but I see his gaze snap to my mother at the question.

"Well, seeing as it requires that I take a queen before I can take the throne..." Ayden's voice trails off, "I imagine it will be about the same time Breyla takes her throne." The number of details he seems to know about our court is unsettling.

"So, the fifth of never? That's fantastic news," Aurelius snaps, his tone dripping with disdain.

"You seem to have lost your diplomacy, Lord Aurelius." Ayden is clearly not amused by Aurelius right now.

"Well, it's a good thing I'm not acting in the capacity of a diplomat presently."

The animosity between them is clear, but the reason is not. Ayden has been pushing buttons all day, but he's been pushing everyone's—not just Aurelius's. No, there's something more to this.

I glance down to my hands, tightly gripping my silverware, to see shadows creeping down my hand and weaving between my fingers. Now is not the time for me to lose control.

"Tell me, Breyla, when do *you* plan to take your place as queen?" Ayden turns the questioning back to me.

I feel my pulse quicken and more shadows crawl down my skin as I fight to gain control of the panic taking over. I glance across the table at Aurelius to see him looking at me with something that looks suspiciously like concern.

As our eyes connect, I instantly feel my heart rate slow. All at once, I can breathe again, and my panic recedes. I close my eyes, taking a deep breath, and call my shadows back into me.

"Oh, probably the sixth of never, seeing as it requires that I take a husband. But you know how that goes, Prince," I chuckle. "There aren't exactly a lot of males lining up for the job of being tied to me."

Ayden leans close and whispers in my ear, "They're all fools."

I turn my head to him and whisper back, "Oh, don't mistake me, Prince—I don't want the job. What would be foolish is assuming I want anything more than what I have right now."

He says nothing, but just smirks and leans back into his seat.

The first course is cleared from the table, and the main course is served. I hear Charlotte engaging Aurelius in conversation about trivial matters, but he smiles at her and carries on as if they are old friends. Which, of course, they are if Ayden is to be believed. I find myself wishing it were me he was giving that smile to.

It's a question from Ophelia that has my attention. "Prince Ayden, I've heard rumors that there is no shortage of willing and appropriate matches in your kingdom. What keeps you from marrying?"

Ayden turns his attention to Ophelia and takes a moment to appraise her before responding. "Willing? Yes. But the rest of your statement is wrong. I would not consider them...appropriate for my kingdom."

"And what would make one the right fit for your kingdom?" I can tell Ophelia is just genuinely curious and perhaps trying to keep the topic of conversation away from me.

"For one, they would need a brain. I'm fairly certain most of the interested parties are missing that. I need a queen who isn't just a pretty face, but someone who is my equal. I don't want someone to bear my children; I want a female who strengthens and pushes me. Power and beauty are nice, but my kingdom needs character."

I'm taken back by his answer, not because of what he says but because it seems like the first genuine thing he's said so far. This is the first I've seen of the true Ayden, and it's not what I expected.

"Why so many questions, Lady Ophelia? Are you interested in the position?" Ayden quips, his mask firmly back in place.

Ophelia blushes, and Elijah shifts uncomfortably next to her.

It's my turn to laugh at Ayden. "Pardon me, Ayden, but Lady Ophelia is far too good for you. Besides, you can't have her. She's one of the few females I care for. You'll have to find another."

He laughs with me and agrees, "Well, you're probably right about that. She seems far above my station."

This has the entire table laughing and the mood shifts to something lighter as we finish the main course.

As dessert is served, Charlotte is deep in conversation with Aurelius, and she places her hand atop his. "Would you care to show me the town tonight, Aurelius?" she asks with a coy grin plastered on her face. He takes notice of the offer in her eyes. There is no heat in the look he gives her.

I'm unsure if I'm more pissed that she's touching him or that she's offering herself in front of everyone in the room, including my mother—his future wife. The pure audacity of this female.

Before he says anything, I let my shadows creep under the table and wrap around his leg, their cool presence a reminder there are other people watching. I feel his muscles tense, and he turns his gaze to me. There is heat in the look he gives *me* as he blatantly ignores Charlotte's offer.

"General, there are some things for the ball that I need to pick up from a shop in town. I heard you were headed there after dinner. Would you care to join me?"

I have no such plans, but I play along. "Yes, I need to see a male about a sword. I'd be happy to accompany you."

Next to me, Ayden rolls his eyes. "I'm sure you can find some other male to give you a tour, Charlie."

Charlotte stays quiet, but her eyes shoot daggers at her cousin.

I pull my shadows back and the rest of the meal continues without incident.

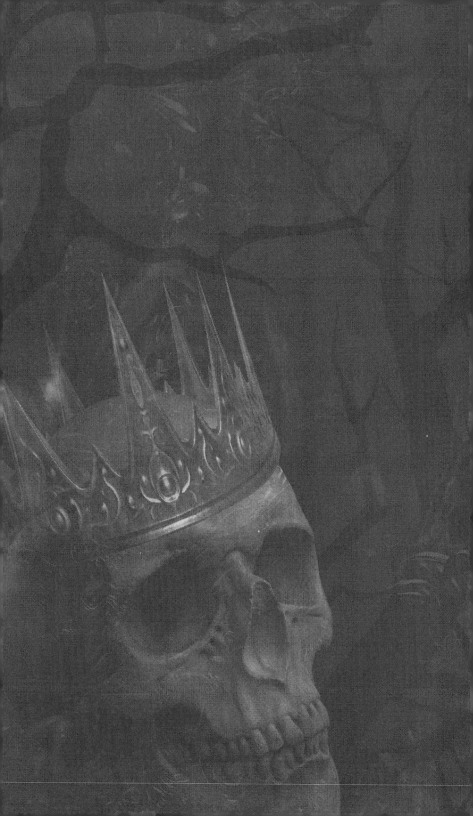

CHAPTER TWENTY

BREYLA

I'm making my way out of the formal dining room, but before I make the turn toward the royal wing, I feel a hand on the small of my back.

"Shall we?" Aurelius asks.

"Oh, you were serious? You actually did have an errand in town?" I quirk a brow at him.

"If the errand is getting away from Charlie, then yes. Now let's go, Princess."

I shake my head in disbelief but let him lead the way.

As we approach the castle gate a sadness settles over me, realizing it's not Nolan's face I'm seeing anymore.

"Good evening, General. Are you headed to town?"

"I am, Samson. Lord Aurelius and I will be going to pick up some items for the ball."

"Shall I fetch Ryder and Zion to accompany you? You do not appear to be armed." He looks uncomfortable.

"That's not necessary, Samson," Aurelius interjects. "She's

perfectly safe with me, but we both know she doesn't need anyone else to protect her."

"Very well, My Lord. The gate is open for you."

"How very un-male of you to admit I'm capable of defending myself," I remark as we pass through the gates.

"You are not some damsel in distress, Breyla. I trust my brother's judgment in appointing you General. So while the male in me will always want to protect you, I have seen that you are capable of protecting yourself. You may irritate the hell out of me, but I also respect you. Plus," he eyes me up and down, settling on my cleavage, "I count at least three daggers on you. You are anything but unarmed."

"Four, actually," I snicker.

We walk the short distance to the town outside the castle in peaceful silence.

"I need to know, Aurelius," I start, and he gives me a questioning look. "Is what Ayden said about Lady Charlotte the truth?"

He sighs. "That prick should have kept his mouth shut. Charlie and I have a history, but—"

Realizing he misunderstood my question, I blurt out, "Oh, no. Your personal history with Charlotte is the last thing I want to hear about." I can't help the slight venom in my voice.

"Then what are you asking, Breyla?"

"In your travels to Prudia, did you get the impression that she had a mind for strategy, as Ayden suggested?" I clarify, then mumble, "Or was she too busy making other impressions on you?"

Aurelius stops abruptly and tugs me down a darkened alley between a shop and the local tavern. Once we're alone, I'm being shoved against a wall. My back hits the cold bricks, and I feel the warm hard muscles of his body press firmly against me. He has one hand against the wall next to my head, the other wrapping around my throat.

"First of all, yes, Charlotte is incredibly clever and strategic. You would be wrong to underestimate her. Secondly, you don't get to play the jealous card tonight."

"Why? Because I'm not really yours?" I spit.

"Make no mistake, Breyla. You. Are. Mine. You may be your own capable person, but the way your body sings for me can't be denied. I'll destroy anyone that tries to take you from me."

I swallow hard as his words cause warmth to flood my core.

"And you don't get to play the jealous card because just last night I had you panting and begging for me, but this morning I find you in another male's clothing, freshly arriving from *his* chambers. Then I was forced to watch not one, but two males openly flirting with you all day."

"Clothes that you burned—" I'm cut off by the sharp sting of his teeth biting the spot where my neck meets my shoulder.

A sound somewhere between a moan and a gasp leaves my throat and all protests are forgotten. He licks the spot, soothing the sting, and kisses up my throat to my ear.

"I don't care that Elijah's your best friend, and I don't blame you for Ayden flirting, but that doesn't mean I like it. Their touches and suggestive looks and comments drive me to insanity. I hate people touching what's mine." A shiver runs up my spine at his words. "I especially hate that I can smell both of them all over you right now. Charlie and I may have history, but that's all it is—history. When she approached me at dinner, I turned to you. You spent all day flirting with Elijah and humoring Ayden in front of me because you knew there was nothing I could do. That, Princess, is why you don't get to play the jealous card tonight."

His words ring true, and I don't have a response that doesn't make me sound like a total hypocrite, so I say nothing. After a long several moments, he eases away from me and takes a step back.

"Come on, Princess. I need a drink." He takes my hand and walks me back down the alleyway to the front of the tavern.

When we enter, I'm greeted by the joyous sounds of my soldiers enjoying a night off and the smell of ale and mead. We take a seat in a corner booth, away from most of the other patrons.

"Evening, General. Been a minute since you last visited my tavern," Luella, the tavern owner, says, greeting me. She's older than both my parents, but you'd hardly be able to tell. Her brown curls hang loosely down her back and frame her warm, tawny skin. She's on the shorter side but has full rounded hips that have most males panting after her. Dark, lined hazel eyes look me over as she notices Aurelius next to me. "And you brought Lord Aurelius!" she exclaims in surprise.

"It was a bit crowded in the castle, Luella. We needed fresh air and a good drink. You were the only logical option, of course."

"Well, I don't know about the fresh air part, but I can set you up with a good drink. What'll it be tonight?"

"The usual for me, and whatever Lord Aurelius wants."

She nods and looks to him.

"Just bring me whatever she's having, Luella. Thank you," he says and smiles widely at her.

"That's brave of you. I could have ordered something overly sweet and frilly," I tease.

"Something tells me you're more of a rum or whiskey drinker."

I shrug. "I guess you'll find out."

Luella sets two short glasses on the table in front of us, each with two measures of a deep amber liquid. She leaves the bottle on the table because she knows better and leaves us to our conversation.

I take the drink and down the first glass in its entirety, savoring the spices and warmth as it races down my throat.

"Rum it is," Aurelius concludes as he downs his own glass and fills them both again.

After the second glass I am feeling bold. "Let's play a game."

He raises an eyebrow at me in question. "What kind of game?"

"Ten questions." Elijah and I usually played two truths and a lie, but that game wouldn't be fair with Aurelius's ability to detect lies.

"That sounds more like an interrogation," he snorts.

"No, this version is much more fun."

"How so?"

"In this version, if you answer the question, you must answer it truthfully. You can choose not to answer it, but in that case, you take a shot instead. The first person to ten answered questions chooses a challenge for the other to complete."

"Sounds simple enough. Let's play."

I'm surprised by how easy it is for him to agree. I expected more of a fight.

"Ladies first," he offers.

"Why do you distrust Ayden so greatly?" I start. I've been wondering about this since he first warned me away from Ayden.

"He wears a mask, different masks for every situation and every person. Though I've spent plenty of time in his court, I never know what to trust when it comes to him because he thrives in creating chaos. He was also in talks with your father about something important shortly before his death. The timing is suspicious. Satisfied?"

I had noticed some of this myself, so it wasn't entirely a surprise to get the full explanation. Though I wasn't convinced that was all there was to it, I let it go. I nod my acceptance of his answer.

"Has there ever been anything physical between you and

Elijah?" He starts with an easy one. Not easy for him, I'm sure, but easy for me.

"Not in the way you're referring to. We've always been tactile with one another, but never sexual and *never* romantic. If you believe in soulmates, know that he is mine. He has and will always understand me on a level that most never will. When I say he is my eyes and ears, I mean it quite literally. That requires a level of trust I would not extend to just anyone."

"I think I understand. You love him, but it's brotherly. Soulmates don't have to be romantic; I understand that. He isn't your fated, your twin flame, so to speak."

"Now you're getting it," I say with a smile.

"I still don't like it when he touches you," he grumbles.

"Get over it." I wink at him. "What is your favorite memory of your childhood?"

"Have you been in the forest behind your grandparent's manor?" he asks, and I shake my head.

"You should sometime. There is a massive, ancient oak tree about a quarter mile from the estate. The woods are dense enough that you probably can't see it from the outside, but it's wide enough to carve out and create a living space inside."

I listen intently as he describes the magnificent tree, wondering how I had never seen it before.

"My powers started manifesting very young, making it hard to make friends. Most of the children feared me because I would accidentally use my abilities on them, and it made them uncomfortable. I would go to that tree and spend hours trying to climb its branches. It's where I went to forget. After a particularly rough day, your father found me there scaling the ancient trunk."

Something inside me softens towards Aurelius as the recounting of his lonely adolescence.

"I don't know if he just didn't want me to hurt myself trying to climb the monster or if he just took pity on me, but he used his earth Gift to carve out steps in the trunk. They wound up the back like a spiraling staircase and ended at the lowest level of branches. I never had to struggle to climb anymore, and I would sit among the branches for hours."

He pauses, seemingly lost in memory, but continues, "Eventually, he even added a little alcove among the branches for me to sit or lay down comfortably. Your father's Gift was truly magnificent, Breyla."

I tear up at the memory of my father. I had never heard this story, and it reminds me how much I miss him.

Aurelius gently wipes the tear from my cheek and continues, "It became my own little world away from reality that I would go to whenever I needed space. He would join me sometimes and let me practice my power on him so I could have a safe space to learn control. Or he'd read with me, teach me how to fight, or just sit with me."

"Is it still there?"

"The last time I checked it was exactly as I left it," he says. "My turn. Do you think I had something to do with your father's death?"

"I did at first, but now I don't know." The look of pain that crosses his face almost hurts me, too. "What's the reason you agreed to marry my mother? The real reason, please."

He reaches for the glass in front of him and tosses the drink back. *Interesting.*

He leans in close to ask the next question. "Tell me your dirtiest fantasy, Princess." His hand trails up my thigh under the table.

I smirk because he obviously thinks he'll get me to pass on this question. I turn to whisper in his ear. "Right now? I can't stop thinking about having you lay me out across this table and bury yourself deep, deep inside me while everyone in this tavern watches."

His nostrils flare, and he shifts in his seat to alleviate some of the discomfort from his hardening length. Under the table I run my hand up his thigh, copying the path his hand had just taken on my own.

"What is your favorite color?" I ask, moving back away from him.

It's not the question he expects."Red, but not the shade you're in now. Red like the wine you favor, deep with purple hues. What's your favorite place?"

"The castle library probably. I love the smell of old parchment and how stories can make you forget your troubles. Is Charlie a regular of yours?"

"Not anymore. You're really hung up on Charlie, why? I have in fact slept with other females, so why this obsession over her?"

I sigh, not wanting to answer this, but also not wanting to lose our little game. I reach for my drink for a shot of liquid courage. I down the spiced rum and turn to him. "You're engaged to my mother, and I can't help but notice that they bear a certain resemblance. They have all the same features that are so...different from mine. I just wonder why you've been openly involved with a certain type of female, but you pursue me in the dark. Hell, I don't even understand why you're pursuing me at all, but I can't seem to stay away from you. I just don't seem to fit your type."

"Is my little demon jealous?" He grins devilishly at me.

"Not jealous..." I mumble. "Just confused."

He grabs my chin between his thumb and index finger, tilting me to look directly into his eyes. "I've tried to tell you before, Princess, that there is nothing between your mother and me. Our relationship is more like your relationship with Elijah than anything remotely romantic. I have my reasons for agreeing to her proposal, but if you would talk to her, you would find that we are on the same page. Her resemblance to Charlie is coincidental. I don't even really care for blondes much, to be honest.

Your crimson locks look so much better wrapped around my fist."

My eyes widen at his confession, my heart beating faster.

"Breyla, you are like fire and sunlight, and I would gladly burn in your heat. Your shadows mirror the darkest parts of me, and I want to bathe in them. You are fierce and brilliant, and I would happily kneel at your feet and worship every part of you."

I had never had any male speak to me like this before, and it makes the breath catch in my throat. His words both frighten and thrill me.

"I can sense the erratic beats of your heart, Princess. You may not be able to understand me now, but you will someday. You are mine, little demon."

I nod—because that's all I can do—and continue our game.

The questions continue until we come to the end, and I have answered ten to his eight.

"What will it be, Princess?" Aurelius sighs.

"You know, I think I need retribution. Take your pants off."

"Princess, as much as I'd love to bury myself in you right now, I will not fuck you in front of all the males in this tavern."

"It's cute that you think that I want you to fulfill my fantasy right now, but that's not what I mean."

"Then why exactly am I taking my pants off?"

"You're going to give them to me and I'm going to return to the castle. You're going to walk back without them."

Realization dawns on him and he groans, throwing his head back.

"Fair is fair, Lord Aurelius. Hand them over," I order, cackling and thoroughly enjoying my sweet retribution.

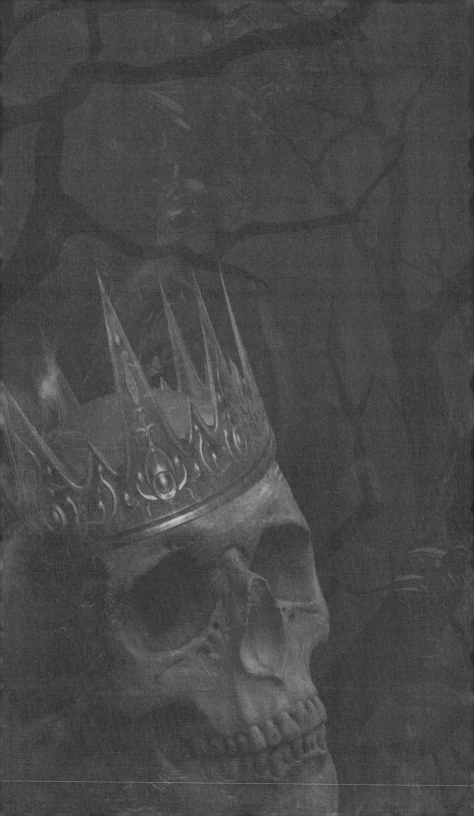

CHAPTER TWENTY-ONE

OPHELIA

The humid, late-summer heat beats down on my back as the clanging of clashing swords fills the air around me. I stand outside the sparring ring watching Elijah and Zion dance around each other. In the next ring, Breyla is engaged in hand-to-hand with Ryder while Jade watches from the side with several other guards in training.

Most of the trained soldiers are still stationed along the border, so the ones in attendance are primarily new recruits and castle guards. They watch intently as we move with practiced deadly precision.

As far as I knew, Elijah had never spent time on the front line, but the way he moved and sparred with Zion made it obvious he had spent just as much time training as any soldier present. I knew he was skilled in politics, but he appeared to be equally skilled with a sword. He moves with a smooth grace, dodging and weaving to avoid Zion's attacks. Zion lunges for him and he parries, narrowly missing his attempt. He spins in a half circle, raising his sword at the back of Zion's head.

"Nice try, Zion. Do better next time."

His shoulders sag in defeat, and he drops his shoulder. "Always a pleasure to have my ass kicked by you, Elijah."

Elijah shrugs. "The pleasure is all mine."

He sheaths his sword and steps out of the training ring, making room for the next set of challengers. It's then that he notices my eyes roaming up and down his naked torso appreciatively. Our gazes meet, and he gives me a wink. A crimson blush takes creeps over my cheeks, but I don't break eye contact.

The sparring continues around us, and he provides a few suggestions for improvement. As the sun approaches midday, we're interrupted by a servant delivering a package to Breyla. Her expression suggests she clearly wasn't expecting any kind of delivery today. It's a larger box, simple in design, and wrapped in brown paper.

She tears off the wrapping and pulls the lid from the box before letting out a scream. Within a heartbeat, Elijah is beside her, and I trail closely behind him. My breakfast threatens to make a reappearance when I finally see the cause of her terror. Blank hazel eyes stare lifelessly up at me.

Julian.

Julian's head is sitting on a black velvet pillow, blood staining the box's walls. I feel my heart crack, my lungs constricting. Breyla is shaking next to me, and I realize she's crumbling. Somehow, Elijah wrestles the box from her hands and places the lid back on so no one else sees.

He wasn't fast enough, though, and Jade's sobs fill the air.

"J-Julian," Jade stutters through her wails of pain. "No, no, he can't be..." She trails off, unable to finish the statement.

Breyla's and Jade's cries fill the air, twining together in one of the most juxtaposed displays of grief. The two strongest females I know are both breaking in front of my eyes. Their pain is a palpable, living thing that fills the air around us, drowning us all in their grief. Tears stream down my face as my soul weeps.

Julian and Elijah had known each other since childhood, and though I didn't know the extent of their relationship, I knew there was history between them. Elijah felt deeply and I could see something break in his eyes as he held Jade's trembling form.

I see Jade start to drop, and Elijah reaches out his arms, catching her as she falls. He gently lowers her to the ground, pulling her into his chest. He wraps himself around her and rocks her back and forth. She's shaking so violently that I don't know how she's breathing at all. Running his hands over her silvery-white braids, they sit there for what feels like hours.

When I lay eyes on Breyla again, it's not Aurelius I see, but Prince Ayden who has her wrapped in his arms. Aurelius isn't anywhere to be found, and it startles me to see Ayden providing any kind of comfort to the daughter of the male he swore revenge against. It doesn't make sense, but I don't have the mental strength to follow that train of thought right now. I'm on my knees next to Jade, rubbing soothing circles on her back.

Eventually, their cries subside to whimpers, and I see Jade's eyelids begin to droop. Ayden is standing with an already passed-out Breyla in his arms. He nods to Elijah as we stand, as if to convey that she's safe in his arms. I don't know why, but I trust him. Maybe not entirely, but with this, I trust him. Elijah moves toward the castle, Jade cradled to his chest. I follow silently behind, opening doors for him as we go.

The deep, even inhales and exhales tell me that Jade has found sleep by the time we reach her chambers. I push the door open, and he enters, placing Jade in her bed. He pulls the covers over her shoulders and plants a gentle kiss on her temple. She looks peaceful in her sleep, and I sigh. This may be the last time she feels any kind of peace for a while. I hope it lasts.

Elijah and I back out of her room, softly shutting the door behind us. He slumps against the stone wall, closing his eyes. The adrenaline is gone, and I watch him deflate. I lay my hand on his cheek, waiting for his eyes to meet mine. When they finally open, they convey all the pain and exhaustion he feels.

"I'm not going to ask if you're okay," I whisper, "but tell me what I can do." It comes out almost like a plea.

"You aren't responsible for taking care of me, Ophelia."

"And you didn't have to take care of Jade, but you did. I want to." Right now, it feels more like a need than a want. Elijah needs someone to just let him be weak. I can be that for him.

"It's always been the four of us," he says quietly. "I can't picture a world without him in it." Elijah sounds so vulnerable.

I don't say anything, just letting him process his emotions. He pulls me into his embrace and burys his nose into the crook of my neck. My arms wrap him, and his muscles finally relax. Something about me gives him enough peace to feel safe, but I still feel his tears run against the skin of my neck.

After several minutes he pulls back just enough to lean his forehead against mine. "Thank you," he says softly.

"I didn't do anything," I reply.

"You are everything."

My breath hitches, and I search his eyes to see if he means that or if it was a slip of the tongue. Suddenly, something shifts in his eyes. The sorrow turns to desire. He reaches a finger under my chin and tips it up, level with his own, and leans in close. Our lips are so close I can feel his breath on my own. His mouth quirks up and I stare into his eyes. There's a question in his gaze.

My lips part slightly, pulse quickening under his touch. I nod ever so slightly, and it's all he needs as he takes my lips in a tender kiss.

It starts slowly and softly as he lets me control the pace. My innocence is no secret, and he doesn't want to scare me away by moving too quickly. My body screams for more. I want him to show me everything I'm missing. I run my tongue along his bottom lip, teasing and testing his resolve. He parts his lips and I deepen the kiss, my tongue pushing into his mouth. He groans, and I relish the taste of him.

His fingers thread through the raven locks at the back of my head, using it to deepen the kiss. He meets my tongue with his own, exploring every inch of my mouth. I bite his bottom lip, eliciting a deep groan from him.

"Fuck my resolve," he growls, spinning us and pressing me into the stone wall. "You are temptation wrapped in perfection and I am weak," he says breathily as his mouth moves down my throat, peppering kisses along the way.

A sharp inhale leaves my mouth as he bites down, soothing the sting with his tongue. The more he sucks the skin into his mouth, the louder my cries get. This will leave a mark, and I realize I *want* his marks all over my body.

I push into him and wind my fingers through his hair, tugging sharply on the strands. His length hardens against me, and I roll my hips into his. I don't know what I'm doing, just going with what feels natural. Being pressed against him, his lips covering every inch of my skin in kisses, feels so incredibly natural.

Suddenly, he pulls back from me. Our chests are rising and falling rapidly as he looks me in the eyes. I can see the desire swimming in his, but it's been eclipsed by something somber.

He pulls away from me, putting some space between our heated bodies.

"Elijah—" I start, a feeling of confusion crossing my face. My brows furrow as I try to read his expression.

"Don't."

"Don't what?" My voice is soft, unsure.

"Don't start to question yourself or if I want you. This space has nothing to do with you or anything you did."

"Then why?" I struggle to believe his words.

He grabs my hand and does something I don't expect, pulling it down to cover his painfully hard erection. My eyes widen as he asks, "Does this feel like me not wanting you? I want you so badly it hurts. I want to bury myself inside you and draw more of those delicious sounds from your lips. And don't mistake me, Ophelia, I will do that. I don't even have a problem taking you right here, in the hallway where anyone can see." My cheeks heat at that statement, but he continues. "But my best friend's head was just delivered to my other best friend in a box. I've wanted you for a while, but if I seek comfort in your arms for the first time right now, you will question if I truly want you or if I was just trying to erase my pain with your pleasure. The first time I have you, there will be no question in your mind. I will not have you questioning why I'm burying myself in you."

I take a deep breath, trying to process his words. I realize he is probably right and that's not how I want it to be between us.

My eyebrow quirks slightly before I ask, "Wanna get a drink?"

"You're speaking my language, doll."

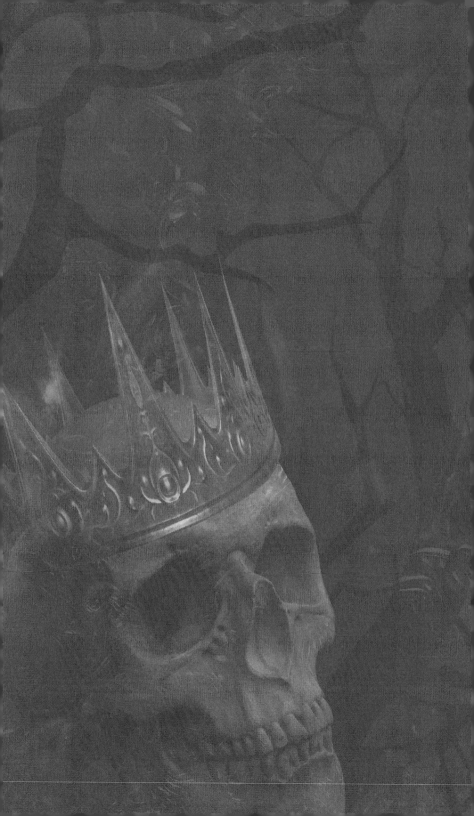

CHAPTER TWENTY-TWO

BREYLA

It's dark as I enter the cold, abandoned graveyard. The moon hangs low in the sky, mostly covered by thick clouds. There's just enough light to make out the crumbling headstones and overgrown plant life that has overrun the graves. Burying our dead is something that hasn't been done in centuries, the common practice now being a funeral pyre. Still, the bones of our ancestors sleep beneath my feet. A slight melancholy strikes me as I think about how neglected the resting place of our forefathers has become, forgotten by the world.

I'm not entirely sure what has called me here, but I know I must heed its summons. I feel it tugging in my gut; I can't ignore this. My bare feet travel the crumbling stone path through the center of the cemetery. It should be painful, but weeds and moss have grown over most of the path, giving it a soft cushion. The hazy moonlight serves as a guide, and I quietly make my way to the back of the area. It's the oldest section, the stones mostly crumbled to dust and completely unreadable. Yet, as I reach the corner,

I find a freshly dug grave. The dirt is piled high with flowers thrown on top.

I glance around the pile to find a pristine tombstone marking the grave. A breeze smelling of fresh rain and hints of leather tosses my hair and causes goosebumps to pebble the flesh of my bare shoulders. There are no dates, no great epitaphs on the stone, just a name. Julian Tanda.

That can't be right, I think. Running my hand through the loose dirt, I try to puzzle out why my second in command would be buried here. I fail to make sense of it as panic sets in. Julian must be under this dirt, but the last time I saw him he was leaving to gather intel on the movements of Lord Seamus. Has someone trapped him under this earth?

I dig my fingers into the cool soil, shifting the dirt aside to reach my suffocating friend. It cakes my fingers, nails ripping and tearing as I move quickly to save him. My heart rate increases as I move layers and layers, frantic to reach him. I've nearly hit the bottom when my fingers touch something hard.

Perplexed, I brush the dirt aside gently, revealing the white of bone. It's a skull.

"Oh, there you are, Julian." I smile with relief. "I was so worried about you, but I'm glad you're safe."

"Of course, I'm safe, B. Why wouldn't I be?" Julian's skull questions, amusement and curiosity thick in this tone.

"No reason, I guess. I just wasn't sure what you were doing under this pile of dirt in an abandoned graveyard."

"Seemed as good a place as any to finally get some rest," Julian sighs. The skull in my hands starts to shimmer and shift. Flesh starts growing where it was once just bone, and after a moment Julian is standing before me.

He's clad in the leathers I last saw him in, sword strapped to his side and a smile plastered on his face. What a beautiful face it is. The clouds must have shifted, because the moonlight now glows brightly against his mocha skin, and the gold in his hazel eyes sparkles.

"That's better," I giggle. "I like you much better in this form."

"What form is that?"

I gesture to him, waving my hands up and down. "This one, the one where you look like my Julian. My fearless second."

"Oh, my dear, Breyla." His smile turns sad. "I'll always be your Julian. Yours, and Elijah's, and Jade's. But I can't be your second anymore."

Confusion twists my face. "Why not? I need you. There's something coming, I feel it." Couldn't he see how much I would need my second? How much I would need him?

"I know it feels that way now, but you don't need me, General." He steps closer to me and pulls me into his chest, wrapping me in his fresh rain and leather scent.

I relax into his hug, my heart calming. "What's coming, Julian?"

"I don't know how to answer that question." It's not really an answer.

"But you do know, don't you?" Julian knew lots of things. His ability to acquire information was part of why I chose him as second.

He tilts my head back so I'm staring into his eyes. "Trust your heart, your gut, but not your eyes. Secrets surround you, some of which will be deadly."

"Will be?"

"And some that already have been." That sad smile reappears on his handsome face. Something ripples across his features, and the vague image of his skull shines through. Like I'm looking at Julian, but also his skeleton at the same time.

"Your non-answers will be the death of me," I grumble.

His face stills. "No, they won't." His tone is deathly serious.

Frustratedly, I demand, "What aren't you telling me?"

"I'm sorry, B. I don't answer to you any longer. That's all I can say." His form wavers again, fading more into the skeleton form momentarily.

"I still don't understand. Of course you answer to me. I am your general and your princess."

"You are my friend and a wonderful general; someday you'll be a fierce warrior queen. But no, I don't answer to you. Death answers to no one. Not even you, Breyla."

In that moment, it finally clicks. Death answers to no one. Julian is dead. The image of his skeleton showing through his skin becomes clearer as my heart shatters again.

"N-No..." I stutter, running my hands up his chest. My fingers run over his jaw, his cheeks, every part of his face as I try to convince myself it's all a lie. Julian isn't really dead; this is all a dream. It's not real. It can't be real.

"Shhh..." Julian soothes me, pulling me back into his chest. He's firm beneath my hands, firm and warm. It's not real.

"Just because it's a dream, doesn't make it any less real. Those aren't mutually exclusive in this case. I am dead, Breyla."

"Why?" I sob into his chest, refusing to let him go. If I hold him tight enough, maybe he'll stay.

"I found something I wasn't supposed to. It's not what we believed, but so much worse. It's okay, B. Everything will be okay in the end."

"You're not usually the optimistic twin."

"Death does interesting things to your perspective."

"When will I see you again?"

"Not for a very long time. You have far too much to do in this world. But we'll all be here for you once you've accomplished it all."

"We?"

"Yes, we. Nolan, me, your father. We'll all be watching you do the impossible."

My chest tightens at his words. The sorrow of their loss fills me. "Any other words of wisdom for doing impossible things?"

THE SORROW OF SHADOWS

"Nobody is who they seem. The next steps will be the hardest Jade has ever taken. I need you to be there for her. We've never lived without each other, but she must figure out how. Don't let her do it on her own. It won't be easy for anyone, but please...Don't let her face it alone."

"You have my word." It was the easiest promise I had ever made.

He places a soft kiss on my forehead, then rests his head on top of mine. We stand there for a few minutes more, listening to the silence of the ancient graveyard.

"It's time to wake up, B."

"No," I plead. I squeeze him tighter, refusing to let him slip through my fingers.

"It's time to face the real world. I'll be watching you kick its ass, so don't let me down."

"No!" I cry again, gripping him harder. I don't want to leave this space. Everything is better here.

"Things are easier here, not better. You made me a promise, and I expect you to keep it. Now go live, Breyla."

With those final words, his form starts to fade again, this time losing its solid state with it. My hands slip through the space where his chest was just moments ago. Tears stream down my cheeks and I shake my head as I look into his honey-green eyes one last time. He smiles at me one last time as his form fades completely and consciousness greets me.

When I awake my chest is heavy, cheeks wet with tears. I suck in a shaking breath, trying to calm my racing heart. There's a heaviness in my center that feels like I'll never breathe deeply again. *Julian is dead.*

The sun hasn't yet appeared, and by my calculations we still have several hours before sunrise. Normally, I would be up at this hour. Most soldiers were early risers. But this isn't a normal day, and I refuse to start it this way.

Julian's words ring in my ears. *"Don't let her face it alone."*

Silently, I crawl out of bed, wrap a thick black robe around myself, and exit my chambers. It's quiet in the palace halls, having reached the hour that finds only the kitchen staff awake, preparing for breakfast. I drift through the halls still half asleep until I finally reach Jade's room.

I don't bother knocking, knowing she's alone and hoping she's still asleep. The room feels heavy as I enter to hear Jade's soft exhales. As I approach, I notice her cheeks are stained with mostly dried tears. Her deep breaths let me know she's asleep now, so they must have come earlier or in her sleep. Either option has me fighting my own again.

I pull back the rich emerald-green covers on her bed and slide in beside her. Jade senses me in her sleep and rolls closer, curling into my side. My heavy eyelids droop lower as I nuzzle into her. I may not be ready to face the day, but I refuse to let her wake up to face it alone. She sighs softly as I drift back into sleep. This time, all I see are bright hazel eyes.

"I definitely think gold is the right accent color for the ball tomorrow." I watch the servants busy themselves with hanging tapestries of crimson and wine in preparation for the engagement celebration. Guests have been slowly trickling in all day and there's not a moment to spare.

Mother quirks a blonde eyebrow at me. "When did you start forming an opinion on accent colors?" she questions, placing the silver candelabra down and holding the gold against one of the deep-red table liners.

"Gold will compliment both your complexion and Aurelius' eyes." I shrug like anyone could see that.

"Mhm," she muses.

232

"You should also wear a gold dress. You'd look like more of a goddess than you already do," I suggest.

"And what will you be wearing, daughter?"

"Haven't decided yet. Probably something black."

"No, I think not. There will be no hiding in dark corners, Breyla. You will help us show a united front to all those in attendance." Her tone leaves no room for argument.

"Would you like to pick out my dress, too?" I snark.

"I don't think you want me to go that far," she challenges. "Why don't you wear our house colors? They flatter you, and it sends a message."

"And what message is that?"

"Strength. And confidence in your rightful place."

"Is that rightful place as princess or general?" I question, not sure her meaning.

"Yes."

Helpful non-answer, yet again.

"Have all the guests arrived?" I ask, changing the subject.

"I believe so." She stops what she's doing, setting the napkins on the table, and places her hand gently on my bicep.

"How is Jade?" she asks softly, as if that will make the topic easier to speak about.

"She'd be better if we actually had his body to burn. She didn't say much this morning, but I left her with Ophelia and Elijah."

"We'll recover his body, Breyla. He will get his proper rights, I promise."

"How can you be so sure of that? We don't even know who is responsible for his murder. There's too many moving pieces and not enough information all at once. We don't even really know why someone would have done this..." I feel my chest tighten. I blink back the tears threatening to burst from me and shove the waves of grief and pain down. I lock it in the little black box that I keep all my pain in.

My mother squeezes my arm reassuringly and strokes my cheek. "Just trust your mother on this. I don't have all the answers, but we will bring your second home."

I sigh and drop the conversation. "So, have you decided what you'll be wearing tomorrow? Something old? Something new?"

It's then that I feel the atmosphere in the room shift, and I know Aurelius has entered. He says nothing, but I feel him watching us from the ballroom doorway.

"I have my seamstress putting the final touches on a new dress. Do I need to send her to you next?" She raises her eyebrow at me. She really isn't going to let me get away with wearing black.

"Absolutely not," I say, trying to protest.

"Very well, I'll send her to your chambers tomorrow morning." She completely ignores my protest.

I groan and roll my eyes. "What about you, Lord Aurelius? What will you be wearing?"

"I wasn't aware you cared about my attire, Princess." His tone is unamused.

"Just trying to make polite conversation."

He scoffs, "You, polite? Unlikely."

At this, my mother actually lets out a low chuckle, which she then tries to cover up by clearing her throat.

"Seriously? You're agreeing with him?" I ask incredulously.

"Well, he's not wrong, dear. Somewhere in your schooling your tutors gave up teaching you proper court etiquette and manners."

"Battle strategy is much more useful," I grumble.

"Breyla, may I speak with you?" Aurelius asks.

"You're speaking with me now."

"In private," he clarifies.

"Very well," I concede, following him out of the ballroom. We walk in silence for a while, passing servants bustling around the castle. It's the busiest I've seen the palace staff in quite some years.

He leads me down the halls until we reach the private rooms the castle guards use to train new recruits. They aren't fancy, but functional.

Once inside one of the rooms he shuts the door and uses magic to lock it. I look at him warily, trying to figure out what kind of conversation this will be. I cross the room and lean my back against the wall, folding my arms in front of my chest.

"What conversation was so important you had to drag me down to the empty training rooms? The twenty other empty rooms we passed weren't good enough for you?"

Aurelius slides his hands casually into the pockets of his black slacks and leans against the wall opposite me. He levels me with a dark gaze. "I anticipate this conversation will get loud and I figured you didn't want others overhearing what's about to happen."

His words would suggest a scandalous meaning, but his tone doesn't. He's being serious.

"That's awfully presumptuous of you," I snort.

He ignores my comment and continues, "When was the last time you were in this room?"

I know the answer, but I'm not playing his game, so I just shrug. "It's been a while," I say with all the nonchalance I can muster.

"How long, Breyla?" Aurelius pushes. "Because as long as I've been back you've trained exclusively outside."

"Your point? I prefer training outside. It's more realistic for battle scenarios and I like the outdoors," I say in a bored tone.

"Liar." He pushes off the wall and quickly strides across the room toward me.

"I'm not lying. You'd know if I was." In my best attempt to ignore him, I inspect the nails of my right hand and refuse to meet his stare.

"That's the problem, Breyla. I can tell you aren't lying to me. But you are lying to yourself. You believe the reason you gave me for not training here, but that's not the real reason you refuse to step foot in this room."

"Excuse me?"

"You haven't stepped foot in here since before your father's death. Don't play me for a fool, Princess. This specific training room was the one your father and Commander Nolan trained you in. Only this one. I know because they trained me here, too. The real reason you haven't come here is because this room reminds you of what you lost—*who* you lost."

My jaw drops, but I can't find the words fighting to get out. My tongue feels like lead in my mouth.

Aurelius steps right up to me, leaving no space between us, and tilts my chin up so I'm looking him in the eyes. I could swear the red in his brown irises is dancing, brighter than normal, almost like live embers lived in his eyes.

"You've lost so much in so little time. You literally received your second's head in a box yesterday—"

"What. Is. Your. Fucking. Point." I grit the words out, my teeth clenched so hard I might crack a tooth. Did he just bring me here to rub in everything I had lost?

"My point, Princess." He leans closer to my face and tightens his grip on my chin. In any other situation this position would be erotic, but I'm just pissed. "Is that you should be grieving, but I found you planning a fucking ball instead."

"How I choose to grieve is none of your business, Aurelius," I seethe.

"That's the problem, Breyla. It *is* my problem, because you aren't fucking grieving at all. You're ignoring, and avoiding, and shoving your feelings down to deal with another day. You push people you care about away, because you fear the pain of losing someone else. You've barely spoken to your mother since you arrived, and when you do it's sarcastic, rude, and surface level.

Did you ever once stop to think she was feeling the same pain you were?"

"How dare you—" I start, but I'm cut off before I can continue.

"No, Princess. How dare *you*." He's glaring at me now. "How dare you refuse to face anything remotely real, refuse to fucking feel your completely normal emotions, and think of only yourself. Everyone else around you is grieving, yet you won't let anyone in when they need you as much as you need them. I get that being General, being surrounded by death on the battle-field, requires you to compartmentalize your emotions so you can effectively lead. But you can't do that here. You have to feel, Breyla." His voice has softened a fraction by the end of his rant.

Hot tears line my eyes and fight to break free. I try to turn my head away so he can't see me. Vulnerability is not my strong suit, and I refuse to look weak in front of anyone.

"No, Princess. Stop fighting it. Look at me and let it all go."

"You want me to let it all go?" I whisper.

"Yes. I need you to let it out."

"It's your fault," I spit at him.

To his credit, he doesn't even flinch. "Come again?"

"It's your fucking fault. Julian's death is on you, Aurelius." Shadows start seeping out my fingertips, but I don't care about my lack of control right now. The fury building in my veins has my blood boiling.

His head tilts to the side slightly as if he is thinking before he speaks. "You need someone to blame? Fine. Blame me. You need someone to rage at? You've got it. I'm right here, I can take what-ever you throw at me."

"Julian wouldn't have even been here if you hadn't gone behind my back to bring him to the palace. There was no reason for him to be here. Now he's gone because of *you*." My voice rises the more I talk. The shadows have now begun flowing from every part of me, slowly filling the training room with darkness.

Aurelius releases my chin and steps back from me, throwing his arms open wide. "Come on, Princess. You can do better than that. I wasn't the one who sent him on a scouting mission alone with so many unknown factors. No, that was all you." His truthful words hurt more than I want to admit.

I let out a frustrated and desperate growl before throwing my shadows at him, letting them wrap around his arms and render him immobile. Before I know what I'm doing, my hand is around his throat. The room is growing even darker, but all I see is red.

"Bodies didn't start dropping until you showed up to court, Aurelius. Why is that?" I whisper in his ear as I apply more pressure. The feeling of his racing pulse under my thumb is intoxicating. I squeeze harder, but he doesn't flinch.

"Try again. The first death—your father's death—was before me. Nobody else died until *you* arrived." I could tell he was starting to struggle for breath, but I was having a hard time caring. He had wanted me to feel, and this was me feeling.

I scream, my rage boiling over, and drop my hand from his throat. "Why?" I half sob, half demand. "Why are you here? Why do people want you dead, Aurelius?" I'm grasping at straws now.

"I've told you before, I'm here to protect your mother and you. I don't know why they're coming for me, but that's not really what you're asking." He is remarkably calm for just being nearly strangled.

I feel the small cracks in my chest widening, ripping themselves apart. My knees hit the floor as I scream again, my fury turning to sorrow. A wave of darkness explodes out of me, shadows covering every inch of the training room as every emotion I've kept bottled away comes to the surface.

They pour out of me, hitting me all at once. Sorrow, fear, guilt, desperation, heartbreak, love, and grief wage a war inside me as I continue to wail.

I sense, more than see, Aurelius hit his knees in front of me.

He reaches a hand to my cheek and pushes me again. "Come on, little demon, I know you've got more in you. Let me have it all."

My shadows become living extensions of the pain I feel, turning into sharp edges and whips that fly around me. I feel the crevice in my chest crack open wider still and more pour out of me. They tear through the room, slicing and cutting through whatever is in their path.

Soft grunts come from Aurelius, and my eyes fly open. I manage to pull back enough of the shadows to clearly see him. He's still kneeling directly before me, his arms open wide and head thrown back. His clothes are in tatters and thin red lines cover his body, blood trickling down the cuts that my shadows created.

I gasp at the thought that I had caused him to bleed, and he looks up at me.

Giving me a wicked smile, he says calmly, "There she is—my little demon. We're not done, give me more. I've tasted your anger and blame, now let me taste your sorrow and grief. Give me your pain."

Who is this male?

I finally voice the question he wanted me to ask before. "Why, Aurelius? Why does everyone I love keep dying? When will it stop?"

A sob breaks free, and I slump as the anger is replaced with grief. I clench my stomach, trying to soothe the ache deep in my core. The pain I've been denying floods my system, and I feel my body crumble to the floor.

Before my head can hit the ground, Aurelius is there, cradling my trembling body. Sobs wrack my body as tears flow freely now.

"That's it, my girl. Let it all out for me," he says soothingly. His long fingers run through my tangled locks as he pulls me closer into his body.

I tremble and curl into his broad chest, soaking up his

warmth. Breathing becomes difficult as I cry so hard I start to hyperventilate.

He rocks me gently, letting me feel whatever comes to the surface. After a few minutes, he looks me in the eyes. "I need you to take a deep breath for me, Breyla. You're struggling to breathe, so either you calm down or I'll be forced to intervene."

"I-I ca-can't..." I struggle to get the words out, letting him know I have no control over my body right now. I sob again, pleading with my eyes for him to make it stop.

"Shhhh, it's okay. I've got you," he whispers as I feel his power wrap around me, my heartbeat slowing to a manageable rate. The tension leaves my body, and I suck in a deep breath.

Tears still stream down my face, snot running out my nose, but I feel like I can finally breathe again.

"Thank you." My voice is a whisper.

"You never have to thank me, Princess."

I nod, but don't say anything more. I curl back into his chest as tears continue dancing down my cheeks. It takes a few minutes more before I feel the last of the adrenaline leave my system, and my spent body slumps in his arms.

The shadows have cleared from the room, but I feel sleep calling me as blackness creeps around the edges of my vision. Aurelius senses the shift in me and moves to stand up, keeping me cradled in his arms as he does so.

Even if I wanted to protest, I lacked the strength to do anything, so I let him carry me out of the training room and through the castle. My eyes flutter shut, and when I open them again, we're outside his quarters. I don't say anything as he carries me through his door, lays me in his bed, and pulls the sheets up around me.

I hear him rustling around his room for a few minutes before I feel the bed dip behind me. His arm wraps around me, and he pulls me into his warm, bare chest.

I can't help myself and ask, "Why are you naked, Aurelius?"

"Because you destroyed my clothes, Breyla. And I'm not completely naked. Now go to sleep, little demon." He chuckles and squeezes me tighter.

As if on cue, I yawn and snuggle closer to him.

"Little demon, I need you to stop moving," Aurelius growls softly in my ear.

"I'm just trying to get comfortable; your bed is harder than mine," I complain while adjusting slightly.

"It's not the only thing. Now quit moving. My restraint can only be pushed so far," he grumbles and pinches my side.

"Fine, fine," I concede, and I still in his arms. I let out another deep sigh and yawn as my eyes flutter shut. Finally, the darkness claims me. I sleep peacefully and without any dreams.

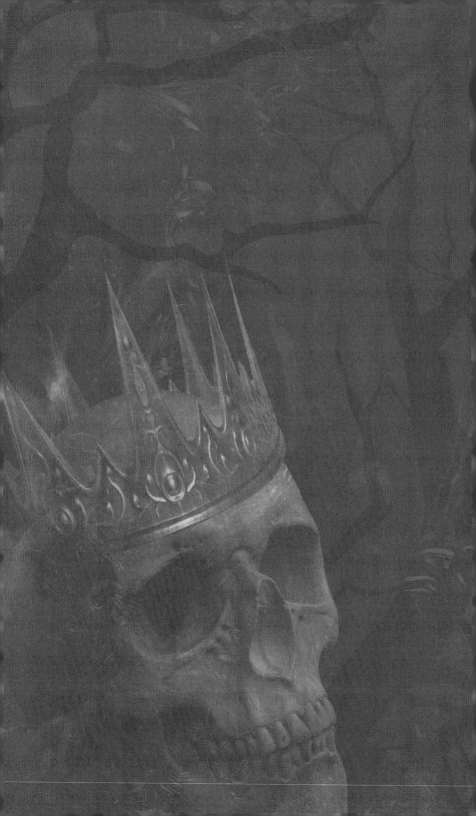

CHAPTER TWENTY-THREE

AURELIUS

Featherlight kisses trailing down my neck and Breyla's honeysuckle citrus scent greets me the next morning. That, and a painfully hard erection. Before she could sense my awakened state, I have Breyla flipped and pinned beneath me, her hands secured above her head and my body between her legs. I slowly thrust against her core, providing just enough friction to frustrate her further.

"Good morning, little demon," I whisper in her ear, my voice gravelly and thick with sleep.

"Good morning," she half gasps, half pants in reply. I feel her legs wrap around my back, and she rocks her hips against me. No doubt she can feel exactly what her wakeup call has done to me.

"I suggest," I pepper kisses down her throat, "you do not start something you can't finish." I leave little bites along her collarbone as my hand finds its way to her ass and squeezes. Lifting her hips up off the bed, I grind my cock into her again and again until she's panting.

"I'm perfectly capable of finishing this, Aurelius." Her voice is breathy and my utter undoing.

I capture her lips with my own and demand entrance with my tongue. She meets me stroke for stroke, moaning softly as I continue rolling my hips into hers. I pull away from her swollen lips to clarify, "I know you're capable, Princess. Trust me, I plan to find out just how capable you are. But what I meant was, you lack the time to finish this right now."

She groans in frustration. "Damn ball. Why does it take all day to prepare for these things?" Her bottom lip juts out in a pout that I find entirely too adorable on her. "Are you sure? I think we could spare a few minutes."

"Oh, Princess. I'm going to make you eat those words. Nothing I do to you will take a few minutes. I will take hours to properly explore, devour, and worship every inch of you." To drive her even crazier I skim my hand down the back of her thigh until I reach the edge of her undergarments. I pull them aside and run my fingers up and down her center. She is absolutely soaked for me.

She whimpers and rubs herself against my fingers, chasing pleasure in any way she can get it. I plunge two fingers inside her without warning and watch her back arch off the bed. I pump in and out several times, listening to the symphony of moans and whimpers she makes. I finally pull them out when I feel her inner walls begin to clench.

Her eyes flare wide at the sudden loss, and I can't help but chuckle. I sit back on my knees, putting some much-needed space between our heated bodies. My lips quirk in a smirk as I suck my fingers into my mouth, savoring the tang of her arousal.

Visibly frustrated with me, she reaches her own hand down to relieve the pressure herself. I use my Hemonia Gift to freeze her hand in place right above her clit.

"No, I don't think so," I tsk. I roll away from her, sitting on the edge of my bed. "Ophelia and Lyla just entered the royal wing. They're on the way to help ready you for tonight. If you want to slip back into your room unseen, I suggest you go now."

A look of panic crosses her face. She isn't ready for others to see us together, but I couldn't give two shits. On any other day, I would hold her hostage in my bed, but it's important to her and Genevieve that tonight goes smoothly. So, I will let her go for now.

She practically flies across the room to return to hers before Ophelia and Lyla can see her. I sigh and drag myself to the bathing room. The magic in our palace provides running water through the pipes that run through the walls. It's a beautiful thing, but a cold bath is probably best for me right now.

I let the cool water wash over my heated body and try to calm my throbbing dick. As much as I want to stroke myself to the memory of her moans, I resist. I left her worked up and wanting, so I can abstain as well. I will have her. *Soon.*

It takes several minutes more, but I finally get my cock to soften. I quickly scrub my skin and wash my hair, combing my fingers through the shoulder-length black waves in an attempt to tame them. Freshly showered, I step out of the bathing chamber and dry off.

I dress in a black button-up dress shirt, rolling the sleeves up to my elbow. Black leathers hug the muscles of my thighs and I tuck my shirt into the waistband, securing everything in place with a black belt. I plan on waiting until the last possible moment to dress for the engagement ball. *Is not showing up an option?*

Fully dressed, I exit my chambers. I have shit to do today, but all I want is to drag the vixen next door back into my chambers and make her scream my name—repeatedly.

Deep in thoughts of Breyla, I nearly miss the figure across the hall from me as I close the door. When Ayden clears his throat, I inwardly roll my eyes.

"Good morning, Prince. Is there something you need? Or do

you just enjoy haunting doorways and creepily staring at other's rooms?" I had no patience for him today—or any day, really.

"Interesting," he muses. "I could have sworn I already heard your door open and someone leave this morning. Yet here you are." His eyes sparkle with mischief.

"Perhaps it was someone leaving Breyla's chambers." It was the most plausible lie I could come up with.

"Mmm, no. You see, I've noticed your door squeaks slightly when opened. Breyla's is silent."

Motherfucker. When did he have time to study our doors?

"Your point?" I say flatly.

"No point, just an observation, really." He shrugs, then continues, "Are you looking forward to your engagement celebration this evening?"

"I'm ecstatic," I reply dryly.

He quirks an eyebrow at me. "You should be. The queen is a beautiful female. And powerful. Quite the catch, if you ask me."

"I didn't, but thanks for your input."

"Well, here's some more input, My Lord. Try to be more discreet when you fuck your future stepdaughter."

My blood heats, but I keep my expression neutral. "I'm not sure what you think you know, but I assure you I haven't fucked anybody." *Yet.*

"Maybe not, but you will. Her scent is all around your chambers; it's not hard to do the math."

I sigh, clearly done with this conversation, but Ayden is not. "Before you go, I have something for you."

He disappears into his room momentarily before returning with a stack of documents. King Raynor's red wax seal sits on the top document, right next to the black seal of Prince Ayden along with both of their signatures.

Fuck. "I thought this matter had been dropped." My stomach sinks at the realization it was not forgotten.

"Not in the slightest. It was actually settled before Raynor's death, but you had disappeared before I could deliver the documents. I wanted to make sure they were hand delivered to you. I'm sure you'll see that the queen gets these?" It's not really a question, but I nod anyway.

"Glad it's settled, then. I'll see you tonight." He turns and leaves me alone with my thoughts.

This is not good.

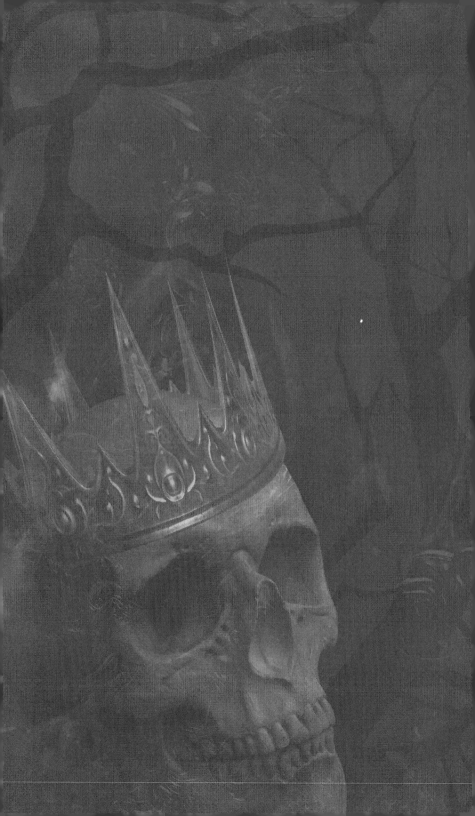

CHAPTER TWENTY-FOUR

BREYLA

Much to my chagrin, getting ready for the engagement ball took all day. But the end result was worth it.

I ended up taking my mother's suggestion to wear the color of House Rozaria. Frankly, I probably would have ended up in this color anyway. It was the color Aurelius described as being his favorite.

A floor-length wine-red gown hugs my curved frame. It was made primarily of a rich velvet that feels like heaven on my skin. A tight bodice accentuates my breasts, remaining respectable, but just barely. The sleeves are a sheer material of the same color that flow loosely down my arms, leaving my shoulders exposed. Tiny crystals accent the neckline and sporadically cover the sleeves. The skirt is loose with a slit up the side, exposing most of my right leg. The real showstopper on this dress, though, is the back. It dips so low that my back was almost entirely exposed. Thin gold chains crisscross from one side to the other across my bare skin.

I had Ophelia style my hair down, but to the side, so it won't interfere with the view. My hair is twisted into a braid around my head, starting at my left temple and wrapping to the right side where it turns into loose curls. A few errant tendrils frame my face, and the golden and ruby diadem sits on top.

Normally, I don't wear makeup, but Ophelia assured me that she knew what she was doing, and I trusted her. She dusted my eyelids with a smokey black color that gradually lightened as it moved from the outside to the inner corners of my eyes. My bottom lids are lined in dark kohl that makes the green of my irises pop. Gold dust covers my cheekbones and the top of my breasts. A deep red that matches my dress paints my lips.

Thin gold bands circle my wrists to finish the look. I smile at the realization that I truly feel beautiful. I normally despised dressing like this, but tonight it feels natural.

According to Elijah's latest update, guests had already started arriving, and the royal family was to be announced soon. I expected Elijah to arrive any moment to escort me to the ball.

A knock sounds on my door and I excitedly open it. When I do, I'm greeted not by blonde hair, but by a brown so deep it's nearly black.

"Prince Ayden?" I look at him in confusion. I'm once again hit with a sensation of familiarity as I take an appraising look at him. He's dressed in black from head to toe and flashes me a wide smile.

"Expecting someone else?"

"Elijah, actually. He always accompanies me to these things."

"Yes, well. He mentioned earlier that Lady Ophelia was in need of an escort, and he seemed particularly enthusiastic to be that for her. So, I told him it would be my honor to escort you in his place."

I smile, happy for his newfound interest in Ophelia and that she has someone showing her the attention she deserves for once.

"I guess you'll do, then," I tease.

"You wound me." He fakes offense, clutching at his heart.

I wrap my arm through his and pat his chest. "I think your ego can take the hit, Your Highness."

We begin our journey out of the royal wing and toward the ballroom. The only people we pass along the way are servants, as all the guests are already present and waiting for us.

"I would be doing you a great injustice if I didn't mention how absolutely ravishing you look tonight. The colors of House Rozaria suit you well. Though, I think you'd look just as amazing in House Mordet colors."

I smile at his compliment, but it becomes a smirk as I quip back, "It's not hard to look good in black, dear Prince."

He lets out a deep laugh. "Touche, Princess. But I bet you'd look even better out of it."

I roll my eyes and ignore his forwardness. He's either trying to rile me or start shit elsewhere, and I refuse to take his bait.

After a few more minutes we finally reach the hallway outside the ballroom. Ophelia and Elijah have just been announced, leaving Ayden and me. Aurelius and my mother will follow, but they have yet to arrive.

I straighten my dress and curls, assuring everything is in its place. Ayden reaches up and adjusts the diadem on top of my head.

"You ready for this?" he asks, and I nod.

He nods back. "Let's go."

The servants open the double doors leading into the ballroom and we step through, halting just inside. "Announcing, Her Highness Princess Breyla Rozaria of Rimor, escorted by His Highness Prince Ayden Mordet II of Prudia."

The ballroom is opulent, draped in gold and red the same shade as my dress. People from all over our kingdom and those around us fill the space. They're dressed in finery, but they're all staring at us. Uncomfortable with this much attention, I usher Ayden away from the doorway and along the side of the room. I may not be dressed in black, but I will hide in the shadows until my mother arrives and forces me to do otherwise.

It's only a few minutes before the doors swing open again and the night's main attraction arrives.

"Announcing, Her Royal Majesty Queen Genevieve Rozaria of Rimor, escorted by her fiancé, Lord Aurelius Rozaria of Rimor."

My mother and Aurelius enter the room, and everyone falls silent. They're truly a sight to see. My mother is dressed in a pale gold dress that flatters her frame but exposes nothing. The gold wrapping around her makes her look like the Sun goddess, Aura. Her strawberry blond hair hangs in loose curls down her back, and light makeup covers her face. A simple golden crown sits atop her head.

Next to her, Aurelius is her dark counterpart. Dressed in all black, he looks like sin incarnate. Gold rings adorn his fingers, and I find I was right—the gold really does compliment him. It shouldn't be possible to look that good.

My eyes lock with my mother, and I recognize that I'm being summoned. Ayden and I cross the room until we stand before them.

"I can see I was right about my suggestion to wear red." She smiles brightly at me.

I return it and say, "And I can see I was right in suggesting you wear gold. You look lovely, Mother."

She pulls me in for a hug, and for the first time in weeks, I finally relax into her embrace.

"Thank you," she whispers before releasing me.

We head toward the front of the room, where two gold thrones await us. My mother steps up on the dais in front of one and clears her throat. The three of us gather around her as she begins to speak.

"Thank you all for gathering tonight to celebrate my engagement to Lord Aurelius. Aurelius and I have been friends for as long as I can remember, and I couldn't think of a better male to help rule this kingdom. While I know no one can replace my Raynor, I have full faith that Aurelius will give his all to protect and lead this wonderful kingdom. To all our guests, no matter how far you traveled to be here with us, thank you. You have made this evening one to remember. So, let's dance, eat, and enjoy this night." She smiles warmly as everyone applauds her speech. There was no way anyone could claim my mother didn't love and cherish this kingdom and all its inhabitants.

I had plans to question some of the guests in attendance to see if I could learn anything more about the attempts made on my and Aurelius's lives, or about the murders of Nolan and Julian. Having this many people gathered in one place was too much of an opportunity to pass up. I doubted the culprit was here, but perhaps I could find someone who had seen Julian before his death. His body was missing, and I was determined to bring it home.

"Shall we dance, Princess?" Ayden asks, breaking me out of my thoughts.

Despite hating nearly everything feminine, dancing was the one activity I loved and excelled at outside of swordplay and battle strategy. I had learned the art at a young age, and it was my first love. It was actually what made learning swordplay easier for me. I was already fluid and graceful from mastering many formal dances. Twirling and swaying across the floor is where I felt most free.

"I would love to." I beam at him, letting him lead me to the dance floor.

We fall into line with the other couples dancing as Ayden places a hand on the small of my back, pulling me close. My arm rests lightly on his shoulder as his other hand takes mine, resting out to our side.

The music begins and we fall into the steps, letting the melody guide us through the twists, dips, and turns of the song. Ayden leads with expert skill, and I follow easily, just happy to have a capable dance partner. They were hard to come by. I close my eyes and let the music take me, enjoying the feeling of the world falling away around me.

"I never suspected you would be such an adept dance partner, love. You are really in your element here. I thought you were all sharp edges and equally sharp words. Who knew you had such a soft side to you as well."

I smile and finally open my eyes to find him staring at me as if he's trying to put together the pieces of a puzzle. "I'm full of surprises, Prince Ayden. You just have to look past all the bullshit you think you see."

"The gods have given you one face, yet it would seem you paint yourself another."

"I think you're actually referring to yourself there."

"More than you even know, love."

"That's the second genuine thing you've said to me."

"Come again? I assure you I've been quite honest with you since the start."

"I'm not saying you're dishonest, but honesty and being genuine are two different things. The first time you were genuine with me was when you expressed what you wanted in a wife, the second was just now."

He smiles and quirks his head as if he knows something I don't. "Three times. I was being genuine when I said you'd look better in the colors of House Mordet."

The first song ends and runs right into the next. This one is a dance where partners are switched throughout until you finally end back with your original.

The music picks up and Ayden spins me to my next partner. I'm surprised, but not upset, to find Ophelia's brother, Lord Layne, waiting for me. He's stiff at first, like he's not quite comfortable, or unsure what to do with me. He obviously knows the dance as he leads us through the steps seamlessly.

"Lord Layne, it is nice to see you back at court," I say, trying my best to make small talk.

"It is nice to be home, Princess." The way he says my title is formal, so unlike the way Ayden or Aurelius says it. I know Ophelia loves him, but he's so hard to get a read on. I can't tell if he despises me, fears me, or if it's something else entirely.

"Was your time away productive?" I try to act casually, but I'm not sure it works.

"It always is." His answer is short, but polite. "How is my sister? I hear you accepted her as your lady."

"Ophelia is more than my lady; she is my friend. She seems good for the most part. She's come out of her shell recently. I think Lord Elijah has a serious interest in her."

He snorts. "Elijah? Seriously? You've got to be making a joke. I've never seen that male serious about anyone."

"While I would normally agree with you, he did ditch me to escort her tonight. He is *always* my partner for these events. It's unlike him, especially when he could still sleep with whomever he wants even while escorting me."

"Intriguing. Perhaps there is hope for him yet."

"Did you just make a joke, Lord Layne? Perhaps there is hope for *you*."

His lips quirk at the corner in the slightest of smiles before he spins me away to my next partner. I'm flung into the arms of the emissary from Lennox.

Lennox borders Rimor to the east and is a relatively peaceful kingdom. I'm not surprised the King and Queen sent their emissary in their stead; they rarely venture outside their borders or engage with other kingdoms.

I make polite small talk and wait to be passed to my next dance partner.

I'm passed several more times before the familiar scent of bergamot greets me. Inhaling deeply, I look up into Aurelius's brown and crimson irises.

He smiles down at me as we twist and turn around the dance floor. "I'll pretend I didn't just catch you sniffing me," he teases.

I shrug unashamedly. "Your scent smells like home."

His eyes sparkle mischievously as he twists me away from him before pulling me back. "And yours drives me feral with a need to cover you in my own."

I blush at such brazen words spoken openly. I then notice he isn't dressed entirely in black like I had initially thought. Deep red, the same shade as our house colors and my dress, peek out from the lining of his jacket. Unnoticeable to most, but the subtle accent color makes me smile.

He leans closer and whispers, "I don't know how you expect me to keep my eyes off you. You look like every deep desire I've ever had. I don't know where you got that dress, but I cannot wait to see what it looks like on the floor."

His words spark warmth low in my belly and make me want to leave this whole godsdamned room of people behind. Before I can act on my desire, I hear Ayden behind me.

"I believe you are monopolizing my partner, Lord Aurelius." His voice has lost its normal flirtatious edge and seems serious for once.

I look around to see he is right, and everyone else has ended back with their original partners.

Reluctantly, Aurelius releases me to Ayden. He looks like he wants to say something but remains silent. I sense tension between them, but that's not all that unusual. Aurelius hasn't trusted Ayden from the beginning.

Ayden pulls me in tight and spreads his hand across the

small of my back. This close I can easily feel the ridges of the muscles, including how tightly wound they are.

"That was tense," I comment.

"I don't appreciate my dance partners being monopolized." He shrugs like that's all there is to it.

I give him a questioning look, but he says nothing. I sigh, and we finish the dance in silence.

"Thank you for the dances, Prince. It's been a pleasure," I say with a curtsey.

"Thank you, Princess. The pleasure is all mine." He grins flirtatiously and takes my hand, leaving a kiss on the top of it.

I take up a position away from the dance floor and observe the guests. For the first time tonight, I notice Elijah and Ophelia. They're on the dance floor spinning and laughing merrily. There are dark circles under Elijah's eyes, but they sparkle as he listens to whatever Ophelia is saying. She's dressed in a satin dress the color of ripe plums, the blue sheen of her hair sparkling beautifully in curls. I can't tell what they're talking about, but whatever it is—they seem happy.

Across the room I catch the sight of Aurelius and my mother dancing. I know this can't be easy on her, but she's handling it all with a grace I envy. He's not holding her in the way he held me in our dance, but there's familiarity between them. Aurelius says something to her that makes her smile and throw her head back in laughter. My mother has been so distant in my time here, I can't even remember the last time I heard her laugh like that. Whatever the nature of their relationship, I'm grateful he has given her that.

"They make a lovely couple, do they not?" I hear the cold voice of Lord Seamus next to me.

Without turning to him, I respond as evenly as possible. "They're beautiful. Not as beautiful as my parents, of course."

"No, of course not. I didn't mean any offense, Princess." His tone suggests otherwise.

"Yes, you did," I say bluntly. "What do you want, Lord Seamus?" I'm still not bothering to look at him as I speak—a fact I'm sure gets under his skin.

He nearly chokes on the wine he was sipping, clearly not expecting me to call him out so blatantly.

"I had heard reports of attacks on palace residents while I was away. I was curious if you had found the responsible party."

"There were several deaths and attempted murders during your absence. I am tracking several leads, but they don't seem connected." A lie on my part. I was sure they were connected, but I just couldn't figure out how.

"One would think finding the person behind the attempted murders of two of the kingdom's future rulers would take priority."

Interesting. "I find your statement intriguing. My attack was never made public knowledge."

"You may not know your enemies, Breyla, but I like to keep close tabs on mine. Lord Craylor mentioned your attack in our most recent meeting."

I scoff. Of course that ass had known about my attack. "And did he mention who he thinks was responsible?"

"He didn't." He responds too quickly, letting me know there's more he's not saying. "But tell me, do you trust the male sleeping next door to you?" Gods, he was obvious.

"If you're referring to Lord Aurelius, the answer is unequiv-ocally yes." I wasn't sure where this was going, but Lord Seamus couldn't think I doubted Aurelius in the slightest. While I knew he still kept secrets, somehow the male had worked himself under my skin and earned my trust.

"And if I was referring to the *other* male?"

I quirk a brow at him and take another sip of my wine. "Prince Ayden? I trust him more than I trust you. Is there anything else you'd like to pry about?"

He looks unamused. "I was wondering if you found my daughter's service as your lady to be satisfactory."

Lies.

"Ophelia is a gem. It's a damn shame you've kept her from my service for so long. We've become quite close."

"Yes, well Ophelia has shown little potential, but I figured she couldn't possibly fail at that task."

I'm growing tired of this prick. "Lord Seamus, I'm afraid you greatly underestimate your daughter. I've found her to be quite capable, but I'm not the only one. Lord Elijah seems quite taken with her." I smile into my wine goblet knowing the truth of my words. I know he attempted to plant Ophelia in my service to spy, but her true allegiance lies with me.

He scoffs in disgust. "He'll lose interest soon enough, I'm sure. She is powerless and far beneath his station. If she weren't my own blood, I would—"

He's silenced by my shadow constricting around his neck, taking the form of a noose.

Finally, I turn to look him in the eyes as I growl my next words. "I would be very careful what words you speak next, Lord Seamus. I don't take kindly to my loved ones being hurt."

I can see sparks dancing on the tips of his fingers. It seems he's stupider than I thought. I loosen my shadows' hold on him just enough so he can speak.

"Are you threatening me?" he gasps.

I chuckle and wrap the shadows around his wrists to hold his hands in place. "No, My Lord. That was a promise. Have I made myself clear?"

He nods in understanding, and I release my shadows' hold on him. He rubs his throat where red lines are now starting to form. Like an idiot, he opens his mouth to speak, but I cut him off.

"You are dismissed." I leave no room for argument, and he turns to storm away from me.

My wine goblet has gone dry and as I turn to refill it, I'm met with the beady eyes of Lord Craylor. I must have a magnet for assholes on me somewhere.

"Interesting conversation you seemed to be having with Lord Seamus, Princess."

"You seem to be having your own interesting conversations with Lord Seamus lately." I shoot him an accusing glare.

"I have many interesting conversations, Princess. It's part of my job, so you'll have to be more specific."

I roll my eyes and reach for another goblet of wine on a nearby servant's tray. "How exactly did you know I was attacked?"

He smiles knowingly. "There are not many things that happen in this castle that I *don't* know about. You would be wise to remember that."

I hear the double meaning and threat laced in his words.

"And there are not many things I wouldn't do to keep my family and people safe. You would be wise to remember *that*." *How many threats was I going to have to make tonight?*

"Of that, Princess, I am well aware. Anyone that doubts you would be a fool." It almost sounded like a compliment.

"Did you find the information I was looking for?" I want to end this conversation.

"It took some digging, but it would appear that the new produce supplier is a farm on the outskirts of Ciyoria. A local family owned it until their untimely deaths about a year ago, at which point it was purchased by the crown. There is no record of who is farming the lands, just that the crown owns it."

"Interesting. Who authorized the purchase?"

"That's where it gets even more interesting. It would appear your father was the one who authorized the purchase. I've left the records in your chambers if you'd like to look at them closer."

I nod my understanding, trying not to let anything show on my face. "Much appreciated, Lord Craylor. Now, I would like to enjoy the rest of my evening. So please find somewhere else to be."

He slithers back to wherever he came from, and I feel like I can finally breathe easily again.

By the time I finish my current wine goblet, my body has started tingling and I decide it's time to enjoy the rest of this unfortunate ball. As if reading my mind, Elijah appears next to me.

"Well, hello there, traitor," I tease him.

He takes my hand and drags me to the dance floor as a new song begins. "I am no such thing, I resent that."

"Where is Lady Ophelia? While I must say it was hurtful that you ditched me, at least it was for someone pretty."

"She hasn't seen her brother since he returned, so they are dancing together now. She wasn't going to come, but Prince Ayden suggested I escort her—assuring me he would have no issue escorting you in my place—and you know I can't resist a pretty face."

"That snake!" I gasp.

"Why? What did he do?" Elijah looks confused.

"He showed up at my door claiming that *you* had suggested he escort me because you wanted to take Ophelia!" I whisper-shout at him.

Elijah throws his head back in laughter and nearly has us crashing into the dancing couple next to us. As he corrects us, he says, "It wasn't entirely a lie, but it was definitely *his* idea. I have to respect the game he plays, though."

"I can't believe you're defending him right now." I smack him lightly on the shoulder.

"Hey now, I'm not defending him. Just saying the prince knows what he's doing. As a fellow male, I respect his creativity."

"Ugh," I groan as he continues laughing at me.

We dance for a few more minutes in silence before I ask the question nagging at me.

"Elijah, what was my father like just before his death?" I keep my voice low, not wanting anyone to overhear.

"What do you mean, B?" He cocks a questioning brow at me.

"I mean...did he make any questionable decisions or behave out of character recently?"

His grip on me tightens, and his face falls. "I don't know where you're going with this, but it's a hard question to answer. He had started making a few decisions without consulting his advisors. They weren't significant decisions, as far as I know. He also had Aurelius traveling to Lennox, Prudia, and Farlain more and more frequently. He didn't disclose why, but I never thought to question him on it."

"Why didn't you tell me?" I try to keep the hurt out of my voice.

"I didn't think it was relevant. He's gone, B. I didn't want to keep picking at that wound." His voice is gentle, and I know he's sincere.

"I know, but I'm starting to think there was more going on than anyone realized."

"What makes you say that?" he asks, curiosity filling his tone.

"I had Lord Craylor follow a lead in Aurelius's attempted poisoning, and the trail ends at my father."

"Are you sure the information is reliable? I thought you didn't trust him."

"I don't, not entirely. That's why I had him leave the records in my chambers so I could follow the trail myself. But something doesn't seem right. I can't tell you what, but my gut tells me something else is going on."

"I trust your judgment. We'll figure this out." He pulls me closer, and I lean my head on his chest as we finish the dance.

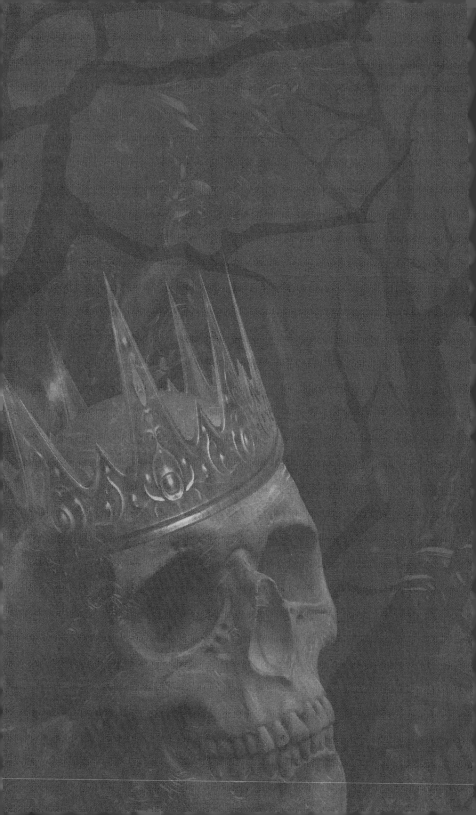

CHAPTER TWENTY-FIVE

BREYLA

I t's well past midnight by the time I'm able to slip out of the ball unnoticed. I'm exhausted, but the rest of the evening continued without incident. I wrap my shadows around me so I can make the trip to my chambers undisturbed.

The information I learned tonight circles my mind enough to distract me from the fact that my bedroom door was unlocked. I realize my mistake as soon as the door clicks shut, and my back is shoved against the wood. My mouth opens on instinct to alert the guards but is quickly covered with a warm, rough hand.

"They won't hear your screams, little demon. Tonight, they belong to me."

Heat pools low in my abdomen at the same time recognition hits. He presses his body into mine, letting me feel his hardened cock against my belly. I whimper at the feeling of him against me.

"I spent all night watching other males dance with you, touch you, stare at you, and it nearly killed me. Actually, it nearly killed *them*." He lays light kisses along my neck and collarbone in between his words. Words that should disgust me but have the opposite effect.

He finally removes his hand from my mouth, and I manage to say, "You can't go around threatening the lives of any male that touches me, Aurelius. I have regular interaction with males, and that won't stop just because you want to fuck me." The possessive behavior of his has my thighs clenching, despite how unrealistic his expectations are. I'll be damned if I ever admit any of this out loud, though.

His fingers wind through the hair at the back of my head and he pulls. The sensation is a delicious combination of pain and pleasure that has me moaning. "Don't you get it, yet? I. Don't. Care. You are mine, Breyla. I'm done pretending otherwise." Butterflies erupt low in my belly. This isn't just physical pleasure he's promising; this is a claiming for him. Feelings that border dangerously close to more than lust swirl in my chest, and I push that aside for now.

His lips are on mine the next second, his kiss hot and demanding. I meet him stroke for stroke, pushing myself off the door and moving us toward the bed. The heat he sparks in me is a raging inferno as I greedily drink from his darkness. I rip his dress shirt open, the buttons flying in all directions as they pop off his shirt.

Without breaking our kiss, I shove him on the bed and straddle his hips, pulling his shirt down his arms and discarding it behind me. His hand is still tangled in my hair as he pulls my head back just enough to drag his mouth down my neck in rough kisses. I groan as he nips the skin along the base of my throat.

Unable to reach my hands lower, I use my shadows to make quick work of his belt and pants, leaving him naked beneath me. His free hand trails up the slit in my dress and he grips my ass tightly, pushing my hips down onto his hardened length. The friction is delicious as he grinds against my oversensitive body.

His fingers trail the undergarments, and he smiles that

devilish way he seems to reserve for me. "You're soaked for me, little demon," he says as he rips my underwear clean off my body.

I gasp at the brutish action and how much it turns me on. Pulling my dress fully out of the way, I lean back until his tip is at my entrance. Before I can sink onto him, I'm flipped onto my back with Aurelius staring down at me, smirking.

"Not yet, Princess. I told you I'm going to take my time devouring you the first time I have you, and I meant it."

In a move that's equal parts infuriating and erotic, he rips clear through my dress, starting at the slit and going up. The dress was very well constructed and I'm in awe that it took him all of a few seconds to destroy it.

"Hey! I loved that dress!" I protest.

"I told you I wanted to see it on the floor. I'll have a new one made for you."

Before I can continue my complaints, his mouth is on me again. He takes a nipple into his mouth and swirls his tongue around it, eliciting a low, breathy moan from me. He nips and sucks my hardened peak until I'm writhing under him, desperate for more.

I feel his fingers trail up my thigh to that spot where I'm desperate to feel him. He circles my entrance before roughly shoving two fingers inside. His fingers pump in and out, then curl toward him, hitting that delicious spot inside that has my back arching off the bed.

My fingers lace through his locks as I demand, "More." I shove his head lower, my intentions clear.

He smiles against me and does what he's told, trailing kisses down my belly until he reaches my center. Wasting no time, he licks a line straight from entrance to clit, his tongue circling the bundle of nerves while his fingers continue pumping in and out.

It's then that I notice his power working through my body. Like the day of our first encounter, I feel him increase the blood flow to all my most sensitive parts. I'm panting beneath his ministrations and the heightened pleasure he's creating.

Two can play this game.

I let my shadows out, making them wrap around his length. I move them up and down as if it were my hand pumping his cock.

He lets out a deep growl and nips my clit in response. I thrust my hips up, grinding into his mouth in a clear demand for more. Aurelius continues his attacks on my pussy, alternating between sucking my clit, swirling his tongue around it, and licking me from opening to clit over and over.

Just as I feel myself teetering on the edge of release, he adds a third finger, stretching me and causing a sweet burn.

"Scream for me, Breyla," he demands, his words finally pushing me over the edge into oblivion.

My legs are trembling as waves of euphoria ripple through me. Aurelius crawls up my still-pulsing body, a sexy, knowing smile plastered on his face. He leans in next to my ear and nips.

"The next time I take you, I'll ask you how you want it, but I want to see your eyes as I bury myself in you for the first time. I want to hear every delicious sound coming out of that pretty mouth."

I groan at his filthy words and thread my fingers into his midnight locks, pulling his lips to mine. His tongue finds mine and I taste myself on him, the flavor intoxicating. I bite down on his bottom lip, causing a moan to slip out of his mouth.

This isn't the first time I've tasted his lips, and each time feels more intoxicating than the last. But something feels different now. Like walls are coming down between us and we're discovering there's more between us than the lust, hate, distrust, and physical chemistry that we've both clung to for so long. There have been plenty of others for each of us before now, but none of them felt like this for me. Like I wanted to erase the memories of all the others from my past. None of them made me want to forget the world just for the male before me.

"Put your ankles on my shoulders, little demon. Right fucking now." He gasps against my lips.

I happily oblige, pulling my legs up and resting my legs along his back. The next second I feel his tip at my entrance and I whimper, begging him to end the anticipation.

He's big; bigger than most, and the slight burn I feel as he stretches me has me moaning. Aurelius slides in slowly at first, then when I've adjusted to his size, he thrusts the rest of the way in. The absolute fullness I feel has me gasping.

"Don't ever stop making that noise," he growls.

"Don't ever stop fucking me, then," I say breathily, my voice caught in my throat.

My words snap something in him, and he pulls out then slams back into me, fucking me at a fierce pace. The angle he has me at lets him hit that spot inside me just right, and I can't contain the moans fighting their way out. I rock my hips to meet his thrusts, my hands digging into the sheets below me.

Over and over, he thrusts in and out, never letting up his pace. His hand reaches around my leg and finds my clit. He rubs in slow circles, the exact opposite of the speed he's fucking me at. I feel another climax build, starting low in my belly, but growing quickly.

My inner walls clench around him as another orgasm tears through me at full force. His thrusts don't slow or stop, though, and he continues his brutal pace, like a male possessed. I can tell I'll feel this in the morning, but I don't care.

My body trembles, my nerve endings overstimulated and overwhelmed by the pleasure. My muscles spasm, unable to handle the waves of pleasure still coursing through me.

I whimper, "Aurelius, please."

His eyes sparkle. "Please, what?"

"I can't take any more; it's too much."

He gives me a sinister grin. "You can, and you will. I'm nowhere near done with you."

He wraps his hand around my hip, tilting me just slightly and allowing him to fuck me at a new angle. I wrap my hands around his neck, tugging on his shoulder-length black waves with one and scraping down his shoulder with the other.

His hiss, then groan, tells me I've broken skin, but also that he likes the pain. I grin at him and do it again. I didn't think it was possible to thrust any harder than he already was, but he proves me wrong as it sends him into a frenzy.

To my surprise, I feel another climax building. My inner walls flutter, and I see his eyes widen at the sensation.

"I can feel you gripping me like a vice, little demon. Be a good girl and come for me again." His words and praise are all I need to find myself tipping over the edge once again. This orgasm is so intense that my vision starts to blur and darken at the edges right as I see his hand twitch, but I'm too caught up in pleasure to think about what lesser magic he was using just now.

"Aurelius!" I scream his name as my back arches off the bed shadows tear out of me, blanketing the room in darkness.

I feel his thrusts turn erratic and desperate before he shutters his release just moments behind mine, my name on his lips. His head drops forward until our foreheads meet, our breathing erratic and hearts racing.

He lowers my legs from his shoulders but doesn't remove his still partially hardened cock from inside me. Tender kisses are peppered along my jaw and cheeks before he finally takes my lips in one last passionate kiss.

"Mine," he growls. Just as I felt earlier—a claiming.

"Yours," I agree, nodding slightly. *A claiming I'm apparently agreeing to in my lust-induced haze.*

"I could stay buried in you forever. I think I might." He chuckles and continues kissing my face.

"You have to let me up at some point."

"Never," he says, nipping my bottom lip playfully.

I shove his shoulder gently, trying to move him off me. "I have to pee, Aurelius."

With that, he finally relents, pulling out of me and rolling onto the bed. The sudden loss of him leaves behind an emptiness I wasn't expecting.

On shaky legs, I stand slowly, relishing the burn and ache in all my muscles. Apparently, it's too quick, seeing that I stumble, my legs still not ready to hold my full weight.

I hear Aurelius's arrogant chuckle behind me. "You alright there, Princess?"

"Wonderful, you cocky asshole." I smile sweetly back at him.

He lets out a full laugh, and I leave the room to relieve myself.

Once I've done my business and cleaned the evidence of our joining off myself, I return to my bedroom. Aurelius is still lounging on the bed, staring at me with hungry eyes. They travel up and down my body as I make my way back to him.

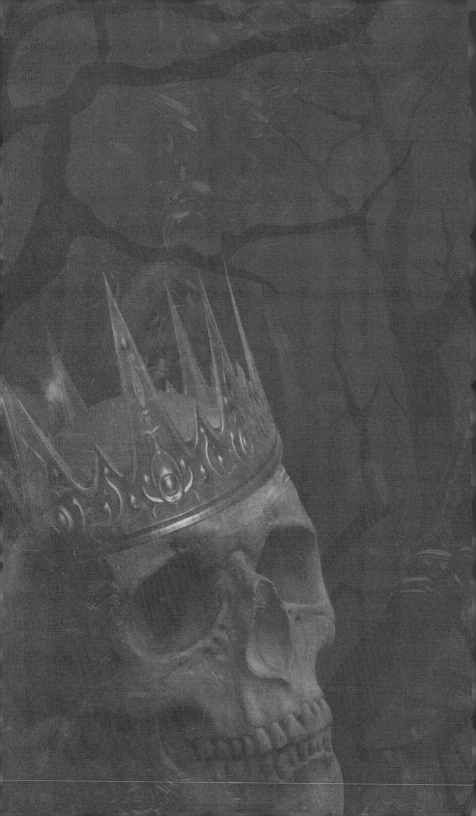

CHAPTER TWENTY-SIX

BREYLA

The warm kisses working down my spine are the first sensation I'm aware of as consciousness slowly greets me. The second is the growing erection pressing against my ass. We fell asleep naked and tangled together, but waking up this way is even better.

I'm on my side, his muscled form tightly pressed against my back. I moan softly and arch my back into his hard length. A low chuckle greets me, but he says nothing, continuing to kiss up and down my spine while pressing himself against my ass. Calloused hands trail up my side and massage my breasts. He bites down on the spot where my neck meets my shoulder, sending shivers of pleasure down my spine.

Whimpers leave my lips as I rock my hips back into him in a clear demand for more. The hand playing with my hardened nipple trails down my side to lift my top leg and swipe a finger through the liquid arousal pooling between my thighs.

"Please," I beg, my voice breathy.

He says nothing but gives into my plea and drives his dick into me in one smooth thrust.

I let out something between a sigh and moan at the feeling of fullness, of rightness, of home I get from being connected to him. We both let out moans as he rocks into me, filling me over and over until I'm panting.

His thrusts become punishing as long fingers tangle in my hair, and he jerks my head back to kiss me. The kiss is nearly as punishing and brutal as his fucking, demanding and hot as his tongue explores every inch of my mouth.

Something feels different about this joining than our first. Everything feels more intense and simultaneously hazy. "This is a dream," I moan. He just grunts in confirmation and increases his pace, retaking my mouth.

I feel my orgasm growing, and my inner walls squeeze around his length. He moans into my mouth as his free hand reaches down for my clit and begins massaging in quick, delicious circles.

I scream my release into his kiss, and he follows me over the edge just moments later.

Our breathing is shallow and fast as we both fight to come down from our combined high. His hand releases my hair at last and the other reaches up to caress my cheek.

"Well, that was one hell of a first kiss, love." I hear his voice for the first time since waking. It's rough with sleep, but it's the use of the endearment that has me freezing. Something doesn't feel right. I twist and take a look at the male behind me.

I'm greeted not by the inky black locks that belong to Aurelius, but by the amber eyes and deep brown curls that are uniquely Ayden.

"What the fuck? Why are you in my dream?

"I don't know, love. It's your dream; you tell me." He smirks before taking my lips in another kiss. Something in the back of

mind screams that I should be fighting, but I can't find it in me to care.

"Little demon, wake up."

I shoot straight up in bed, panting and gasping for breath.

Aurelius sits up next to me, his hair mussed from sleep and eyes growing more alert as he scans me for clues to my distress.

"Aurelius?" I question, still not sure what to believe. The dream was so vivid, it *felt* real.

"Of course, Princess. Who else?" he questions curiously.

"N-no one. I was just confused," I mumble.

He brushes a lock behind my ear as his lips turn downward. "What's going on, Breyla? You were moaning in your sleep. I only woke you to help make your dreams become reality but found your shadows out thrashing wildly." What would have normally come off as cocky is now concern.

"I—I was having a dream."

"And?" he prods, encouraging me to continue.

"I thought it was really happening; I thought *you* were really fucking me. I—" I'm having trouble finishing my sentence, fully feeling embarrassed and guilty.

He grabs me by my chin and turns me to look him directly in the eyes. "Who was fucking you, Breyla?" His tone is dangerous, but not threatening.

I try to force my chin out of his grasp, but his grip tightens as I mumble "Ayden."

Before I can fully process what's happening, Aurelius is across the room, pants already hanging loosely off his hips as he reaches my door.

"Aurelius, where the hell are you going?" I demand as I throw on my robe and follow him out of my bed chambers.

He says nothing to me but pounds his fist on the door across from mine—Ayden's.

"Open the fucking door, bastard!" he yells as he continues pounding.

I'm too stunned to speak when Ayden finally opens his door, full smirk in place.

"Can I help you, Lord Aurelius?" he asks.

"Fuck you," Aurelius spits and wraps his hand around Ayden's throat, throwing him against the closest wall.

Ayden doesn't even look surprised or angry. He looks amused, proud of himself even. *What the fuck am I missing?*

He doesn't fight Aurelius, instead laughing and grinning maniacally.

"Whatever is the problem, My Lord?" he mocks.

"Stay out of her fucking head." That has my attention.

"Excuse me? What the fuck do you mean by that?" I ask, my eyes darting between the two males. They're both wearing nothing but sleep pants, full chiseled chests on display. In any other situation I would be feeling a completely different way.

"Yeah, you lost your right to be pissed when you fucked her across the hall from me and dropped your sound shield right as she climaxed and screamed your name. We both knew what we were doing, Aurelius." He's still looking at him in that cocky way, but he's no longer laughing.

I feel my anger rising that no one will explain what's going on, but even more so at hearing what Aurelius did.

"You. Did. What?!" I grit out, turning my glare at Aurelius.

"Don't look at me like that, Princess. I told you that you were mine and I was done pretending otherwise. The prince just needed that message as well." He doesn't even flinch under my gaze.

"We'll circle back to why you found it necessary to broadcast my screams to the castle—"

"Not the castle, just the prince here," he interrupts to clarify.

"And why the fuck would he care?"

Neither of them says a word, their gazes locked in a battle of wills.

"To answer your earlier question—Ayden is a dream weaver,

Breyla. He can manipulate and cast dreams, infiltrate them at will. He did it to fuck with you, to fuck with both of us."

I turn my glare to Ayden. "Is that true?"

He winks at me and shrugs but says nothing. He's still pinned to the wall, but he's about to be on the receiving end of Aurelius's anger if I don't do something.

I feel shadows creeping from my fingers, flaring with my anger. With great effort, I manage to wrestle them back. "Why would you do that? *How* could you do that? My mental shields are nearly impenetrable."

"The how is simple—your shields mean nothing to me, love."

I know I've lost control of the situation when Aurelius's fist lands on Ayden's jaw, his head snapping back. "Stop calling her that."

The crazy bastard lets out a laugh, like the *pain* means nothing.

"The why, darling, is much more interesting. Aurelius here needed to be reminded that you aren't actually his."

My stomach clenches in understanding of what he's saying. The one thing I've struggled with the most since our first encounter—his betrothal to my mother. I open my mouth to speak, but Ayden beats me to it.

"Don't worry, darling. I won't be telling mommy dearest about your transgressions. But you'd do well to remember who you're dealing with."

There's a thinly veiled threat in that statement, but there's not much Aurelius or I can do in this situation.

Finally, Aurelius drops his hold on Ayden and steps back.

"Stay the fuck out of her dreams," he demands and pulls me to him, kissing me deeply as if to show Ayden he's wrong.

I stiffen in Aurelius's hold at Ayden's next revelation. "In all fairness—Breyla was already having the dream; I just decided to make her partner more...*interesting*. It's also worth noting that I didn't hear any complaints when she figured out it was me."

"We're done with this conversation," I growl, resisting the urge to punch the prince.

As Aurelius pushes me from Ayden's chambers, I hear him call out, "Oh, and Breyla?"

I stop mid-step and glance back at him but say nothing.

"You sound so beautiful when you come," he purrs and winks at me one last time.

This time I'm the one pulling Aurelius back to my room, trying to keep him from killing the prince.

"What the fuck was that?" I demand as the door closes.

"You'll need to be more specific."

"Let's start with, oh I don't know, you dropping the sound shield as I screamed your name?!" I'm damn near shrieking by the time I finish.

He smirks. "Like I said," he starts, backing me against the wall with a glint in his eyes, "I'm done pretending you aren't mine. I just needed him to get the message."

"You insufferable male," I seethe.

"Maybe," he grins at me, "but I won't apologize for it. At least I'm *your* insufferable male."

"Are you teasing me right now?" I tilt my head, trying to understand what's happening.

He steps closer to me, my back fully pressing against the stone of the castle wall. "Maybe just a bit," he whispers, and I feel his hands trail up my stomach, pushing aside the robe, so he can access my bare skin.

I'm at a loss for words when he grips my hips and rolls his into mine, his cock hard and ready for me. He trails his nose up my neck, his hair tickling me just slightly as it trails over my sensitive naked flesh. He peppers light kisses up the column of my neck until he reaches my face.

"You can't end this conversation early by...distracting me." My protests sound weak to even me.

"No? I'm going to try anyway. I need to feel you, Breyla."

Goosebumps dance over my flesh at his words, and I notice myself warm in need to feel him the same.

He grabs my left leg and pulls it up so that I'm wrapped around his waist. My robe falls to the side, leaving me completely exposed below the waist. His fingers trail the space where my thighs meet, and I shiver in anticipation.

I moan loudly as he wraps a hand around my throat, tilting my head back and leaning in to whisper, "Tell me, Princess. How did he fuck you in your dream?"

"From behind. Rough." I don't even try to keep the answer from him.

The next moment I'm being ripped from my spot against the wall and thrown on the bed, face first. Before I can try to flip around, he has a hand on the middle of my back, pushing me down into the mattress.

The crown of his dick rubs up and down my pussy, gathering the slickness already forming for him.

"I suggest you find something to cover your mouth if you want the prince to not hear you scream my name again. I already told you I'm done pretending, so you better brace yourself for what comes next." The next moment I'm filled completely in one thrust, and I find I don't care if Ayden can hear right now— not when it feels so glorious to be claimed by this male. Because there is no doubt in my mind, I am his.

"And in case you were wondering, you'll be what's coming next," he growls as he begins thrusting in and out of me. The pressure from having him behind me is exquisite, probably my favorite angle so far.

There's nothing I can do but take every ounce of pleasure he gives me as he drags his dick in and out in a seamless motion that leaves me gasping. I'm suddenly pulled up flush against his chest as he continues his motions in and out. The new position has me moaning loudly as I meet his thrusts with my own. He pinches and rolls my nipple with one hand and bites down on my neck as

I scream his name for the second time tonight, my orgasm crashing through me without warning.

"Fucking beautiful, and all mine." He claims me as his thrusts grow erratic, his own release nearing. It hits him moments later as he moans my name then bites the same spot on my neck. I have no doubt it's enough to mark me, at least for a few hours. Long enough that I'm sure he'll find some way to flaunt it in front of Ayden.

We both collapse in a sweaty mess of limbs on the bed, thoroughly exhausted from our combined release. I don't even bother cleaning myself before I drift off into a deep sleep. This time I'm unbothered by any dreams of mischievous dark-haired males.

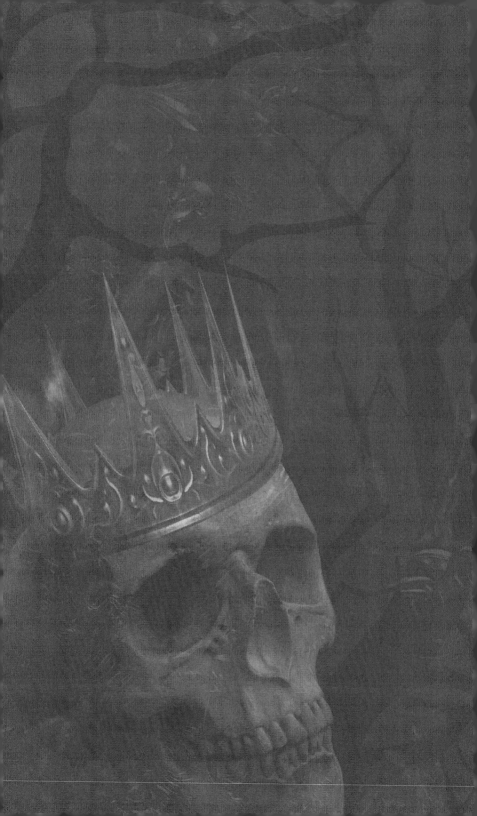

CHAPTER TWENTY-SEVEN

AURELIUS

When I awake next it's to the feeling of Breyla's fingers drawing soft patterns down my abs, dancing dangerously close to my dick. I don't think she's trying to be erotic, but everything this female does turns me on. I could spend all day with my dick inside her or my tongue tasting every inch of her freckled skin.

Without opening my eyes, I pull my little demon into my chest, leaving a kiss on the top of her head. "Good morning," I say, my voice raspy.

Her fingers still, and she lays her hand flat on my lower stomach. "Good morning," she whispers. Her voice lacks her usual bravado and confidence. She sounds like she's deep in thought.

"What's on your mind, little demon?"

She turns her head to look up into my eyes. "Where do we go from here?"

"I don't know about you, but the bath sounds like a good place to start." My voice is full of insinuation of what I'd like to do with her there.

She doesn't respond to my suggestive tone but slaps me lightly on the stomach. "That's not what I meant, Aurelius. I mean what comes next for us?"

"I grow tired of repeating myself. How many times must I tell you you're mine before you finally believe it?"

"That's just it—I *do* believe you. You've made it clear that you aren't going to let me go, but how exactly are we supposed to be together when you're betrothed to my mother? There would be a scandal if we were seen in that way together while you're supposed to be marrying her. You can't exactly just choose me instead. She'll be forced to abdicate the crown to me if she doesn't remarry. Gods know nobody wants me on the throne."

My eyes roll at her undervaluation of her own worth or ability. I can practically see the wheels turning in her pretty little head. She's both overthinking and not seeing the full picture at the same time. It's driving her insane.

"I know you don't feel anything romantic for her, but I can see how she is around you. She obviously cares for you," she continues, spiraling out of control.

I slide my palm over her mouth to silence her rambling. "That's enough of that nonsense. Come on, let's go." I sit up and slide out of bed, pulling her to her feet with me.

"Where are we going?" she asks, quirking an auburn brow at me.

"To settle this once and for all." I pull on my discarded clothes from the floor.

She slides on a long nightgown, then wraps a robe around herself right as I finish putting on what clothes I can. She had ripped the buttons off my dress shirt in her lust-fueled frenzy last night, and now I have no choice but to let it hang open, baring my chest.

I'm pulling her out of her chambers and further down the royal wing at a pace that forces her to jog to keep up with my long strides.

Recognition of where we're heading registers on her face. "Aurelius, why are you taking me to my mother's chambers?"

"Because you need answers and refuse to ask the questions yourself. You've left me with no choice."

I bang on Genevieve's door three times, then say, "Gen, open up. It's me."

The door opens to reveal a sleepy Queen Genevieve, her hair mussed and eyes rimmed in red. *She's been crying again.*

"Aurelius, what is it?" she asks and opens her door wide, inviting us inside.

I drag Breyla in behind me, our hands still clasped together.

"Gen, I need you to clear something up for us."

She gives me a questioning look, but nods for me to continue.

"Do you love me?"

"Of course I do, Aurelius. I've always loved you." She states it as if it's obvious, and Breyla tenses next to me.

"But do you have *feelings* for me?" I continue, trying to clarify what I mean.

Instead of responding she breaks out into a full-belly laugh. The way she laughs more freely fills me with hope for her future happiness.

"Yeah, they range somewhere between you being the little brother I never asked for and you being my best friend despite that fact." She grins widely at me.

"Haha, very funny," I say, rolling my eyes at her.

"What's the reason for the questions? You know all this already."

"Breyla didn't get that message, apparently. I have a point to prove to her." I think it's then that she first notices our linked hands and gives me a questioning look.

I have to be careful how I word the next question. "And is the reason I agreed to marry you to protect Breyla and keep you from losing the throne or being forced into a less-desirable match?"

She yawns, "That's the gist of it. Is there a point to this?"

"I'm getting there. Now, do you plan to ever go through with our wedding?" This question has Breyla's attention. Her eyes flare wide in anticipation of what her mother will say next.

"Not if I can help it. It's a political move, but I thought we already established this."

"Fantastic, now don't kill me for what I'm about to do." Before she can say anything more, I yank Breyla to me and wrap a hand around the back of her neck, fingers tangling in her auburn curls. I pull her lips to mine and kiss her in a way I hope shows my complete obsession and dedication to the fierce female in my arms.

A startled gasp leaves Gen, but it doesn't sound like she's angry. More like she's surprised I would be as bold as to kiss her daughter right in the middle of her bed chamber.

As I pull back from Breyla, I catch the subtle pink that stains her cheeks, and it might be the most adorable thing I've seen on her. She can't seem to form words but directs her gaze to her mother, gauging her reaction.

Gen just chuckles. "I suppose I shouldn't be surprised. The energy between you two has always been something that toed the line between wanting to murder or fuck the other."

"You aren't mad?" Breyla asks incredulously. The guilt she's been carrying for weeks is evident in the way she looks at her mother.

"Mad? No. Actually, I think I'm relieved. Maybe I should be horrified that you're kissing your father's brother, but you've never really looked at him that way, have you?"

"Not really." Breyla is clearly uncomfortable with this conversation. I, on the other hand, am highly amused. "Could you not say it like that?" Breyla pleads. "He's adopted. There's no blood relation."

"Breyla, this is Aurelius. Aurelius, meet our daughter, Princess Breyla." My father introduced me to the male he called brother. They looked nothing alike. Father had hair like mine but even brighter, and Aurelius had hair as black as shadows. His eyes were dark. The only thing they had in common was they were both tall.

"Hello, Princess." Aurelius said with a smile. He doesn't look nearly old enough to be Father's brother. Older than me, but not that old.

"Don't call me that," I said with an eye roll.

"Then what should I call you?" he asked curiously.

"I don't know, just not princess," I replied with a shrug.

My father chuckles behind him. "She has never cared for her title. Just call her Breyla."

"You look nothing like Father. Are you sure we're related?" I asked.

"Blunt little thing you are," my father said.

Aurelius took a deep breath, debating how to answer me. "No, I wouldn't look anything like him. We're not related by blood."

"What's that mean?" I asked.

"Aurelius was found as an infant without any parents, so mine took him in and raised him as their own," my father elaborated.

"It's like how Elijah isn't really your brother, but we take care of him because his parents are gone," my mother added.

I tried to wrap my head around how that worked, but all I could figure out was, "So you're not actually my uncle."

"No, not technically, I suppose." Aurelius didn't look upset by this.

My mother bent down to my level and said, "Sometimes family is blood like with you and me and your father, but sometimes family is chosen. Both are precious, Breyla."

I looked Aurelius up and down, trying to determine if he fit

*into my family. After several moments of silent thought, I said,
"Well, I don't choose you for my family."*

*"Breyla!" my mother said, frustration and embarrassment
clear in her face.*

*I pulled away from her as my father's deep voice boomed, "To
your room, young lady. That is not the way we behave."*

*"I was already going there," I replied as I skipped out of the
room and back to my own. I didn't care if I was confined to my
chambers; Aurelius wasn't family, and I didn't regret saying that.*

"Why are you relieved?" I ask, my curiosity piqued.

"Well, for one, it saves me from having to ever bed you." She
visibly shudders at the thought, doing *great* things for my male
ego. Not that the thought of sleeping with her doesn't elicit the
same reaction from me. "For two, maybe the tension between
you two will finally ease and we won't have to endure your
constant bickering."

I chuckle. "Not likely. She's still the most infuriating female
I've ever met."

Breyla punches me hard in the shoulder at that comment,
which I mostly deserve, but I wasn't lying.

"Yes, well, she gets that from her mother," Gen teases.

"Like mother, like daughter, I suppose." I reach out and
catch Breyla's fist before she can land a second hit. Stop it, little
demon. There are much better things I can think of to use your
hands for."

Gen clears her throat behind us, as if to say she doesn't want
to hear this. I turn to face her again, and her face is sullen.

"What's wrong?" I ask, immediately on edge.

"You can't tell anyone, at least not yet." I'm not surprised to
hear her say this, but I don't like it all the same.

"It might be too late for that," Breyla says, fidgeting
nervously.

Gen levels an impressive glare at me. If I didn't know her so well, I might be afraid of the queen in front me. "Who did you tell, Aurelius?"

"Why do you assume it was me?" I ask in an exasperated tone.

She gives me a look as if to say she knows better. She does, but I'm not going to tell her that.

"It may have been both of us, actually," Breyla admits, and it takes me by surprise.

I tilt my head at her in question. "Who did you tell, Princess?"

"I may have lost a bet with Elijah and he got me to show him...one of my memories that exposed us." She seems wholly embarrassed, probably because she's having to admit this to her mother.

"Of course, it's fucking Elijah," I grumble.

"Hey!" she snaps at me. "It's not as bad as what you did." She jabs an accusing finger into my chest.

"What I did was necessary, and you know it," I huff back, brushing her finger off my chest.

"No, what you did was a show of territorial male bullshit. You were basically a dog pissing on a tree to mark its territory."

"Silence!" Genevieve demands in a tone that has us both hushing. "You two are insufferable." She rubs her temples, trying to release the headache we're causing her.

"Somebody just tell me who you told." She sighs, looking between the two of us.

"Prince Ayden was..." Breyla's voice trails off as she tries to find her words, "made aware of Aurelius's feelings toward me last night."

I smirk at her word choice, but it quickly turns to a frown when I see Gen's face.

Pissed would be too light a word to describe the emotion on her face. She's irate, but there's also something akin to fear in her eyes. She begins pacing back and forth, muttering to herself about idiotic males.

"Why in the hell would you do something so stupid, Aurelius? Can you imagine what someone like Prince Ayden would do with that information? The danger you've put us all in by giving him leverage like that?"

I take a deep breath, trying to find an answer that will satisfy her, knowing I'm in trouble either way. "The prince is a nosey bastard and already suspected something before I exposed the truth. He would have figured it out either way, but I needed to send a message that he couldn't misinterpret."

"Ah, so territorial male bullshit, just like my daughter said." She rolls her eyes, clearly irritated with my reasoning.

I couldn't really explain it any other way but a need to claim my little demon and make sure no one else would dare touch her. I can't say that, though, because that's the literal epitome of 'territorial male bullshit'.

"What's done is done. If it helps, he gave us his word he wouldn't tell anyone." I shrug as if that's supposed to help. It doesn't.

"And you believed him?" she asks incredulously. "You were obviously thinking with your dick. Honestly, I should strip you of your position as emissary after this stunt."

I tense at her suggestion, never considering that was something she would do.

"But I won't," she sighs. She finally ceases her pacing and stands directly in front of us.

"As you said, what's done is done. Moving forward, no one else can know. I trust Elijah, of course. Ayden is a wild card, no doubt. I'll find some way to end our betrothal, Aurelius, but until then you must keep your relationship with Breyla a secret. I need time."

Then she does something I'm not suspecting and wraps her arms around both of us in a group hug.

"I'm happy for you both, truly. But you're both idiots. Don't do anything else stupid for a while," she says, squeezing us tightly.

"No promises," Breyla responds and hugs her back.

As we pull away from the hug, Gen's face softens. "Breyla, now that the ball is over, we need to decide what to do for Julian."

"I can't lay him to rest knowing his body is still out there, but not knowing what happened to him...Don't ask that of me."

I pull her into my side, wrapping my arm around her waist as she leans her head on my shoulder.

"We won't ask that of you, little demon. We will get you answers," I promise, not sure it's one I can keep.

Genevieve runs her hand up and down Breyla's arm in a soothing motion. "I think we can manage here without you for a few days. Why don't you follow his trail and see if you can find anything? Aurelius can accompany you."

Breyla nods at her mother before adding, "Do you think you can spare me for a few more? I think I'd like to visit Father's parents. They're on the way Julian would have taken, so it shouldn't add much time to the journey."

Gen smiles brightly at her request. "I think we can handle that. It's about time you saw them; I know they'll be ecstatic to see you both. Though, maybe don't mention the nature of your relationship to them. That might be too much for them to handle right now."

"That's fair. That's not a conversation I want to have with them," she says, chuckling lightly.

"Not sure they'd really be surprised by anything after raising me."

Breyla shoves her elbow into my ribs and sighs. "That's not helpful. We are not telling them anything."

"For now," I say, but keep to myself that I don't think I can keep my hands off her for long. I understand why we can't tell anyone, but now that I've had her, I don't think I can return to life without her. Consider me addicted.

Breyla ignores my comment and continues, "We'll leave first thing tomorrow morning. Just Aurelius and I; I don't want anyone else knowing what we're up to."

"If anyone asks, I'll just say Aurelius is making an extended visit home and you wanted to see your grandparents."

"Perfect, it's settled then."

And with that, we part to prepare for the journey.

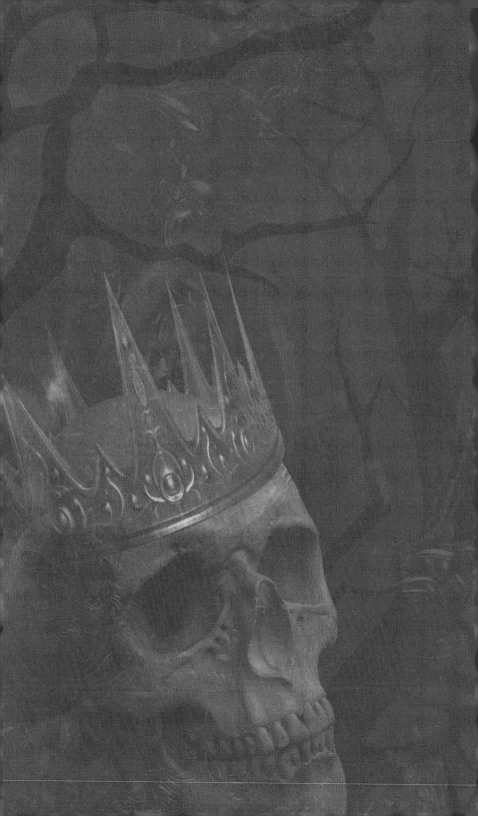

CHAPTER TWENTY-EIGHT

BREYLA

The next morning we stood in the stables, packed for a journey to find the body of my second and visit my grandparents. The sky is overcast, and it feels like a storm is brewing. It's not unusual for this late in the summer season, but inconvenient for traveling. There's anticipation and heaviness in the air as if the weather can sense my mood and is mirroring it.

I wish I could say I'm not nervous, but in truth I'm filled with anxiety as I think about what we are about to do. Jade stands silently on the other side of Luna as I finish saddling her. I hate that I have to lie to her about the purpose of our journey. I want nothing more than to tell her we're going to find and bring her twin home, but I know if I do, she'll insist on joining us. I can't allow that. Not only would it alert others that there's more going on with this trip, but she's in no emotional state for this journey. Given the nature of Julian's death, we could very well be walking into more danger, and she would be more of a risk than an asset at the moment.

Jade's hazel eyes are bloodshot and puffy. She goes between a state of hysterics and a cold shell of the female I know. She's strong, and I know with time she will come back to us, but I refuse to subject her to any more heartache for the time being.

Julian's last words to me play on repeat as I remember the promise I made to his spirit. *Don't let her face this alone.* I've instructed Ophelia and Elijah to remain close by her side in my absence. Knowing their hearts, it probably wasn't necessary, but I gave the command anyway.

"Are you ready to go, Princess?" Aurelius asks from the stall over. His all-white mare, Crea, stands next to him.

"Almost," I say, circling Luna to embrace Jade. I hug her tightly, rubbing my hands up and down her back.

"I'll be back soon. I love you, Jade. Stay with Elijah and Ophelia. They need you, too."

She hugs me back, nodding in understanding, but doesn't say anything.

I slip my left foot in the stirrup, then lift myself onto Luna, swinging my right leg across her back. I lead her out to the front of the stables to meet Aurelius. We make our way to the castle gates at a casual pace. It'll take us most of the day to reach my grandparents, so we'll increase our pace once we are outside the castle walls.

We pass by the guards at the gate, and they salute me, then raise the gate to let us pass.

"I've never heard you speak to your friends like that," Aurelius says, startling me.

"Like what?" I ask.

"I've never heard you tell them you love them. I didn't know you even knew those words."

I roll my eyes and watch as the expression on his face shifts to one of irritation laced with intrigue. I know he doesn't like me rolling my eyes at him, and he's probably thinking of all the ways he can punish me for doing it to him again.

"Is there a question there?"

"What changed?"

"You," I answer simply, hoping it frustrates him.

"Me? How?" he asks, obviously confused.

"What you told me that night in the training room—about me keeping people at a distance, people that are hurting just as much as me—you were right. After Julian died, I realized the last words I said to him weren't anything of substance, and I regret not telling him I loved him. I don't know what he felt in his last moments, but I hope he knew I loved him, even if I never told him. I just never want anyone to have to question that."

We've reached the city's edge before Aurelius says anything in response to my explanation.

"I think he knew you loved him, Breyla. Maybe you didn't say it, but you make people feel it with your actions. You're loyal to a fault and protective in a way that scares me sometimes. You care about those around you fiercely. There's no way he didn't feel it."

I fight the tears welling in the corners of my eyes, tipping my head back in a refusal to let them fall.

"Come on now, Princess. We've been through this; you need to feel. It's okay to cry, so don't smother your emotions." Aurelius's voice is calm and comforting.

"I'm the general of the royal army, I'm not weak, and I hate feeling vulnerable." I'm trying to express my feelings now, but it's quite possibly more uncomfortable than admitting to my mother that I'm sleeping with Aurelius.

"Feelings don't make you weak, Breyla. Vulnerability is a strength, and it makes you relatable. No one expects you to be some emotionless creature; they expect you to be real."

With that, I let my tears fall.

We continue the ride in relative silence, increasing our pace as we go. As we make it further from the capital, the trees become fewer and farther between. Red and orange leaves appear amongst the green, signaling the upcoming seasonal change. Autumn is my favorite season, but I hate what comes after it. Winter is harsh and cold here, making it difficult to do just about anything. The sky eventually opens and rain begins to drench us. Luckily, it's a warmer day, and the effects of the rain aren't as harsh. There's nothing we can do about it and no reason to stop for shelter. Between here and my grandparents' estate there isn't much in the way of forest or trees, only open fields, and the occasional cottage. The sun has begun its descent by the time we reach the outskirts of my grandparent's property.

The rain has slowed, but we're still soaked when we knock on their front door. Warm smiles and tight hugs greet us as I lay eyes on the people I haven't seen since before my father's death.

"It's so good to see you, Breyla. We missed you at Raynor's funeral," my grandmother says, her honey and lemon scent wrapping around me. She's basically the female spitting image of my father—fire-red curls, hazel eyes, and freckles dusting her cheeks. The sight of her is both comforting and painful.

"I know, Grandma. I've missed you, too." A pang of guilt rattles through me for staying away from them for so long. She passes me over to my grandfather before setting her eyes on Aurelius.

"I guess we know who the favorite is," Aurelius grumbles behind me.

"Obviously. I mean, have you met you?" I snicker.

"I think you mean, have you met *you*? I'm an angel." His tone is overly sweet, letting me know he knows he's full of shit.

"Knock it off, you two. We are delighted to see both of you. Our wayward son and granddaughter returned home at last."

I inwardly cringe at her comment. Yeah, this is going to be difficult.

They usher us inside, taking our rain-drenched things to dry by the fire and escorting us to our rooms. Dark wood lines the halls as we're led from the entry. If the sun were shining it would cast brilliant rays through the numerous windows that line the manor. We go up a set of carpet-lined stairs, taking a left down the first hallway. The manor is large, but it has nothing on the size of the castle.

"Your room is the same, Aurelius. I had the servants make up the guest room down the hall for you, Breyla. We'll let you get bathed and into dry clothes, and some hot food will be waiting for you once you're done," my grandfather says, and they leave us to do just that.

Aurelius waits until they're just out of earshot before speaking. "Those riding leathers must be a nightmare to strip out of when wet. They're clinging to your skin in the way I want to be right now." He trails a finger seductively down the center of my chest, below my breasts, and down to my navel.

"Not happening." I grin and push him away from me with one hand. "You heard the queen's orders—no one else can know. *Especially* not your parents."

"No one has to know. We can be very discreet." His lips quirk up in a smirk as he pulls me by the hip into him. I feel his already hardened dick through my leathers as he holds his hips against my lower belly. It has shivers racing down my spine, and I nearly give in.

I somehow find my willpower and shove him away again. "Absolutely not," I say with as much bravado as I can.

I turn from him before he can tempt me any further and enter my room. I lock the door behind me, but not before I hear a self-satisfied chuckle behind me.

Aurelius is right—wet riding leathers are an absolute nightmare to get out of, but I refuse to go to him for help, because I know he would turn it into something far less innocent. I manage to get out of my top, but the bottoms become an issue as I find myself dancing and wiggling around the bathing chambers to remove them from my thighs.

My thighs are toned and muscular partially from genetics,

but mostly from years of training. There's never been a gap between them, but I never cared. They're curved in ways that males want to worship and females pretend to judge but secretly envy. But right now, I wish there were less of them as I struggle and fail to get the leathers off. I end up taking a misstep, hitting a puddle of water that my discarded top had left behind, and I slip.

My ass hits the tiled floor with a heavy *thud* and pain throbs in my left cheek, leaving me groaning. That must be the least graceful thing I've done in years.

"Thank the gods no one was here to see that," I mumble, then hear a muffled laugh from behind me.

I whip my head around and look up to find Aurelius in the room behind me, sitting on the bed and laughing at me.

"What the fuck, Aurelius!" I demand from my place on the bathing room floor.

"Still don't want my help getting out of those leathers?" he taunts.

"No! Well, maybe. How did you get in here? I locked the door."

"Did you really think a locked door would stop me in my own home? Princess, I've been sneaking in and out of here since I was twelve. You'll have to try harder to keep me away." He gives me that self-satisfied grin that's equal parts infuriating and sexy.

"Ugh, you're incorrigible. As long as you're here, get these damn things off me," I demand.

"As you wish," he answers and prowls across the room to me. I reach up a hand and let him pull me to my feet. I rub my sore ass cheek and wait for him to help.

He drops to his knees before me, a sexy grin plastered on his beautiful face. His thumbs slip inside my leathers and begin slowly pulling them down my thighs. The slow movements are oddly intimate and arousing. Or maybe that's the sight of him on his knees for me.

He works them past my thighs, easily slipping them over my knees, but his pace is torturously slow. It's completely intentional, I have no doubt, but I'm not going to call him out on it. As he begins his journey down my calves, I feel him trail kisses down my thighs as he goes.

A sharp jolt of arousal hits me in my core, so strong I bend forward, gasping at the intensity.

"Aurelius," I pant, "stop using your powers on me. Right fucking now."

"No, I don't think I will." His kisses continue, moving higher and toward my center. I still have my undergarments on, but that doesn't stop him from laying a kiss right at the apex of my thighs.

My pants have finally reached the floor, and I step out of them, kicking them to the side. I grip the curls at the top of his head and sharply pull his head back to look at me.

The increased thrumming in my clit from his power has spread to my nipples, hardening them into stiff peaks. I nearly moan from the sensation. "I. Said. Enough," I grit through clenched teeth.

His eyes flare, but he obeys my command and gets to his feet. He's not touching me anymore, but he hasn't released his power's grip on me. I'm nearly to the point of begging him to take me, despite our surroundings and the people in this house. He spares me, though, and takes a step back.

"Have fun imagining me on my knees for you when you slip into that bath and come on your fingers, little demon."

With those parting filthy words, he finally leaves me.

I'm still unbearably aroused when I slip into the warm water of the bathtub. I slip my fingers below the water, and do exactly as he said I would, finding my release within minutes. It's his name on my lips as I come undone.

Freshly bathed and dressed in silk sleep pants and shirt, I go down to the parlor to meet my family. It's well past the time for dinner, so my grandparents have had food brought here, rather than the formal dining room.

Aurelius is already there, standing to the right of the fireplace. Sleep pants similar to mine hang low on his hips, and a loose tunic hangs off his shoulders, untied and leaving glimpses of his toned chest visible. I have to catch myself before I'm caught drooling over him.

"Have a nice bath?" Aurelius smirks at me, knowing in his eyes.

"It was quite satisfying," I respond without missing a beat.

My grandparents, clearly missing what's happening between us, call for the servants to place the food on a low table in front of the blazing fire. I take a seat in one of the wing-backed chairs and pull it close to the table.

The savory scent of roasted pork belly wafts my way, causing me to salivate. I haven't eaten since breakfast, and I am starving. The plate is filled with roasted vegetables and creamy potatoes. An indecent moan leaves my mouth as I bite into the steaming food in front of me. I pick at the vegetables, moving the carrots to the side, but devouring everything else.

Once the food is gone, my hungry belly satisfied, I look up at the people staring at me.

"I don't think we've seen anyone with such an appetite since the boys were still at home," Grandfather chuckles.

"I haven't eaten all day," I say sheepishly.

"It's quite alright, dear. Your grandfather was just teasing you. There's more if you'd like me to fetch you another plate," Grandmother offers.

"Oh, no! I'm quite satiated now. It was delicious. You must give my compliments to your cook. He might be better than the palace cook!" I'm not exaggerating. It was one of the best meals I've had in a while.

"I'll be sure to," Grandmother says, smiling. "So how long do you plan to stay?" Her question is directed at me, but it's Aurelius that answers.

"We'll leave the morning after next, Mom."

"Oh, I do wish you'd stay longer; we hardly get to see either of you. It's been so hard after losing Raynor..." Her voice trails off, and I'm filled with guilt for not seeing them sooner.

"I know, Grandma. I promise we'll be by more often. We just have a lot of work to do right now." It's the best answer I can give without saying too much. Tears slip down her cheeks, and I reach out a hand to her, taking hers into my own. I squeeze gently to let her know I'm here, that I feel her pain.

"I hope you know how proud of you we are, Breyla. I know your father would be proud of you, too."

This time it's my turn to tear up, and the salty bastards stream down my face. I knew my father was proud, but hearing it said out loud does something to me. An overwhelming sense of sorrow laced with satisfaction washes over me.

After a few moments of silence, my grandmother says, "It's late and I'm sure you're both exhausted from the journey. We'll leave you two and see you in the morning. Goodnight, my dears."

"Good night," Aurelius and I say at the same time.

They exit the parlor, leaving Aurelius and I alone by the fire.

Tears are streaming down my face still as the weight of being in my father's childhood home bears down on me.

"Come here," Aurelius says softly. He doesn't demand, but it isn't a question, either.

I walk over to him, and he pulls me into his lap, wrapping his arms around me and allowing me to curl into his warm chest. I pull my knees to my chest, and he runs a hand in soothing circles on my back. The dam breaks and I don't fight it as tears stream down my face steadily. Full sobs and tiny hiccups escape me as he just lets me break in his arms. He kisses my hair softly but stays silent, letting me work through my emotions. Heartbreak, guilt, and nostalgia all fight for dominance in my chest. It still feels like there's a cavern in my chest where my father, Nolan, and Julian used to fit. Bit by bit I'm putting myself back together with Aurelius's help. Like an open wound, not still bleeding, but raw and painful starting the process of scabbing over.

Eventually my cries quiet and my eyelids grow heavy, the exhaustion of traveling and emotional turmoil taking its toll on me. I don't fight it and let my eyes shut, falling asleep against Aurelius's chest.

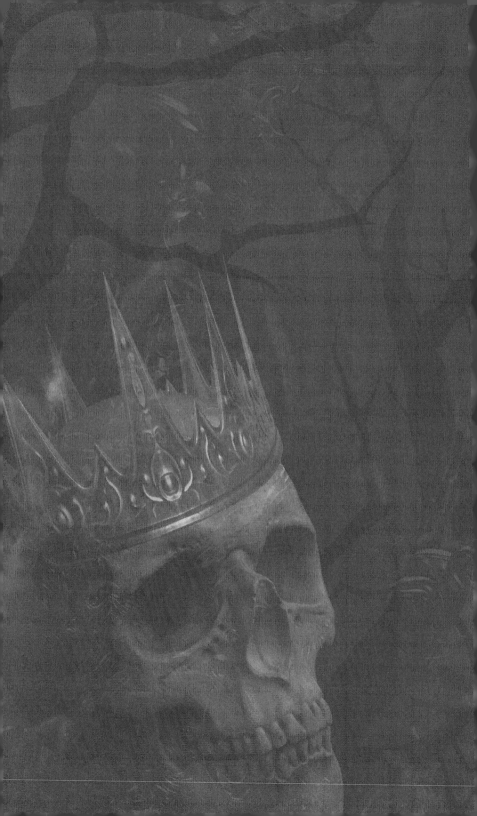

CHAPTER TWENTY-NINE

BREYLA

At some point in the night Aurelius must have carried me to the guest room, because I awake there the next morning, surprisingly alone. My clothes are still slightly damp, so I dress in a spare dress left in my room by the servants.

It's emerald green and pairs perfectly with the color of my eyes, while allowing my hair to stand out in stark contrast against it. To my relief, it's simple, lightweight, and easy to move in with a sweetheart neckline, sleeves that come to my elbow, and a slit up the leg. Because I go nowhere without my weapons, I slide a holster onto my right thigh and slip in my dagger for easy access. It's high enough that it's undetectable, but still within quick reach should I need it.

I braid my hair to one side, securing it with a strip of leather, and opt for no shoes. Aurelius greets me as I open the bedroom door to leave for breakfast.

"Good morning, beautiful." The way my heart flutters in my chest at his greeting is something I've never experienced before.

"When did you become so charming?" I tease, letting out a light laugh.

"Contrary to your opinion, I've always been charming. You are just so infuriating that you never get to see it. It's hard to charm someone when you want to wrap your hands around their throat."

"How am I infuriating?" I scoff in disbelief.

"From age fifteen to seventeen you insisted I bow before speaking to you just because you could. You challenged me to duels every other week, but knew I was better, so you cheated. Speaking of cheating, I'm pretty sure you cheat at cards. The first thing you did after arriving at court was insult me unprovoked and call me a devil. You challenge me at every turn, fight me every chance you get, openly flirt with others where you know I can't react, and you made me walk home from the tavern with no pants. Shall I continue?"

"First of all, you deserved most of that. You are not better at swordplay than me, and I definitely don't cheat at cards. Perhaps I was a bit of a handful when I arrived home, but you are equally as infuriating. And you *definitely* deserved to walk home from the tavern without pants." I cross my arms defiantly.

"Let's not forget the game you made of interrupting me whenever you knew I was with someone. It lasted for *years*."

"That was a game you started," I scoff.

"I don't know why you can't just admit you're a brat."

"I don't know why you can't just admit that you like that I'm a brat," I say, grinning.

He rubs his temples. "The name 'little demon' could not be more fitting for you."

"I think you need a nickname, too. I wonder what would fit," I muse. "Grumpy uncle? That seems accurate."

"Please no," he says, his tone flat.

"No, you're right, you're a terrible uncle. Oh, I know!" I grin mischievously. "Stepdaddy dearest!" I repeat the words I had used for him with Elijah, following through on his bet to call Aurelius that to his face.

"Absolutely not," he growls.

I know the sound is not meant to turn me on, but it does.

"What? You don't like being called *daddy*?" I drop my voice to a seductive whisper.

His eyes flare wide, and I almost see a hint of interest in them. Suddenly, he turns to face me mid-step and wraps his hand around my throat, pinning me to the wall. He shoves his knee between my thighs, rubbing right against that sweet spot in a way that has me biting my lip to keep from moaning. Leaning close to my ear, he nips my lobe before saying, "How about this? I'll let you scream daddy in bed when the day comes that your womb swells from my child growing in you."

My mouth drops open in astonishment at what he just said. He takes that opportunity to steal a kiss from me, his tongue diving deep and claiming my mouth like he claims everything else from me.

When he finally breaks away, I'm breathless. "Does the thought of me being with child turn you on, Aurelius?"

"The thought of you pregnant with *my* child, yes. Very much so," he admits easily.

"That's unexpected," is all I can muster in response.

"It will happen one day, Breyla. I respect your autonomy and your decision for when you're ready for that, which is why I've been taking a tonic. But I will see you pregnant with my children someday."

With that he releases me and steps back from the wall, giving me space to breathe and digest his words. I knew someday I would have to provide heirs for the kingdom and accepted that, but I never stopped to consider if I *wanted* them. Though I can't say the idea turns me on like it does Aurelius, I don't find myself opposed to the idea of having his children.

I can almost picture their dark curls, green eyes, and light freckles. Or maybe they'd have my auburn locks and his crimson flecked dark eyes. Either way this plays out, they're absolutely beautiful in my mind.

Shaking myself out of that daydream, I continue our walk toward the dining room, eager for breakfast. I can smell the freshly cooked sausage and pastries before we reach the room.

My mouth waters as I take in the spread before us on the table. It has everything from poached eggs, sausage, and bacon to fresh fruit, sweet pastries, and flapjacks. I eagerly sit down, waiting for everyone to join before I dig in.

"We weren't sure what you preferred now, so we had the kitchen prepare a bit of everything," my grandma says, smiling.

"Everything," I reply hungrily. "I like everything."

My grandfather chuckles. "Take after Raynor with that one. That boy could eat. Our kitchen never could keep up with two growing males with that kind of appetite."

I laugh because he's not wrong. I do get my appetite from my father. Most females picked at their food, while I held no such reservations. I would always gladly devour what was put in front of me. I had absolutely no shame when it came to food.

Finally, everyone is present and seated, so I begin dishing food onto my plate. I shovel a bite of sausage covered in sweet syrup, followed by a piece of a blackberry Danish into my mouth. I moan in contentment around the food in my mouth. Aurelius stifles a laugh with a fake cough, and I catch him adjusting uncomfortably in his seat.

Curious, I send my shadows under the table to crawl up Aurelius's leg. They take the shape of hands as they inch higher up his thighs. I watch his face, but it's infuriatingly passive. He is clearly not as unaffected as he would have me believe, though, as my shadow hands find his dick rock hard beneath the table.

My lips quirk at the corner in the slightest of smirks. I hadn't meant to turn him on, but the temptation to mess with him is too great. I use my shadows to rub slowly over his erection. His brow furrows, and he drops his fork to rub circles on his temples, as if nursing a headache.

"Are you alright, son?" Grandfather asks, noticing his discomfort.

"I'm fine, Dad. Just didn't sleep the best." The lie slides easily off his tongue.

"Do you need some more rest?" Grandmother offers, her tone concerned.

"No, I think I'll be fine. I'm just going to get some fresh air. There's actually something I wanted to show Breyla."

They nod in understanding, dropping the subject, and I giggle internally at the distress I cause this male.

We finish breakfast in silence, and I don't bother him anymore with my shadow fiends.

He leads me out the back of the estate, exiting through one of the servants' entrances. We walk into the woods behind the home, the trees thickening as we travel further in. I have a feeling I know where he's leading me, but I stay quiet.

I know what this place means to him; the memories he shared with my father here. I'm flattered and excited that he would want to share it with me in person.

After a few more minutes of walking—my feet starting to sting from traipsing over twigs and rocks barefoot—we reach the tree he described to me our night at the tavern.

"Welcome to my first home away from home, Princess," Aurelius says with a soft smile.

I marvel at the sheer size of the tree. He didn't overestimate its size; if anything, he underplayed it. It's massive, and I wonder how it's the only one of its size in the woods. The others surrounding it are large and show signs of weathering that would suggest they're just as old, but none compare to the beast in front of me. I estimate it to easily be a hundred feet in diameter.

Carved in the trunk is a staircase that spirals up the side, leading to the place where the branches begin. These are the steps that my father carved with his magic. I lay a hand on them, feeling how smooth and perfect they are. They are not quite natural, but they are still a part of the tree through the help of his Gift.

"This is magnificent, Aurelius," I say in awe.

"Just wait until you see the top." He grins, tugging on my hand to accompany him.

I follow him up the smooth steps until we reach the top, roughly thirty feet in the air. Thick branches shoot out in all directions around us, but in the center is a space carved out into the perfect hideaway for a young Aurelius. It's probably twenty feet wide in both directions, the branches forming a smooth and mostly flat floor to walk across. More branches curve around the top, creating a cave of sorts; like a chrysalis made of tree limbs.

It's probably seven feet in height, leaving just enough room for adult Aurelius to stand easily. He pulls me into the center, a wide smile on his face. I turn in circles, looking up and in all directions to marvel at the beauty of this place.

"My father did all of this?" I ask in astonishment.

He nods. "All of it. He was truly talented. The most talented I've seen with his particular Gift. Never tell your mother this, but his power to manipulate earth was stronger than hers. Though she possesses all the elements, his control over this particular one was much stronger."

My father's other Gifts, that very few knew about, were astral projection and the ability to speak telepathically. It allowed him the ability to hear others' thoughts if the person near him was unable to shield their minds or keep from broadcasting their thoughts. It was his control of three powers that made him such a good match to marry the princess of Rimor, making him the King. We kept that knowledge limited to very few individuals, though.

"Gods, it's magnificent," I say, my voice full of reverence.

"It's still only the second most magnificent thing he's ever created," Aurelius says quietly.

"What's the first?"

He wraps an arm around my lower back, pulling me into his chest and using his other hand to tip my chin up. Aurelius stares intently into my eyes as he whispers, "You."

I thread my fingers into his hair and claim his lips softly. The kiss is different from every other kiss we've shared. It's soft and full of emotion, creating a sweet juxtaposition to our usual kisses' normal fire and passion. His lips massage mine tenderly, his tongue tracing my bottom lip.

Our kiss gradually turns more heated as he nips my bottom lip, eliciting a soft whimper from me. I use my grip on his hair to deepen the kiss, my tongue meeting his and exploring his mouth. I break from the kiss to trail my lips down his jaw, then his throat, eventually reaching his exposed collarbone.

His fingers trail down my ribs, sending goosebumps across my flesh as he reaches the underside of my breasts. The pad of his thumb circles my nipple, making it harden beneath his touch.

I alternate my kisses with bites and eventually suck the skin into my mouth, desperate to taste him. He reaches down the front of my dress and pulls it to expose my breast. Rough fingers pinch and grab my nipples, twirling them in a delicious motion that has warmth building in my core.

I roll my hips against him, begging for more sweet friction to ease the ache between my legs. He pulls the dress down my shoulders and exposes both of my breasts.

"These are so fucking perfect; I could spend hours playing with them," he groans.

I smile and trail my lips further down his chest, slowly dropping to my knees before him.

"I need to taste you, Aurelius." I open the fastening on his pants and work them down his hips, his heavy erection bobbing out to meet me.

"Fuck, Princess. You have no idea what it does to me when you say these things," he pants.

"Oh, I think I have an idea." I smirk before trailing my tongue along the underside of his cock. My tongue circles his tip in teasing laps before I finally wrap my mouth fully around him.

He moans loudly, and I hollow my cheeks, sucking him in deeper.

"Fuck, little demon. Your mouth feels like heaven."

His words of praise heighten my arousal. I feel the wetness spreading between my thighs, working its way down.

I move my mouth up and down his cock, increasing my pace as I go. I wrap one hand around his balls and squeeze them gently.

"Oh gods, don't stop, Breyla. Look at you taking my cock like such a good girl."

I increase my pace, occasionally letting my teeth graze him, since I know he too likes his pleasure laced with pain.

I take him to the back of my throat, swallowing as much of him as I can fit, and tears roll down my face from the size. At the sight of my tears he snaps, losing all restraint.

He fists my hair and uses it to guide me up and down his cock, setting a punishingly sweet pace that has more tears falling and my jaw aching.

The next moment he pulls me back, removing himself from my mouth.

"I'm about to come, but I need to feel your pussy wrapped around me first."

He sits down, leaning against one of the tree branches that forms a wall behind him. He pulls me to him, not bothering to remove my dress, just pulling the skirt to the side. I straddle his lap as he runs a hand up my thigh to move my undergarments to the side.

"You've been bare this whole time?" he asks, eyes wide.

I nod and roll my hips against him.

"Fuck, the ways you find to torture me. Sit. Now. Ride my cock, Princess."

I obey, happily sliding onto his waiting cock. We groan in unison at the connection. I take a moment to adjust to his size at this angle.

"I swear to the gods, Princess, start moving or I will throw you on your back and fuck you until it hurts."

His command has me moving, rolling and grinding my hips against him. This position has his dick easily hitting that spot inside me that sends pleasure to every inch of my body.

I switch from rolling to an up and down motion, and Aurelius thrusts his hips from below to meet me. I'm bouncing in his lap, my breasts perfectly level with his mouth as he sucks one.

He circles my hard nipple with his tongue, then lightly bites, quickly lapping away the sting with his tongue.

"Fuck, Aurelius. I feel so fucking full. It's hard to even breathe," I gasp out.

"Shit, Princess. You can't say those things when I'm buried in you. You're going to make me finish before either of us is ready."

"Come for me, Aurelius," I beg, rolling my hips again.

He wraps his hands around my hips so tightly I know there will be bruises. He directs my hips against his own, hitting that earth-shattering spot inside me again and again. He slips one breast back into his mouth and moves one hand to my clit, rubbing fast circles over it.

"Fuck, fuck, fuck. Don't stop, I'm so close," I whimper, delirious with the pleasure he provides me.

Refusing to release my breast, he doesn't respond. Instead, he bites down harder on my nipple, making me scream.

I feel my body tightening with the impending orgasm as I rock my hips faster and faster against him. I chase my own pleasure as I ride him relentlessly.

Finally, right before I tip over the edge, I feel his other hand circle to my back, and he slips a single finger into the wetness between us, coating his finger. Then I feel his finger slide right into my puckered hole and I can't help but scream my release as he gently works it in and out. The foreign feeling stings slightly but isn't unwelcome. I feel even fuller than I thought possible, and it causes euphoria to take over my body.

I'm panting as I come down from my release, finding him grinning like the cat that got the cream.

"I knew you liked it rough, Princess, but who knew you were so fucking filthy. I can't wait to explore that little turn-on more."

Even though I've just come, his words spark new arousal in me.

"That was unexpected," I pant. "That might be the hardest I've ever come."

His eyes sparkle with delight. "Then I can't fucking wait to have my dick in that tight little ass. Gods, the way you would feel wrapped around me, clenching down on me."

I moan at the mental picture he paints for me, throwing my head back.

"Oh shit, my filthy little demon likes that, doesn't she?" He leans in and nibbles my neck.

He's still fully hard inside me, not having reached his climax. I rock gently against him and nod in agreement.

"I'm going to need you to hold on, Princess," he warns, flipping me from his lap onto my back.

Then he's fucking me just as hard as he has before, his hips snapping against mine in a glorious, frantic pace that has another orgasm building. He pins me down by my throat, applying just enough pressure to make me lightheaded, but not lose consciousness. It takes my arousal to an even higher level, my body tingling from the lack of oxygen mixed with the pleasure from his fucking.

I scream my second release; this time he comes with me.

He releases my throat, and I suck in a needy breath, fighting off the blackness dancing at the edge of my vision. Our breaths mingle as we come down from our combined release, eventually returning to even after a few minutes.

He rolls off me, pulling me onto my side and wrapping an arm around me.

"You're awfully cuddly post-fuck," I say fighting off a yawn.

"Are you complaining?" he asks, his fingers drawing patterns across the skin of my back and sides.

I giggle at the tickling sensation. "No, it's just unexpected."

"Did the general of the Rimorian army just giggle?" he asks in mock surprise.

"I happen to be incredibly ticklish," I say through another giggle as his ministrations on my side continue.

"Oh, you are, are you?" he teases, then goes from light touches to full-on tickling my side.

I squirm, struggling to breathe through my laughter, then push against him. "S-stop. Please," I gasp through my laughter. "I can't handle it!"

He's on top of me now, tickling both sides, showing me no mercy. I'm pinned between his legs, unable to escape.

"No, I don't think I will." He laughs and continues his attacks. "It's just too damn adorable that someone as fierce and terrifying as you can be brought down by tickles."

I'm gasping for breath and fighting the urge to pee from laughing so hard, while simultaneously hitting him in the chest every chance I get.

"Mercy! Mercy, please," I beg. "I'll give you anything."

He stills above me and quirks a brow. "Anything?"

One hand has both of mine pinned above my head, while the other hovers right at my side, ready for another attack should I disagree.

"Anything," I promise.

"Sleep with me tonight. I don't care that we're in my parent's house, I need you in my arms."

I consider his request—demand, rather—and nod. "On one condition," I offer.

"And what is that?"

"It's *just* sleeping. I'm not willing to risk any other lewd behavior being discovered."

He grins and says, "I accept your terms. Just sleep." The look on his face has me doubting his intentions, but I agree anyway.

"Now get off me, you pain in the ass."

"As you wish," he says, rolling off and resuming our previous position.

"Aurelius?"

"Yes, Princess?"

"Don't you dare tell anyone I'm ticklish," I say, deadly serious.

"Are you telling me nobody knows?"

"Not many."

"Not many?" His voice trails off, as if in deep thought, before he asks, "Elijah knows, doesn't he?"

"Yes."

"Why am I not surprised?"

"Because it's impossible to keep anything a secret from him. I don't even try anymore." I yawn, thoroughly spent by our late-morning escapades.

"Noted."

We lay there for a while more, him telling me more stories of my dad, me just listening. Eventually, I doze off to the sound of his heartbeat.

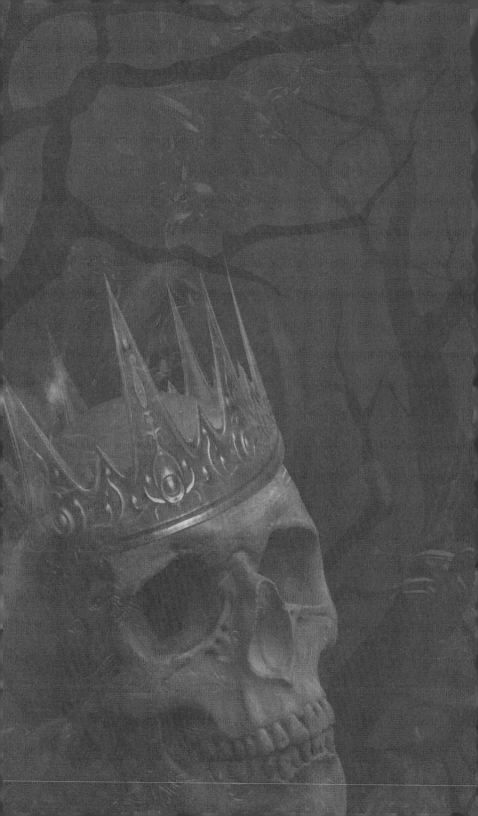

CHAPTER THIRTY

AURELIUS

We spend most of the afternoon touching, reminiscing, and falling in and out of sleep in my hidden oasis. I could spend all day wrapped up in Breyla's arms, but I know we're here for more than that.

It's approaching dinnertime when we finally make it back to the estate. I had to carry Breyla on my back since her feet were raw and blistered from walking out here barefoot. I wrapped her feet in thick wool socks to cushion them and lessen the discomfort while her body worked to heal the blisters and cuts. We ate a quiet dinner of lamb stew with my parents, and now sit around the parlor table playing cards.

Either my mother or Breyla has won every damn hand. It's honestly too much of a coincidence, and it's starting to piss me off. It's statistically improbable that they would win every. Single. Hand. I'm starting to wonder if Breyla gets her card-playing skills from my mother.

When Breyla lays down a pair of kings and three aces, winning yet again, I call bullshit.

"There is absolutely no way you won again. You are obviously cheating, and I'm pretty sure you got that skill from my mother." I dart glares at them both.

"Nonsense, dear. I play by the rules, just as everyone else does. I can't help it if you and your father aren't as good as us ladies." My mom shrugs in an all-too-innocent gesture.

Breyla just laughs at my expense and agrees with mother, "What's wrong, Aurelius? Are you jealous you can't win against a couple of females? Can your fragile male ego not handle losing?"

"My male ego is anything but fragile, Princess," I snap back. "But you forget one thing."

"And what is that?" she challenges.

"I can tell when you're lying, and you both reek of deception right now."

At this, my father lets out a full belly laugh, throwing his head back.

"Thank the gods for you, son. I've been waiting for someone to call your mother out on her cheating for years now!"

"Mallum!" Mother cries in outrage. "I do not cheat!"

"Stop lying, Mother. You're fooling no one. You obviously passed that trait on to Breyla," I say, side eyeing the guilty princess.

"If you want to be accurate, I learned my card-playing *skills* from Father," Breyla declares as if she's proud of the fact that her father taught her how to cheat at cards.

"And let me guess, Raynor learned to play from you?" I accuse my mother.

She shrugs as if to say yes but doesn't want to admit it out loud.

I collect the cards from them all and throw them aside. "Enough of this. We're playing a game you two can't cheat at."

They both huff and fold their arms across their chests. It's cute to see Breyla sitting there, looking like the younger version of mother. Her auburn hair is just a shade off from my mother's fire-red, same freckles, and annoyed look in their eyes. Mom's are hazel, but flecked with the same emerald green that fills Breyla's irises.

Raynor looked like the male version of Mom, taking on very few features from our father but all his personality. He was stoic for the most part but absolutely fierce if provoked, loyal beyond belief, and selfless. I was always the black sheep of the family, quite literally. My dark curls, tanned complexion, and odd crimson-flecked irises always stood out against the fair quality of their features. It was always obvious I was adopted—my parents never tried to hide it—but they loved me all the same.

They had always done their best to make me feel the same, but in so many ways I just never quite fit. My Gifts had developed early and quickly. There were so few instances of my Hemonia Gift that I had no one to help me learn to control it. My ability to read intention and sense lies was slightly more common, so my parents were able to find a tutor for me to hone that ability. It was lonely being the only one like me.

Breyla is a perfect balance of both her parents. While physically she resembles her father more—except for her complexion—her personality was equal parts her father and mother. Her quick wit and sharp tongue came from her mother, but her fierce devotion, loyalty, and interest in all things dangerous came from her father.

I can remember no less than a dozen times I thought I might die from stunts or adventures I was dragged on by Raynor. He passed on his desire for adventure and experiences to his daughter.

"So, what game are we playing?" Breyla asks, shaking me out of my mental assessment of her.

"Remis and Goblets," I say, confident that she can't cheat at this one.

"The drinking game?" Breyla asks.

"That's the one."

"I'll grab the goblets and the ale!" My father dashes from the room, excited to play a game he can finally win.

"I don't know what you expect to gain from this," Breyla starts while picking at her nails as if unbothered by my challenge. "I excel at all drinking games."

"Well, so do I. Game on, Princess." I lean over the table and meet her eyes with a stare of my own.

Father returns with the goblets and pitchers of ale, pouring us each a hefty glass. I pull a Remi from my coin purse and bounce it toward the cup in the middle of the table. It lands directly in the middle, the coin ringing against the metal of the cup.

I smirk up at Breyla, her face less than impressed.

Father goes next, landing his coin directly on top of mine. An excited yelp escapes him as he demands, "Drink up, ladies!"

They both take a drink, then line up for their shots. Both land the Remis in the goblet, much to our dismay, and we drink. *Shit, this might be harder than I thought.*

The play goes back and forth, with each of us making the most of our shots and barely missing any. At the end, though, we come out victorious, and the girls have to finish the pitcher of ale.

My mother looks at the pitcher with disgust, clearly not wanting to take another drink.

"Don't worry, Grandma. I'll take this one," Breyla offers and tips the half-full pitcher to her lips. She gulps it down, little drops escaping the sides of her mouth and running down her chin. I find myself wanting to clean them off her and find out what the ale tastes like on her skin.

"Thank you, my dear," my mother hiccups. "I can't hold my ale like I used to."

Breyla finishes the drink in record time and sets the pitcher on the table with a triumphant grin.

"What's next?" she challenges.

"Nothing for me, dear. I'm retiring for the evening," my mother says between hiccups.

"I'll join you, darling," my father says, joining her as she exits the parlor.

"What do you say, Aurelius? Up for another game?" Her words are slightly slurred, and I can tell the alcohol she just chugged is starting to hit her.

"I say, it is also time for bed, my drunk little demon."

"I'm not drunk, you're drunk!" she exclaims, then giggles.

"We've hit the giggling stage; it is time for bed." I laugh, pulling her behind me down the hallway toward my room.

We pass her room and she looks at me, confused. "That's my room, where are you taking me?"

"Did you forget our bargain, Princess? You promised to stay with me tonight."

"Oh!" she yells, just a bit too loud for my liking. If there were servants nearby, they definitely heard that.

"Shhh. You don't want anybody to hear us, remember?"

"Oh yeah," she whisper-yells, barely any quieter than before. "Gotta be quiet, so they don't know we're fucking."

"We're not fucking tonight, Princess," I whisper as we finally reach my room.

"Why not? I love it when you fuck me." Her words have me instantly hard, and I groan. I throw up a silencing shield before I say my next words.

"I promised I wouldn't fuck you tonight. It was your condition, if you remember. But gods, Princess, if you keep talking like that, I might just have to break that promise."

She pushes me backwards until my legs hit the edge of the bed. "What if I want you to break me, instead?" She bites her lip in a seductive move that has precum leaking from my tip.

"Princess, I'm about two seconds from cleansing that alcohol from your blood and letting you go to bed sober so you come to your senses. I don't have any restraint when it comes to you."

Just when I think she'll see reason, she pushes me backwards onto the bed and straddles my hips, rocking against my erection.

"Really? 'Cause I think you want to fuck me, just as much as I want you to. Sobriety won't change that reality," she whispers as she grinds her hips down on me.

"That's it," I snap, but not in the way she's expecting. I let my Hemonia Gift course through her, stealing her inebriation and instantly sobering her.

She shakes her head, the fuzziness clearing and her senses returning.

"Sorry about that," she grimaces.

"You don't need to apologize. You just need to know, that's the last time I'll be holding myself back from taking you. Test my resolve again, and I'll fuck you just to remind you what I'm capable of."

"Understood," she gulps, removing herself from my lap.

I stand with her, then pull her dress over her head as she lifts her arms. I walk to my dresser, looking for some sleep clothes that will fit her. I settle on an old tunic that hangs low, almost reaching her knees.

"Sorry, I don't have any sleep pants for you, but gods, I love the sight of you in my clothing," I say as she pulls the shirt over her head.

I lay down in bed, pulling her into me. I lay on my side with her in front of me, my arm wrapped around her stomach. She sighs against me, and I nuzzle into her hair, inhaling her scent.

It takes us no time to fall into a deep, peaceful sleep.

Breyla's screams startle me several hours later. She's thrashing from side to side, tears streaming down her face as she cries

Julian's name over and over in her sleep. Her body trembles violently as I try to shake her awake.

"Breyla, wake up!" I whisper-yell, before ensuring the sound shield I had placed earlier is still in place. The last thing I need is for a servant to hear her screams and find her in my room.

She doesn't respond to my attempts to wake her, still crying Julian's name on repeat. I can't imagine what horrors haunt her, but I want to chase them all away, erase them from her soul.

I change tactics, now shaking her firmly, but not so much it will hurt her. "Breyla, please. Wake up!" I beg as her thrashing and tears continue.

Still nothing. I straddle her hips, laying my forehead against hers and cup her cheeks.

"You're safe. Please, my love. Wake up," I whisper, my voice relaying the desperation I feel internally.

Her breathing evens, tears eventually ceasing. The trembling stops, and her eyes open. I stare into her emerald greens, wishing to drown in them, if it only meant she never screamed like that again.

"Aurelius?" she croaks.

"Yes, Princess?"

"Thank you."

"Of course. You want to talk about it?"

I'm still straddling her, my forehead resting against hers.

"I will if you lay back down," she offers.

I oblige her and roll back to my side, wrapping her tightly into my chest.

"Every time I close my eyes, I see him. His lifeless eyes stare back into mine, his head laying on the velvet pillow of that damn box."

I'm unsure if she's done, so I stay quiet, giving her time to decide.

"I can still see every part of him in vivid detail. Sometimes, I swear it looks like his face moves, his lips twitching as they try to talk to me."

"What do you think he's trying to tell you?"

"The dead don't speak, Aurelius."

"Are you sure about that?"

"No. I'm not sure about anything, anymore."

My chest tightens at her pain and uncertainty. I want to take it away, make it all okay. But that's not my job; it's hers. I can be her support, but only she can fight this battle.

"Is it always the same?"

"No," she says, her voice coming out softly.

"Do you want to talk about that?"

"Not tonight."

"What do you need?"

"Just hold me and chase away my nightmares."

"Always," I promise and mean it with my whole being.

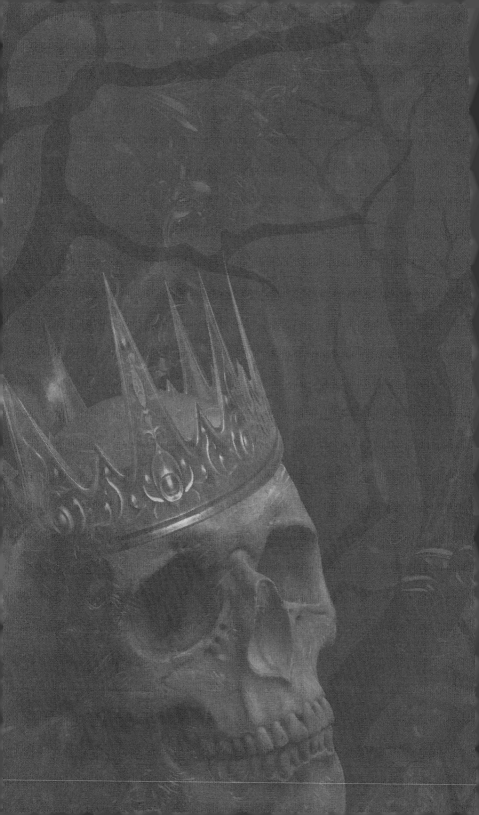

CHAPTER THIRTY-ONE

OPHELIA

"She won't eat, Elijah." What I'm telling him isn't new information, but it's been three days since Jade has had anything to eat, and she won't leave her chambers. It's like she's shut down entirely.

She lost her twin, the other half of her heart. I can't say I understand how she's feeling exactly, but I do feel for her. If I lost Layne, I would probably react the same way. He was the only family I really cared for and that loved me. Though we weren't twins, he was my best friend, and I would be heartbroken if he was gone. I don't know how to reach her. I promised Breyla I would watch over Jade in her absence, but I am failing miserably.

"You just aren't using the right tactic. You're far too sweet, but tenderness will not motivate Jade to respond."

"Then what will?" I ask, at my wit's end.

"Anger, more than likely."

"You want me to make her mad?" I ask in horror.

"Nah, doll. I want you to get me chocolate cake from the kitchen, then let me make her mad."

We've been sitting in the castle library all morning, mostly reading to ourselves, just enjoying each other's company. The castle has been quiet with Breyla and Aurelius gone, leaving very little for us to attend to.

"Why chocolate cake?"

"That's Jade's weakness. If she'll break for anything, it'll be that."

"You know so much about your friends," I observe.

"Of course I do. They're my family." He shrugs as if it's obvious.

"Alright, chocolate cake it is. I'll meet you at her room."

It takes me no time at all to find the chocolate cake once I'm in the kitchen. The benefit of being ignored by most is they rarely care where you go or what you do. The kitchen and I were well acquainted as a result. Grabbing two pieces, because I couldn't leave without one for myself, I exit the kitchen. Elijah is already by her door when I arrive, cake in hand.

"Two pieces?" He quirks a blonde brow at me.

"You expect me to say no to chocolate cake when it's right there in front of me? Clearly, you know very little about females."

His grin turns flirtatious as he says, "Oh, I know quite a bit more about females than you might expect." The statement is full of innuendo, and my cheeks heat.

He opens the door without knocking and enters. I follow behind, setting a piece on the dresser and holding one in my hands.

"Jade, you smell like shit," Elijah says bluntly.

All we receive in return is her middle finger thrown up in the air toward us.

"You know what Julian would say to you right now?"

"Go away, Elijah." Her voice is weak and hoarse from crying.

"Mmm, no. Julian never told me to go away. If anything, he was begging for me to come—"

A pillow hits him square in the face, cutting off his current statement before it could get uncomfortable for us all. "Shut the fuck up, E. I'm not in the mood."

"Not in the mood for what? Living? Yeah, sure seems that way." He's provoking her, and by gods, it's actually working.

"Fuck you, Elijah. You have no idea what I'm feeling." She spits the words at him.

"I'm not pretending to know how you feel, Jade. I can't possibly fathom what it feels like to lose the other half of my soul. But I do know how it feels to lose my sometimes lover, my forever friend, and companion. You don't think my heart is shattered, too?" A rogue tear streaks down Elijah's cheek as his voice softens.

Jade's shoulders sag, and her head hangs low. "I'm sorry, I didn't—"

"You don't have to apologize, but you are disappointing him. You know he wouldn't want to see you like this. You have to eat, you stubborn ass." And just like that Elijah is back to pissing her off.

She snaps out of bed and storms toward him, her hands balling into fists. Just as her fist rears back to let a punch fly, Elijah catches it midair and stops her in her tracks.

"Ah ah ah," Elijah tsks. "You can have one free shot once you eat."

"Excuse me?" She's as confused as I am at Elijah's bargain.

"One punch for one meal. I brought your favorite, but you have to eat it first." He pulls the chocolate cake from behind him and holds it right next to her face.

Her stomach rumbles loud enough that we all hear it. She rolls her eyes, grabs the plate, and gives into Elijah's demand.

She shovels the chocolate cake into her mouth, faster than should be possible. I wish we could have gotten her to eat something more substantial, but I'll take what I can get at this point.

"Happy?" Jade grumbles.

"Ecstatic," Elijah says, grinning.

"Can I punch your dumb ass now?" Something sparkles in her eyes at the request.

"A deal's a deal, just please not the nose."

She strides across the room, a slight grin on her face. I hear a sick crunching sound as Jade's fist meets the flesh of Elijah's face. He lets out a low grunt but doesn't resist or say anything else.

"Now get lost, both of you. I need to bathe."

We both grin, knowing we got two wins out of this visit. Without needing to be told twice, we back out of her room to let her bathe in peace.

"Well, that was an interesting but effective tactic," I muse once outside her room.

"I've known Jade for a long time. I'm rather good at getting under her skin when I want to."

"Am I going to have to let her punch me each time I want her to eat?" I ask, my eyes comically wide.

Elijah lets out a loud, boisterous laugh. "If you keep having issues, just come get me, doll. I'm happy to oblige. She's too weak from not eating to really hurt me right now, anyway."

"Oh, thank the gods." I sigh in relief.

We're back in the library, Elijah lounging on a cushioned bench, as I'm bent over, inspecting the purple bruise spreading under his left eye. My fingers trace the edges of the bruised skin tenderly.

"Need a closer look, doll?" His voice is flirtatious, and the next second his hands are on my hips, pulling me into his lap.

I'm straddling him, his arm banded around my lower back, holding me close.

He grins at me. "If I tell you it hurts, will you nurse me back to health, Ophelia?"

I still at his words; there's no way he could know about my abilities.

He senses my hesitancy, and his lips drop. "I was only joking, Ophelia. Did I make you uncomfortable?"

"N-no, it's not that." I lay my hand on his cheek. I make an impulsive, probably reckless decision. "Put up a sound shield."

He does as I ask, then cants his head in question at me.

I take a deep breath before speaking. "You can't tell anyone."

"Can't tell anyone what?" he asks, but I'm already pushing my healing power into his skin.

The prickling sensation passes from my fingers into the skin of his face, and his jaw drops. Tentative fingers prod at the space beneath his eye that was bruised and swollen just moments ago.

"Did you just—" His words cut off like he can't believe what just happened.

"Heal you? Yes," I say softly.

"That's...that's amazing." His voice is full of awe.

"Only a few know, and I'd like to keep it that way."

"Your secret is safe with me," he promises with a smile. "But I have questions."

I playfully roll my eyes. "Of course you do."

"I guess the first is a bit of a confession." He looks at me sheepishly. "I've known about your Gift since the day I ran into you in the hall...I wasn't wearing gloves and I accidentally read your memories. I saw you heal Lyla."

My jaw drops, and I stare at him. "You've known for weeks?"

He nods in confirmation, looking almost nervous.

"And you haven't told anyone. Not even Breyla?" My mind races at this revelation. Breyla knew about my Gift, but that's because I had saved her life with it. I was sure she didn't know about it prior.

"I just figured there was a reason you hadn't told anyone, and it wasn't my place to say anything. Selfishly, I wanted you to trust me enough to tell me yourself." His large brown eyes stare up into mine, begging me to believe him.

"I trust you, Elijah," I whisper, and he smiles at me. "You said you had questions?"

"First, why do you keep this a secret? Your power is amazing and easily makes you one of the most powerful in the kingdom. There are so few healers—none even in the capital. The ones Rimor has are treated like royalty."

I don't bother to correct him that I'm not technically a healer; I'm something different, something more. "Because my father would find some way to use it to his benefit; he always finds a way to use me."

"Your father is a piece of shit," Elijah spits.

"Well aware," I say, sighing.

"Next question—why did you decide to tell me?"

I smile shyly, my cheeks flushing. "Like I said—I trust you, Elijah. I don't have many people I can trust, but you have always treated me as an equal even when you thought I had no power."

His face falls, and I'm left momentarily confused before he speaks. "That's because you *are* an equal, Ophelia. Hell, you're better than most people, and it has nothing to do with you having power or not. You are worthy despite your Gift, not because of it."

"No male, except for maybe Layne, has ever spoken to me this way," I say as my lip quivers.

Elijah growls low in his throat, "Then you weren't talking to males; you were talking to boys."

"How do you keep saying all the exact right things?"

"Oh, I can say plenty of *wrong* things." I don't miss the slight heat in his words.

"Oh yeah? Like what?"

"Like I know right now is the exact wrong time for this," he starts, leaning in and hovering his lips just inches from my own, "but I'm going to kiss you now, Ophelia."

Shivers run down my back, and my breath hitches. I whisper, "No, that's still the exact right thing."

His lips are on mine, soft and tender, not like the first kiss we shared several nights ago. It's patient and slow, warm and sensual. He doesn't push me any further, letting me set the pace. I tentatively run my tongue along his bottom lip, begging for him to open to me. He obliges, letting his tongue meet mine and tangle together.

One of his hands threads through the black strands hanging down my back and cups my head reverently. I repeat the gesture and tangle my fingers in the dark blond waves at the base of his neck. My fingers tug gently, trying to bring him even closer to me, and he lets out a small groan into my mouth.

"Fuck, Ophelia. What are you doing to me?"

"I don't know, Elijah. You're the only male I've ever kissed." I feel my cheeks flame at the admission.

Elijah throws his head back and lets out a loud groan this time. "You absolutely *cannot* say things like that, especially while I have you on my lap."

"W-why? What's wrong?" Uncertainty fills me.

"Absolutely nothing, doll. You're fucking perfect. But it's taking every ounce of willpower to resist your specific flavor of temptation. Now you're telling me I'm the only one that's kissed you? Heard those beautiful noises you make? It's too much and not enough all at once. I want every piece of you."

I reach out my hand, dragging his face back to mine, and kiss him deeply. Breaking it, I offer, "Then take every piece of me, Elijah. I want to know what that feels like."

The next thing I know, the library door is slamming shut and locking. He flips our position so I'm pinned between his hard body and the bench seat below us.

"Don't say things like that unless you mean it, doll." He is hovering his lips above mine, so close I can feel his breath on my lips.

My response is only to roll my hips into him, rubbing against his erection pressing against my core. *Holy hell, how big is it?*

He chuckles, "I'll make it not only fit, I'll make it feel so good you scream for me."

Oh crap, I must have said that thought out loud.

"Now lay back and let me worship you, Ophelia."

I drop my head, my ebony locks cascading over the edge of the bench like a waterfall of midnight. His lips trail my jaw up to my ear, and I gasp as he nips at the lobe. He sucks it into his mouth as his hands trail up each side of my ribcage, stopping just below my breasts.

His fingers brush over my nipple and it hardens. The sensitive buds ache to be touched, and I thrust my chest forward, chasing more of him.

"So eager and responsive," he hums against my skin, moving his kisses down my neck. He alternates bites and kisses in a blend of pain and pleasure, sharp and tender that leave me hot.

One of Elijah's hands moves from my breast down to my hips, stopping just short of the apex of my thighs.

He stops his assault on my neck to ask, "Tell me, Ophelia. Have you ever touched yourself here?"

My neck flushes at his words, the heat creeping up my face. I shake my head, and he grins.

"Such a good girl. You won't stay that way once I've had you. I need you to be absolutely certain you understand what you're agreeing to. I'll break you in the best ways, my sinful little doll."

I don't hesitate before nodding my understanding.

"I need your words, Ophelia."

THE SORROW OF SHADOWS

"I understand, Elijah." My voice doesn't waver as I give him my consent.

Fire sparks in his brown eyes, and he captures my lips in a passionate kiss. He wastes no time pushing his tongue into my mouth and meeting mine, deepening the kiss with every push and pull of his lips.

The hand that was hovering above my center is now pushing up the skirts of my dress, baring my legs to him. He quickly finds my undergarments and runs a finger along the edge, dipping one finger just barely inside them.

The teasing sensation has me shivering in anticipation, driving me to pull at the bottom of his tunic, lifting it over his head.

As we break our kiss to remove his shirt, I get the chance to admire the body beneath. My mouth might be watering, staring at the hard lines and ridges of each defined muscle along his arms, chest, and abdomen. I'm pretty sure the gods sculpted this male, because there's no way they can look *that* good.

He has that delicious vee that leads down to his pelvis, and I find myself wanting to run my tongue along it. I've seen plenty of males train shirtless, but Elijah is something else entirely. I will never understand how someone of his build ended up as an advisor to the king. You can't even compare most males to him.

He is the perfect opposite to my petite frame, and I love the way he dwarfs me, yet I feel like I fit perfectly against him.

"You done staring, darling?" he teases.

"Never," I reply, biting my lip.

He leans down and pulls my bottom lip from between my teeth into his own, biting softly.

I let out a soft moan, the sudden sting soon soothed by the lapping of his tongue. He runs a knuckle down my center over my undergarments. I'm surprised by how sensitive it is, even through a layer of fabric.

He resumes our kiss, letting himself explore every inch of my mouth. His fingers continue their motion against my center, and I feel myself moaning every time he drags a knuckle over that sensitive bud at the top of my sex.

After a few minutes of his torturous pace, I start rolling my hips against his hand, desperate for him to touch more. I need to feel more.

"When I remove these, am I going to find you wet for me?" he asks against my lips, his fingers teasing the edge of my undergarments.

"I-I don't know," I say honestly. This is all new territory to me.

"Let's find out, shall we?" He winks and hooks a thumb through them, pulling them down my thighs.

He works them off me easily and brings them up to his nose, breathing in deeply. The dirty act is oddly erotic. He moans at the scent, then tucks them in his pants pocket.

My back bows off the bench when he finally drags his finger from my entrance to that bundle of nerves. His touch is like ecstasy, and I find myself craving more of it.

"I love your reactions. I can't wait to see what others I can create," he says before rubbing circles around that magical spot, then running his fingers down around my entrance. He alternates the motions, driving me to the point of insanity.

"Please, Elijah," I whimper. I don't even know what I'm asking for at this point. I just know it's not enough.

"Please, what?" He grins at me.

"Please..." I start, not sure how to finish the request. "Put your fingers, um..."

"Put my fingers where, Ophelia? I need to know where you want them." He's enjoying making me squirm entirely too much.

"Inside my um..." I start but hesitate with what to call it. So, I go for the safe, "Inside me."

He traces from the bundle of nerves down to my entrance, then further down to the puckered hole, and chuckles. My eyes flare wide at the sensation. "There's more than one place I can fuck you with my fingers. You'll need to clarify."

He's really going to make me say this, isn't he? I sigh in frustration, "Please put your fingers in my p-p-pu—" I still struggle to get the last word out, feeling horrified at the way the dirty word feels on my tongue.

"Say it with me, beautiful: Elijah, please put your fingers in my *pussy*." He smirks, letting the word roll off his tongue.

"Elijah, please put your fingers in my pussy," I say as quickly as possible.

"I'd be happy to," he says, pushing the tip of one finger in my tight channel. I already feel so full, I'm not sure how I'm supposed to fit more. There's a slight burn as he moves the finger all the way in.

"I'm going to need you to relax. You're so fucking tight, Ophelia." Elijah groans, then uses his thumb to rub circles around my clit. The pleasure erupting from that motion is enough to distract me, and I let the muscles of my inner walls relax.

"I promise to make you feel good, but you'll have to trust me," Elijah reassures me, his finger pumping in and out of me in slow strokes. After a few minutes, I find myself rolling my hips, chasing the pleasure his fingers provide.

"I'm going to give you more, now. Let me know if it ever gets to be too much." His words are full of concern, and it touches me that he would care so much.

A second finger teases my entrance, but he doesn't push it in. Instead, he moves down my body, leaving tender kisses along the way.

When he finally reaches my hips, he lays a soft kiss on my clit, before running the pad of his tongue from entrance to clit. I let out a loud sound I didn't know I could even make.

This is enough affirmation for Elijah to continue using his mouth to lick every last inch of me. I cry out at the sensation of him flicking his tongue over my clit quickly. Finally, he slides in a second finger and uses both along with his mouth to continue pleasuring me.

"Fuck, Elijah." I writhe under his touch, a tightness building low in my belly. It's a foreign feeling of pressure unlike anything I've experienced before. I chase it, letting my hips rock against his hand and mouth.

"That's it, doll. Fuck my face. You're so close, I can feel it in the way you grip my fingers." He continues pumping them into me, increasing his pace. "I can't wait to feel you grip my dick like this," he says between licks up and down my pussy.

"There's so much pressure," I whine, unable to handle the tightness building in me for much longer.

"I know, sweetheart. Just let go, and it'll feel so good." I feel his tongue swirl around my clit again, then he sucks it into his mouth and nips it lightly. It's enough to send me hurtling over the edge, and a world-shattering wave of pleasure consumes me as I scream his name.

The pleasure goes on, rippling across my body in waves of ecstasy. I'm panting hard by the time he raises his head from between my legs and smiles at me.

"You're welcome," he says, full of cockiness.

"For what?" I quirk a brow at him.

"Your first orgasm," he replies, winking at me.

I flush at his words, then ask, "Can we do it again?"

He throws his head back in laughter. "Anytime you like, sweetheart. Right now, though, I think you need a nap."

"Nonsense, I want all of it, Elijah." I yawn as I say this, proving his point.

"You'll get all of it, but we might need to work up to full-blown fucking. You just had your first orgasm, and you can barely keep your eyes open."

I wave him off like he's crazy.

"You're going to need to build stamina before I can fuck you

properly. Don't worry, I have no problem helping you with that."
He nips at my inner thigh, and I giggle deliriously.

"Fine, but you better not keep me waiting long, Elijah." I do
my best to give him a serious look.

"Oh, don't you fret, Ophelia. I'll be fucking you *very soon*,"
he says seductively.

He leans back and pulls my dress down to cover me. My
eyes flutter as I fight sleep, and he lifts me from the bench. He
scoops me up and carries me bridal style out of the library. I
think he takes me to my chambers, but I don't know for sure
because sleep claims me before we make it there.

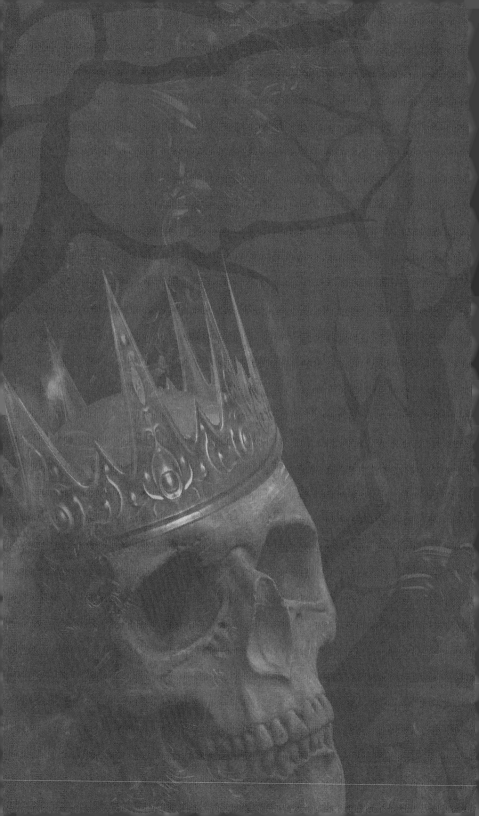

CHAPTER THIRTY-TWO

BREYLA

We had been riding all day after departing my grandparents' estate, much to their disappointment. We had to promise to visit and bring Mother next time to get my grandmother to release us from the death grip she called a hug.

We closely followed the path we believed Julian would have taken. The rain had washed away any traces of a potential trail he would have left. Unfortunately, he had been trained well and probably hadn't left much to go off despite the rain. I had also instructed him to avoid major cities and establishments when possible, something I was now regretting.

There had been a few inns and taverns that he might have stopped at, but when we stopped to ask the tavern owner if he remembered seeing Julian, he had no memory of seeing a soldier matching his description within the last week.

"It seems Julian did *exactly* as I commanded, stopping nowhere he could be recognized, and I've never been more displeased at him for following orders." I sigh, the frustration seeping through me.

Aurelius rides close to my left side and has remained quiet for most of our journey. When he speaks, it's not what I expect. "Keep your eyes forward, General. We're being followed. They've been on us since we stopped at the last tavern."

I stiffen but follow his instructions. "Do you have any idea who it might be?" I keep my voice barely above a whisper. What I don't ask is how he managed to sense it when I hadn't noticed anything. That thought was more unsettling than being followed.

"No, they haven't come close enough for me to get a look at their attire."

"How many?"

"Just one."

"Plan?"

"I don't know what they want, but I don't think they mean us harm. I don't sense any ill intention on them."

"The trees are getting thicker up ahead. I could wrap us in shadows and ambush them as they pass through."

"That'll do. When they're close enough, I should be able to render their limbs motionless so we can question them."

I nod in acknowledgment of our plan. We ride another ten minutes until the trees start to thicken. Once the horses pass through a particularly shady patch, I wrap my shadows around the both of us, allowing us to blend into the natural shade of the trees.

We wait for another ten minutes until our tail appears. It's not at all what I expect to see when a mousy young female peaks her head around the grouping of trees. I'm sure she's looking for us since it probably seemed as if we disappeared into the shadows in front of her.

I take a moment to observe her before either of us move. She has chestnut hair and deep blue eyes. Her body is tall and willowy, limbs thin and dainty. It's what I imagine my mother would look like if she were severely underfed. The girl has slight curves, but it's hard to find them with the lack of meat on her bones. Still, there's a brightness in her eyes; a determination.

I give Aurelius a nod to signal it's time to enact our plan. He holds up his hand, twisting his fingers in a motion to freeze her in place. At the same time, I release the shadows keeping us hidden.

"Hello, little mouse," I say, greeting her with a smile. If she's scared, she doesn't show it.

Aurelius has left her control of her neck and head, so she can turn it to look us in the eyes. She twists her head around, examining her frozen body.

"Hmm. How intriguing," she hums before turning her gaze back to us. "Hello, Princess and Lord Aurelius."

"So, you *do* know who we are," I reply, confirming she knows who she's been following. "But care to share who you are and why you're following us?"

"The name is Nameah Galvin. I'm following you because I overheard you in Mo's tavern, and I have something I think you'll want to see."

This piques my interest—she had heard us asking about Julian. It would be our first real lead, and I couldn't let it pass.

Aurelius seems less convinced. "Why should we trust you? You could have approached us at the tavern, yet you followed us all the way out here instead."

"I'm not from that town. My family lives about a half day's ride to the south, but I come into town for supplies and trading when necessary. I don't trust everyone in town, and I have a feeling you don't want news spreading about what I'm about to show you."

My hackles rise at her words, something in my gut telling me to believe her. I look to Aurelius for confirmation that she's being truthful, and he nods.

347

"Very well, Nameah. I believe you. Lead the way." I nod to Aurelius so he'll release the hold he has on her body.

He relaxes his hand, and movement returns to her previously frozen limbs. She wiggles her fingers and stares at them in awe.

"What an interesting Gift. I've never seen one quite like it, though I've never seen much of any Gifts with how far away from most people we live." Nameah rambles on, and I'm unsure if she's speaking to us or herself. "I've heard tales of your power, General. Of course, I've encountered the occasional shadow wielder, but none nearly as strong as what you're rumored to be."

I chuckle lightly. "Are you trying to flatter us, Nameah?"

"No!" she exclaims a bit too quickly, then reconsiders. "Well, maybe a bit. I have always wanted to join the Rimorian army, so I figured it best to get in your good graces."

That bit of information surprises me, but I keep my face neutral. I decide to question her as we ride. "How old are you?"

"Twenty-one, Your Grace."

"If you want to get on my good side, don't call me that," I say with an exaggerated eye roll that has Aurelius snickering behind me.

She nods enthusiastically, and I continue my questions. "Do you possess any powers?"

"I do. I can bend light. I'm not the strongest, but I can do this." She demonstrates her Gift, her hand raising and disappearing before my eyes. Her power seems to work similarly to my shadows, but with light; she's bending the particles around her body in such a way that she appears invisible. It's quite impressive, but rather useless in the dark.

"How far does your ability extend?"

"I can manipulate my entire body, but I can't do anything beyond that." There's potential she could make for a decent spy with some training.

"Can you create light?"

She shakes her head. "No, sadly I cannot. I've tried, but it seems I'm not strong enough."

"Your strength is not defined by your power, little mouse. It's quite the opposite, actually."

She quirks a brow at me. "How so?"

"Everyone is born with certain talents, but *skill* is developed. Those with raw power, but no discipline to learn control over that power are wild and useless. Most of the time, they're dangerous. Therefore, they are actually the weakest because I can do nothing with them. Those born with less natural 'talent,' but the discipline to learn control and grow their powers are far more useful. Our Gifts are like our muscles; the more we exercise and train them, the stronger they grow."

"I had never thought of it like that, but I guess that makes sense. So, are you saying I could grow my abilities beyond what they are now?" There's a hint of excitement in her question.

"I think it's possible. Whether or not you do is dependent entirely on you."

She nods in understanding, and I continue my questions. "Can you fight? Have you been trained?"

"I have two older brothers, so I've spent my fair share of time wrestling and sparring with them. I wouldn't say I've been trained formally, but I can hold my own."

A few moments pass in silence as I consider her potential. She'd be starting later than most soldiers and she's severely underfed, so the training would take everything from her until she started gaining muscle. It wouldn't be easy, but she seems eager.

"I'll consider it, but only after I see what you have to show us and once I've had a chance to evaluate your abilities myself. I won't lie to you; it will be difficult. You'd be starting at a disadvantage, but I'm not one to deny anyone a chance."

Nameah nods enthusiastically. "I understand! That's good enough for me. I won't let you down, General."

We ride for another hour before Nameah announces, "We're almost there. It's in the clearing just beyond this group of trees." Her face is serious and sullen.

A nervous energy consumes me as we make it through the trees to the clearing beyond. What we see has a sob fighting to break free and bile racing up my throat. I dismount Luna in a hurry and fall to my knees as I empty the contents of my stomach on the ground.

Aurelius is behind me, rubbing soothing circles on my back. "It's okay, Princess. I've got you," he whispers for my ears only.

After another minute, I find the strength to look up and fully take in the site before me. On a wooden cross hangs the headless body of my second. His arms are stretched out to the side, nails driven through his wrists to keep his body in place.

The stench hits me as soon as I take a step closer. Close to a week has passed since his head was sent to me in a box—and there's no telling exactly when he was killed—so the process of decay has fully begun. The putrid smell of rotting flesh invades my nostrils and has me gagging. If I had anything left in my stomach, it would surely be coming back up. My eyes water from the smell at first, but quickly shift to actual tears streaming freely down my cheeks.

Up close, I can see his body more clearly. It doesn't appear that he has any other significant injuries, which leads me to believe he wasn't tortured. I pray to any gods that will listen that it meant he had a swift death. If he wasn't tortured, it means they weren't looking to get any information from him.

So, then why was he murdered at all? Was he just in the wrong place at the wrong time? Did he see something he wasn't supposed to?

I turn to Aurelius. "Who would do this?" It's all I can manage to get out.

"I don't know, Princess. But we'll figure it out." He pulls me into his warmth and places a soft kiss on the top of my head.

"I'm glad Jade isn't here to see this," I whisper.

"No one saw who did it, in case you're wondering. He was just here one morning. My family lives close enough that we would have heard something if there was a fight, but there was nothing."

"Why didn't anyone try to take him down?" I feel anger rise in me that they would leave his body like this. The wildlife has already started picking at his corpse; they should have done something.

"We did," she sighs. "There's some kind of shield around his body that wouldn't let anyone pass through. It didn't protect him from the elements or animals, but no person could reach him."

I hadn't heard of any shields like that before. "I don't understand," I say, furrowing my brows.

She walks up to his body and reaches a hand toward him. Before she can touch him, her hand just stops. It's as if there's an invisible barrier that she can't pass through. "I don't understand either, but we all experienced the same thing when we tried.

I reach out a hand to see if I get the same resistance. My hand passes through whatever barrier is there and meets his body. As soon as I make contact, a burning sensation races up my fingertips, causing me to jerk back and cry out in pain.

"What the fuck was that?" I hiss out, shaking my hand. Aurelius grabs it tenderly, turning it over and looking for signs of injury. There's nothing there, and the burning has receded to a slight tingling sensation.

"Is your hand okay?" Nameah asks. "I swear that didn't happen to any of us that tried before."

"It's like it was meant for only you. Like it was waiting for you to touch his body," Aurelius muses. "I wonder..." His voice trails off as he reaches his hand out toward Julian's body.

Like mine, his hand passes through the invisible barrier,

allowing him to touch Julian. As soon as he makes contact, he grunts and pulls his hand back just as I had done with mine.

"There's something there," Nameah says. I find where her eyes are pinned and notice a piece of parchment nailed to his chest, right above where his heart would be.

"That wasn't there before..." My voice trails off as I reach for the note. Careful not to make contact with his body again, I rip the parchment free.

Written in elegant script are the words:

The Crimson Prince and Queen of Shadows will fall.

"What the—" My words are cut short by the whistling of an arrow as it flies by inches from my face.

"Get down, Princess. We're under attack!" Aurelius roars as he draws his sword.

I roll my eyes. "I'm the fucking general, this is just another Thursday." I pull my own sword, dragging Nameah behind me. She's untrained, and I refuse to have her blood on my hands.

Four males surround us, seeming to have appeared out of thin air. There's no way they would have escaped the notice of both Aurelius and I, so they must have been cloaked somehow. They're all dressed in leathers identical to each other, red cloaks pinned to their shoulders, and all armed to the teeth. All four males tower over us, even exceeding Aurelius's height by a few inches. I stare down the one who shot the arrow at me, studying his features.

His red hood is pulled high over his head to hide his hair and obscure his features. His eyes are a shade of red I've never seen before. It's unnatural and unsettling. I can't make out anything else on his face as a black cloth covers the bottom half.

The group remains silent as they continue circling and closing in on us.

"What do you want?" I demand, using the voice that always has my soldiers falling into line.

"You are attacking the General and Princess of Rimor and

the Royal Emissary. I suggest you carefully consider your next move. You wouldn't want a war on your hands." Aurelius speaks in a way that would make lesser males quake.

Still, our assailants say nothing, but I hear a few muffled snickers. These males have no fear.

The one I was studying finally speaks, his voice low and smooth like liquid velvet wrapping around my senses. "War is coming for you whether anyone wants it or not," he says pointedly before finally attacking.

He swings his sword straight for me, and I raise my own to meet his at the last possible second. He's fast. They're all incredibly fast. Aurelius and I work to fend them off, keeping our backs together and Nameah between us.

Except she's not between us anymore. From my peripherals I catch sight of her engaging one of the males not currently attacking Aurelius and me. She has a dagger in her hand, and while she has very little range, she can at least stand a fighting chance if he chooses to attack.

My attention snaps back to the two males charging me. I meet the first, fending off his blow and pushing him back, then swing right as the second thrusts his blade at me. I narrowly miss his attack and manage to make one of my own, my sword slicing through the air where he stood just a moment ago.

These males are skilled, obviously highly trained, and clearly just toying with us. If they wanted to kill us, they'd be trying harder.

Aurelius grunts from somewhere close by, his sword clashing with the male currently attacking him.

When it's clear I'm not taking any ground against my assailants, I change tactics. Instead of thrusting my sword at him, I wait until he charges me. I twist out of his path, then use my shadows to create a blindfold around his eyes. I have a feeling it won't hold for long, so I take my shot while I can, slamming my heel into the center of his back. He stumbles into his companion and lets out a startled grunt.

They clearly didn't expect that move, and they're unhappy about being outmaneuvered.

I hear Nameah struggling against her attacker, but she's doing better than I expected. She's still alive, which is more than I could have hoped for at this point. I cast shadows in her direction, doing what I can to lend her the strength of my Gifts without leaving myself vulnerable.

A realization dawns when my shadows reach her, and the next second, she disappears. *There we go, little mouse. That's thinking on your feet.*

I turn my focus back to my fight, my attackers having fully recovered from my last trick. The warrior on the right raises his sword and steps toward me, but then freezes. His eyes drop down, and I follow their path to see the tip of a blade sticking out the front of his chest just below his heart.

The warrior on my left bellows in rage, swinging his sword wide and thrashing at the enemy he can't see. His sword makes contact, and I hear Nameah's pained gasp, followed by the flickering form of her body coming back into view.

The remaining three warriors halt their attack and retreat from us. They lay hands on their fallen comrade as their forms start to waver and disappear in a cloud of smoke.

Just before they disappear completely, I hear, "The prince sends his regards."

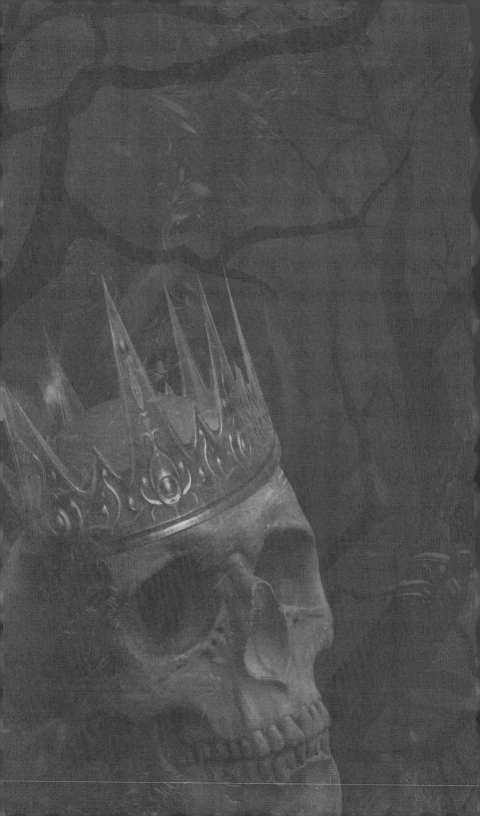

CHAPTER THIRTY-THREE

OPHELIA

"I thought I'd find you here." Layne's voice startles me out of the world I was in reading my latest romance novel. It's about a female scholar living in a world so unlike our own, caught between two lifetimes; an ancient civilization drowned by the gods, and a love story that follows her through the lifetimes.

"You know me well, brother." I smile and scoot over on the settee to make room for him.

"Whenever we played hide and seek as children, I found you in the library. You were incredibly predictable." He laughs softly as he recounts the memory.

I close the book in my lap, noting what page I'm on. "Fictional worlds were always far better than our own reality."

A saccharine smile crosses Layne's face and he sighs. "I have something for you."

"A gift?" I perk up in interest.

"Just a little something I found at a local market in my latest travels." He winks at me and pulls a package from behind him. It's wrapped in brown paper, twine tied into a bow on top.

I unwrap the paper carefully and grin. It's a leatherbound book, with pages lined in gold. I examine the title and flip open the cover.

"No way," I gasp. It's my favorite book; one that I've read a dozen times over.

"Yes way." He smiles at me. "Flip to the next page."

I do as he suggests and squeal, "It's signed by the author!"

"And it's a first edition print. The edges were hand painted by a local artist. It's one of a kind, for my one-of-a-kind sister." He's grinning widely at me now, his blue eyes sparkling.

The tears pool in the corners of my eyes, and I whisper, "Thank you, Layne. It means more than you know."

He pulls me into his arm and hugs me tight, his apple and sage scent wrapping around me. Layne is all the family I've had for so long, the only one who truly cared about me until recently. I relax into the embrace that feels like home.

After a few more moments, Layne finally releases me and says, "So, tell me what I've missed out on during my time away from court."

"I don't know where to begin; you've missed a lot." I contemplate what to tell him first.

"Let's start at the beginning. Last we spoke, Father had commanded you to get close to Princess Breyla for his own gain. How is that going?"

"It should come as no surprise, but Breyla saw right through that. She knew from the start that he sent me. So we formed our own agreement instead, and I feed him false information, just close enough to the truth to not be obvious. In return I tell Breyla what I can about his movements. Breyla and I have come to form a friendship."

Layne looks contemplative as he says, "I still don't know that I trust her, Ophelia." I open my mouth to defend her, but he holds his hand up to stop me. "But I trust Father even less. So, please just be careful. I don't want to see anything happen to you. I can't stand seeing you hurt."

"Yeah, well, I'm used to the pain. I'll be okay, Layne. I know you don't trust Breyla, but I do. Neither she nor Elijah will let anything happen to me." I do my best to reassure him.

"Lord Elijah? I wasn't aware you were close with him." Layne raises a brow at me.

I fight the blush claiming my cheeks, thinking about just how *close* Elijah and I have become. "He's Breyla's best friend, so we've spent considerable time together. They're kind of a package deal most days." I pray to the gods that the explanation is enough to let him drop it.

"Uh huh, I see," he hums in disbelief. "So, you and Elijah haven't spent any time together outside of when you're both with the princess?"

"There's been a few occasions I've enjoyed his company without Breyla present," I say as evenly as possible.

He narrows his eyes at me. "But you're just *friends*, right?"

"We're friendly, yes."

"That's not what I asked, O."

"Your question was unclear, then," I say, shrugging.

"Ophelia, stop dodging my question."

"Ask clearer questions, brother."

"Is there something...romantic between you and Lord Elijah?"

"Something like that," I mumble, my cheeks flushing.

Layne leans forward, gently taking my chin between his finger and thumb, forcing me to look him in the eyes. "Something like *what*," he nearly growls, his jaw clenched.

"Ugh, you overprotective ass. I am an adult, fully capable of choosing with whom I share my time and body." I roll my eyes.

His nostrils flare. "You're sleeping with Elijah?" he nearly screams.

"Not that it's any of your business, but no. We haven't slept together, yet. We haven't exactly defined what we are, but he's made his interest clear. I don't believe he's spending time with anyone else like he does with me. He's actually interested in me. He's sweet and kind; he gets me. He doesn't even care that I have no power." Something twists in my gut at the fact that I'm still keeping Layne in the dark about my Gifts.

Layne grumbles and mutters something unintelligible under his breath.

"What was that?" I challenge.

"I still kind of want to punch him in the face for touching my baby sister, but if you're happy and he treats you right, then that's what matters most."

I chuckle at his overbearing older brother act. "I am happy. He makes me happy."

"I still might punch him," he mumbles.

"Not that I don't have faith in you, brother, but I don't think that's a fight you want to pick."

"Fine, I won't punch him. But you can't blame me for trying to protect my favorite sister," he concedes.

"I'm your *only* sister, you ass."

"Still my favorite," he shrugs. "When did you get such a foul mouth?"

"You can thank Breyla and Elijah for that. I sometimes wonder if they received any lessons in manners at all."

"I'm sure you're not the only one wondering that," he says, laughing.

"Tell me about your time away. Did you have any grand adventures?" I lean in closer to hear his stories.

"Grand adventures? No, not this time. Father sent me to Lennox on business. It was mostly stuffy meetings with even stuffier nobles and merchants. He's been busy making deals and allies all over the continent."

"Sounds absolutely dreadful," I giggle.

"Oh, it most definitely is. The most dreadful," he exaggerates and throws his head back.

"Well, when you're done running all his awful errands, you must take me with you on a grand adventure."

Layne pulls me into his chest, my back to his front, and lightly plays with my hair. My midnight strands wrap around his pointer finger, and he twirls them. It's a soothing sensation for me, one he picked up from our mother; it's one of the only things I remember about her. I think it soothes me as much as it does him. "And where would we go on this grand adventure?"

"What about Amara?" I suggest.

"In Lennox? Why would you want to go there?"

"I've read that Amara has white sand beaches that sparkle like diamonds in the sun and turquoise waters. This time of year, it's the perfect level of warm and sunny all day. I've never seen the ocean, but I think I'd like it. It sounds peaceful." I sigh at the daydream.

"It does sound peaceful, but do you even know how to swim?" he teases lightly.

I pinch him on the thigh. "Of course I know how to swim! I spent time in the river behind the palace grounds, just like every other child at court."

"That is barely a river, Ophelia. The ocean is a different beast. It can be beautiful, but it can also be wild and unforgiving. Some let its beauty distract from its lethality."

"Well, you certainly sound like an expert. I shall rely on you to teach me everything I need to know for this grand adventure."

"Very well, dear sister. I shall be honored to teach you to swim in the ocean and all the other necessary skills for our grand adventure." He smiles at me.

We continue our conversation, catching up long into the night. I tell him of all the weird happenings at court, Father's questionable actions, the arrival of Prince Ayden, and everything else in between. I fall asleep listening to him talk, right there in the library, and it feels just like we're children again.

CHAPTER THIRTY-FOUR

AURELIUS

"What... the fuck... was that," Breyla pants as her eyes frantically search the area for our attackers. They were there one second, then gone the next. I had never seen anyone with a Gift like that, let alone four of them together. Even the body of their fallen soldier is gone.

My eyes roam up and down her form, assessing her for any injuries. When I find none, I turn my attention to the feisty one. Nameah surprised the both of us with how well she held her own in that fight. The trick with the light bending was clever.

"Are you okay?" I ask, gently wrapping my hand around her bicep and pulling it close for inspection. "This doesn't look too deep; I think you'll be fine after we get you to a healer."

"I'll be fine, it just burns like a bitch." She hisses as I run my hands over the edge of the wound. "So, did I prove myself enough to you, General?" She turns her attention back to Breyla.

"Yeah, little mouse, I'd say so. You're still alive, and you managed to take one down, which is more than the rest of us can say. Nice trick with the light," Breyla says with a wink, her breathing still heavy as the adrenaline wears off.

"You like that? I thought it was pretty great." She grins ear to ear.

Breyla chuckles and pats her on the shoulder. "I'll make a soldier out of you; I just have to get some muscle on these bones first."

"That would be easier with more food," she sighs. "Unfortunately, it's not something my family has a lot of. Not since Pa died, at least."

Breyla's smile drops into an understanding frown. "I'm sorry you lost your father. Has your family petitioned the crown for help? We have resources in place for situations like this."

"We have," she says solemnly.

"And that was not enough?"

"Unfortunately, being given nothing doesn't go far." Her voice is hardly above a whisper.

"You were turned away? By whom?" Breyla's voice rises in frustration.

"I was not with my mother when she went, but I believe it was King Raynor."

"When was this?"

"Pa died two years ago, and Ma visited court to request assistance the spring before last. We've survived, but it hasn't been easy." Nameah's voice is sullen, her eyes downcast.

While they've been talking, I've been evaluating. Before Breyla can respond, I interrupt, "I'm sorry, but we have a problem."

Emerald and bright blue eyes stare back at me, and I fear what I have to say. "The blade Nameah was cut with was laced with poison." I sigh, before continuing, "But I don't know what kind."

"Then purify it from her blo—" Breyla starts.

"I've already tried, my Gift has no effect on whatever this is."

"Okay, so then we get her to a healer. How quickly is it spreading?"

I bite my tongue because I can't bring myself to voice my doubts. The truth is that if my Hemonia Gift won't remove the poison, I doubt the healers will have the ability to help. The few healers we have come to me when they encounter a poison they can't treat. "We have a day, maybe two by my estimate."

"Well, fuck."

We'd spent all day and most of the night riding at top speed in hopes of reaching Ciyoria in time to save Nameah. After our attackers had disappeared, we were able to touch Julian without being burned. In order to transport his body home, Nameah had ridden with me so her horse could carry him. Had it been just Breyla and I, we probably could have ridden faster, but this was our only option.

Still, we made decent time and reached my parents in the middle of the night, leaving us just a day's ride away from the capital. Our horses needed to rest and refuel, if only for a few hours before we pushed them to make it the rest of the way home. My parents were startled to see us pounding on their door in the middle of the night, but ushered us inside without question once they saw Nameah's state.

She had spiked a fever sometime around dusk, and I'd been monitoring her decline closely. Sweat drenched her forehead as she lay quietly resting in the parlor. Breyla, being the stubborn female she is, refused to rest, opting only to eat as she kept watch over her *little mouse*. The tiny female had endeared herself to the General in the short time we'd been with her.

367

I'm startled out of my thoughts by Breyla's soft question. "How is she, Aurelius?"

"She's fighting it. I can feel her body giving its all. But the poison is spreading. It's keeping the wound from healing, so thank the gods that cut wasn't deep."

"Let us pray that's enough," she sighs.

"Little demon," I start, trying to find the words to convey the reality of the situation to her.

"Don't," she commands. "I can't bear the thought of bringing two bodies home, Aurelius. My heart can't handle it."

I say nothing. I fight the urge to tell her that she has the strongest heart of anyone I know; that it will bear it because it must. That her heart is one of my favorite things about her, and that it breaks my own to know how much pain it has already endured. As much as she's already been hurt, she could be bitter and calloused, close her heart off. Yet, she still made room for one more. With Breyla, there always seemed to be room for more.

The soft thud, followed by the clamor of steel hitting stone, caught my attention as I turned the corner. I had come down to the training rooms to work out the tension in my shoulders. Gen and Raynor were helping me train with my Anima Gift, preparing me for a role in politics, but I was exhausted. The energy it took to hone this skill was far greater than anything it took to wield my Hemonia Gift. I had gained access to the ability to bend and control blood when I was very young and had spent years practicing. When this new Gift had manifested it had taken all of us by surprise. All of us being me, Gen, and Raynor. There were others with similar Anima Gifts at court, but none that I trusted. Raynor possessed one very rare Anima Gift, and he was helping me to learn mine.

I had not expected to find Breyla down here. More surprisingly, I hadn't expected to find her looking so distraught. She hadn't noticed my presence; something very unusual for her. The sound had come from her knees hitting the ground and her sword dropping. A breeze rolled in from the open door in front of us as she knelt there, just staring out into the distance.

"Princess," I started, carefull so as to not startle her. I had never seen her in a state like this, so I wasn't sure how she would respond.

She said nothing. "Princess, is something wrong?" I tried again, a little louder this time.

"He's gone," she whispered solemnly. Who is she referring to?

"Who's gone?" I asked, kneeling beside her. Her eyes were red and her hair disheveled. She's not crying now, but she might have been earlier. I had never witnessed Breyla cry over anything. During a challenge I had once sliced her hand so deep a healer had to be summoned, yet she hadn't shed a tear. She was livid and promised to return the favor. But she hadn't cried or whimpered in pain.

This side of Breyla was truly unsettling. She had sharp edges and even sharper words. Vulnerable and broken wasn't a look I had ever seen on her. I hated it. More than that, I hated that I cared at all.

"It doesn't matter. He wasn't who I thought he was," she mumbled.

It obviously mattered, but I was afraid to push her in this state. "Then he wasn't worth your time," I said anyway. Then it occurred to me that perhaps I didn't think any males were worth her time. That I didn't want any others to be worth her time. And that thought terrified me.

Nameah groans and blinks open her eyes. She sits up slowly, her movements sluggish. Her skin has taken on a gray hue, and her eyes are bloodshot. The symptoms suggest the poison is progressing faster; we don't have much time left.

"Time to go," I announce, knowing we've stayed longer than we should have.

I give Nameah my arm to help pull her to her feet, and we exit my family's estate right as the sun is rising.

Beautiful shades of pink and orange paint the sky in an ethereal morning glow. Nameah stares at it as I hoist her into the saddle and take my place behind her. I wrap a steadying arm around her, holding her gently to my chest. The rising sunlight catches the tears pooling in her sapphire blue eyes, making them shine.

"You know, I never was a morning person. I regret that now. I never realized this is what I was missing. It's breathtaking." Her voice is reverent and regretful all at once.

"Hold tight, little warrior," is all I can say as I kick Crea into a fierce pace, hoping and praying this isn't the last sunrise she'll see.

By the time we reach the castle gates, the sun is setting and Nameah is barely conscious. We halt only as long as it takes for Breyla to immediately yell at Samson to fetch Lady Ophelia. As we pull into the stables, I dismount Crea and pull Nameah with me, cradling her limp body in my arms.

I'm not even sure if she's conscious, but she's shivering, a fever ravaging her body. Ophelia appears in the stable as I lay Nameah on a fresh pile of hay.

"I don't have time to explain, I just need you to trust me. She was cut with a poisoned blade, and I need you to heal her, Ophelia. Please." Breyla's voice quivers as she pleads with her lady to save this stranger's life.

Without a second thought, Ophelia drops to her knees on the other side of Nameah. She grasps her limp hand between her own and closes her eyes. I swear I see a light glow coming from her hands as she pushes her magic into Nameah's body. I blink, and the light is gone. Ophelia remains quiet for several more minutes until a loud groan comes from the little warrior's lips.

It's not one of relief, though. She's in pain. Nameah's body begins thrashing as her cries grow louder. I catch tears running down Breyla's cheeks as she shushes Nameah.

"Hold on, little mouse. Ophelia is trying to help you," she whispers as she brushes sweat-drenched locks out of her face.

"I-I'm sorry, Breyla. My magic..." Her voice trails off. "It's not working. I don't know what this is, but I can't fix it."

I see tears well in the raven-haired female's eyes as she delivers the news I've been trying to convey to Breyla for the past day. There is no saving Nameah. Whatever this poison is, we don't have the power to cure it.

"No," Breyla wails. "No, it can't be. There has to be something we can do!"

Nameah's tortured moans grow louder as she cries, "Please, make it stop!"

"There's one thing..." Ophelia whispers. "Send for my brother."

I find the nearest servant to the stables and instruct them to bring Lord Layne at once. He arrives a few minutes later, and a look of anguish crosses his face.

As an empath, he's probably feeling every emotion rolling off the dying girl and the three of us surrounding her. I can only imagine how overwhelming it feels.

"Layne, she's dying. There's nothing that can be done to stop it, but can you please lessen her suffering?" Ophelia looks at her brother with pleading eyes.

He nods and drops to his knees, taking the side opposite Ophelia. Breyla has Nameah's head in her lap as she gently plays with her chestnut locks.

"What's your name, beautiful?" Layne smiles sadly at her.

"Nameah," she groans.

"Okay, Nameah. I'm going to make the pain stop. It's going to be alright."

He places his hands on each side of her face, cradling it gently. "Shhhh, beautiful," he hums.

Slowly, her body stops trembling and her cries diminish. Her breathing evens out, and she opens her eyes. Beautiful sapphire eyes stare back at us, free of pain for the first time since she was injured.

"Brave little mouse, I am so proud of you," Breyla praises, her fingers still twisting through Nameah's hair.

"Thank you," she croaks as she holds Layne's gaze.

"You don't need to thank me," he grimaces. "No one should feel that kind of pain in their last moments."

"How long do I have left?" A stray tear rolls down her cheek.

"Not long," I say softly. "The poison is nearly at your heart, so you may only have a few minutes remaining."

"Then I'd like to see the sunset one last time, please."

"As you wish," I reply, scoping her into my arms once more. I look to Layne before lifting her. "Can you maintain your hold on her without touching her face?"

"I can hold her hand and that will be enough." He takes her left hand from Ophelia and stands with me as I lift Nameah.

We walk out of the stables and into the empty courtyard. The sun has moved past setting and has begun its evening gloaming hour. How fitting she should get to see both on her last day. As the sun makes its final descent, brilliant shades of pink, blue, and orange dance across the sky. Purple and black start to creep in slowly.

"I think I like this one the best," Nameah whispers.

"Any final requests, little warrior?"

"I think I'd like to go out on my own terms. Does your power allow you to stop my heart?" Her question surprises me, but I nod.

"It does."

"Will it hurt?"

"No, it'll feel like falling asleep."

"Then I think I'd like that, please."

"Are you ready now?" The poison is nearly at her heart, but I want this last choice to be hers.

"Yes," she sighs.

I let my Hemonia Gift creep under her skin and wind its way through her veins. I will her heart to slow its beating until finally it stops altogether. Those dazzling blues drift closed for the last time as she takes her final breath in my arms.

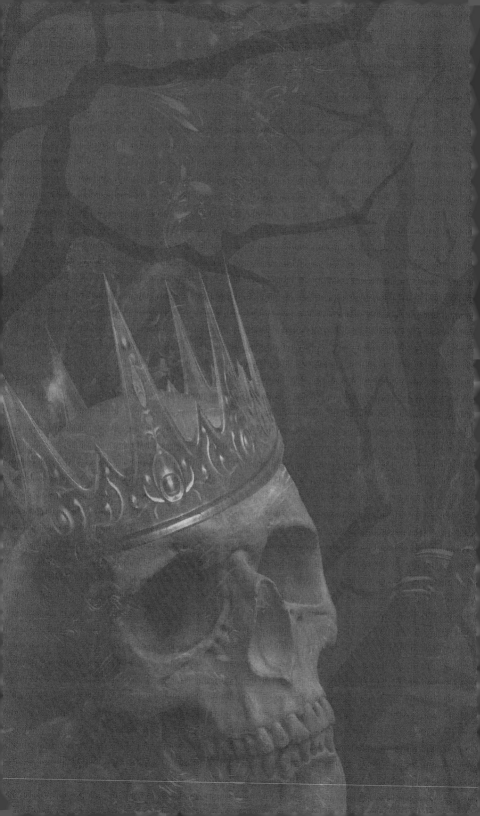

CHAPTER THIRTY-FIVE

BREYLA

Clouds hang low in the sky, the air thick with the humidity of a coming storm. In this late summer heat, it makes everything feel sticky. The sun has yet to make its appearance, and I beg the gods to hold their tears until after we're done. This time, the weather mirrors how I feel inside about what we have to do today.

I find myself once again dressed in all-black full armor, sword strapped to my side, surrounded by the warriors that follow me. It was barely weeks ago that we stood in front of Nolan's funeral pyre, but this time there are two.

It wasn't even a question that Nameah would be given the honor of a warrior's last rites. I mourn the young female and all the things she'll never experience. I had delayed the funeral long enough for her family to arrive. They deserved to say a proper goodbye.

Her mother, two older brothers, and younger sister stand beside me, all dressed in black. Their features vary, but they all share those dazzling blue eyes. Every one of them shows the signs of exhaustion and going too long on an empty belly. I've insisted they stay in the palace tonight and for as long as they wish before returning home. They don't know it yet, but I've also arranged for a healthy stipend to take care of them moving forward and will offer both her brothers a place in the army should they desire it.

To my left is Jade, followed by Elijah, Ophelia, and Layne. My mother and Aurelius stand behind me. Further down the way is Prince Ayden.

The prince sends his regards. Fury churns in my gut as I think of the assassin's last words to me. I've repeatedly played the scenario in my head, and that's the only conclusion I can draw. Ayden is responsible for Julian's death and our subsequent attack. We were not far from the Rimor-Prudia border; close enough his warriors could have snuck in unseen and attacked.

To what end? I cannot say; I haven't worked it out yet. There's a lot about the prince I haven't been able to work out, and it's driving me crazy.

Fighting the urge to make a scene by confronting him, I turn my attention back to the pyres before me.

I clear my throat, waiting for the crowd to silence. "Today we honor two fallen warriors. Both courageous beyond measure, gifted beyond compare, loyal to a fault, and loved beyond words. I was blessed to fight alongside both, and I owe them each my life. I can never truly repay those debts but will spend my life trying." My voice begins to crack, and I take a moment to compose myself.

"Julian Tanda, my warrior, my second, my friend. You lived like you fought—fiercely. There is no word that encompasses how much you will be missed. From your first breath until your very last, may the gods grant you peace." The crowd echoes my words back.

"Nameah Galvin. My brave little mouse. Though our time together was short, it is clear that you were fearless, loyal, brave beyond compare, and possessed a fire in your veins. Your light shines the brightest, and I will remember you always. You made me proud, and I wish I had a hundred more with a spirit like yours. From your first breath until your very last, may the gods grant you peace."

As my words are echoed back, a heartbroken wail erupts from Nameah's mother. The sound is something I will never forget.

My mother's flames begin the process of lighting the torches carried by the guards surrounding the pyres. As the wood begins to catch, ribbons of red and gold climbing their way up to the top, I hear Jade's smooth alto voice start the ancient song, the voice of Nameah's mother joining her just a moment later.

May the mother keep you close
And the father protect you now
The tears that once were shed
Make the flowers grow
When the night is darkest
And the sun has ceased its shining
May you remember
My love for you is eternal
From your first breath
Until your very last
May the gods grant you peace

Thunder roars in the distance, alerting us to the impending storm, and I watch my mother send her air magic to feed the flames more oxygen. There's nothing quite like only getting halfway through a funeral and having to wait for the wood to dry out so you can burn the bodies again.

The flames burn brighter, consuming the wood and bodies at an increased rate. Jade steps closer to Julian's pyre, tears streaking down her tawny cheeks and glistening her hazel eyes.

Closer and closer she creeps, her hand stretching out like she's reaching for her twin. When she's as close as she can bear, I watch her drop to her knees and sob. She sinks lower, her entire frame dropping with the weight of her grief. I can see it like a physical thing sitting on her shoulders.

Elijah drops to his knees beside Jade and wraps his arm around her back, letting her bear her weight on him as violent trembles wrack her body. She slumps against him, burying her head against his broad chest. He doesn't bother trying to hide his tears. Elijah has never tried to hide, justify, or apologize for any part of himself. He owns his emotions and wears them for everyone to see. And right now, I see despair painted across his face.

I follow them to the ground next, my knees hitting the hard dirt as I lace my fingers through Jade's. It goes against everything ingrained in me by my father and Nolan to openly show my emotions in front of my soldiers. *Never let them see you break.* I can hear it in my father's voice even now. But pretending I'm unaffected by the death of one of my closest friends? That does his twin no good; it only hurts her. Pretending Nameah's death doesn't mean anything to me? That dishonors her memory and disrespects her family.

Having emotions doesn't make me weak, but pretending I don't makes me cruel. So, I do what feels right, and I let the dam break. Hot, salty crystals pour down my face as I remember the male Julian was, and I mourn the fierce warrior Nameah never got the chance to be.

Just as the last of them has turned to ash, I feel the first drops of rain. The skies open up, drenching us in a matter of minutes. It's a warm summer rain, and I embrace the feeling of it on my skin. The rest of the attendees have cleared out when I feel Aurelius pull me to my feet.

"Come on, Princess. Let's get your dried off so you can continue the warrior's celebration with the rest of them."

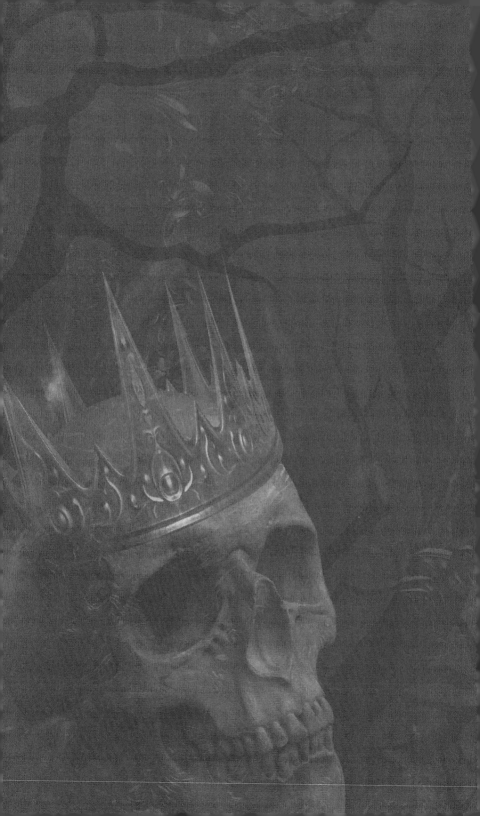

CHAPTER THIRTY-SIX

BREYLA

"So, what did you find, General?" Elijah asks.

It's been three days since we burned Julian and Nameah. Now, I'm surrounded by Elijah, Ophelia, Aurelius, and Jade. I'm not sure Jade's ready to hear this, but she insisted on being here. She watches me intently but remains quiet.

We're seated in one of the training rooms below the armory. It's not the same room Aurelius took me to and forced me to confront my emotions in all those weeks ago, but it's nearly identical. I didn't want to have this conversation anywhere we could be overheard, and I had my doubts on how secure even this space was. They were supposed to be spelled to be soundproof, but there were several people in this castle who knew more than they should already.

"It wasn't pretty," I sigh. "Are you sure you're okay with hearing this conversation?" I direct my gaze to Jade.

"I need to hear this. I can't continue not knowing what happened to my twin." Her voice is weak from disuse.

"Aurelius and I weren't having much success tracking down Julian's last known whereabouts. We had a vague idea, but he covered his tracks a little too well. Then we noticed we were being followed." I smile slightly at the memory of discovering Nameah on our tracks.

"By Nameah?" Elijah guesses.

"Yeah. Spunky little thing, that one. Anyway, she was able to lead us to his body. It was left not far from her home."

"Why did they just leave it there?" Jade asks.

"I asked the same thing, but it turns out they had no choice. They had tried to move it; her whole family had given it a try, but there was some sort of force field surrounding his body that wouldn't allow them to touch it."

Confused gazes meet mine but I continue. "When we found his body..." My voice trails off, and I fight the urge to look at Jade. Despite what she says, she doesn't need to hear this.

"Stop treating me like a child, Breyla, and just fucking say it." Jade's words are laced with venom.

"I'm not treating you like a child; I'm protecting you! What I saw will *never* leave my mind. I don't want you to bear that same burden."

"How about you let me decide what burdens I bear? Tell me, or I'll force it out of you."

My eyes flare at her threat to use her Gift of coercion on me. It's something she's never done and promised she never would. Aurelius and Elijah both stiffen. I assume Elijah's having the same reaction I am, but I look to Aurelius. He nods, as if to convey he can sense she's serious in her threat.

"We found his body hanging on a wooden cross. There were nails driven through his wrists to hold it there. The smell was so putrid I vomited as soon as I was within twenty feet of it. The barrier that kept all others from touching it didn't protect him from the elements or animals. It had been picked apart, but at least it didn't appear that he was tortured before his death. Small blessings, I suppose. Is that what you wanted to hear?" I nearly spit the last words, frustrated that she would force me into telling her that.

Jade just grunts in response and waits for me to finish.

"So how were you able to get him home?" Ophelia asks.

"And that's where it gets ominous. Someone *knew*, without a shadow of a doubt, that it would be Aurelius and I to find him. We could both touch him, but it burned us to break the barrier holding him there. It was like the magic was keyed into us specifically."

"Hurt like a bitch, too," Aurelius adds, and I nod in agreement, remembering the burning sensation lighting up my nerve endings.

"As soon as we broke the barrier a note appeared pinned to Julian's chest, then we were attacked." I finish the story, telling them every detail of the attack and the strange males behind it. I spare nothing, hoping someone picks up on something I may have missed.

"The Crimson Prince and Queen of Shadows will fall?" Elijah repeats the ominous note's wording back to me. "I can't be the only one thinking it, right?"

"That it sounds an awful lot like Aurelius and Breyla," Ophelia pipes in.

"The thought had crossed my mind," I admit. "But I'm not Queen, and Aurelius never had, nor ever would have the title of Prince. Even when he marries my mother, he'd assume the title of King. It doesn't quite add up."

"You're leaving out the best part, Princess," Aurelius says with a pointed look.

"I wouldn't call it 'the best'," I mock.

"The strange warriors' parting words, 'The prince sends his regards'."

"Well, that's not ominous at all," Elijah mumbles.

"It's Ayden," Jade says bluntly.

"That's the first place my mind went as well," I agree. "We were close to his border, and we know Ayden has held a grudge for years since King Raynor killed his father in battle, so he has a motive."

"I don't know," Ophelia adds, voicing her doubt.

For how vehemently against bringing Ayden to the castle he was, Aurelius has remained suspiciously quiet on the matter.

"And you, Aurelius? What do you think?" I push him to share his thoughts.

"I think it was a coincidental circumstance at best. While I don't trust Prince Ayden, I don't think he's the prince they were referring to." More cryptic answers. Why did I let this male fuck me, again?

I hear Elijah stifle a laugh as I stare down the frustrating male. "What other prince could it be?"

He just shrugs. "There are other kingdoms around us, Princess."

"Well aware, Aurelius, but you can't tell me you think Lennox is more inclined to attack than Prudia. That makes no sense." I cross my arms and roll my eyes, which has Aurelius's temper flaring from the looks of his clenched jaw.

"I didn't suggest that. I just said there were more kingdoms."

I clench my fist, resisting the urge to punch him. "Could you be more vague right now?"

"If you'd like—" he starts but is cut off by Jade.

"Enough. You two are acting like petulant children, and it's getting us nowhere. If we're done here, I'm going to find a bottle of red to have for dinner." She rolls her eyes and saunters toward the door.

"Don't you mean *with* dinner?" Elijah asks.

"I said what I said," she replies without looking back.

As she exits the training room, Elijah moves to follow her. "I better make sure she finds something else to consume for dinner."

Ophelia looks around the room, avoiding eye contact. "I think Layne wanted my help with something," she mumbles and finds anywhere to be but trapped in a room with Aurelius and me.

The door clicks shut as Ophelia leaves, and I hear the lock turn.

"Are you trying to be difficult?" I shriek at him.

"No, I excel at it naturally."

Before I can blink, he has me pinned, my face turned and pressed against the cool stone of the training room wall. I try to catch my breath as he laces his fingers through my hair and pulls, holding me in place. His other hand is trailing down my lower back to my ass.

"What the fuck are you doing?" I snarl through clenched teeth.

"Following through on my word," he says as he hooks his fingers into the waistband of my pants and yanks them down. He pulls them just far enough that my ass is bare to him.

"What are you talking about?" I try to squirm away, but he has such a tight grip on my hair that I can't move.

"I told you the next time you rolled your eyes at me, you would find out what the end of my patience looks like."

Oh fuck, I think to myself. I had rolled my eyes at him, but I had completely forgotten his threat.

"You're infuriating," I seethe.

"Likewise" is all he says before I feel his hand come down on my bare ass. I hiss at the slight sting from his palm, but a new sensation takes over with his next slap.

A warm tingling starts low in my belly and moves to my pussy as he spanks me a third time, and I let out a soft moan.

He chuckles low in my ear, "I should have known you'd like that, little demon."

"Fuck you," I hiss, fighting the urge to rub myself against him.

Slap. His hand comes down on my bare ass again, and I bite my lip to keep from moaning. I refuse to give in to him.

"That won't do," he tsks before ripping my pants the rest of the way down.

"Fuck. You," I grunt.

"You said that already." I can't fully see his face, but I can see the hint of a smirk from the corner of my eye. "Tell me, Princess, will I find you wet for me?"

His fingers run up my inner thigh, stopping just short of my pussy. He lightly traces his fingers along my bare ass cheek and chuckles, then shoves my legs further apart using his own foot. I'm spread wide for him, the air hitting my heated sex as I squirm in his grip.

"Answer me," he demands when I continue to say nothing.

"No," I grit out.

"*Liar,*" he whispers in my ear right before he plunges two fingers into my dripping pussy. He pumps them in and out slowly, eliciting an involuntary moan from my lips.

"Does the end of my patience turn you on, little demon?" he purrs as he continues pumping in and out of me. I roll my hips in time with his hands, chasing the pleasure only he can provide.

He bites down on my earlobe, growling, "Answer me." His fingers leave my heat, but before I can miss them, he lands a light slap right on my clit.

"Yes," I gasp out at the sudden wave of pleasure his punishment provides.

"Good girl," is all I hear him say before I hear him pull his pants down.

"You're not going to fuck me, Aurelius," I bite out, still furious that he's punishing me when he was the one being intentionally difficult. Still furious that I *like* his brand of punishment.

"Still lying, Princess?" He lines the head of his cock up with my entrance. "Didn't your parents teach you not to lie?" he continues as he slams into me in the next breath, burying himself to the hilt in one thrust.

We let out a collective sigh at the feeling of our joining. He trails kisses down the side of my neck as I catch my breath and adjust to him. After a few moments, I rock my hips back into him, attempting to relieve the ache in me.

"If you're going to angry fuck me, then you better make it hard, My Lord."

My words set him ablaze as he pulls out and slams back into me, thrusting in and out over and over at a relentless pace. His hand finally leaves my hair as both find their way to my hips, using his hold to fuck me harder.

I moan with each thrust and the building orgasm.

Aurelius continues peppering kisses and bites along my neck and shoulders as his thrusts increase in pace. He has me gasping, sucking to bring in air through the overwhelming pleasure he's forcing through my body. I'm lost in the pleasure as he purrs in my ear, "Be a good girl and touch yourself for me."

I'm beyond any ability to deny his commands, so I drag my fingers down to my clit and rub in long slow circles. The building pleasure in my low belly turns into a raging inferno as I hover on the precipice of bliss.

"I can feel your tight little pussy clenching down on my cock. So fucking tight, Princess." He groans as his cock continues slamming into me, hitting that delicious spot deep inside me.

My fingers increase their pace as I chase my orgasm. Within moments I shatter, falling over the edge and shuddering through my release. I scream my pleasure for the infuriating male behind me.

"Fuck yes, little demon," Aurelius grunts as his own release finds him. His hot cum fills me as his dick pulses inside me.

He stays buried in me for several more minutes as our breathing returns to normal. Finally, he slips his softening dick out of me, and the warm liquid runs down my inner thighs.

I can't help the moan that slips out as I feel his fingers slip back into my oversensitive pussy.

"What are you doing?" I whimper.

"Just making sure my seed stays where it belongs," he whispers.

"You're incorrigible," I half-heartedly complain.

He just shrugs and pulls his fingers out, then pulls my pants back into place. Flipping me around to fully face him, he commands me, "Open."

I cock a brow at him but do as he requests, opening my mouth for him. He feeds me the fingers that were just buried deep inside me and are covered in his cum.

"Now suck," he says, grinning at me.

I close my lips around his fingers and suck, savoring the mix of his salty release and my own tangy arousal. My tongue wraps around each digit, cleaning them thoroughly before he's satisfied.

He takes my face between his thumb and forefinger. "Good girl," he praises, leaving me with one last punishing kiss.

As he opens the training room door, I storm after him. "We aren't done with this conversation, Aurelius."

"We are for now. I have places to be, Princess." His lips quirk up on one side, clearly entertained with my lingering frustration toward him, then disappears down the hallway.

It's sometime after midnight as I lay in bed, wide awake and staring at the ceiling. Aurelius lays beside me, sleeping soundly, an arm draped over my stomach. I've been tossing and turning for hours, unsure what is keeping me awake.

Maybe it's restless energy, maybe it's the images of my friend's decapitated and crucified body that won't leave my head, or the fact that every time I close my eyes, I'm reliving Nameah's last moments as she dies in Aurelius's arms. Maybe it's all of it.

I slide out of bed, leaving Aurelius sleeping peacefully, and silently pad across my room to the door. The door clicks shut softly, and I drift down the hall in search of something to drink.

When I reach the kitchens I find I'm not the only one who can't find sleep.

"Prince Ayden, I didn't expect to find you here." I give him a questioning look as I take in his sleep-mussed state. He's dressed in loose-fitting linen pants and a black silk robe that hangs open, leaving his chest bare. The deep brown waves that grow longer on the top are tousled and messy, like he's been running his fingers through them.

"That makes two of us, Princess. What brings you to the kitchens at this hour?" he asks as he pulls out a second mug and sets it on the counter in front of him.

"Tea, of course." I round the counter and stand next to him as he prepares tea for the both of us.

He smiles softly. "Then you're in luck."

It's too easy for me to forget I don't trust this male, that I suspect he has something to do with my friend's death, when he's so charming. The mask he normally wears has been dropped; this is the real Ayden I've glimpsed a few times. I see so many sides, I never know which one to expect.

He stirs in a healthy amount of honey and raises the mug to his lips. I reach for mine but hesitate.

"How do I know this isn't poisoned?" I ask, staring at him.

He sighs, "Poison isn't really my style, love." He takes the mug from my hand, takes a sip, and then hands me his own in exchange.

"There. Now if it's poisoned, we'll both die."

"So dramatic," I tease and sip the tea. The warm liquid runs down my throat and makes my taste buds dance.

Our conversation is interrupted by the screams of a nearby resident. Both our heads snap toward the sound and we are headed for the door, our tea forgotten.

It doesn't take long for us to locate the source of the screams. We reach Jade's room and see Elijah already standing outside, his hand on the knob, preparing to enter.

He pushes open the door and the three of us enter together, our senses on high alert and looking for the danger. Her room is empty aside from her, though. She's asleep but screaming and crying out.

"I think it's a dream," Elijah whispers.

"It's not just a dream; it's a night terror. She's been through quite an ordeal. I'm not surprised she's having them," Ayden says.

"How do you know that?" Elijah questions.

"Dream weaver, remember?"

"More like dream *manipulator*," I mumble.

"Only for you, darling," Ayden chuckles.

Ignoring his comment, I ask, "How can we help her?"

"*You* can't," he replies. "But I can." He moves toward her bed on silent feet.

I reach out and grasp his wrist. "Wait," I whisper-yell. "How do I know you won't mess around in her dreams and make it worse?"

He glares at me. "You really don't trust me, do you, Princess?"

"I don't have a lot of reason to trust you," I quip back.

"You don't have a lot of reason not to trust me, either," he says, his eyes softening. "I would never intentionally make someone hurt worse than she already is. Trust me when I say, there's not much worse I could do than what she's already seeing in those terrors."

Right then, Jade screams and cries again in her sleep.

"Can you see what she's seeing?" I ask.

"Yes," he replies softly, his voice laced with melancholy.

"Okay," I nod at him, "I trust you to help her."

I release his wrist and let him cross the room to her bed. Kneeling beside her head, he takes her head between his hands and lets his magic work.

I can't see any physical manifestation of his power, but Jade's body immediately ceases its thrashing and her screams quiet. She stills and falls into a peaceful slumber.

The door clicks shut behind us, and we breathe a collective sigh of relief.

"How long will your magic hold?" I ask him.

"Only for the night," he replies solemnly.

Silence blankets us as we find our way back to our forgotten tea, and I'm filled with conflicting emotions for the Prince of Prudia.

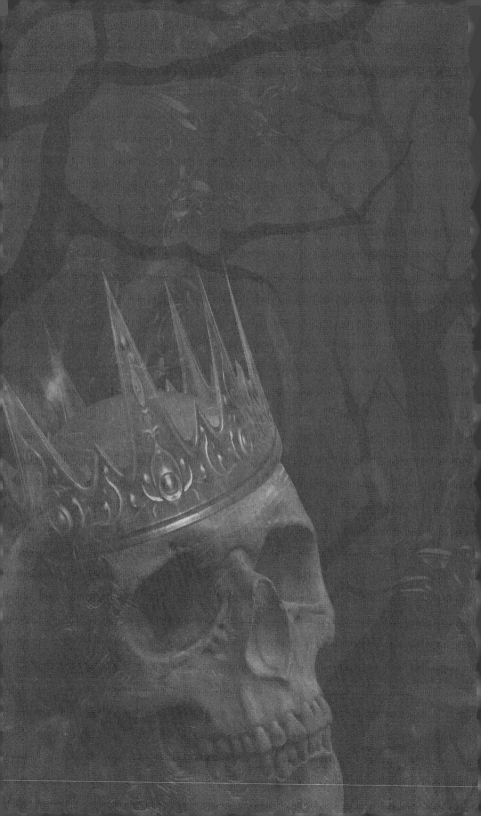

CHAPTER THIRTY-SEVEN

BREYLA

"What are we doing?" I whisper to Elijah, who is currently leaning on the door to my mother's chambers.

He startles, jumping back from the door. "Shit, Brey. Warn a guy when you're sneaking up on him."

"What fun would that be?" I scrunch my nose and grin.

"What kind of fun are we having?" Aurelius asks as he rounds the corner.

"Will you two be quiet?" Elijah whisper-yells, leveling a glare at us. He leans into the Queen's door again, trying to hear the conversation.

Suddenly, he jerks back and ushers me and Aurelius down the hall and around the corner. Just as we are out of sight, the queen's door slams shut, and the muttered curses of Lord Seamus can be heard moving in the opposite direction from our hiding place.

After a few more seconds, Elijah turns to Aurelius and me. I wave my hand to say, 'Go on, tell us.'

"The Queen summoned me to her chambers, but when I got here, it was obvious someone was already there."

"She summoned us as well."

"I overheard a conversation between her and Lord Seamus. It seemed...tense."

"What was said?" Aurelius inquires.

"I didn't catch all of it, but it might be easier to show you." He beckons us closer, lifting a hand to each of our temples to replay the memory into each of our minds.

"Your Majesty, you cannot expect the council to continue supporting your rule when you refuse to set a date for your wedding to Lord Aurelius," the slimy voice of Lord Seamus sneered. He sounded angry.

I wasn't purposely eavesdropping, but it would be rude to interrupt such a juicy conversation. Eager to hear the Queen's response, I maintained my position outside her chamber doors. The queen had summoned me to her chambers but didn't provide a reason. I didn't anticipate walking in on such a tense conversation.

"I expect you to remember your place, Lord Seamus. I demand for you and the rest of the council to respect your queen and the timeline in which she remarries." The Queen's voice was muffled, but clear enough I could hear the venom in her tone.

"Admit this engagement to Lord Aurelius is a sham; a lie meant to appease the council but lacking intention to follow through." Lord Seamus's words were bold, bolder than I've ever heard anyone except Breyla use with her.

I felt the queen's icy powers drift through the door at the same time as Lord Seamus's pain-filled hiss could be heard.

My brow furrows as the memory finishes, and I look to Aurelius.

"Did any of that make sense to you?" I ask, my voice wavering.

He shakes his head, a frustrated look on his face. "It's

nothing she's brought up to me." His jaw clenches, and a look of hurt briefly flickers in his eyes before he casts them downward.

"Well, since she called us all here, maybe we're about to find out what that was about," I muse, but I'm not entirely sure.

"Well, let's find out," Elijah suggests as he moves back down the hall to my mother's chambers.

His knuckles wrap on the queen's door a second before it flies open, like she was waiting for us. The queen's normally bright-blue eyes are dull, dark circles framing her blonde lashes.

"Come in," she says sternly, ushering us in.

Once we're inside, she uses her magic to lock the door and immediately throws up a silencing shield.

"So, what's this meeting all about?" I start.

"I wanted to discuss what you and Aurelius discovered on your journey to recover Julian's body," Queen Genevieve explains. I just don't think it's a conversation the whole council needs to be a part of."

"Because you don't trust them?" I guess.

"Not all of them," she admits.

"Lord Seamus?" I push.

"I haven't trusted Lord Seamus in years, but he's become even harder to trust since your father's death."

"Do you think he had anything to do with Raynor's death?" Aurelius asks.

"Why would you ask that? There was nothing to suggest foul play with his death; just an unfortunate, much-too-early passing." Her voice is hard as she answers. This is a sore topic for her.

"You didn't answer Aurelius's question, Mother." I narrow my gaze at her .

"No, I don't think so. Now drop it." Her tone brokers no room for argument. I resist the urge to roll my eyes. She's not saying something, but now isn't the time to push.

We all take a seat in the chairs occupying the queen's receiving area. "Now tell me everything," she commands.

I spend the next ten minutes relaying the same information I had shared in the training room two nights before. The entire time my mother stays silent, ingesting the details and considering them all before she speaks.

"How interesting," she finally says. "I've never encountered magic or a shield like you described."

"You don't think it could be one of our own?" Elijah asks, voice full of uncertainty.

"No, I think we would have heard of someone with abilities like that before now. You can't hide that kind of power for long. They must have come from one of the neighboring kingdoms, but..." She trails off, deep in thought.

"But what?" Aurelius pushes.

"It doesn't mean they aren't working with someone within the kingdom. There's too much coincidence for me to believe it was happenstance. They had to have knowledge that would be impossible to know without an inside source."

Anxiety churns in my gut at the implications. There was likely someone in the castle that we couldn't trust.

"Any guesses who?" Elijah asks.

Mother contemplates for a moment, before sighing. "It's hard to say for sure. Only because there are several I don't trust lurking in these halls."

I grunt in agreement, but Aurelius asks, "Could it be Lord Seamus?"

"You really don't like him, do you?"

Aurelius snorts. "Does anyone?"

Mother chuckles. "No, I don't think so. But that brings me to another point. I may have found a way to end our engagement."

A feeling sparks in my chest that I don't want to acknowledge and will have to inspect later.

"Oh?" Aurelius asks, his voice full of intrigue.

"Lord Seamus is convinced our engagement is a ruse." She laughs, but it lacks real humor. "He has offered himself as an alternative."

"That snake," Aurelius hisses.

"What do you care? You're fucking my daughter, and it would leave you free to do so openly," she scoffs.

"I care because you're still my best friend, Gen, and he's a shit male," Aurelius snaps back. "You'd be in a loveless, miserable match. He's got ulterior motives."

"Of course he's got ulterior motives," Mother says, rolling her eyes. "*Anyone* who offers themselves for the job would have ulterior motives. That's why I approached you first. I knew you wouldn't be like them." Her voice softens as she finishes her explanation.

Elijah's bewildered gaze finds mine, a question in his eyes. I shoot him a look that says, '*I'll tell you later*'.

"I'm sorry, Gen," Aurelius says, his voice apologetic. "You know I'd do anything to help or protect you. I just..."

"Fell in love with my daughter?" she offers softly. I stiffen at my mother's bold words. We hadn't named this thing between us, but apparently she had.

Aurelius reaches for my mother and wraps her in his arms. She returns his embrace as he mumbles, "Something like that."

Unsure of how to respond to the scene before me, I clear my throat and ask, "You're not seriously considering his proposal, are you?"

"What other option do we have?"

Aurelius pulls back from Genevieve and gives her an incredulous look. "You just said you don't trust him! Tell me you're kidding. You deserve so much better."

"Aurelius, I wouldn't really trust anyone offering themselves for the job at this point." Her face falls at the admission. "I don't know that I really do deserve better," she whispers. Seeing her so vulnerable and defeated is new, and I don't like it.

"Of course you deserve better!" Aurelius bellows.

A tear forms at the corner of her eye, and I watch as it runs down the porcelain skin of her cheek. "The decisions I've had to make..." she says, her voice trailing off. She catches herself, clears her throat, and sits up straighter. "Regardless, I will accept Lord Seamus' proposal. I don't have to love him; he will be a king in name only. I'll be damned if he thinks he can take control of my kingdom."

There she is, my fierce mother.

"Mom, there's something else I need to ask you about." My voice is hesitant, not wanting to talk about this.

"What is it, dear?"

"I need to know how Father was behaving before his death."

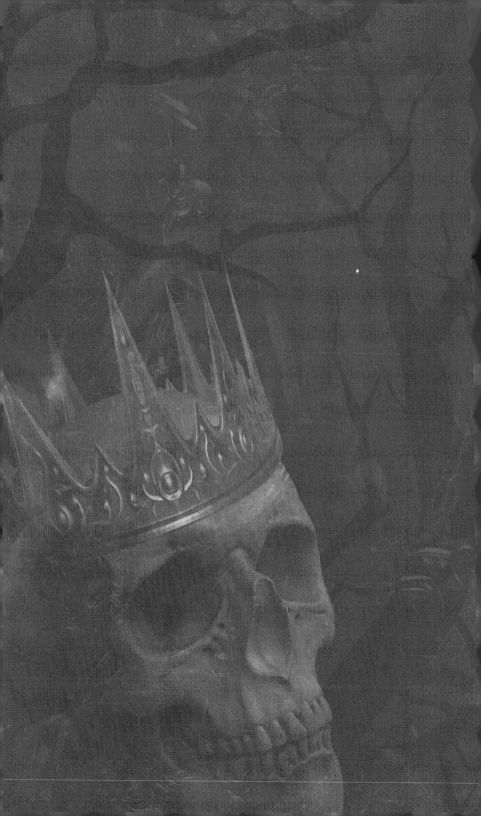

CHAPTER THIRTY-EIGHT

OPHELIA

It's nearly empty when we enter Luella's tavern late into the evening. Breyla wanted to discuss the next steps, but no longer felt safe to do so in the castle. I'm not sure how a public tavern is any more secure, but here we are.

We take the furthest booth in the back corner, Aurelius, Elijah, Breyla, Jade, and I piling around the table. Luella drops off each of our preferred drinks, and Breyla slips her a few gold Remis to keep the other patrons seated far away from our dark corner. Breyla throws up a silencing shield, but it wouldn't be impossible to read our lips if someone were close enough. Thus, the bribe to Luella.

Breyla relays the information from our conversation earlier today with Queen Genevieve to catch me and Jade up to speed.

"I don't like this," Jade comments. "I feel like we have more questions now than before."

"I agree," I say. Elijah is seated next to me, his thigh pressed against mine. His rich cinnamon and chocolate scent fills my nose, overwhelming my senses. Under the table, he rests his hand on my leg, lightly caressing my knee.

A slight flush creeps up my cheeks, and I see Elijah smirk next to me. My mind wanders to all the ways he has and could make me blush.

"—do we feel about Ayden?" Jade questions and I realize I've lost track of the conversation in my daydreaming.

Luckily, Breyla saves me and pipes in with, "As much as I hate to admit it, I don't think Ayden is behind the attacks. Not that I trust him, necessarily."

"What did I miss? Why are you suddenly doubting Ayden when you were yelling at me for doing just that days ago?" Aurelius asks.

Breyla sighs. "I forgot to mention that. I still don't trust that he isn't up to *something,* but Ayden doesn't seem that malicious. There was something he did later that same night that showed another side to him."

Aurelius drums his fingers along the tabletop and takes a generous drink of his ale. "What did he do that made you suddenly so fond of him?" he asks, tone even, but I can sense the underlying anger in his words.

"I couldn't sleep, so I went to the kitchens for tea. When I arrived, he was there as well. There was a blood-curdling scream coming from Jade's room."

Jade stiffens, looking confused. "I don't remember—"

"You were having a night terror. I heard it, too," Elijah answers before she can ask the question.

"Right. When we got to her room, he didn't hesitate to make it...stop. You were thrashing and crying and couldn't be woken, Jade." Breyla's eyes look apologetic, and Jade says nothing.

"When I asked him why I should trust him not to make it worse, he told me he would never intentionally make someone hurt worse than Jade already was. That there wasn't much worse he could do than what she was already seeing in the nightmare."

"So, what? One good deed done, and you suddenly trust him?" Aurelius says, his tone accusatory.

Breyla bristles beside me and growls, "I just said I don't trust him. I simply think there's more to him than meets the eye. He's up to something, I just don't think that something is assassination attempts and murder."

Jade takes that opportunity to point out, "You were literally the one who argued that Ayden wasn't behind it when we talked two days ago, Aurelius."

"He still believes that; he's just being insecure about me possibly trusting the prince," Breyla clarifies.

"Why would Prince Ayden make him feel insecure?" I ask mischievously.

"I'm not insecu—" Aurelius starts while Breyla says, "Because we're fucking, and he's possessive."

I lock eyes with Jade across the table and blurt out, "Ha! I told you so. Pay up!"

Jade slaps a coin purse into my open palm and huffs.

"Wait, did you two have a bet going on if we were together or not?" Breyla asks.

"Maybe we did, maybe we already suspected and had a bet on who would be the first to admit it."

"Why didn't you let me in on this bet?" Elijah asks, offended.

"As if you didn't already pry that secret out of Breyla," Jade replies, shaking her head at him.

He smiles wickedly. "True. She lost a bet to me and had to give the memory over."

"Gross," Jade shudders.

Elijah raises his ale to his lips before muttering, "It was really hot. Our Aurelius here is hung like—" His description of Aurelius's male parts is muffled by his drink being dumped on his face thanks to Breyla's shadows tipping the mug.

He wipes the ale off, and I catch Breyla staring daggers at

him, her cheeks flaming. Aurelius is trying to hide a smile, pure male ego sparkling in his dark eyes.

"Temper, Princess," he tsks and pulls her closer to him, laying a kiss on her cheek.

"He deserved it," she mutters, relaxing into his hold. "Why do you always have to dampen my anger?"

"I don't, but you're incredibly easy to get worked up, and that won't help us right now. You can be mad at me later," he says with a suggestive wink.

She groans and throws her head back. "Anyway...what are our next steps?"

"I'll see what I can find out about my father's intentions and whereabouts over the last several months," I offer, chewing my bottom lip. Elijah's eyes are locked on it, a heated look in his eyes, and I find myself wishing to be alone with him. "Good, but if it comes down to your safety or answers, you will choose your safety, Ophelia. Am I understood?" Breyla's face is deadly serious.

I nod in understanding.

"Elijah, were you able to learn anything else about the servant we found in the river?"

"While you were gone, I was finally able to track down who she was. Her name was Delilah Howard. She had spent most of her time in the kitchen but had been recently reassigned to serve Lord Seamus Delencourt." My leg bounces nervously under the table at how that sounds.

Breyla chokes on the ale she was drinking, the droplets spraying out of her mouth. "I can't be the only one that thinks that's more than a little suspicious." She turns to me and asks, "Do you know anything about this?" Her tone isn't accusatory, but my eyes widen at being put on the spot.

"No, I swear I've never heard of her before. My father rarely shares details with me about anything," I say quickly, nearly tripping over my words.

"Calm down, Ophelia," Breyla says softly, trying to assuage my nerves. "No one is accusing you of anything. I was just curious if you had seen her around your father before. You will always be safe with me, regardless of your father's actions."

My shoulders slump and I let out a sigh of relief. "No, I hadn't ever seen her around my father, but I can see if there's anything in his records that mentions her."

"Thank you," Breyla says, turning her attention back to me. "Is there anything else?"

"The last bit is just servant's gossip, but you know how that is. It usually holds some truth. Word is her family was recently gifted a large sum of money from an unknown benefactor."

Breyla nods, taking a sip of her drink. "I think it's past time we paid her family a visit."

"Consider it done, General."

Breyla turns to Jade next. "We're still missing something from Nolan's death. Can you see what you can find out from the castle guards? Discreetly, of course. Try not to need your coercion, but if you must use it, you have my full support."

"I can handle that. They'll probably trust me more than the rest of you, anyway." She's not wrong.

"I will continue looking into Ayden's movements, just in case we're missing something. My mother plans to announce her engagement to Lord Seamus at a dinner in three days' time. We must have something more to go off by then."

It's quiet by the time we return to the castle from Luella's. Elijah is walking me back to my chambers when his restraint finally snaps. Right before we arrive, he grabs me by the hip and presses me back against the door before I can open it.

His large frame and hard muscles feel heavenly pressed against me. He stares down at me, brown eyes sparkling in the low light. My lips part slightly, and he seizes the opportunity, leaning down and capturing my mouth with his own.

The kiss is slow and exploring, his tongue tracing my lips

and begging entrance. I open for him and let my tongue dance with his, tangling and tasting every inch of his mouth. I whimper softly when he presses himself against me, and I feel his hardness against my lower belly. I've wanted him alone all evening, and now I have him.

He breaks our kiss and trails his lips down my neck before asking, "How do you plan on looking into your father's whereabouts and intentions, O?"

"Hmmm?" I hum, not totally processing his question in my lusty haze.

"Tell me your plan, Ophelia," he demands as he nips my earlobe gently. I whimper softly, my back arching off the wall.

"I'm going to break into his study. He keeps meticulous records." I wind my arms around the back of his neck and pull him closer, trying to direct his lips back to mine.

"Then I'm coming with you." It's a statement, not a question.

"Why?" I pant between the kisses he peppers down my throat.

"To keep you safe, of course."

My body stills, and he pulls back to look me in the eyes. I'm filled with pure awe, surprised someone would care enough.

"I will never not keep you safe, Ophelia. Always," he vows, stroking my cheek gently.

"Okay," I agree quietly. "Now fucking kiss me, Elijah."

He replies, "Yes, ma'am," then takes my mouth again in a fevered kiss.

I melt like butter under his touch and savor every bit of his dark kiss before he bids me goodnight.

CHAPTER THIRTY-NINE

BREYLA

The next day Elijah, Aurelius, and I leave the castle walls in search of Delilah's family. Elijah was able to locate the part of Ciyoria they live in, but it will take some time to find their home. Having never been there, I rely on neighbors and other residents to point us in the right direction.

Today is the first day I can feel the coming autumn. There is a slight breeze that rustles the multicolor leaves that fill the trees around us. It's the first day that I'm not sweating by midday, and I can finally let my hair hang loosely down my back without it sticking to my neck. I let out a contented sigh, relishing in the momentary peace.

"You seem happy today, B," Elijah says, nudging me in the shoulder as we walk.

"I'm just enjoying the peace while it lasts. And the weather is beautiful," I say with a smile.

"Autumn has always been your favorite season," Elijah says.

"It never lasts long enough," Aurelius adds.

"Agreed," I say, grinning at him.

We walk a few more minutes in silence, just taking in the sounds and scenery of the capital. The area we're going to is a less affluent and older part of the city. I hate that anyone in my kingdom would want for anything, but I'm also not naïve enough to believe it doesn't happen. I hadn't given it much thought previously, but my conversation with Nameah shifted my perspective. Her family had struggled, asked for help, and were denied by the people sworn to protect them. I couldn't continue to live in denial. This kingdom isn't perfect, and there are people that struggle, but I want to change that.

The houses gradually decrease in size, the paint more weathered, and some showing signs of damage. I wonder how much of it is truly neglect and how much is due to the owners not having the resources to fix their homes. We reach the section of the city that Delilah was from and split up to speak with the people who live there.

I knock on the first door I come to. The paint is chipped away, and the glass in the windows is cracked. I make a mental note to send masons into this section of the city to make repairs before winter arrives. A thin female with wispy brown hair answers the door. There's a baby on her hip and a toddler hiding behind her legs.

"Can I help you, Your Highness?" she asks, her eyes cast downward.

"I hope so, miss...?" I ask, waiting for her name.

"Emilia, Your Highness."

I smile, trying my best to put her at ease. "Well, Emilia, I'm trying to locate a family that lives in this area of the city. Do you know the Howards?"

"I'm afraid I don't. There's a lot of us in this neighborhood. Hard to know everyone." She shrugs, shifting the baby from one hip to the other.

"Of course, thank you," I say, and she nods, moving to close the door.

"Can I ask you one other thing?" I ask, using my hand to stop the door from closing.

"Of course, Your Grace," Emilia says respectfully.

"Is there anything you need help with?"

"I don't understand what—" she starts with a confused look on her face.

"Like anything that needs to be fixed on your house, more food, or clothes for your children? Anything like that?" I clarify.

"I, um...I don't..." Her voice trails off.

"You can be honest with me, Emilia."

"Yes. We always need more. My husband works from sunup to sundown every day and still we struggle to make it. But we aren't the only ones. Everyone here—in this part of the city—we could all use more. We're hungry, and cold, and tired." She finishes, and my face falls at her response.

"Thank you, Emilia. You've been a great help. I hope you have a good evening," I say solemnly.

She closes the door, and I continue to the next house. I talk to several more people, but none know where the Howards live. After a few more I catch up with Elijah and Aurelius.

"Have you found anything?" I ask them both.

"I talked to one male who said he didn't know where they lived but had heard they had left town suddenly. No one has seen them in at least a week," Elijah supplies.

"I spoke with one family who said they lived a few streets over and several others who have complained about the smell of this area," Aurelius adds.

"Well, both of those are far more than I found. Let's start with the houses nearby. Not sure what we can really do about how this area smells. I can't say I've noticed anything, though."

They both shrug, and we head toward the street Aurelius indicated. As we approach, I start noticing an odor, but I can't place what it is. I ignore it as we knock on the first door.

An older male, with graying hair and bright eyes, answers the door.

"My Lords, Your Majesty, how unexpected. Is there something I can help you with?" he asks.

"Yes, sir," Elijah says, smiling at him. "We're looking for the Howard family. Have you seen them?"

"Not in several days, I'm afraid. The others say they came into some money and disappeared into the night. Off to better places, I suppose."

"Can you tell us which house was theirs? We'd really like to locate them, so maybe they left something behind to let us know where they went." Elijah just has a way of getting people to open up to him.

"Sure thing, they lived in the house three down from here. The one with the red door," the male answers, smiling at us.

"One last thing—does it always smell like this?" I ask.

"No, not usually. That's a pretty recent development."

"Very well, thank you so much for your time," I say.

As we near the house he specified, the smell intensifies. It's rather unpleasant and has my stomach rolling. I don't bother knocking, since everyone here seems to think they disappeared. The door opens easily and swings open. The stench becomes unbearable, and I suddenly realize what it is we're smelling.

It's the scent of decaying flesh, and I don't know why I hadn't recognized it sooner. I gag, trying to keep the contents of my stomach from coming back up. Raising my arm to my face, I try to block out the smell of putrid flesh. My eyes water as I attempt to breathe through my mouth.

"Dear gods, this is awful," Elijah remarks, covering his nose as we enter the home.

"It doesn't matter how often you smell rotting flesh, you never get used to it," I remark.

"I wouldn't want to..." Elijah's voice trails off as he bends over, dry heaving. Luckily, nothing comes up, but I can tell it's a fight to keep it down.

We move toward the bedrooms at the back of the small house. I push open the door and reach for the wall to balance. The sight that greets us has my heart sinking. "I think it's safe to say we found the Howard family. But we weren't the first..." I sigh.

A male and female I assume to be Delilah's parents lay in bed, their throats slit and eyes closed. From the looks of it, they were probably slaughtered in their sleep, completely unaware they were being hunted. Red soaks the sheets below them, the blood long dried. Flies buzz around their bodies, the skin bloated.

I move onto the next room with Elijah and Aurelius behind me. This room belongs to the Howard children. The body of a teenage female lies on the floor, eyes open and staring at the wall. It appears she was not as lucky as her parents.

"She saw her death coming, and from the looks of it she tried to fight. Her throat isn't slit cleanly like her parents. There are stab wounds in her chest and crimson blood has pooled down her nightgown and on the floor beneath her body." I nearly choke on the words.

Moving further into the room, I lose the battle to keep my breakfast down. The contents of my stomach reappear on the floor before me. I'm bent over, heaving as tears stream down my face.

"My gods..." Aurelius's voice trails off in horror.

"They slaughtered them all in their sleep, even..." Elijah starts, but can't seem to finish his sentence. The contents of his stomach join my own on the floor.

"Even the babes," I whisper through sobs as I stare down at the body of a female infant and male toddler in their beds.

"Who would do this?" Elijah asks, his voice full of dismay.

"What could they possibly have known or done that would put a target like this on their backs?"

"I doubt there is anything that could ever justify this." My voice is quiet as tears continue streaming down my cheeks.

Aurelius pulls me into his chest, turning my face away from the scene before us. Silent sobs wrack my body, and I mourn for the lost lives of my people. His hands trail up and down my back in a soothing motion.

We say nothing more until we're back outside the house. "Who do you think is responsible, Breyla?" Elijah asks.

"Who I think is responsible and who actually wielded the blade are two different things." I chew my bottom lip as I work to puzzle it all out. "We need proof before we can accuse Lord Seamus of this, but I need to pay a visit to a certain king. This wasn't carried out by soldiers. This is the work of mercenaries. Of that, I am sure."

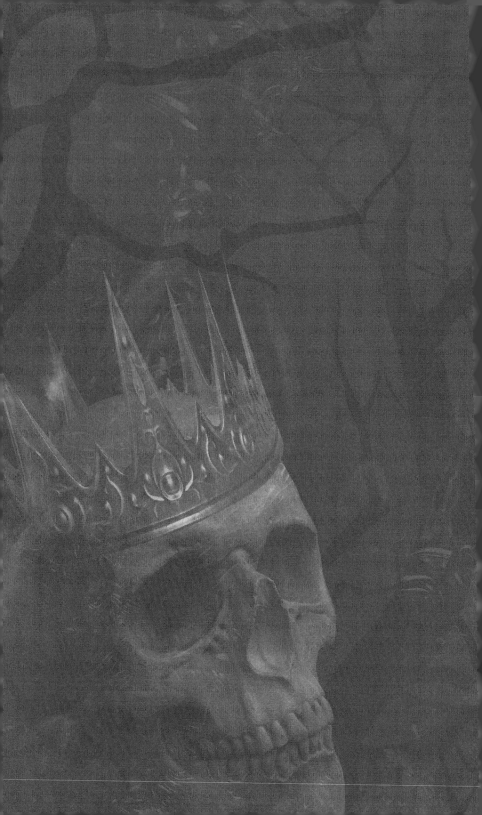

CHAPTER FORTY

OPHELIA

It's nearly midnight when I hear the door to my father's chambers creak open and a click as the door shuts again. Elijah behind me, I slip out of my own room to face the young female exiting his room. Her hair is disheveled, and she looks exhausted, but I see no physical injuries.

"Are you okay?" I ask quietly, and she nods.

"He didn't hurt you?" I ask just to be sure.

"No, not really. He was rough, but the sedative in the wine took hold of him before he could do any real damage. I ensured he drank plenty, so he will think it was just too much wine that knocked him out." She straightens her hair, wrapping a cloak around her shoulders. I had paid her an exorbitant amount to drug my father under the ruse of sleeping with him. I had paid her even more for her silence in the matter.

"Good," I say, nodding. "Thank you so much for your help. Speak of this to no one."

She visibly shudders. "Please, I would never tell a soul I bedded Lord Seamus. I'd like to forget it myself."

Elijah stifles a laugh behind me, and I dig my elbow into his ribs. I drop the last half of the coins into her hand and watch her leave the castle.

Once she's gone, Elijah nips my ear and whispers, "Clever minx. I can't believe you pulled this off on such short notice."

I lean into his touch and respond, "I almost didn't. I was hoping I could just sneak in when he left the palace, but the bastard has been hiding in his study almost all day. This was my last resort."

"Either way, you still pulled it off. You're brilliant, O. Now, let's go break into his study." Elijah pats my side, then leads me into my father's rooms. I can hear him snoring heavily from his bed and know that he'll be out until morning. Still, it's best to keep as quiet as possible.

We move from the sitting room to his study, and I reach for the handle.

"Shit," I mumble when the handle refuses to budge. "It's locked. I'm going to have to sneak into his bedroom and look for the key." I nearly groan at the thought.

"Not to worry," Elijah whispers. He pulls an iron key from his pants pocket and kisses my forehead. He slides it into the lock and turns it until it clicks open. We step into the study, shutting and locking the door behind us.

"How did you get a master key to the castle?" I ask.

"Oh, you know..." he looks at me mischievously, "I swiped it off Commander Nolan like two years ago."

"Why?" I ask.

"Why not?" He shrugs.

I shake my head in disbelief at him.

"Okay, you go through the desk drawers, and I'll go through the records in the cabinet. He keeps very detailed notes, but I'm not sure how they're organized. He rarely lets me see this room." I don't add that he does that because he doesn't believe females have a place dealing with finances, business, or any real decision making.

"You got it, doll," he says and goes to work opening the desk drawers. I open the cabinet, trying to decide where to start. I finally pull out a stack of parchment from the top and start reading through the records. Most of this seems like correspondence with business contacts in other cities and countries, but nothing comes off as suspicious.

Nearly an hour passes in silence as we read through his records but find nothing. I sigh in frustration as I drop another letter that proves to be a dead end. Elijah sets down what he's reading and moves behind me. My heart beats fast as he wraps a muscled arm around my waist from behind, pulling me into his chest. His cinnamon and chocolate scent wraps around me, and I relax into his hold.

"We'll find it eventually; we just have to keep looking." He places a kiss on my cheek, then one behind my ear and squeezes me tightly.

"I know, I'm just so frustrated, and my eyes are going cross from looking at all these letters and numbers." I let my fingers trace a pattern over his hand as he runs the other over the curve of my hip.

"I can feel how tightly wound your muscles are, Ophelia. Do you want me to help you relax? We can take a quick break from looking." His tone borders on seductive.

"What do you mean?" I ask softly, unsure of where this is going.

He kisses down my neck, while running his hand down my leg. The skirt of my dress begins to rise as he slowly bunches it up one side and whispers, "Let me help you *release* some of that tension. Maybe once you're relaxed, you'll be able to look at this with fresh eyes."

My cheeks flame at his meaning, and I gasp as my skirt is lifted high enough for him to slip a hand between my legs. His finger traces around the spot at the apex of my thighs that makes me see stars.

"We c-can't." I stutter, trying to maintain my focus as he continues to tease me. "Not here. Surely my father will hear and find us."

"Your father is passed out cold until morning, doll. He's not going to find us. But if you're that worried, we can be very quiet." Elijah continues kissing my neck, peppering soft bites in between.

As I open my mouth to speak, a moan leaves my lips instead when his fingers finally press down on my clit. All ideas of denying him are gone as he begins rubbing in slow circles.

"That's what I thought," he chuckles, moving his finger further to my opening. "Gods, Ophelia. You're soaked for me."

His words have me groaning quietly as I roll my hips back into him, feeling his erection pressed against my lower back. One of his fingers enters me slowly, and I suck in a breath.

"Elijah," I whimper, reaching a hand back to find his erection. "Are you going to make love to me right here?"

The thick digit inside me moves in and out, and a second joins it. I groan louder as his thumb circles my clit and I roll my hips again, savoring the friction between us.

"Fuck, Ophelia. You've got to be quiet," he says, covering my mouth with his hand. "No, I'm not going to make love to you here. Because when I take you, you will scream and there will be nothing quick about it."

I nearly scream out of frustration at this male. I don't know how else to express that I'm ready and want him. Since our first last encounter, I've thought about it several times. More than once I had to find release with my own hands as I imagined what it would be like to be taken by him. And he was denying me—again.

"Soon, Ophelia, I promise." He picks up his pace as his fingers slide in and out of me, working me closer to the edge of bliss. "Tonight, you will come on my tongue, and I will savor every fucking drop of your release."

A shutter rolls through me at his words. Keeping his fingers still inside me, he moves us to my father's desk. After quickly shoving aside some papers, he lifts me and places me on top. His lips find mine in a fevered kiss that has me gasping for breath when he breaks it. He places a hand on my chest and pushes me back so I'm lying on the desk.

Elijah pulls my undergarments down my legs and slips them into his pocket. *What does he do with them...*I wonder, but the thought is quickly lost when his hot mouth finds my center. His fingers slide back inside me as he licks me from opening to clit. He was slow and tender the first time he did this, but I find none of that now as he works his fingers in and out of me, quickly building speed.

I writhe beneath him, covering my mouth with a hand to keep as quiet as possible. Elijah flicks his tongue over my clit repeatedly as his fingers continue building that sweet pressure inside of me. He sucks my clit into his mouth right as he curls his fingers and hits that perfect spot inside me. It has my back arching off the desk.

"Elijah," I pant, completely lost to the pleasure of his touch.

He continues the motion of curling his fingers until I'm finally about to burst, then nips my clit, forcing me over the edge of bliss as wave after wave of euphoria washes over me. I'm lost in the sea of his pleasure, my breaths coming in short pants as I see literal stars dance across my vision.

"Fuck, Elijah," I say when I can finally breathe again. Just as my heart rate comes back to normal, I feel his tongue make long, slow strokes up my thighs. He alternates sides, thoroughly licking every inch of me. "What are you doing?" I ask in confusion.

"What I told you I would do—savoring every drop of your release," he replies with a smug look on his face. Despite what just happened between us, I find myself still blushing at his words.

He stands up, pulling my dress back down, then brings me to a sitting position. "Now let's get back to work," he says, kissing my lips softly. This male just made me come on his tongue in a matter of minutes, but I find myself still wanting more of him.

Another hour later, we finally stumble upon something helpful. I pull out several letters all bearing my father's signature and several with wax seals I don't recognize. Carefully, I open the first letter and read over the flawless script that implicates my father. The further I read, the more my stomach churns. I'm both relieved to have found something to help Breyla, but nervous for what this means for Layne and me.

These letters undoubtedly prove my father is a traitor. The letters aren't signed by the other party, instead they just bear an unknown seal in red wax. Every single letter is addressed to Lord Seamus Delencourt. Swallowing hard, I turn to Elijah.

"Elijah, I found something," I say, my voice barely more than a whisper.

His concerned eyes find mine, and he takes the letter from my trembling hands. Reading it over, he sighs. "Well, this is what we were looking for. This doesn't just prove your father is trying to overthrow Queen Genevieve, but that he's working with another country to do so. I don't recognize this seal, but maybe the pieces will all come together once we turn this over to Breyla."

My heart thuds rapidly in my chest at the implication. Not only is my father a traitor to the crown, Layne and I will be marked as traitors by extension. I knew this was a likely possibility, but now I had to face what this meant for me. What my next steps would be. Could I stay here? Would Layne and I ever be safe again if we ran?

Elijah must sense my warring emotions, because the next thing I know, I'm being pulled into his hard chest. A soothing hand runs down my back as I tremble in his arms. Tears stream down my face while I cling to his chest, my lungs burning as I struggle to pull in air. The room around me spins, and I sob hysterically into his chest.

"Shhhh," he says, trying to soothe me. "You're panicking, Ophelia. I'm going to help you through it, though."

I'm too lost to my panic to respond verbally, but I nod.

"I need you to tell me five things you can see in the room," Elijah says in a firm but kind tone.

I glance around the space, trying to focus on anything I can. "Desk, c-candle, chair, tapestry, parchment."

"Good. Now, four things you can touch." He gives the second command with the same gentleness as the first.

"Um," I start, trying to feel for four things, but all I feel is him against me. "Your shirt," I say as I grip it tighter. "My dress," I add, running a hand over the sleeve. "The rug, and your muscles."

He chuckles softly. "I shouldn't count that last one, but I'll take it. Now give me three things you can hear."

I take in a breath, finding it easier now. "The wind outside, my father's snores..." I struggle to find a third when it hits me. There's a steady beating I hear coming from his chest. "I can hear your heart beating."

"Good girl," he praises. "Now give me two things you can smell."

"Cinnamon and chocolate," I blurt without thinking.

"Cinnamon and chocolate?" he asks, clearly confused.

"It's what you smell like," I explain. I feel his chest move slightly as he stifles a laugh.

"One thing you can taste, now."

"I-I don't know." I haven't had anything to eat or drink in hours, and I don't typically go around just tasting the things around me.

"Here, I'll give you the last one," he says as he tilts my chin up, so we're making eye contact. Then he places the softest of kisses on my lips. It's a kiss so tender, I never want it to end. But it does, and when he pulls back, he smiles at me.

"There she is," he says softly.

"Thank you," I whisper.

"You never have to thank me for that, or anything. Except orgasms, you can thank me for those any way you like," he says with a wink.

I roll my eyes and take a step back from him. "Elijah, I have to leave." It takes everything in me to utter those words, because I know he can't come with me.

"No. You don't." His words are firm and leave no room for argument.

"But, I—"

"—No, Ophelia. Your father is a traitor. That word does not apply to you. You had no part in this, and I won't let them touch you."

His words should be comforting, but they're not. "It's not up to you, Elijah. And what about Layne? You can't protect me, let alone both of us."

"Do you honestly believe your brother had any part of this?" he asks.

"Layne would never," I say resolutely. I had absolute faith in my brother.

"Then you have nothing to fear. I know Breyla better than anyone. She would never hold you—or your brother—accountable for your father's actions. That's not how she thinks." He says this with the same certainty I had about Layne.

"But the law dictates that Layne and I should share his fate.

History would tend to agree," I argue, referring to the story of Myer, Elythia, and their children.

"Breyla is the law, Ophelia. She would never let something happen to you. I promise." I don't know if I'm totally reassured, but it's good enough for now.

"There's something else I found—I think." He says this cautiously, I'm sure to keep from triggering another episode in me.

"What is it?" I ask.

Elijah pulls me over to the desk and the record he was looking at. It's a ledger of all my father's accounts. Something I wouldn't have thought to look over.

"At first, I almost looked over it, but I'm glad I didn't," he starts, running his finger down the page. "Here—just a week ago there were two suspiciously large transactions made close together. One is recorded as 'H' and the other as 'M'. I'm fairly certain the 'M' is for the services of the Midnight Brotherhood, but I'm wondering if he did pay the Howard family."

I scan over the records, trying to make sense of them. My eyes snag on one other transaction, dated several weeks prior. "Here," I say pointing to it. "It looks like he paid the salary of Delilah Howard shortly before Aurelius's attempted poisoning."

Elijah's eyes widen. "I'm not the royal treasurer, but I can tell you that is far more than any other servant makes, Ophelia."

I pull the ledger sheet out, folding and tucking it carefully in the bodice of my dress. Elijah then slips the letters into his pocket, and we return the room to its original state. "We need to get these to Breyla, immediately." I say it with more confidence than I feel.

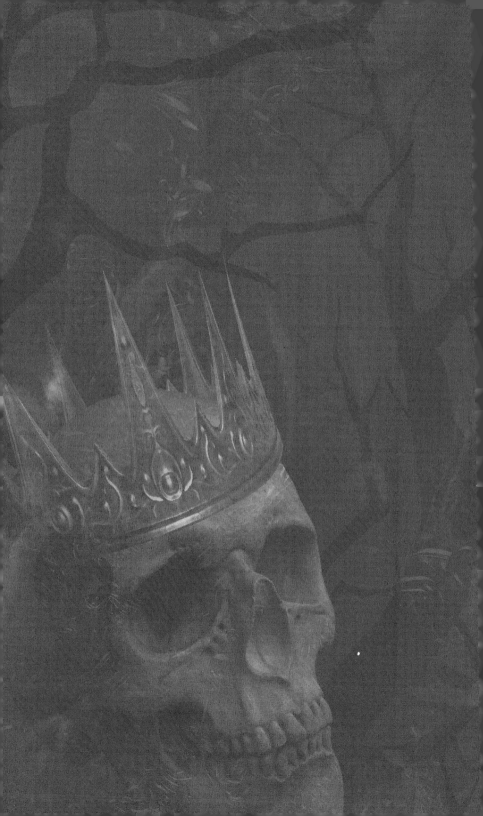

CHAPTER FORTY-ONE

BREYLA

I wait until nightfall to track down the mercenaries I suspect are behind the Howard family's deaths. Tomorrow is when my mother plans to announce her engagement to Lord Seamus, and I am running out of time. My auburn curls are braided tightly and tucked under a black hood, and I'm dressed in all black to help me blend in. My knives are strapped to their normal places, plus a few extras. One can never be too careful around mercenaries and assassins.

Shadows wrap around my body, helping me to blend in even more as I make my way through town. I duck and weave, moving as quickly as possible without being noticed. Finally, I come to an unassuming building on the outskirts of town. The citizens recognize it as a brothel, but it is so much more than that.

I slip in the front, careful to keep my hood pulled low. It's not the first time I've been here, but I don't need to be recognized right now. Sitting on a stool at the bar, I lean over to the madame as she greets me.

"Good evening, miss. What are you drinking tonight?" she

asks. She doesn't mean liquor; she's asking about my sexual preferences.

"I'll take a gin with lavender," I respond as quietly as possible.

Her brown eyes widen slightly in recognition of the phrase only used by those seeking *other* services. She leans over the bar to speak low. "And will that be with honey?" Another code.

"Honey and cinnamon, please," I respond, letting her know I need to speak with the mercenary king.

"I'll have that out in just a minute, miss." She nods and steps back from the bar top, leaving through a door in the back.

A few minutes later, a young female with olive skin and black hair and a silver-haired male with onyx eyes step up on either side of me. The female's lips are painted red and she wears a sheer matching colored gown. Her hair hangs low enough to cover her nipples, but nothing else is left to the imagination. I can see every beautiful curve of her lithe body. The male is topless, wearing only silk sleep pants low on his hips. He's fair-skinned and has well-defined muscles that most males work years for.

They press into each side of me, their body warmth cocooning me.

"You ordered a gin with lavender?" asks the female directly in my ear.

I nod ever so slightly and lean into her embrace. The male presses in closer, burying his face in my neck, then whispers, "With honey and cinnamon?"

Again, I nod in confirmation, wrapping an arm around each of their backs. The male places a tender kiss on my neck, and I fight the urge to stiffen in his hold. It would seem suspicious behavior, but I know the fury he'd face if Aurelius finds out. It doesn't matter that this is all part of the process for gaining entry to see the mercenary king. With my luck, Aurelius will smell another male's scent on me and go feral.

"Come with us," the female says. Her voice is low and sultry. To anyone else, this would look like exactly what people come to brothels for. But these two aren't your typical courtesans. They're part of a specially trained group that works for both the mercenary king and the brothel's madame. They function primarily as spies and bodyguards for the other courtesans that reside here.

I stand, letting them lead me out of the main room to the hallway. We travel to the back, up a flight of stairs and down another hallway. The male opens a door at the end and ushers us inside, locking it behind him. Immediately, I'm pushed against the wall and the female's lips are on mine. They're soft and full as she explores my mouth.

I don't kiss her back, but let her hands roam my body as the male joins her. He pulls down my hood and kisses down my throat, his hands also exploring my body. This little inspection used to thrill me, but now I feel nothing. Now that I've had Aurelius, I'm afraid no one else will compare.

Right as the male finds my first dagger, a throat clears.

"Claudia, Jaret, that's enough. The General can keep her daggers. We both know she's quite capable of killing me even without them." The mercenary prince's sweet lilt rolls through the room.

The male and female—Jaret and Claudia, apparently— immediately cease their search and back away from me.

"You are dismissed." The command is clear. Jaret and Claudia nod their heads in understanding and back out of the room, the door locking again behind them.

"Hello, sweetheart," he says, his melodic voice rolling over my skin. I keep my place against the wall, letting him approach me. He prowls closer, like a feline stalking its prey. But I am no prey.

"Hello, Cillian," I reply as he finally reaches me. The male leans over me, his forearm on the wall above my head, leaving his face mere inches from mine. This close, I can see the deep teal of his eyes and the freckles that line his cheeks. Copper ringlets hang loose around his face, and most of his hair is pulled back into a knot on the top of his head.

"To what do I owe the pleasure of your company, little General?" he asks, his tone somehow both playful and condescending. Cillian had once been a member of the Rimorian army before my time as General. We had grown close as we trained together and eventually found ourselves frequenting the other's bed. That was until I discovered he was the son of the most notorious mercenary in our kingdom.

He had been planted in the army as a spy, but growing attached to me was never part of the plan. I wouldn't call what we had love, but more of a heated companionship. Part of me had always wondered if it could have been more if we were different people or had met under different circumstances. Until Aurelius strolled back into my life, that is. It was becoming harder and harder to deny the feelings stirring in my chest every time I looked at the broody male that had claimed me as his.

Once I had learned Cillian's true identity, I had made the decision to spare his life. Elijah had insisted it was because I had cared for him, but I knew it was really because Cillian had cared for me. I knew he would one day take his father's spot as the self-proclaimed mercenary king. If he didn't, someone else would, and I figured the devil you know is better than the one you don't. Cillian owed me his life; a fact I rarely let him forget.

His father was long dead now, and Cillian ruled as King of the Midnight Brotherhood. They were assassins and swords for hire but somehow had their own twisted morals. I had maintained contact with him through the years, occasionally still winding up in his bed when the loneliness was too much for one of us to bear. I suspected he still harbored feelings for me, but we both knew where that would lead. Which is why we never spoke about it. My heart was not his.

"I'm not here for pleasure, Cillian. I need details on a slaughter the brotherhood was behind," I finally say.

He tilts his head in question at me, eyes running over my face and assessing me.

"You know that's not how this works, sweetheart," he tuts. One of his fingers traces my jaw, tilting my face up to look at him. Cillian is tall—taller than even Aurelius—and dwarfs me in every way. While it may look like a sensual position, this is very clearly a power play to me. Though I hold power over him through his life-debt, he has information I need, and he's going to make me work for it.

Doing my best to brush him off, I say, "There was a family of five that we found slaughtered in their beds. Surname was Howard, lived in the eastern part of the capital—small house with a red door. Ring any bells?"

"If you brought no coin, no secrets to barter, and you don't want to cash in that life-debt you've been holding over my head...I could arrange a more *pleasurable* exchange for the both of us." I don't miss the insinuation or him ignoring my question all together.

My shadows slither along the floor, trailing up his toned legs until they reach his hips. His eyes sparkle in excitement, and I know I have him distracted enough. With the help of my shadows, I flip our positions, slamming him into the wall. I have a dagger pressed against his throat, and a wicked smile creeps across his face. If this were anyone else, they'd be afraid. But there was a reason they called him king of the mercenaries. I glance down at the dagger he has pressed against my throat. But much like him, I'm not afraid.

He winks at me and says, "If you're trying to turn me off, you'll need a different tactic."

"I told you, I'm not here for pleasure, Cillian. This is official business, and it's important. I'll pay you if I find the information worth it."

"Yet, that's never stopped you from taking pleasure from me before," he hums.

"My pleasure isn't yours to have anymore," I say evenly. It's not meant to be cruel, but I need to get the point across.

I catch the way his lips fall just slightly at the corners of his mouth. "Is it possible the little general has found her match?" His words are laced with just the smallest bit of bitterness.

"I have found the one that makes my shadows sing and my heart beat faster." It's the first time I've confessed something of this magnitude out loud.

"You used to sing for me, sweetheart. I had hoped that one day you would again." His voice is soft as reality hits him that it never will.

"Don't go there, Cillian," I beg him. I had put the thought of us together to bed years ago. It was time now that he did the same.

"You deserve all the happiness, Breyla. I'm glad someone was able to get through that thick wall you keep built around your heart. Too bad it wasn't me. Whoever he is, he's one lucky male." He drops the dagger from my throat and sheathes it at his side.

"Thank you," I say and smile softly at him. "You deserve the same. I know one day you'll find her." I lower the dagger from his throat, stashing it back in my thigh holster.

"Yes, well, you should know the fee for information has just gone up. Now what would you like to know?" He chuckles at the glare I shoot his way.

"Bastard," I mumble before taking a step back from him.

"Most definitely," he says with a smirk.

"The Howard family," I start, trying to get back on track. "What do you know about that hit?"

"I know a member of your court showed up at my establishment offering to pay double the normal fee. He didn't say why, but it's not my place to ask those questions."

"They had three children, Cillian. Did you not think to ask about that?" I fight to keep my tone even as the emotions tighten my throat.

"I was aware of the children, yes. I did not care to—"

"What happened to not harming children, Cillian? They were all slaughtered in their beds. Every one of them. When did you start taking contracts on the young?" I demand, tears pooling in my eyes. My shadows flare, blanketing the room in darkness in response to my emotions.

Light slowly creeps out of his palms, causing my shadows to recede. Cillian is the only other light wielder I know since Nameah had died. But his power is far greater than hers had been. He could create light, much like I could create shadows. If she had lived, I would have asked him to train her.

A mix of fury and grief wash over me as I stare into his eyes, waiting for him to answer me.

"I didn't take the hit, Breyla." He reaches a hand up to my cheek and strokes it softly. "Nothing has changed. I'm still a dark, twisted, ruthless killer. But I would never harm children."

My shoulders sag in relief. I would have run my sword through his heart if he had said anything else. "Then who did?" I ask, straightening my shoulders.

"There are a handful of mercenaries that don't agree with all my views and have defected. My guess is it was one of them. They're somehow operating under the Midnight Brotherhood name. It's created quite the headache for me."

"Why is this the first I am hearing of them?" I ask, frustrated that he didn't tell me this sooner.

"I'm dealing with it, Breyla." I get the feeling there's more he's not saying.

"Just know that when I find them, I will not hesitate. Their lives are forfeit."

Cillian grins wickedly. "I would expect nothing less, little General."

"One last question, and this is important. Which member of my court ordered the hit?" I'm not leaving without this answer.

"Lord Seamus Delencourt."

I can't say I'm surprised; just relieved to have someone able to confirm his guilt finally.

"Thank you, *Your Highness*," I say, mocking his self-appointed title, and he rolls his eyes. "Your information has been most helpful." I take out the coin purse full of gold and drop it in his waiting hand.

He drops it in his pocket and says, "Pleasure doing business with you, sweetheart. Try not to get yourself killed before I see you next."

"No promises," I say with a wink as I pull my hood back over my head.

As I reach for the door handle, Cillian calls out, "Oh, and Breyla?"

"Yes?"

"I meant what I said about you deserving to be happy. I'm sorry it wasn't me, but if he ever fucks it up, I'm only a raven away."

I let out a chuckle. "Sure, Cillian. I know I can always count on you as plan B." I slip out of the brothel and back to the castle.

The palace is still quiet by the time I make it to my chambers. My hand is on the door to my room when I hear the low, deep voice of Ayden.

"Evening, love." The door clicks shut behind us as I turn to face him.

"Evening, Prince." I keep my voice low, trying not to wake Aurelius or catch the attention of anyone else that might be wandering the halls. I take in Ayden's appearance and determine that he was probably not asleep. His well-defined chest is on display, and it's a damn shame I'm the only one here to see it. The male looks like he was sculpted by the gods. His hair isn't mussed from sleep, and his eyes are bright. He's alert and smirking at me. He's been awake this whole time.

"What troubles you at this late hour?" he asks as his eyes roam over me.

I keep my voice even as I reply, "Nothing troubles me. I was visiting an old friend."

Ayden takes a step closer, his eyes still assessing me. His lips quirk up on one side, and he runs his fingers down my neck. My hand shoots up on instinct, gripping his wrist tightly. I'm tired of being touched by so many people that aren't Aurelius tonight. I want to wash the feel of everyone else's touches off my skin.

"Your friend has a lovely shade of lipstick, love." The bastard smirks at me again, bringing his fingers in front of my face. The red color of Claudia's lips stains the tips. "What was her name?"

Fuck. I had forgotten about that.

"I don't owe you any explanations, Ayden."

"Perhaps not," he says as a wicked smile takes over his face. He leans down and whispers in my ear, "But I would love to know what Aurelius thinks about your friend."

"Our relationship is none of your concern," I grit out.

"We'll see about that," he says, stepping back. "Try to remember the silencing shield tonight. It's late, and I need my beauty sleep."

Before I have the chance to respond he's back in his room, door shut and locked behind him. I roll my shoulders, trying to ease the tension building between them.

I'm muttering something about stupid insufferable males as I finally enter my own room, locking the door behind me. All I want is to bathe and sleep through what little I have left of the night.

"It's late, Princess."

My heart beats faster as I lay eyes on Aurelius stretched out across my bed. He's wearing loose sleep pants, but nothing else. The toned lines of his muscles catch my eyes, and I find myself staring.

"I'm aware," I finally manage to say. "I was just about to bathe."

He looks me up and down, his gaze assessing, but I can't tell what he's thinking.

I turn toward the bathing chambers and make it all of two steps before I feel him behind me. My hood is down, and his head is buried in the crook of my neck. His arm wraps tightly around me, and I feel his chest move as a low growl rumbles through him.

"Where were you and why do you smell like shit, Princess?"

I flip in his arms so I'm facing him now. "I had to pay a visit to the Midnight Brotherhood. We needed information about the Howard family, and I knew I could get it there."

"That answers the where, but not why you smell like so many *others*." The way he says others is laced with threat. He doesn't like their scents on me or how they got there.

"There is a certain protocol for speaking with a mercenary king," I explain, keeping my temper and tone even. "One that not even I'm able to bypass. I did what I had to do, Aurelius."

"There's lipstick on your neck, Breyla," Aurelius snarls. "Why didn't you take me?"

"Cillian never would have spoken to me with you there. We have a history, and he owes me, so he agrees to see me. But you? He never would have let me through the door with you there." I explain it the best I can, trying my best to remain calm, but it's becoming increasingly more difficult.

His nostrils flare as he processes my words. "What kind of history?"

My patience finally snaps as I blurt out, "Enough of this. Control yourself!" I shove against him, trying to create space.

He's having none of it, though, and pulls me back into his chest. "I'm not jealous, Princess. Jealousy would imply that you aren't already mine, and we both know I hold every piece of you. Your pleasure, your sharp words, your moans, your insults, your laughter, your tears and sorrow, your anger, and even one day—your love—are mine."

An excited thrill runs through me at his words, and I can't help the heat growing low in my belly as I realize how true those words are. I never wanted any piece of this male—if anything I wanted him gone from my life—but something changed, and I'm so tired of fighting it. I don't understand it, but the heart doesn't obey the laws of logic.

"My history with Cillian is the ancient kind. I made that very clear to him tonight. When he asked me if I had finally found my match, do you want to know what I said?" My heart beats erratically in my chest at what I'm about to admit to him.

"I'd very much like to know, Princess." Aurelius's eyes search mine as I take a deep breath.

"I told him that I had found the one that makes my shadows sing and my heart beat faster." The admission comes out barely above a whisper. "I'm not proclaiming love, but this is the closest I've ever come. "Never have I felt like this for anyone, Aurelius. I don't understand it, I sure as hell didn't ask for it, but here we are."

His jaw drops as his eyes widen, the moon making the crimson flecks sparkle in its light. "Those are awfully poetic words coming from you, my little demon."

"That's all you have to say?" I ask dumbfounded.

"You're not yet ready to hear what I have to say." His response leaves me stunned. I just admitted that I care for him—that this isn't just something physical between us—and I'm somehow not ready to hear his response?

"Excuse me?" I ask, trying to understand.

He moves us toward the bed, never breaking eye contact with me. When the backs of my knees finally hit the mattress, he tilts my chin up and kisses me softly. I melt into his kiss, relishing the feel of his lips on mine in a touch that's so at odds with our normal heated embraces.

He finally breaks the kiss, and his hands wander up my body, landing on the string that keeps my cloak tied. He tugs it free, letting the cloak drop.

"It took me weeks to get you to feel anything, Princess. You've been suppressing your emotions for so long, they were literally exploding out of you in uncontrolled waves of power." His fingers work to unstrap all the daggers hidden on me next, dropping them one by one to the floor. "I've known from the first time you barged into my room and I had my first taste of you—that one taste would never be enough. If I had you every day from now until the end of our days, it wouldn't be enough, Breyla." My heart flutters at what he's implying by the words he's not saying. Next, he unlaces my leathers, pulling them down my shoulders. The tunic underneath comes off next, leaving me exposed to him. My nipples harden as he stares intensely at me. His words are doing something to me I wouldn't have expected. "I've known the depth of my feelings for you for longer than I want to admit. This thing between us may have started as just a physical connection, but it's so much more than that for me. The difference between us is that I've had no trouble admitting that, and you're just now coming to that realization." Lastly, he tugs my leather pants down my legs, letting me step out of them before shoving me roughly to the bed. He drops his sleep pants and steps between my legs. His cock is hard, and the tip glistens with precum as I lick my lips. He lines himself up at my entrance but doesn't move. "So no, Princess. You aren't ready to hear what I actually want to say to you right now. You'll get there, though. Because if there's one thing I'm certain of in this world—it's that I am *never* letting you go."

I moan as he thrusts straight inside me in one fluid motion. My back arches as I adjust to him and the sudden intrusion. It burns slightly, but I would be lying if I said I didn't also love the pain. He gives me very little time to adjust before he pulls out and thrusts back in again. "Tonight, I'm going to show you everything I want to say to you," he says with another thrust that has me clenching the sheets beneath me. His hand winds around my throat as he thrusts again and again at a pace that has my toes curling. "I'm going to fuck you until I'm the only thing you feel. I'm going to cover you so thoroughly in my scent that I can't smell the others on you. Then I'm going to bathe you and do it all over again." His promise has my inner walls clenching around him. "Fuck, Princess. Do that again," he demands as he thrusts harder into me, leaving me gasping for breath.

Completely lost to pleasure, I do as I'm commanded. I clench down on him hard as his thrusts grow faster and harder. A scream erupts from me as I barrel over the edge into my release. I fight to catch my breath, but Aurelius doesn't slow his thrusts or let me come down from the high of my orgasm. He just keeps fucking me until I'm a shaking, trembling mess. I dig my nails into the skin of his shoulders, and he moans. Blood trickles down from the crescent moons left behind in his skin.

"Yes, little demon, I will gladly bleed for you." His thrusts grow erratic as the crimson drops onto my chest.

"Good," I say breathlessly. "Now fucking come for me."

He chuckles, the sound deep and sensual, as he says, "All in good time." Before I can let out the snarl building in my throat, he's pulling my leg up to my chest and fucking me at an angle that has me screaming again. "That's a good little demon. I love the sound of your screams when my cock is buried so deeply in you. Now come for me again."

It takes all but a few more strokes at this new angle to have me doing exactly as I'm told and coming so hard I see stars. A few thrusts later and he follows me over the edge into ecstasy. My name is all he moans as he spills himself inside of me. After a few minutes of heavy breathing, we both finally come down from our high.

"Bath time," he whispers as he leaves a gentle kiss on my cheek.

"Yes, please," I say sleepily as he lifts me from the bed, cradling me in his arms, and carries me to the bathtub. A few minutes later, after the tub is filled, he lowers me into the warm water, then follows behind me. He washes every part of me, then does exactly as he promised earlier and fucks me again. This time it's soft and full of reverence, his body telling me everything he refuses to say out loud. For the first time in my life, I feel cherished.

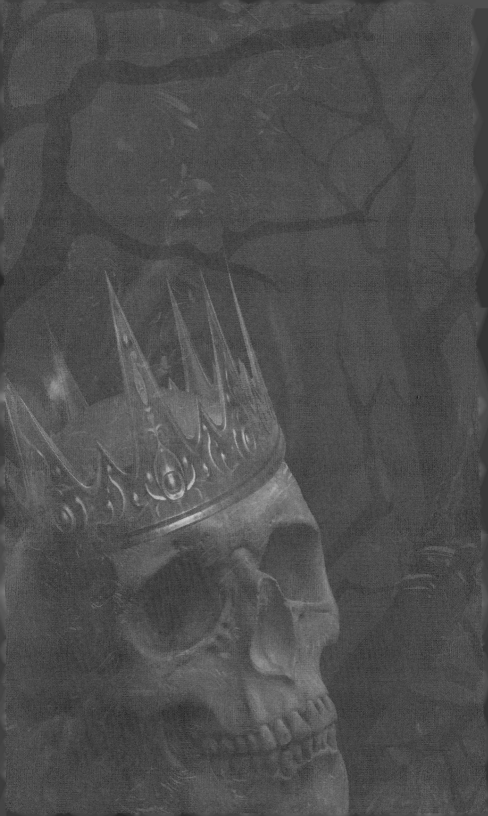

CHAPTER FORTY-TWO

BREYLA

What I'm doing is undoubtedly the most reckless thing I've done in a long while. But I'm desperate, and I need to know what Prince Ayden is up to. Even if I don't believe he's responsible for the slew of deaths and attempted murders recently, he is up to *something*. It's just a matter of finding out what. My mother plans to announce that she'll marry Lord Seamus instead of Aurelius tonight, so I've run out of time.

It's midday, and the eyes I have on him show him in the library with his cousin, Charlotte. They are elbows-deep in old parchment and weathered leather books. I'm not sure what they're researching, but it's given me the opportunity I need to break into his rooms.

I didn't tell Aurelius about my plan because he reacted so strangely anytime Ayden was mentioned, and I don't trust him to not try and stop me. He was busy trying to convince my mother not to accept the engagement to Lord Seamus, so that left me free to do what I needed.

I stand in front of Ayden's door, letting my shadows out just enough to fill the lock on the door. Once they've entered every crevice in the lock, I will them to take a more solid state, essentially creating a shadow key. It works like a charm as I twist my hand and the lock clicks, the door swinging open.

I slip through the door and shut it behind me. When I was in here before, I had noticed Ayden had large stacks of scrolls and letters scattered across the desk in the corner. Fate shines on me as I notice that nothing has changed. The papers still lay in haphazard piles on the desk, devoid of any clear organization.

I get to work shuffling through the documents, trying to find anything of interest. Most of them are letters I'm familiar with—reports on his army and any battles. I'm unaware of any conflict between Prudia and any kingdoms outside of my own. Still, there are numerous reports from who I assume to be his general.

There isn't time for me to look through those reports fully, but I make a mental note of it. I continue looking through the papers until something catches my eye. A familiar seal and signature sit at the bottom of a letter that makes my blood boil. It's unaddressed, but as I read the contents my heart sinks at the words.

The King is dead. Though untimely, the people believe it was of natural causes. We know the truth. The princess hasn't returned home, and the people are restless. I have taken steps to ensure the throne will be ready for you. Now is the time to strike.

Lord Seamus Delencourt

The breath catches in my chest as I read it over and over. Prince

Ayden has been working against me the entire time, and I was too stupid to see it. I let the brief moments and small acts of kindness cloud my judgment when it came to him. He's been working with Lord Seamus to take over my kingdom. Was he behind the attempted assassinations of Aurelius and me? Was Lord Seamus behind my father's death? I still had so many questions, but one thing I knew for sure. Neither Prince Ayden nor Lord Seamus were to be trusted. They were actively working to take the Rimorian throne.

Not bothering to look through the rest of the papers, I fold the letter neatly and tuck it into the front of my bodice, ensuring it is out of sight.

I exit the room, my heart full of despair and fury.

I arrive at dinner dressed in my leathers, much to my mother's disappointment. But I know what is about to happen, and I don't expect it to happen smoothly. This court is full of vipers, and I will not underestimate any of them.

My mother is dressed in a fine navy-blue dress, her straw-berry-blonde locks pinned back with a golden crown sitting on top. She looks put together, proper like one would expect from the Queen. But I can see the purple that haunts her under eyes and the red that rings them. I see the weight she's lost and the way her cheekbones are more prominent. I see her sorrow, and I feel how it echoes my own.

Everyone is present now, each person in their respective seats. I sneak a glance at Lord Seamus out of the corner of my eye. He's wearing a smug grin, knowing he's won and eager to let the rest of the room know as well.

As the main course is served, I raise my glass and tap my fork on the side to capture everyone's attention. Everyone, including my mother, turns their gaze to me.

"I have something to say," I smile sweetly, trying to fake my excitement.

At my words, the doors open quietly and fully armed guards step in right on time.

"Since my return to the capital there have been three murders and assassination attempts on my and Lord Aurelius's lives. I have evidence to suggest it was all in hopes to usurp the throne of Rimor." I pause, and startled gasps sound around me. I turn a malicious grin at Prince Ayden.

He's smirking back at me as I give my next command, "Guards, arrest Prince Ayden II of Prudia for conspiring against the crown and the attempted murders of Lord Aurelius and me."

The smirk on his mouth doesn't even falter as he stands and offers himself over to my guards. He even winks at me as they yank his arms behind his back, shackling them in place.

Lady Charlotte stands abruptly with a furious look on her face. "This is preposterous! What proof do you have that Prince Ayden is behind any of this?"

"Stand down, Charlie," Prince Ayden commands.

"Yes, *Charlie*, sit down," I growl. "Before I find charges against you as well."

With that, she sits, glaring daggers at me.

I pull the letter from Ayden's room and unfold it. "This letter was recovered from Ayden's belongings. I think you'll find the evidence damning." I recite the letter word for word, finishing it with a "Oh, and guards. This letter is signed by Lord Seamus Delencourt, so arrest him as well." I say it as an afterthought, but this is the part I'm most excited for.

The smug look from Lord Seamus's face is gone, but a look of pride shines on Ophelia's. The letters she and Elijah recovered from her father's study were the final piece of evidence I needed to arrest him. While none of them were ever signed from or addressed to Ayden, it was enough for me to make the connection.

I pull the letters and throw them down in the center of the table. "These were recovered from Lord Seamus's study."

Lord Seamus stands abruptly, the chair falling backwards and hitting the floor with a loud thud. He opens his mouth to speak, but I'm not done.

"Oh, and the servant that died from eating the poisoned food meant for Lord Aurelius? The poison was water hemlock slipped into the produce shipment from the farmlands owned by Lord Seamus. That took some digging to find out, but you have Lord Craylor to thank for helping me discover that."

Seamus is apparently too stunned to speak, so I continue, "I discovered the servant we found in the river—her name was Delilah in case you were wondering—had been reassigned from the kitchens just days before her disappearance. What I found interesting was when I tried to pay a visit to her family, the neighbors were under the impression that they had all disappeared in the night. But when I entered their supposedly empty home, I found them all right there. Slaughtered in their beds, even the babe."

"There is no possible way you connected all of that to me," Seamus spits. "Especially not from a few letters stolen from my study."

"Oh, that's right. I forgot that because I'm female, I'm somehow less intelligent. That I couldn't possibly read your ledgers and piece together that the large sum you paid to 'M' was the standard fee that the Midnight Brotherhood charges for mercenary services." I pause for added effect. "Please, My Lord, do not insult me. You may have paid them well, but I pay them better." It also helps that the head of the brotherhood was an old friend of mine who owed me a favor.

"You think you're so clever, Princess. You know nothing," Seamus snarls.

"Wrong, I know I'm clever. I may not know everything, but I know enough to have you executed for your crimes." I smirk at him. "Kind of like how you executed Commander Nolan for coming too close to the truth."

The guards close in on Lord Seamus, pulling his arms behind his back, but he won't go easy. He thrashes in their grip, desperate to not be shackled.

His eyes dart to the letters on the table, and it finally clicks how I was able to gather this information. Electricity dances in his eyes as he turns his gaze to his daughter.

"You traitorous bitch," he spits at Ophelia. She doesn't even recoil from him, just meets his stare and crosses her arms.

"No, Father. *You're* the traitor, and I'm done living in fear of you." Her voice is steady and full of a confidence that wasn't there when I first met her.

"You will pay for this!" he screams as lightning bursts from his hands into the bodies of my guards. They drop to the floor, their hearts no longer beating.

Everyone else takes a few steps back, not wanting to be his next target. It's pointless though, because the next target is the raven-haired beauty standing next to Elijah.

Before I can process what's happening, Lord Seamus pulls a blade I didn't know he had and throws it straight at Ophelia's chest. With expert precision, it hits the target with a sickening crunch of steel piercing flesh and bone.

Ophelia's scream echoes through the room, but it's not one of pain. I blink rapidly, trying to make sense of what I see before me.

The dagger is protruding not from Ophelia's chest, but Layne's. He had stepped in front of the blade to save his sister from their father. Layne drops to his knees, then collapses completely on the floor, blood pooling around him.

"Aurelius!" I shout, and he seems to read my mind. His

Hemonia Gift instantly seizes hold of Lord Seamus's body, keeping him immobile and unable to use his power.

I turn back to Ophelia who is on the floor with Layne, tears streaming down her face.

"Why did you do that?!" she screams, but he just stares up at her and smiles.

"I will always—" he chokes on blood pooling in his lungs, "protect my baby sister." He reaches up and brushes a strand of her hair behind her ear.

"I'm going to save you, okay?" Determination set in her eyes, she reaches to remove the dagger from his chest. Since he was considerably taller than Ophelia, it didn't hit him directly in the heart, but rather just below.

I notice a familiar scent surrounding the blade, and my shadows dart out and halt her hand before she can touch the handle. "Ophelia, stop."

"Breyla, I only have minutes before he bleeds out. I have to act now."

My heart sinks at the words I utter next, "No, you have minutes to say goodbye. That blade is laced with the same poison that claimed Nameah. I'm so sorry."

Her beautiful gray eyes fill with tears as she turns back to Layne. She cradles his head between her hands and sobs.

"You promised me a grand adventure, brother," she whispers, tears streaming down her face full force. "You can't leave me yet."

"You'll still go on a grand adventure, O. You'll just have to do it without me," he chokes again, blood spilling from the corner of his lips.

"I love you, Layne. How am I supposed to do this without you?"

He shifts his eyes behind her until they land on me, then moves to Elijah's next. I understand his unspoken words and nod at him, tears filling my eyes. "I love you, too, little sister. So much." He coughs again, more blood spilling from his lips and covering Ophelia's face in small splatters.

"No no no," she cries, and I swear I can hear her heart break in her chest. She leans down until her forehead rests against his.

In the softest whisper, Layne's final words to her are, "I'll be waiting for you in Amara."

Sobs wrack her tiny body as he takes his final, pained breaths. When she pulls back, I see vacant blue eyes staring at the ceiling. Ophelia closes his eyelids and lays one last kiss on his brow. A pained wail crawls out of her shaking body. It's a sound I've never heard at such intensity before.

Elijah reaches for her hand as she passes, but she pulls it out of his grasp and continues moving past him. She rounds the table and stops in front of her father, still immobilized by Aurelius's power.

"Consider this your final lesson in life, Father." She grips him by the throat, thin fingers digging into the flesh below his jaw and drawing blood. "You never should have underestimated me," she says as a black glow wraps around her fingers.

It's reminiscent of the glow her hands take when she heals, but this is black where her healing is white. The black aura spreads down her arms and covers her body in an ethereal, dark glow. Her raven strands lift and float around her, her eyes emanating the same black aura.

Lord Seamus gasps as if struggling for air. His skin begins to lose color and whither as if he's aging in front of our eyes. The color leeches from his hair next and the muscles on his body sag until his body goes completely limp in her grasp.

A heavy thud sounds as Ophelia drops her father's dead body to the floor. When she turns to me, the dark has receded, but she's still glowing. I'm not sure if it's just me or if she somehow looks healthier. Younger even, perhaps. Something snapped in her and released a new power. Or had she always had this ability?

Many of the faces in the room look at her in horror, but she doesn't even notice them. She makes her way back to the other side of the table, everyone giving her a wide berth. She reaches Elijah, and he stares at her in awe.

"My dark goddess," he whispers reverently.

She stares into his eyes, her own grays glowing as she takes him in. "Not a goddess, but still yours."

Elijah pulls her into his chest, wrapping an arm around her lower back to hold her close. She relaxes into his grip and goes limp in his arms. The overwhelming use of a new power drags her to sleep.

"So, Lord Seamus and Prince Ayden were behind all the recent deaths? Even the King's?" Lord Jaeson questions.

I nod. "I believe so, yes. I—"

"No," my mother's voice echoes into the room.

"Mother?" I turn a questioning look to her.

"At the risk of causing more death, I need to set the record straight," she says as she stands and clears her throat.

Lord Craylor steps up to her, laying a gentle hand on her shoulder. He hands her a wine goblet and whispers something in her ear. She nods and takes a sip of the wine before continuing. "The only one responsible for the king's death...is me."

Chaos erupts around me as a chorus of voices ring out, all indecipherable in the cacophony that fills the room. The guards look to me for direction, but I have nothing to give them.

I stare at the female who birthed me and try to piece together what she just said. *She killed Father?* How could that be possible?

I move toward her, desperate for her to say she's lying, that she had nothing to do with his death. Before I can ask any of my questions, she drops to the floor.

"Mother!" I scream and drop to my knees before her. In the next beat, Aurelius is on her other side, holding her left hand in his own.

451

Blood trickles her mouth and nose. I know what Aurelius is going to say before he opens his mouth. "It's the same poison, Breyla. It's coursing through her veins. She must have ingested it." He looks at me with panicked eyes.

I hold his stare as we both grapple with the reality that we have to hold *another* person as they die from this mystery poison. There's nothing we can do but watch our hearts die before our eyes.

When my mother opens her mouth, she calls out a name I wasn't expecting. "Elijah," she croaks.

He's next to her a heartbeat later. She reaches a shaking hand to his cheek, and he grasps it. Elijah says nothing as she shares something with him. He nods at her, tears in his own eyes.

She turns her gaze to me next and strokes my cheek. Tears are falling full force down my face. I brush a strawberry-blonde curl from her face as I tell her, "I love you, Mom. I'm sorry I never said it enough."

"I love you, too. We were both so proud of you, keep making us proud." Her breath is wheezing, and it's growing harder for her to speak.

Slowly she turns her head to Aurelius. "I love you, too. Take care of my daughter, or I'll find a way to haunt you."

Aurelius trembles and strokes her hand still clutched between his. "I love you, Gen. I'm sure you'll haunt me, regardless."

She takes another wet, choking breath and looks back at me.

"I'm going to make it stop now, Gen," Aurelius says before looking at me. "She's choking on her own blood, Breyla. Let me give her peace."

"Just like falling asleep, okay?" I nod to him but keep my eyes on her.

He lays a hand on her chest, and her eyes fall closed the next moment, her heart slowing to a stop. As her heart ceases beating, I feel my own crumble in my chest. That gaping wound left by my father, Julian, and Nameah is ripped open. The female who had loved me longest, who had given me life and been there for me even when I didn't want it—is just gone.

The next sound I register is the slow clap coming from the other end of the dining room.

"I must say, I'm impressed that you figured out as much as you did, Princess." Prince Ayden's voice grows louder the closer he comes. I'm filled with confusion as I try to understand how he's walking free, not shackled. "You missed a few key facts, though. I didn't have anything to do with the murders or the botched assassinations," he says, picking an invisible piece of lint from his shirt. "In fact, you'll find that the one Seamus was working with is much closer to home than you might have imagined."

He turns his gaze to Aurelius, and his next words shake the foundation of my world. "But we can fill my fiancé in on that during our trip home. Can't we, brother?"

MORGANA'S LITTLE MASOCHISTS

You okay there? I know that ending was a bit of a wild ride. What did you think of the little twist at the end? If you want to vent, theorize, or perhaps cry with other readers, I invite you to join Morgana's Little Masochists reader group on Facebook. You'll also get sneak peeks and writing updates, plus access to giveaways and incentives.

https://www.facebook.com/groups/808677844456576/

ACKNOWLEDGMENTS

Holy hell, I did it. I wrote an entire book. I couldn't have done it without my amazing support system! A massive thank you to the amazing authors who answered every question I had about writing and publishing: Chloe I. Miller, Luna Laurier, and M.A. Kilpatrick. I couldn't have done it without you. Thank you, Chloe, for being an amazing Alpha reader, for making me think critically, for helping me connect the dots, and for answering every crazy question I've had. Luna, I wouldn't have had the audacity to do what I did if you hadn't first traumatized me with chapter 47. You've given me so many tips and advice about self-publishing, sprinted with me, and helped me develop my craft. I'm so grateful for you. M.A. Kilpatrick, thank you for going before me, for letting me learn from every success and mistake along the way, for proofreading and formatting my story, and for listening to every crazy idea I've had as this story unfolded. Most of all, thank you for being the most amazing mother and friend.

To my incredibly talented editors, Sam & Sarah, thank you for helping me create a wonderful, polished story and for encouraging all the chaos along the way.

To my friends—Riki, Sam, Audrey, and Joanie—thank you for supporting and loving me through this process. You've shouted about my book to people I don't even know and made me feel so loved throughout this journey.

Thank you to my wonderful beta readers, every ARC

reader, and every other person who has read or shared my book with the world.

Lastly, to my husband, Johnathan. I love you so much. I know you don't always understand my excitement over books or why we're paying so much for character art (it's a real problem, okay. I need the whole thing illustrated.), but you took it all in stride and supported me through it all. You're better than any book boyfriend.